THE MALCONTENTS

THE
MALCONTENTS

A NOVEL BY REGINALD KEITH

TATE PUBLISHING & *Enterprises*

Published by Tate Publishing & Enterprises, LLC
127 E. Trade Center Terrace | Mustang, Oklahoma 73064 USA
1.888.361.9473 | www.tatepublishing.com

Tate Publishing is committed to excellence in the publishing industry. The company reflects the philosophy established by the founders, based on Psalms 68:11,
"The Lord gave the word and great was the company of those who published it."

Book design copyright © 2007 by Tate Publishing, LLC. All rights reserved.
Cover & interior design by Leah LeFlore

Published in the United States of America
ISBN: 978-1-60247-537-3
07.07.05

DEDICATION

Dedicated to my wife and family, especially my daughter, Janine, who spent hours proofreading. Many thanks to Dan Cleary of the Coffee Beanery, who provided the "quiet niche" those early mornings.

PROLOGUE

ANDRE WATCHED AS THEY CAREFULLY LOWERED Hannelore's full-length portrait from the wall behind where her desk had been. It was the last article packed for storage. Andre didn't know what he was going to do with her possessions, but one thing he did know was that they would be kept; why was another question. His desk was yet to be removed and placed in the gallery office downstairs next to Otto Kranz. He was glad he would be working with the old man and friend of years. He got up just as the portrait disappeared into its packing crate, if ever to be seen again.

He walked to the window overlooking the garden that held memories of youth and love. *They would never meet there again*, he knew. *How could these past few days have altered the course of so many lives so drastically?* And the cost was laid to his account, and the debt he could never repay began to mount that night not so very long ago.

CHAPTER 1

ANDRE WAS MESMERIZED BY THE SWIFTLY GLIDING bow as it caressed the violin nesting between cheek and shoulder. He was no lover of classical music by any means—not that he did not enjoy some of the concerts that Hannelore expected him to attend with her for appearances' sake. But tonight the first violinist and her intimacy with the violin captivated him almost annoyingly. He did not understand why it should, but it did.

"I'm amazed at your rapt interest in tonight's performance. It's refreshing not to worry about your embarrassing habit of nodding off," Hannelore whispered. Andre was amused at her reaction.

Andre acknowledged the compliment with a smile, inwardly hoping Hannelore would not press for the reason of this current interest.

Andre was surprised at his own fascination with the accomplished violinist. She was ending the performance with an electrifying intensity that carried to the audience. Her bouncing bow in the last movement of Paganini's *Violin Concerto No. One*, a technique feared by many violinists, brought the audience to its feet. Andre was among those first to stand, joining in the crescendo of applause. Although Hannelore also rose, it was with an air of distinct diffidence as she cast a look of amused surprise at Andre.

"My," she whispered in his ear, "I am indeed interested to hear why you have suddenly taken a liking to this performance."

Andre, with a corresponding whisper, said, "Hannelore, you have often scolded me for my lack of interest in concerts. I suppose this is as opportune time as any to begin to develop that interest, especially with such a fine performance as this."

Hannelore's raised eyebrows told Andre that more would be forthcoming on this subject.

Leaving the theatre, Andre overheard Count von Linglesdorf remark to Hannelore that the concert had performed reasonably well considering it was a Polish orchestra.

"However," he added, "it is entirely too soon to welcome those who where enemies of our country just a short twenty less years ago. Remember, it was the Poles who, in '39, attacked our radio outpost and forced us to retaliate to protect our land."

However, Andre was too engrossed in thoughts about the violinist to pay much attention to the current opinions of the Count or any of the others who continued to believe in an event long proved a lie. In fact, he had to admit to a surprised self, he was already planning for an opportunity to hear or, better yet, to meet the violinist herself. The published schedule called for a performance in Mainz the following week. Andre kept the thoughts of Mainz in mind as he endured a boring after-theater dinner. He was hard put to restrain commenting while members of the Kreis discussed the inferiority of the evening's performance. Von Lingelsdorf wondered if indeed it was not an affront to allow a Polish orchestra to even play works by German composers. Von Bruback added that it was all a plot of the Socialist to further weaken the German national spirit.

"Well, I knew by her name, Katya Presnoski, that the violinist was Polish," sniffed Hannelore in derision.

CHAPTER 2

AFTER ANDRE'S FATHER HAD TAKEN IN HANNELORE'S father as a partner, they decided to convert the large second floor, largely unused, into two very luxurious apartments. They were separated by a well-appointed entrance hall reached either by elevator or stairs, the latter being Andre's choice to keep fit. In elegant script, the names von Kunst and Hasenfeld graced the fruitwood doors to the respective apartments. A beautiful Oriental rug bordered by white marble completed the impression of affluence to any visitor coming into the hall. A marble table was always graced with fresh flowers provided by Annalise, who had served both families since Andre could remember.

He and Hannelore enjoyed a good relationship as partners in the gallery. Both enjoyed the living quarters their parents had provided that afforded access to the gallery and to each other without any invasion of privacy. A rear stairway led from the office space to the garage housing the cars Andre loved for speed, Hannelore for prestige.

A visitor would immediately observe upon entering the office space Andre and Hannelore shared the distinct dividing line between their areas. Hannelore's decided preference for remembrances of Germany's recent past and Andre's fascination for the fairy tale world of castles and stories of a Germany long past was not to miss.

Most striking was the life-size painting of Hannelore in her Nazi Maidenkorp uniform hanging behind her desk. The portrait displayed the medals she had achieved and the coveted insignia of a group leader.

The smile she wore was one of exceeding pride and pleasure, and the beauty captured in the painting remained hers to the present day.

Andre's walls reflected his love of ancient times in the paintings of gray castles brooding over Father Rhine winding northward. Much of his love for these scenes was because of Hannelore. When, as children, they played in the courtyard garden, she would relate tales of heroic Germans.

She would sit with him on the bench facing the playing fountain and tell him how lucky he was to have been born into such a great nation. While he would listen, it was not because he was impressed; it was because his older playmate, by three years, took an interest in him. For Andre, memories of those days of their youth never dimmed. The passing of time only brought sadness as their age of innocence ended. There was little time now to spend in the garden.

CHAPTER 3

WHEN KARL VON KUNST HAD ASKED HEINZ HASENFELD to join the gallery, it was with the knowledge that Heinz was much more the businessman than he was. Karl had seen good growth as he took over from his aging father, but needed the help Heinz could lend. However, the influx of artworks during the early war years caused Karl unease and asked Heinz to explain.

Heinz said with pride, "You see, Karl, I told you sometime ago when you were upset about political developments, all of this would work to our advantage. I had early on made contacts with brokers in neighboring countries. They made contact with people who were nervous about the political situation and wanted a safe place for their artworks."

"You're saying then that these are legal purchases?" Asked a doubting Karl.

"Of course," was the quick reply.

Karl said no more until the larger shipments of art from within Germany began to arrive shortly after the Krystalnacht tragedy, as Karl termed it. Heinz explained to Karl that sadly enough many of the Berlin families affected thought that they could not risk their art treasures being damaged by these street hooligans. Of course, Heinz, also deplored these developments. But he was pleased that so many of these families requested that their gallery take these objects for safekeeping. "After all," he told Karl, "it is a tribute to this gallery's reputation that should make you proud."

CHAPTER 4

THE MORNING AFTER THE CONCERT, ANDRE TOLD Hannelore his travel plans over their morning coffee. He said he would be leaving for Mainz Sunday night. Hannelore nodded disinterestedly at Andre's announcement; his trips were often spontaneous and very beneficial to the gallery. He was well respected in the art world for his expertise and integrity and had established a large and profitable clientele. Not the least of his sales talents was the value his clients placed on the personal contacts made on these trips.

Andre had spent a long time during the night trying to analyze or, better said, rationalize this unexplainable fascination for the dark-haired violinist. He allowed she was attractive enough, but Andre was drawn by another force he could not readily identify. It was the unexplainable he wanted explained. Perhaps a face-to-face meeting with her would lead to the discovery of a very talented but ordinary person, not mysterious at all.

He rehearsed several scenarios; calling her hotel direct seemed too abrupt an approach, waiting at the stage door, too immature; writing a note was chosen. He decided it would be the most polite and least offensive tack. He would take a bouquet of flowers to the concert with a note, his business card attached, requesting her presence at dinner the following evening. He would also extend the invitation to whomever else she might wish to invite. This would allay any concerns that she naturally might have meeting a total stranger.

Andre arrived early in Mainz after an uneventful but enjoyable fast drive over the almost empty autobahn. He reviewed again his plan to reach her and could not deny the growing excitement at the prospect. He admitted that to defend his desire to meet someone who had played a violin some forty feet away as a rational act was not possible. But he was here, and the ticket he held confirmed his irrationality.

He took his reserved box seat accompanied by a boyishly pounding heart as in the days of early youth when asking a pretty fraulein to dance. His seat overlooked the stage nearest the first violinist's chair. Arriving guests looked somewhat curiously at the well-dressed young man sitting alone with a rather large bouquet of flowers on his lap.

He had arrived early at the theatre to inquire of the floor manager the possibility of presenting his card of introduction and the flowers during the intermission. He had no desire to be part of the crowed pressing toward the stage at the concert's end or waiting at the stage door.

The manager said Andre should go immediately to the small door to the left of the platform; he should present his card to the attendant with a request that Herr Karpinski, the conductor, meets him. Of course, Herr Karpinski's compliance was entirely up to him, the manager reminded Andre.

Andre had rehearsed many times the short greeting he would say to the conductor while presenting his card and bouquet, requesting they be presented to the violinist Fraulein Katya Preznoski. He would be careful to explain that he was well aware that the tradition of honoring performers was at the end of a performance, but would beg for an exception in this case.

The concert was about to begin, and Andre watched with still pounding heart as Kayta walked with grace to the podium. She was stunning, dressed in a long black sheath with a black onyx necklace lying serenely above the modest cut of her gown. She mounted the podium and, raising her violin, began to lead the orchestra in tuning their respective instruments.

Her profile was to Andre; her raven hair pulled back accented a translucent skin worthy of a living cameo. Her movements mesmerized Andre as they had in Berlin. Leading each section of players in tuning their instruments, it seemed her bow became a fairy's wand. She stepped down lightly to stand by her chair as the players and audience welcomed the maestro Mylovic Karpinski to the podium. At his signal, and absent the traditional bow to the audience, which Andre had also noted at the Berlin concert, he raised his baton to begin a series of Italian baroque airs.

As the concert progressed, it was evident she knew the music by heart, her gaze almost entirely fixed on the Maestro. His reputation for perfection without quarter was well known. Many a musician had suffered his temper after a performance in which one false note had been detected. Any repeating of a mistake could lead to an instant dismissal. He was often questioned about this harsh treatment of a mistake that the majority of the audience, if not all, would not have noticed.

His reply was that while a painter, a sculptor, an architect could repaint, re-chisel, or redraw in the privacy of their studio, the miscue of a note did not allow that luxury. Once the note was played, had left the instrument, it could never be recalled, any more than the bullet or arrow sent.

No doubt, this philosophy was well understood by his musicians, whose quality of playing was rated among Europe's best. Anyone achieving the first violinist chair would be held to that same perfection. That Mylovic held jealous guard over his first violinist was to become quite apparent to Andre.

At the intermission, Andre proceeded to the designated door and asked the attendant to please present his card to the Maestro with the request that he meets him for a very short word. No doubt, the young man holding the large bouquet justified the quizzical look on the attendant's face at this unusual request. He took Andre's card with a nod, entered the doorway, and returned rather quickly with Mylovic following. The expression on the Maestro's face was one of distinct dislike. Before Andre could deliver his practiced speech, Mylovic spoke, "So you are Herr von Kunst of Von Kunst Gallery." It was said as a statement not a question. The Maestro continued, "I respected your wish to see me because I wanted to see for myself a living member of the von Kunst family."

It was very evident to Andre that this curiosity was not intended to be complimentary. Andre decided on the moment not to respond to this opening other than to compliment the Maestro on the performance. Then he simply asked if the Maestro would be so kind as to present these flowers and his card to Fraulein Preznoski. He acknowledged that this imposition was unusual during the intermission. He knew the press of the crowd following such an excellent performance might result in his appreciation being lost.

Mylovic studied Andre intensely, and then retorted, "Herr von Kunst, acts of appreciation are not lost even if presented at inopportune moments. However, while inconvenient, I will accept these on her behalf."

Without a further word, he took the flowers, card, and left. Once inside the door, he turned to the attendant and told him to give the bouquet to whomever he pleased. He proceeded back to the rehearsal room tearing open and reading the note attached.

"Dinner indeed," he muttered, tearing it to pieces and dropping it with the card into the nearest waste receptacle.

Andre returned to his seat in hopeful anticipation of a favorable reception of his invitation. What perplexed him was the Maestro's comment about meeting a member of the von Kunst family. After the concert ended, Andre waited for a while at the same door where he had met the Maestro, hoping perhaps for an immediate reply.

After a time, he felt self-conscious standing before the door like a forlorn suitor. The theatre was now empty. No doubt, the number of persons pressing backstage made it nearly impossible to expect a quick reply. He had noted his hotel number on his card and decided to await a reply there. He realistically had no reason to expect a positive response to his invitation, but he fervently hoped there would be one.

There was no response that night but by late morning with still no response, Andre was puzzled. It did not seem in keeping with common courtesy to not at least have received a polite response. At least a thank you for the flowers and an expression of regret in having to decline the dinner invitation was the least to expect. At noon, with still no response, he checked out of the hotel but requested any messages for him be held for at least two hours. He would return then for a final check.

CHAPTER 5

THE WEATHER WAS BEAUTIFUL, THE PEACEFUL ATMO-
sphere created by the sun and flowing river lent itself to Andre's reflection again on the reason he was even here. It was evident that there was
to be no response to his invitation. That surprised him. But even more
troubling was the Maestro's comment that he only met him because he
wanted to see a living von Kunst. He offered no explanation while giving the distinct impression that there must have been a reason, which he
cared not to reveal. It was evident that he must have known of the gallery,
or of someone connected with it.

The afternoon wore on and as he looked at the concert schedule,
noted the orchestra would be in Köln Wednesday for a single concert.
The thought of going there came as a reflex that he immediately dis-
counted as further irrationality. It was now evident, after asking once
more at the desk, that he was not going to receive any reply.

The silence was a signal to accept that the pursuit had ended. He
should accept that as evidence to close the matter and go back to Berlin.

As the valet brought his car from the garage, the thought of going to
Köln forced its way back into his resisting mind. Irrationality seemed the
stronger force; however, as he again entertained seriously the idea. He left
the hotel and entered the main road heading for the autobahn that would
take him back to Berlin, but the sign pointing to the Rhine road became
a command and the Mercedes obeyed.

He had to accept that no response from her in Mainz was a definite
signal of no interest, what reason would there be to expect a better recep-

tion in Köln? But he still found it difficult to accept this rejection without some explanation. He decided to take the Rhine road, fully intending to take it only to Koblenz. Intentions, while well meant, are no match for irrational desires.

As he drove, he thought *it did not seem unreasonable to make one more attempt at a contact. He would politely inquire if there was a particular reason his invitation was inappropriate and if so make an apology.* He found this reasoning logical and passed the turn off at Koblenz in good conscience.

He realized, of course, this decision was not at all in keeping with his usual behavior with respect to women. Yes, he enjoyed their company and spent many a pleasant evening with one or the other of his acquaintances and oft times especially with Elsa. Hannelore did not count as an acquaintance; she was a long-time companion and full business partner, their relationship stood apart from any other.

He found many women attractive, but the word fascination would not apply to any of them. *But is it fascination behind this current compulsion?* He thought further, *If indeed there is no rationale to this desire to know a stranger then is not that even more reason to explore its irrationality? Wouldn't making contact, a personal face-to-face encounter, perhaps reveal the answer?*

Driving along the Rhine road at a more leisurely pace fit his contemplative mood better than the more intense driving on the autobahn. This was the road that followed the river of legends, Father Rhine, on whose banks the great castles of the robber barons still kept their spectral guard and where the heroes of Wagnerian fame fought their fatal wars.

As he passed the Lorelei rock, he thought of the luckless sailors lured to their deaths by the songs of the maiden combing her golden hair. Of course, only a legend, Andre still wondered if indeed he was any better than those sailors who chased a fantasy to their sorrow.

He stopped for an evening meal at a gasthouse in St. Goar. While enjoying his meal, he began to think about his own ambivalence toward things political.

Andre usually gave little thought to the war years. For Andre, the question was always how to be a part of a new Germany, a Germany of free people living in peace and enjoying the God-given beauty of the land; the pleasure of coffee and cake after an afternoon's walk along a river or through a green forest. There was the joy of listening enraptured by an orchestra bringing to life some of the world's most beautiful music written by native sons. These he knew to be the true pleasures held in the hearts of his people. It was not a lust for war; it was not a hatred for others of different cultures .

The gasthouse was still relatively empty as he waited to pay his bill. As he finished his wine, his thoughts turned again to the pursuit that had so far led him to this table. He smiled to himself at the reaction Hannelore would have if she knew his sole purpose in driving to Mainz and now continuing to Köln was solely to gain the acquaintance of the striking Polish violinist.

Andre paid the bill and started toward his car but not before pausing at a small balcony overlooking the verdant green valley and the swift flowing Rhine below. He listened to the strained chugging of the southbound cargo-laden house barges and the softer sounds of those going with the northward flow. Wisps of mist were slowly leaving their nesting in the trees and moving out onto the water, slowly obscuring his view. Was this what Kayta was doing to his mind? Clouding his vision of reality? Was Hannelore, whose presence was reality, personified, but Katya only the mist of illusion?

As he drove on, keeping to the Rhine road he watched the fields and forest fading into darker shadows of green, now turning to blackness. Across the river, the reflecting lights of the small towns were the only evidence of the Rhine's presence.

He loved this Germany. The small towns were surrounded with an air of tranquility that he never sensed in Berlin. That city never rested; its cafés and bistros offering hospitality throughout the night, although now only a shadow of the glory days when it rivaled Paris.

He enjoyed the night; top down, warm wind, lights reflecting on the river, little traffic, giving time to think about Hannelore and her "friends'" involvement in his life. He thought of the many times he had sat with her and her friends at a restaurant, forced to stay until he felt his obligatory presence had been fulfilled. He would tire early of the repetitive political tirades about the dangers of socialism. What was so odious to the Kreis was the constant demand for Germany to apologize to the world for imagined grievances.

But now as he drove through the evening toward Köln with growing anticipation, he began to realize that Hannelore's control over his life had been his own doing. It just had not mattered. Yes, her friends were boring and her own political views beyond comprehension, but when he and she were alone, the mood could be entirely otherwise and Hannelore a pleasure to be with. Their conversations would center on the gallery and then, oftentimes, fond memories of their past childhood would evoke laughter. Hannelore would invariably make some oblique reference to a certain beach in Spain that Andre would feign not to remember.

There were other enduring memories; a trip to Paris or London combining pleasure with business as they visited gallery auctions or strolled along the Seine or Thames. At times she would gently say that her reprimands were not meant to embarrass him, but these friends, she would remind him, had suffered and sacrificed much during the war. If Andre remained silent at these comments, the evening would remain enjoyable. However, there were times he could not resist a counterargument. If he tried to point out that, it was time to move on, to accept the new Germany that was finding its place on an international level, enjoyment faded quickly. Hannelore would not accept his explanation that he was not intending to insult her or them, but only to bring reality into focus.

The politics of her friends, he would say, had no place in this present time; they had already been proven as unworthy of merit. From this point on, the evening would become quite serious. Hannelore's tone would be soft and tinged with sadness telling Andre how she and her friends could not accept injustice, and wrongs had to be made right. If not through war, then at least by political means that would resurrect the pride of a nation whose superior people and culture had been so shamed.

A silence would follow, neither one at the moment having more to say that would break the impasse. They'd come to this point many times, Hannelore not understanding how Andre could be so ignorant about so important an issue. Andre not comprehending at all why this long disproved philosophy of racial superiority could possibly appeal to her. Perhaps it was this inability to find a common ground on this issue, the disappointment of conflicting ideologies that kept Andre from responding to Hannelore more intimately.

He thought again sadly of those occasions, when Hannelore's closeness was drawing him in only to repel him when politics or twisted philosophies intruded. He knew this present journey would not meet with her approval, especially if he had the good fortune to find this fascinating creature to be one he would like to know more closely. He needed to disengage himself from Hannelore's domination.

His mind was growing weary from all the thoughts crowding for attention. He was tired from driving as well. *Time to seek out a hotel*, he thought as he passed the Markburg Castle perched high on the bank to his right.

He took a room in a small hotel overlooking the Rhine, placed a chair in an alcove, and sat in the darkness watching the lights of the Village reflecting on the river. *Same river but always new water.* He thought about the river needing renewal from its origins in the Alps as the White Rhine, then tumbling into the valley on its northern journey to the sea.

Is this quest just a refreshing of my life? Doesn't this mighty river need the inflow from the melting ice of the mountains and the contribution of each tributary along the way? Yes it does, in order to reach the sea in undiminished fullness. However, what then? It reaches the sea and at once its identity is lost, yet on that journey its flow carried ships; watered vineyards. So is this feeling arising in me at no bidding of mine, much like the river having to accept what flows into it in order to survive? Do I simply need this experience? With thoughts foreign and wearisome, he fell asleep in the chair.

Finishing his breakfast, he checked out and started north following the Rhine. Above the river were the castles of his youthful fantasy; ghostly sentinels standing their sad eternal watch over the river that once was their private domain.

The kilometer sign announcing his nearness to Köln brought him back from romantic musings to the reality of his probably misguided purpose of visiting this city. If nothing else he would, politely as possible, learn why his invitation in Mainz was never acknowledged and why the Maestro had met him only because of his name, a name the Maestro clearly detested. However, this time he would insist on a personal, if short, face-to-face few moments with the violinist in spite of any less than friendly reception by the Maestro.

Traffic had been light, permitting him to arrive in Köln well before noon. There was ample time to find a room and perhaps spend some time visiting the Kölner Dom, a magnificent cathedral centuries in the building. Recent excavations had revealed remnants of a Roman military fort or encampment. Andre wanted to visit this historic find as well as the Dom itself.

He was able to obtain a room at the hotel where the musicians were staying. A ticket to the almost sold-out concert was fortunately available although for a seat not to his liking; he had wanted one nearer the front.

CHAPTER 6

THE NEED TO CALL HANNELORE, WHO HAD LAST HEARD at breakfast his intention to go to Mainz, was quickly dismissed. He had no desire to enter a long conversation trying to justify his presence in Köln.

The weather was warm and sunny, permitting him to enjoy a lunch at a small open café across from the Dom. As he gazed at the ancient structure, he remembered Hildegard of Bingen's story of St. Ursula's martyrdom. She had been slaughtered together with more than a thousand pilgrim English virgins murdered on the nearby riverbank centuries ago. He envisioned the descending pagan hordes with flashing swords slaughtering the innocent on their pilgrimage for God.

Ironic, thought Andre, *that such an unexpected tragedy would send them to their maker this early in their journey.* Surprised at his theological musings, he finished his lunch, walked over to the Dom, and entered its spacious Gothic interior.

A few elderly ladies were kneeling in the front pew; otherwise, the Dom was empty. Saints from stained glass windows shared their sun-lit colors with a sculptured penitent kneeling at a station of the cross. Andre almost felt a compelling urge to kneel and pray in the reverent silence. He realized he had never given much thought to God in his life, his brief reflection earlier about God and the slain virgins did not seem to be prerequisite enough for such an act of piety. He sat down in a back pew and with certain awe surveyed the magnificent soaring columns supporting the vaulted ceiling.

What was it about the early society that compelled the building of such a structure? Did the ancient worshippers actually believe God came and lived in it? Certainly today, people did not. The icons of saints surrounded by cherubs and winged angels seemed to know this as they gazed sadly down on the empty pews below.

He enjoyed the quiet, but it was not long before his thoughts left God to His empty church and returned to his much more secular concerns, how to meet Katya. Again, the cool reception of the Maestro and his comments about meeting a von Kunst family member disturbed him. Perhaps the Maestro had said something to Katya that had been reason enough to merit no reply. Well, he was determined to try again although recognizing his first thought of going to the hotel without asking the Maestro for an introduction might only cause more friction. Andre decided it would be more prudent to try again at the intermission to ask the Maestro to please allow him the opportunity to express his compliments. If the Maestro declined, then the Maestro be damned; he would make his own opportunity!

Satisfied with this newfound determination, he left the Dom and studied the artifacts on display at the site of the excavation of the Roman camp. To think of that ancient empire having once reached this far and even farther north to Hadrian's Wall was astounding. How great a power had been Rome! Conquering the known world by legions of foot soldiers enforcing the rule of an emperor seated in Rome. The imperial eagle had fluttered over many foreign camps like this one.

Did those ancient soldiers, leaving family and friends behind, believe in their cause or have any idea there was a cause? Much more probable is that they gave little thought to any question of right or wrong; they came simply because they were told to.

Andre checked himself, *I think*, he said to himself, *this chasing after Katya is taking on more of a retrospective nature than I would have imagined. I rarely give much thought to questioning my motives or my life's direction, and in some ways, this is very disquieting. Much better to enjoy my present life and quit these musings.* Yet he felt a certain bond with those ancient soldiers. They must have, at times, wondered about the purpose of it all. What justified suffering, the deprivation of home and family? Certainly, these relics of their time at this camp gave no evidence of an easy life. Andre knew he was exaggerating this comparison to his own quest. He was under no orders, just an inner compulsion to do the irrational.

The ancient world from which they came was always a fascination for him. For while they served in a primitive land of barbarians, the world they left was one of opulence. It was graced with paintings unequalled today. The sculptures so perfect in detail, one waited for their waking to life. The cathedral's gravity defying spires touched heaven's floor, their beauty eclipsed today's sterile cement and glass rectangulars.

Was the ancient soul, spirit, closer to nature and life? Andre mused. *Have the material demands we place upon ourselves caused an inevitable distancing from spiritual powers that feed the creative nature? Is it some remnant of that nature that draws me to Katya? Is there something beyond her obvious physical attraction? Is it to be found in the music that her gliding touch calls forth from the violin? Does she awaken the spirit the ancient maker breathed into the instrument, her touch the one long awaited?*

He brought himself up short, as he had to do too many times on this trip. *My mind is certainly exaggerating this girl and her effect on me. No doubt, once I meet her, I will find her ordinary. I will find proof enough that, had I never met her, there would have been no great loss. Perhaps the truth is I have seized on this desire to meet her as simply a diversion from my mundane and unexciting everyday life.*

Later he would often ask himself a question that would always beg his answer, *Would he have pursued Katya as he did, had he any inkling of what would be the final outcome? But that is an exercise in futility,* he would think when the question crossed his mind, *to speculate on actions taken facing an unknowable future. One did what one did based on the known not the unknown.* He knew at the time that he had to meet this lovely creature, even if he did not understand the fascination. The events that followed could not be laid upon his conscience.

After a few more explorations of the ancient city, he returned to the hotel. He took some coffee on the terrace, thinking again of the intriguing girl that had captured his attention. He rejected again the impulse to call the gallery; the coming concert was far too much the focus of his thoughts. He looked forward to the evening with growing anticipation.

The concert, of course, was superb. Herr Mylovic's predilection to choose many of his countrymen's compositions was evident. However, he would often choose lesser-known composers he felt deserved wider recognition. This evening Katya's virtuoso performance of the English composer William Walton's *Violin Concerto* would have brought Jascha Heifitz to his feet as it did the entire audience. At the intermission, he hurried to the stage door and implored the hesitant attendant to please give the Maestro this note and his card. A visibly irritated Maestro met him and cut short the compliment Andre offered about the performance.

He said very curtly that he spoke for Fraulein Preznoski and himself, and neither he nor she had time or inclination to honor his request. Andre was incensed at this lack of civility.

He asked the Maestro why his request was received with such evident displeasure. He certainly had done nothing to offend by this simple request. In fact, he thought performers were pleased at receiving compliments. The Maestro stared at Andre, somewhat taken aback at this unexpected rebuff.

Overcoming the desire to turn and go without another word, the Maestro said somewhat mollified, "Herr von Kunst, this is neither the time nor the place for me to discuss or even defend our right to privacy. However, you are right, regardless of my reasons not to see you, I need not be impolite or rude, and I apologize should my tone have been so received. But this does not change my answer to you that Fraulein Preznoski is not available to receive your personal congratulations."

Andre, quite surprised at his own persistence, inquired as to what conditions would be acceptable. He couldn't imagine that his request for a few moments with such a brilliant artist was not possible. If his timing was inconvenient his apology, but certainly, there must be another time that would be appropriate.

"Herr Mylovic, I attended your recent concert in Berlin. It was magnificent. Then I drove to hear you again in Mainz, and now I am here in Köln. Your violinist is absolutely without peer, a fact, of course, well recognized by you I am sure. As you see from my card, I am deeply interested in art, not only that which hangs in my gallery, but also that which is manifest in performances such as yours, especially when presented so excellently. Therefore, I think my sincere wish to meet you and Fraulein Preznoski is not without merit and should not be so abruptly dismissed."

The Maestro hesitated, somewhat impressed by Andre's manner and apparently sincere compliments. Yet he could only answer,

"Herr von Kunst, I have no doubt you are personally a gentleman of character, but your association with the Von Kunst Gallery is the reason I must ask you to please desist in any further efforts to contact myself or Fraulein Preznoski. Now the intermission is about over, good evening and yes, thank you for the kind words about our performances, especially Fraulein Preznoski's and I shall relay that to her. Again good evening."

With that, he turned and left. As Andre returned to his seat, he knew it was futile to think of reaching Katya through the auspices of the Maestro, but more puzzling was the Maestro's antipathy toward the gallery. Why?

He watched her graceful movements with the bow. Her fingers trembling above the strings like hummingbirds enjoying their nectar. Her presence fired all the more his desire to meet her. The concert ended with Katya's outstanding performance of Mendelssohn's *Violin Concerto in E Minor*. It was a daunting piece even for the most expert violinist.

He had to know this girl. He almost laughed to himself at his envy for the violin that enjoyed such an intimacy with her. Was he actually jealous of her love affair with her instrument? It was clear that there would be no meeting her after the performance. He dared not be so crude as to force a meeting at the stage door. He walked back to the hotel much disturbed by the Maestro's comments and even more so by his inability to meet her. There would be a way, and he would find it.

He ordered a light 'abendbrot' in the hotel restaurant and, while enjoying a glass of Rhine wine, his reverie was abruptly interrupted as the Maestro and Katya entered the restaurant and were guided to a table a short distance from his.

Her profile at this close distance clearly revealed the luxurious blackness of her hair softly curling behind her ear, eyelashes nearly touching brow and cheek. Her face rested on gracefully folded hands. She was listening to the Maestro, who seemed rather agitated as he spoke. As the waiter approached their table, the Maestro turned to accept the menu and, at that moment, caught Andre's eye.

A fleeting look of recognition and annoyance was evident to Andre as the Maestro quickly turned to face Katya. He held the menu much like a shield against any possible acknowledging glance from Andre. To Andre, fate, chance, or perhaps even some foreordained destiny had charitably provided the long-sought opportunity to meet her.

There was no denying the Maestro had recognized him. While the Maestro was obviously not going to make any overtures from his side, Andre felt it perfectly in order to approach their table. He walked to their table and, almost before they were aware of his presence, he spoke first to the Maestro.

"Herr Karpinski, how very nice to see you again." Presenting his card, he continued, "May I say that the evening performance was as superb as usual." Turning to Katya, his breath almost failed him. Her nearness, her sculptured face, and deepest hazel eyes added even more to her beauty. She looked up with some curiosity at the handsome young man who evidently knew the Maestro.

"Fraulein Preznoski," Andre fought desperately against giving in to a nervous urge to swallow, "May I offer personal thanks to you for sharing such a virtuoso performance with us? You are indeed gifted beyond what one would dare expect to find on this earth."

Katya's initial reaction to this extremely flattering compliment was that it was a bit overdone. However, she had not failed to notice his evident nervousness that she found charming and gave credence to his sincerity. Her voice was low and soft as she thanked him for the kind words. Before Andre could offer any further comment, the Maestro quickly intervened, "Yes, thank you," he said curtly. "Now, if you will excuse us, we need to order quickly to assure that Fraulein Preznoski may retire early." Andre noted that Katya was about to say something when the Maestro almost rudely said, "Good evening," in a tone of unmistakable dismissal. Andre, with a nod to them both, gave a slight bow and went back to his table.

Katya knew how short-tempered the Maestro could be with an orchestra member whose performance failed to meet his standard. She was not accustomed to this display of rudeness. Yet the young man now retiring to his table after giving her a warm smile seemed to completely ignore the Maestro's impoliteness.

She looked questioningly at the Maestro. "Why were you so rude? He certainly was polite and his compliments seemed genuine, and you are always so pleased when compliments come our way. Besides, he seems to know you."

"I vaguely remember meeting him somewhere briefly after a concert. It is of no consequence. I don't know him personally, but as you can see from his card, he is connected with an art gallery in Berlin. I have heard of it but that is little enough reason to allow his disruption of our dinner. Enough talk about him or his gallery, except that he serves to remind us where we are. Katya, do you know where we are?"

Katya puzzled at a question with so obvious an answer hesitated as she said, "Köln."

"Of course," he said rather impatiently. "But where is Köln?"

Katya frowned, "I do not understand you. We are in Köln, and Köln is in West Germany and we are performing at the Staatsoper. Whatever else you expected as an answer to such a silly question I cannot imagine."

"Silly?" he almost raised his voice. Andre could not hear what they were saying, but it was obvious that the Maestro was agitated. He noticed how Katya reached over and placed her hand on his in a calming gesture.

I, too, would like to feel that hand on mine, thought Andre.

"Silly?" The Maestro could hardly contain his frustration with his protégé and her perpetual naiveté. "Nothing more to add, nothing? You fortunate child, how convenient to have a memory that recalls only that which is pleasant. You must have an innate sensor that filters out the realities of the past that could cause pain. You are now barely thirty, still so young. Yet that, perhaps, is a blessing. You can forget so quickly because you were so young the events back then, seen through eyes of innocence, saw not the evil rampant in this land."

Katya's eyes misted. "Maestro, you know I have never forgotten the evil of those early years that left me with no family. I thank God that He gave me you, and if not for your care these many years, I would not be here. No doubt, I would have suffered the same fate as my beloved parents. You confuse my supposed faulty memory with a decision I made long ago. I resolved to embrace those things my dear father taught me about facing life in an imperfect world. I do not choose to go back in my mind to events that cannot be altered and have no value other than to make me perpetually sad. That I will not accept for my life."

"Katya, it's remarkable that you can face those memories with such equanimity, I cannot! Although it is an economic necessity that we accept these invitations to perform in Germany, I feel a traitor to my beloved Poland. Our land was crushed as a beautiful flower is under the foot of an ignorant tramp.

"And that is why I must hate; it is that hate which drives me to be superior in my work. It is the need to be recognized as a musician and conductor of an orchestra that receives the praise of critics the world over. It is that recognition that places us above any of our peers, most importantly, those in this country! I bask in that reward, a Pole 'untermensch' actually receiving acclaim of the world. Katya, that is my revenge."

"Maestro, please, you're making yourself too upset to eat. There's no reason for you to react so just because a young German, who I'm sure was as young and as innocent as I was in those years, paid us a compliment. Certainly your revenge shouldn't be directed toward him."

"Katya, he is not just any German! He is a von Kunst. Well, you are right; we must eat, but please do not look his way and give any indication that would encourage his return."

Andre was not too surprised at the less than friendly reception by the Maestro. Their prior meetings were sufficient to make him aware the Maestro would not be inclined to extend any warm greeting or welcome. Yet for reasons unclear, the name von Kunst seemed to be the cause of this coolness.

While trying not to be obvious, he could not avoid watching them as they ate and conversed. It was clearly a very agitated Maestro, whose emphatic gestures punctuated the emotion in his remarks. Katya would at times reach to still his trembling hand.

He watched with envy how the exquisitely tapered fingers entwined with those of the Maestro. The brief encounter, the softness of her voice, the beauty of her face, the eyes of deep hazel only intensified the drive that admittedly was becoming an obsession. He felt in that brief moment a presence that went beyond her physical beauty, a certain divinity. The thought startled him.

Please, man, control yourself, you must not allow such exaggerations. You are only setting yourself up for a very emotionally devastating let down should you succeed in meeting her again…Certainly, it will prove her to be no more than a talented, young lady yet with the flaws we all have as simple humans. You won't find her to be the image your romantically fevered mind has conjured up.

He ignored this rational voice. Instead, he vowed to see her again. *It may be true that what I feel is contrary to all reality, but I doubt my mind, my senses, have misled me; she is a creation of no ordinary kind.*

Andre told the waiter to add their bill to his. The waiter said, "With pleasure," but was quite surprised at the displeasure shown by the Maestro when he told him the young gentleman who had just left had paid his bill. Katya could hardly suppress a smile at this gracious expression by the young German. The Maestro mumbled a "thank you" to the waiter. He gruffly told Katya that this show of apparent generosity was merely German arrogance. He had simply wished to embarrass the Maestro.

Katya, remembering Andre's polite manners and genuine compliment, could not agree with the Maestro, but she said nothing more. She could not help thinking that the young German did not fit the image the Maestro had portrayed to her of these people. Yet, polite or not, Katya had to recognize that he was, after all, German. She had tried all her life to live in the present and not dwell on the past, but he did belong to a nation with an unforgettable past of evil.

Andre went to his room more determined than ever to meet Katya. No matter the Maestro. While there was little said between Katya and Andre, Andre didn't think that Katya was in any way upset by his visit. He saw no reason to believe that she would take unkindly to another polite advance from him.

Certainly, he thought, *she was not so tethered to the man that there were times she wouldn't be free to do what pleased her.* He fell asleep devising various ways of meeting her.

CHAPTER 7

KATYA SAID GOOD NIGHT TO THE MAESTRO WHO, STILL out of sorts about the encounter, barely replied. Entering her room, her mother and father looked out at her from their picture placed on the nightstand by her bed. She always carried it with her. It wasn't to purposely remind her of her loss, but rather it was to make sure the warmth, love, and teaching they had given her was never forgotten. The picture kept their memory as close as when she was twelve years old.

She was aware back then of fearful events surrounding her, but was always assured by her parents that God would protect her as He had their ancestors in ancient times. Katya often reminded herself that her questioning why God had failed them, if not her, would not have pleased her parents. After all, had not God through their prayers seen her safely through those horrid times?

Perhaps God made choices she need not question. Perhaps He saw the future of a young girl with a long life ahead weighed against two elderly parents already nearing the close of their natural life. Perhaps God had to permit humankind to make choices no matter how contrary they would be to His divine plan. Otherwise, there would be no free will, the most exceptional gift God could give. He could have held all creation captive to His will. Did God see that through the Maestro's teaching her natural talent would emerge, bringing a gift of music to inspire a needy world?

If tempted to have bitterness about the events of those early years, the reassuring words of her father and mother remained to sustain her resolve not to succumb to that temptation.

Evil, they said, had always been present and at times gained possession of people who would use this evil power against mankind. For reasons known only to Him, God allowed evil to have its way, perhaps to show the world how much God was needed to combat the destruction evil could bring. But in the end, God would triumph, for goodness was greater than evil, even if that triumph seemed long in the coming. "Remember, Katya," her father had said as she prepared to leave Poland with the Maestro, "do not let the hatred brought against us enter your heart, for then you become just as capable of the evil they do, yourself."

As time passed, it became clear to Kayta that her parents were not going to be found. When the war ended, the sad confirmation of her fears caused a pain that never ceased. As she gazed at her parents' picture, these past remembrances flowed like a stream refreshing the memories living in the valleys of her mind.

She thought about the young polite and well-mannered German who had approached their table expressing his appreciation for their music. His acceptance of the Maestro's abruptness without any evidence of resentment impressed her. His assuming the cost of their meals was an unneeded show of kindness especially considering the Maestro's rudeness. She didn't agree with the Maestro's comment that he did it to embarrass him. Yet, although he had been polite enough, she couldn't ignore the fact that he did belong to a nation that countenanced the slaughter of millions of innocent people, especially those of her own faith. Did his parents justify to him the need for such crimes that he willingly accepted?

Somehow, without the burning hatred that consumed the Maestro, was there not justification for placing collective guilt on a nation? Where were the voices that should have cried out? Were there not enough persons for good conscious' sake brave enough to cry out against a program to annihilate entire ethnic groups for no other reason except that they were in the way? Was it fear that silenced them, if so, then forgivable? Or worse, was this young German in some way an active participant in these crimes? Or perhaps, when pressed, would offer the excuse most odious to the Maestro, "I didn't know?"

Yet, as Katya stared at the photograph, she couldn't imagine the couple looking back harboring a cancerous hatred toward people and the evil they caused as terrible and as unjust as it as.

No, thought Katya, *her father wouldn't allow hatred to destroy his faith in humanity. He would, in fact, express only sorrow for their actions and let the God of his faith render whatever judgment there was to be.* They would not allow, nor would she, this hatred to destroy the hope of any future happiness. They wouldn't have wanted her to allow such hatred to continue to work its evil in her own heart, although thoughts of how they may have died, to what tortures they may have suffered, began again to crowd into her mind.

"No," she said out loud as she gazed at their loving faces, "I'll not allow it, God be with you. In the morning I shall take an early walk and be thankful. Thankful for life and your early teachings that have saved me from the hate that keeps our good Maestro from seeing anything good in life." She fell asleep admitting that the young German was indeed attractive.

CHAPTER 8

ANDRE, FEELING LIKE A YOUNG "REALSCHULER" WITH
a crush on an unattainable beauty showered and dressed. Following an
idea that came to him last night, he walked over to a small café facing the
hotel. He seated himself where he could watch the hotel's front entrance
in anticipation of seeing her.

Of course, he had no assurance she would even be leaving the hotel
at this early hour and chided himself for this immature, even juvenile
lying in wait. But he decided it was worth the effort. He had to find an
opportunity to see her without the Maestro's presence.

Katya woke early, showered, and dressed for her morning walk, leaving a message for the Maestro that she wouldn't be joining him for breakfast but would be back before lunch. The Maestro was never comfortable
with her early walks alone. But while Katya was usually very compliant with his wishes, there was an element of independence he couldn't
conquer.

As she entered the lobby, she noted the hotel breakfast room was
quite crowded and decided to forego her usual light breakfast. Exiting
the hotel, the little café across the square caught her eye. It seemed an
appealing place to get an early coffee before her walk.

Andre saw her as she emerged from the hotel and his heart started
its uncontrolled racing as the chance to follow his planned encounter
seemed at hand. He beckoned the waitress to give him his bill and rose to
leave when he noticed Katya coming in the direction of the café. He sat

down, his thoughts suddenly reorienting themselves to meet this unexpected good fortune.

He watched the slim figure in black slacks, a white pullover, and black suede jacket striding purposely toward him. He caught his breath as she reached the café door; whether fate, destiny, or accident was in play, he was thankful for it.

She entered the café as Andre deliberately avoided looking at her and pretended to be deeply engrossed in reading the newspaper. Katya, upon entering, looked for an empty table when she saw Andre. Somewhat startled, she decided it wasn't her place to address him and sought out a table near the rear of the café out of his line of vision. Andre, without lifting his head, had still enough visibility to note her hesitation and was sure she had seen him.

Katya seated herself and ordered a coffee. She had a good view of him, and unless he were to deliberately look back, he wouldn't notice her intent gaze. She admitted to a curiosity about him. It was, of course, flattering to receive compliments and attention. But something about his coming to their table and accepting graciously the Maestro's rudeness was unusual.

At least, she thought, *it would be in order to thank him for the compliment and dinner; I'll do that as I leave. He should not be left with the impression that I was ungrateful.*

Andre decided he would go, but just as he was leaving he would pretend to inadvertently happen to see her. He would then, quite innocently go to her and wish her a good day.

Katya, considering whether or not to carry through her thoughts, saw him rise to go and realized the opportunity would be lost unless she acted now. As she took her first steps toward him, she noted he had turned and was advancing her way. They stopped a few feet from one another, each rather at loss for the correct first words.

Andre decided it was his duty to avoid any prolonged or awkward silence.

"I was just about to leave the cafe when I saw you, how fortunate for me," he said warmly. Katya smiled, feeling at ease at once.

"Well, just as I stood to leave I saw you and was just coming to tell you how much I appreciated your generous gesture last evening. I must apologize for the Maestro's somewhat impolite attitude. He's usually irritable after a performance, which never meets his own high expectations.

He'll always find some fault, yet the critics will have given an excellent review."

"I fully understand," said Andre. "I certainly take no offense especially since it gave me an unexpected opportunity to tell you in person that it was a magnificent performance. Your playing was absolutely without peer." Katya felt a slight blush rising.

"How nice of you to say that, but I'm afraid I didn't respond to your compliments last evening as I should have. I was embarrassed by the Maestro's curtness."

"Please," Andre smiled, "there's no need for any further apologies. I was the intruder into your privacy, and for that I really should be the one apologizing. Perhaps I should extend that apology for what may have been interpreted as an intrusion in Mainz when I extended that offer for dinner. I just wanted to thank you personally for providing such enjoyment through your talent. Evidently, the flowers were not your favorite. I must admit that receiving no response to my invitation was disappointing, but I really had no right to expect one since I was a perfect stranger."

Kayta raised questioning eyebrows, prompting Andre to offer another attempt at an apology.

"Fraulein Preznoski, forgive me, I had no right to mention that, it certainly lies within your pleasure to respond to such invitations or not. Again, I'm afraid I was a bit too bold in the asking."

Katya was at a total loss at Andre's reference to an invitation; she was sure she would have remembered had she received one. Katya felt awkward at continuing this conversation while standing in the aisle, and she was curious about his reference to an invitation she was sure she didn't receive.

"Herr von Kunst, please, let's go back to my table. I just ordered another coffee and perhaps you can help me remember the occasion you are referring to with a bit more privacy than here in the aisle!"

Andre nodded a quick agreement, pleased at the opportunity to speak with her further, yet not yet quite convinced she had no recollection of his invitation. *Could be*, he thought, *she is embarrassed at the oversight and would rather not admit to ignoring me.*

As they were seated, Andre said, "Your coffee is no doubt cold by now," and signaled the waitress for two more coffees. Katya protested that hers was fine but Andre insisted.

He said, "It gives me reason to keep you here for a few moments longer."

Katya felt a slight blush beginning again; it was evident that this young man was paying more attention to her than was warranted if he simply wanted to compliment her talents as a musician. She didn't really quite know how to react. The Maestro very much controlled her private life. It wasn't in a deliberately restrictive way, but his constant demands for practice and her importance as first violinist always dictated time priorities. The tour schedule itself was very demanding, leaving little opportunity for outside social contacts. That there was any motive on the part of the Maestro to deliberately keep her from making contact with anyone outside of his influence did not occur to her until Andre explained his dinner invitation.

"Well," Andre continued after Kayta asked him to explain more about the missing invitation. "Since you are so polite to ask, I was hoping to hear you enjoyed the flowers."

"You personally gave the flowers and the invitation to the Maestro?" she asked almost incredulously. "When, how?"

Andre explained that he met the Maestro during the intermission and gave him the flowers and the invitation.

Katya was silent and thankful that sipping the fresh coffee allowed her time to collect her thoughts. She was certain she had never received the flowers or the invitation to which Andre referred; would he be making this up just as an excuse to talk to her? She didn't think so; besides, his explanation could easily be verified, and that she intended to do.

"Herr von Kunst, I am terribly sorry that there was no response from me. I do at times receive such shows of appreciation, and if I cannot honor an invitation, I always respond with an acknowledgement and a thank you."

Andre didn't wish to pursue a topic that was evidently disturbing to her. "Well then, let's just assume that whatever happened to the invitation was a result of the press of time. I am sure you never received it, but I just wanted you to know that I had desired to express my thanks to you and meet you in person. And now I have. In Shakespeare's words, 'All's well that ends well.'" Katya could not suppress a quiet laugh.

"Now what do you find so funny in that?" he asked puzzled.

"Please excuse me, I mean no offense, I just didn't expect a Shakespeare quote from you."

Andre was somewhat taken aback. "Is it so surprising that a German would be conversant about Shakespeare and be able to read it in English?" Katya sensed the note of hurt in his reply.

"Herr von Kunst, I truly meant no offense. I suppose I am so provincial at times I forget the good contributions of one culture to another. Others like yourself understand that and readily accept those contributions regardless of their origin. Please excuse my ignorance."

Andre studied the beautiful face before him. He saw no guile there. Perhaps he was overly sensitive to comments that all too often were echoed in the foreign press and other sources that kept referring, if obliquely, to Germany as a land of aggressive barbarians.

"Fraulein Preznoski, forgive my sensitivity. I know we Germans carry a heavy burden of negative opinion especially from those who suffered during the tragic war years. I can offer no adequate apology that doesn't sound self-serving."

Andre paused and felt again the bitterness of having always to be on the defensive about his nation's past, and worse having no adequate defense. Katya heard the frustration in his voice, saw the pained expression on his face, the pleading eyes asking for an understanding that he already doubted was possible.

Katya was perplexed; she felt the sudden chill that descended on their pleasant conversation. The innocent remark about his English knowledge had a reaction she could not have expected; his apology was heartfelt, she was touched.

What can I possibly say? she thought. There was no denying that the young man was pleading for what she was hardly able to give. How could she reconcile the suffering of her nation and her own parents and let the past be buried and forgotten by the simple passing of time. Was it fair, however, to hold a new generation hostage to a past they could not control?

Should we who suffered simply put aside our personal loss and leave the past to historians who would write about it with so-called academic distance?, She wondered.

Andre watched her in silence, regretting words that evidently found little sympathy, as there was no response. He knew the opportunity to meet her that he had so eagerly awaited was now ending and possibly with little chance of another meeting.

"Fraulein…" he struggled to find words that would save the moment.

"Fraulein Presnoski, please, we cannot change what has been, I know that, and what I am asking is no doubt unfair of you. Your silence is just; you need not say what cannot be said with truthfulness to appease my own guilt."

She couldn't deny she was touched by his sincerity. She remembered again her own vow to not let the unfortunate events of the past destroy her hope of a better future.

"Herr von Kunst, do not take my silence as a rejection of what you say, but there are memories that I cherish. They call from the past to remind me that while I struggle to not let them control my life, neither do they want to be forgotten. It is a difficult balance, believe me."

"Indeed I do believe that." Andre nodded. "I would in no way wish to infer that we simply ignore the reality of the hurts that will always be with us. But I would regret to my life's end that the past could be so powerful as to prevent any chance of a better future. A future that, I pray, will give me the opportunity to meet you again and enjoy a friendship while still honoring those whose memories you rightly hold so dear. I am not asking you to forget what has caused you pain or hurt, but I am pleading for another opportunity to see you again."

She studied him, wanting to believe in his sincerity. *Anything that caused me pain or hurt?* She thought for a moment of telling him of her parents, yet she hesitated; he seemed so earnest, and to hurt him further at this time seemed unnecessary. Truthfully, to see him again was not an unpleasant thought.

"Herr von Kunst, we hardly know each other, and it cannot be denied we come from two different social cultures with a marked difference in our recent past histories. I come from Poland, a nation that has suffered much, add to that I am Jewish, not at all the best credentials for acceptance into much of western society." She raised her hand to stop the suspected voice of protest coming from him. She went on, "But somehow, if these barriers are too strong to knock down, perhaps friendships could build bridges over them. At least that way those who cared could reach each other. Herr von Kunst, I believe such friendships are possible, and yes, to meet you again would be pleasant, but I am afraid our schedule will not allow that. We leave for Warsaw after tomorrow's performance."

Her first words filled him with hope, only to be followed by a sense of despair when she finished. Suddenly he asked, "What is your schedule in Warsaw? I mean, what will you be doing?"

Katya smiled at his intensity and apparent earnestness in finding a way to see her again; she admitted to herself she was flattered. She knew, however, after their return to Warsaw and a few days' rest, strenuous rehearsals in preparation for a United States tour would allow little personal time.

When she told Andre this, she was touched by his deepest look of disappointment. Andre was desperate; although this brief meeting had not allowed much time for getting acquainted, he felt a deepening attraction. He was more convinced than ever to know more of this entrancing girl. He wasn't about to give up; he seized the comment about the period of rest she mentioned.

"Fraulein Preznoski, please listen to me. I do not wish to be an annoyance, but our parting here cannot be a final farewell. As you know, in German we have two good-byes, 'Lieb Wohl' and 'Auf Wiedersehen.' I cannot bear to say the former, but if you will listen to my idea and agree, the second will be said gladly.

"I must confess at the expense of my pride that from that first evening in Berlin where I heard you play, I was determined to meet you. That is why I drove to Mainz, tried to reach you without success. Refusing to give up, I drove here to Köln. My persistence has been rewarded. The proof is having you here, sitting across from me in this little café."

Katya wasn't sure how to respond; she didn't understand why he would be so interested in her.

"Herr von Kunst, I must say I am flattered, but certainly much more puzzled why you should go through so much trouble to meet a simple violin player from Poland."

"Fraulein Preznoski, I wish I had a rational explanation. Suffice it to say for the present that your playing, your very presence on the stage so fascinated me that I knew I had to know you. Strange as it may sound, I felt drawn to you, and it was not your beauty alone, which would be reason enough, it goes far beyond that, and yet to put that into words, I cannot. Please, I must assure you that if you have no wish to have further contact with me, a simple word to that effect and I will indeed promise to say 'Lieb Wohl.'"

Katya felt his intensity and yet was not disturbed by it. She sensed an honesty that encouraged her to say, "Well, Herr von Kunst, for conversation purposes after such flattering comments, I should at least accept your offer to listen to this idea you mentioned, but I cannot promise acceptance, agreed?"

Her acceptance to listen delighted Andre so noticeably that Katya had to fight back an urge to laugh out loud.

"You mentioned," Andre leaned forward speaking so earnestly that Katya drew back a little, " that there would be a short period of rest when you returned to Warsaw."

She nodded assent.

"Why not take this opportunity to spend a few of these rest days as my guest in Berlin? True, it's not the city it once was, but still has much to offer. My gallery has a collection of some of the world's finest art that I would be pleased to show you and the Maestro." He ended with an undisguised note of hopefulness in his voice.

Katya was quiet and at a loss to understand this interest in her. She had little contact with men other than those the Maestro would introduce her to from time to time. Whether he prescreened them or not, she suspected he did, none of them impressed her as did this young German. His politeness, his openness was not that of one trying to make a favorable impression for superficial reasons. She sensed a sincere desire to be accepted at face value, to be taken at his word.

Yes, she would like to know him better, but an invitation to visit Berlin? Hardly possible knowing the Maestro's feelings toward all things German.

"Herr von Kunst," she spoke rather slowly, and perhaps a touch of sadness was already evident in her voice, "you are most persuasive. Truly I am flattered that you find me so interesting to have made such an effort to meet me. I doubt there is any chance the Maestro would be inclined to accept your invitation. Nevertheless, I will ask on your behalf."

As she rose to go, Andre could hardly suppress the urge to reach for her hand and physically hold her longer, but instead he made one last plea as he handed her his business card after quickly writing his room number on it.

"Fraulein Presnoski, may I ask a personal question?"

She hesitated, but then smiled and said, "Of course!"

"If it were your decision alone, would you accept my invitation? It is important for me to know that."

"I suppose my saying the Maestro would not agree might indicate I am not capable of making my own decisions. I certainly can, but my reasons for considering what he would want to do, as it affects my own personal wishes, reaches a far distance back in my personal history.

"While I am not obligated to follow his wishes, I do owe a debt of gratitude for what he has so selflessly done for me. I'm sorry, but I don't feel it to be in order to say much further; it is a very private matter. Please take no offense. Now I must really go. Again, I am very pleased to have met you and am surprised at much of what you have told me about your efforts to meet me. Perhaps another time, other circumstances would have held more possibilities for knowing each other better.

"I really must go, I can make no promises, but I have enjoyed meeting you and much appreciated your kind remarks." Turning as she went, she gave what might be considered a coy smile as she said, "Auf Wiedersehen."

She was determined to take the walk the visit had interrupted if not unpleasantly. She needed to gather her thoughts, to rightly assess her feelings. She couldn't deny her interest in him.

As she walked enjoying the brisk morning air, it seemed to help clear the questionings in her mind. The comments Andre made about trying to reach her in Mainz pressed forward in her thinking. It was clear she needed to know whether or not the Maestro was aware of Andre's attempt to reach her in Mainz. If he did, then certainly an explanation was due her. Yet she was sure that if he did know, there would be a good reason for not telling her.

Yet whatever his motive or personal feelings, she felt courtesy dictated she be told when someone wanted to see her; he had to recognize that she was old enough to decide whether or not she wished to see who was inquiring.

She was a bit surprised at her own irritation toward the Maestro, that he would have made such a decision concerning a private matter. She owed him so much, but Katya reminded herself she was still an individual in her own right. She was determined to avoid her thankfulness to him become that of total subservience.

Yes, it was time to face the Maestro and his hate. Katya entered the hotel refreshed and considering the best way to suggest a Berlin visit to the Maestro. Yes, she'd ask as a personal favor, not as a demand, and if the Maestro was not prepared to grant her this wish, then she would not press the issue. That would be unfair to him. However, she was still determined to know if the Maestro was aware of the young man's attempt to contact her in Mainz, and if he did, why she was not told.

It was still quite early in the morning; she knew the Maestro would be having breakfast in his room. He never indulged in the bountiful breakfast hotels offered, content with a "kannchen kaffee und zwei brotchen" while reading the morning news, especially any reviews of his last performance.

Katya knew his mood was best at this time. The reviews were rarely negative. The orchestra had so established itself that a critic put himself in danger of losing creditability if he didn't have excellent grounds for his criticism, substantiated by other colleagues as well. As for Katya, the Maestro knew full well she was a tremendous asset, and her virtuoso performances were a major public draw.

He answered her light knock with a cheerful, "Come in." He quickly offered coffee and one of his rolls while beckoning her to take a seat.

CHAPTER 9

AFTER SHE LEFT, HE LAID THE PAPER ASIDE; POSITIVE reviews now held little interest after his conversation with Katya. He could justly take some credit for his excellent teaching, but her innate talent was exceptional. Without a doubt he was overly protective of her and his jealous guarding of this musical talent understandable.

He was pleased that she had been and was such a willing pupil, aware that this willingness did not hide the fact she had a strong will of her own. This will was demonstrated by her disciplined attention to his instructions. Without this determination, she never would have achieved such a high level of performance. He often reflected on these past years of their companionship and the joy she brought him.

With her visit with him this morning came the first dark clouds of doubt. How long could he shelter her from a hostile world? Berlin? To spend a few days in Berlin at the invitation of a scion of the hated von Kunst family was not to contemplate. His inner response was to dismiss out of hand this pleading of hers. It had actually hurt him deeply, but there was no doubt she really wanted his agreement to make this visit. He could have reasoned more strongly against the idea had she not asked as a personal favor and said she would understand if he did not agree.

He had been tempted to go further than ever before in explaining to her his hatred of Germany in general, and particularly the von Kunst family. They epitomized for him the evil in this land. Yet her sweet spirit had, as always, dissuaded him from telling her exactly how her parents had died. He was fearful her grief might so overcome her that her interest in music would be lost and she would sink into a deep depression. Until now she knew only that her parents had been swallowed up in the chaos of events. She assumed they had died through one of the tragic accidents of war. She wouldn't have the slightest inclination to believe the von Kunst family had any connection with their death.

But the Maestro had never been so close to telling her the truth as he was today. Revealing the truth would be a desperate effort to convince her that any connection with the von Kunst family or Germany was unthinkable. He thought that a full revelation would finally break through her incomprehensible optimism. It might cause her to finally understand the justification of his hatred and change her unwillingness to take it upon herself. Learning the truth of the past tragic events would certainly dispel any wish she might have to spend time in Berlin with him. Yet he had hesitated to say anything. He listened to her pleading to allow this small wish to venture beyond the established routine of their lives.

Inwardly, he was all the more furious that the young German had been so brazen as to tell Katya of his failed attempt to reach her. He explained in answer to her questions about the Mainz invitation that he had not told her because of his usual concern not to let unknown persons bother her with unsolicited advances.

"After all, Katya, my first concern is to make sure you are not deluged with pestering young men."

Katya had laughed. "Maestro, perhaps I would enjoy a little pestering. Would it be too much to ask you to at least tell me about those wanting to 'pester' me? From time to time it would be interesting to have dinner or a short conversation with someone wishing to compliment my playing. You know how gratifying it is to hear compliments that a performance was enjoyed, and that it gave the listener such pleasure that they made the effort to tell us personally."

"Katya," he had replied, "perhaps I have been too protective of you. You are a grown woman; I have no right to intervene in your world as I did when you were a child. All that I have done was for what I believed to be for your good. Not telling you of Herr von Kunst's attempt to visit you was with that purpose in mind. However, he has succeeded quite cleverly, I must say, in circumventing my obvious desire that he not contact us, or specifically, you."

"Cleverly?" she'd asked, surprised at this open admission of his wish to keep the young man away.

"Katya, don't you find it a little strange that he sits by pure chance in a café directly across from the hotel where he can watch whoever comes and goes?"

"Maestro, I find it totally coincidental. When I left the hotel, I really had no intention of going to that café; it was a spur-of-the-moment decision. My, but you are the suspicious one!" she said laughingly. Secretly, she rather enjoyed the thought that he had deliberately positioned himself for an opportunity to meet her.

The Maestro had struggled with the thought of having to spend any more time than necessary in Germany, let alone in Berlin as a guest of this von Kunst. Getting back to Warsaw and a well-earned rest from the rigorous demands of touring was too compelling a reason not to give in to Katya's request. But perhaps the time had come for her to learn for herself what the true reaction of these people would have toward her when she was among them simply as a visitor. Perhaps exposure to Herr von Kunst in his home environment might reveal a far different character than the one now presented to her.

He decided he would give in to her but not without some definite preconditions. He would offer to go with the condition that the stay be three days; or less, should he decide it was not in both their interest to stay longer. He would tell her so at dinner.

Katya returned to her room after her talk with the Maestro. She was a bit perplexed; he had made little comment one way or the other, but he had not given the adamant "no" she had expected. He had appreciated her less than demanding manner. He said only that it was a decision he could not make lightly. He needed to consider all aspects including the personal nature of her wish, the demands on their time, and the need to get back to Warsaw. As she thought about the possibility he might agree, she began to have reservations about whether or not she wanted him to say yes. A no would allow her to tell Herr von Kunst she had tried but to no avail. The Maestro, she would say, had said their schedule simply would not allow the time. This might at least give him the satisfaction she had not rejected his request outright, but she could not deny the excitement a "yes" would bring.

Admittedly, she was aware he was very physically attractive, but Katya was too much the pragmatist to expect that attribute alone to be sufficient for an enduring relationship. The Maestro had, surprisingly, not responded as she had expected, not withstanding the good mood she found him enjoying. She had calculated a good mood would simply temper the more vehement rejection she really expected. Instead, he had listened to her as she unsuccessfully tried to hide her desire for his approval. When she had ended, he had simply said, "Katya, this is not an easy matter. There are many reasons why we should not accept, but please let me think this over and we can discuss this over dinner this evening."

She had thanked the Maestro for listening and the promise to talk more later about her request, irrational as she knew it appeared to him. That he would approve, she doubted.

Andre returned to the hotel after Katya left. From what she had said, it appeared her bond with the Maestro was not going to be broken with an appeal to visit an obviously unwelcome stranger. Well, he would remain for the day and evening in Köln in the vain hope she might call. He had waited this long and was not willing to give up until the last ray of hope faded away.

As Katya sat down with the Maestro for dinner, she tried hard not to show any of the tension gripping her. She already prepared herself for the inevitable denial of her request, recognizing that it would be best if he did, yet she couldn't deny the anticipation that he might agree. She always used Andre's full family name when thinking of him. She didn't allow even in her private thoughts the intimacy of his first name. After placing their order, the Maestro looked intently at Katya when he asked, "Katya, does Herr von Kunst know you are Jewish?"

This startled Katya, who replied quickly, "Yes."

The Maestro raised his bushy eyebrows in surprise and followed up with, "And of course he knows you are Polish?"

The "Yes" came almost with a touch of defiance. It was becoming more evident to the Maestro that she and Andre had had a more in-depth conversation than he had assumed.

"Katya, perhaps I have been remiss in sheltering you from a world that historically has not been friendly to Jews, let alone Polish ones. Above all, countries like Germany, Russia and, yes, even England, France, and the United States have strong elements that hold no abiding love for us. I have tried, perhaps too subtlety, in many ways to make you aware of this. I have explained to you that the loss of your parents and my taking you to England were all events that were a result of this abiding hatred of us."

Katya took his pause as a chance to interrupt. "Maestro, I do not believe you have been subtle at all. I have heard you express many times your hatred of Germany. Indeed, it now seems that you place the entire world as arrayed against me just because of the accident of my birth into the wrong culture and nation. I have always resisted, while always respecting you, this disdain, no, your hatred of Germany.

"Yet, may I respectfully ask, is your hatred good, theirs evil? It seems to me, as I remember my father's teaching, that hatred is a fire that consumes the soul, leaving only ashes of despair. I cannot believe that in all fairness you can hate individually people of a nation because a political power has misled, lied, or in any other way manipulated circumstances to serve admittedly evil purposes."

The Maestro had too often heard her unreasonable belief in the goodness of most people. Would it not now be appropriate to tell her the full truth, a truth that should be enough to destroy her evident belief that Herr von Kunst was one of the good individuals in a corrupt nation? After all, whether it was this young man personally or others in his family, it was impossible to believe he was not aware of their involvement with the loss of her parents. But would his word alone suffice to convince her?

He knew she had explicit faith in him and would probably take his word as well meaning, but without true conviction he was right. There was little doubt that the young German had stirred more than a passing interest in her. Words of reason, even facts, would be hard pressed to convince a heart already inclined to disbelieve any evidence contrary to what the heart wanted to believe.

Perhaps the visit to Berlin was the best solution. By giving in to her wish, he would be placing her in the very environment of hate he had wished to avoid. Observing Herr von Kunst in familiar surroundings might be what was needed to have her experience personally the depraved culture the Maestro had been unable to convey in words. Yes, he'd give in, but not for the reasons she might think.

"Katya," he finally continued after her defense, "I have always considered what I felt was in your best interest whatever decisions I made. Perhaps this has led to my being overly protective. If so, my apology."

Katya quickly protested, "I never doubted your intent, Maestro. I'm sure my parents couldn't have given more care for my welfare than you have. But I must learn for myself some of life's lessons that you have explained to me but I failed to grasp. No doubt it's because I have not experienced them as you have. Perhaps the experiences I seek will only confirm much of what you have told me, but I accept that even at my own peril."

"Katya, that is bravely said, so it is time for me to accept your bravery, your challenge to me to let you venture into an environment that I cannot see holding anything of positive value. So we go to Berlin."

He saw with some dismay the surprised but happy smile form on her pretty lips. *Well,* he thought sadly, *perhaps the lesson she will learn in Berlin will erase forever such an innocent look, but so be it, it must finally come.* The initial excitement she felt at his words was tempered by the awareness of his strong reluctance.

"Maestro, I promise, should it become unbearable for you, we can leave at anytime. I will make this clear to Herr von Kunst, but thank you."

"Katya, I can only hope that you won't change your 'thank you' to a sorrowful 'why did you?'"

"No, never, Maestro, you have made your concerns perfectly clear, but I must be woman enough to accept all consequences without any blame on your part."

They went to their separate rooms. He for a restless night, Katya pondering when to call Herr von Kunst, now or in the morning? It wasn't exceptionally late; she doubted he retired very early. She reached hesitantly for his card and with a somewhat shaking hand lifted the receiver. She was still uncertain what she should say as the import of what she was doing began to feed her persistent doubts. Shouldn't she consider further the Maestro's concerns and warnings? After all, even if the Maestro agreed, he did so very reluctantly. Perhaps it would be better not to accept the invitation, to end the matter right now. She dialed his number; it was busy.

It suddenly occurred to Andre that he had not called the gallery since he had left. While it was not unusual for him to be off traveling, he had always called the gallery at least every other day or left word where he could be reached.

I truly find this neglect to be out of character, he thought to himself. *I must get this situation under control and accept the reality that my behavior has been irrational. From all indications, the matter is ended. I doubt Katya will receive any support from the Maestro to accept. I had better get on with attending to the daily routine of business.*

Elsa never minded his late calls; it gave her more time to talk. He reached for the phone and dialed her number.

CHAPTER 10

IT WAS EVIDENT SHE WASN'T GERMAN, ALTHOUGH she spoke the language fluently, but with an accent that Elsa detected to be east European. Her companion was obviously American, easily identified by the style of dress, or lack of it. He was looking admiringly at the gallery's art objects while his companion introduced herself as Maria Skorkia. She told Elsa they needed to speak with either Frau Hasenfeld or Herr von Kunst.

Elsa replied in perfect English that Herr von Kunst was traveling and Frau Hasenfeld was not presently available. However, she would be glad to take any message and was sure one or the other would get back to her at the earliest opportunity.

Elsa's reply in English was deliberate; she already assumed the young man was American and the lady before her would also be conversant in English. Elsa was very proud that she spoke French and English as well as her native German tongue. She rather enjoyed the reaction of people who, assuming no doubt she was simply the receptionist, were surprised when she answered in their native language.

One of Elsa's unique talents was the ability to quickly assess by discrete questions if a first-time visitor was a dealer, broker, private buyer, or a 'just looking.' Elsa noted Maria's two-piece gray suit over a bright, highly starched white shirt and thin black tie and the giveaway large black portfolio/handbag. *No doubt an insurance agent*, surmised Elsa.

It wasn't unusual for insurance companies to inquire about certain works of art and their market value. Usually, most requests were by mail or phone; this personal visit, without any prior appointment was unusual.

It was clear from the expression on her face that Maria Skorkia was not pleased with the information Elsa gave her. Elsa, noting this, offered to help in any way she could. If it were a matter about some work of art the gallery possessed, she herself was a registered appraiser and perhaps could provide some assistance. She noted with some pleasure, the surprised reaction shown by both of them at this information. Elsa was always amused that people seemed to assume that a receptionist was usually a pretty face placed to offer a human touch to the entering public, but of not much value beyond that. Elsa was aware of her natural good looks, but much more pleased that it was her knowledge of art that gained her immediate respect.

Maria thanked her for her offer but explained that she and her colleague, Greg Summer, were representatives of International Gallery, New York, and the information they needed could only be supplied by one of the partners. It was important to meet with one or the other as soon as possible.

Elsa knew from Maria's introduction that her company insured not just individual works of art, but the galleries themselves against fraud, theft, or physical damage. When Elsa asked again the nature of their visit, Maria said, not unkindly, but emphatically, that it was a matter that could only be discussed with an owner or authorized partner of the gallery.

"When," she asked, "would they be available? We have come directly from New York and would like to finalize our work here as quickly as possible."

Elsa was surprised; if a visit of such importance mandated a direct flight form New York, why wouldn't an advance appointment have been made? In answer to the question of availability, she said she would place a call to Frau Hannelore Hasenfeld and inquire if she was accessible.

When Hannelore answered and Elsa told her of the visitor's request, Hannelore responded quickly that she would check her appointments and call back in a few moments. Elsa told Maria and Greg that Frau Hasenfeld would call back in a few minutes; meanwhile they could wait in the small lounge or browse around the gallery. Maria nodded and took a seat in the well-appointed lounge and proceeded to review some papers she took out of her handbag. Greg smiled at Elsa and commented upon the large inventory on display of not just paintings but sculptures and other objects of art.

"Yes," replied Elsa. "The gallery is noted for its wide-ranging repertoire and has a resident restorer whose expertise in repairing damaged works of art is without peer. In fact, many insurance companies call on his services for claim repairs."

Hannelore did not like surprises. She was annoyed that Elsa had not been able to determine the reason for their visit. Elsa had hoped that she could pass on some further information by the time Hannelore called back. She was not intimidated by Hannelore, but was constantly aware that Hannelore viewed her as no more than a necessary employee. Elsa liked to take every opportunity to counter that opinion.

Hannelore recognized at once the name of the insurance company Maria represented. This unannounced visit disturbed her. While International Gallery insured galleries for many forms of coverage, their expertise was investigating fraud.

With this in mind, Hannelore quickly reviewed the publications the gallery received for any information of current events indicating some activity that would lead the visitors to Kunst Gallery. If she had any concern at all, it would be centered on Kunst Gallery's affiliate in New York, Art World. She had opened the New York gallery several months ago, forming a partnership with Kurt Kohl that had more to do with using his compliant nature and personal affection for her than any business skills he had. What are these agents looking for? While she normally took care of all the Gallery's business affairs, the insistence of the visitors to talk only with either of the partners, she decided, it would be better to have Andre here as well.

She also needed to check with Otto in the event he had any news that had escaped her. A quick call to him resulted in his answering he knew nothing of importance. Hannelore couldn't see the look of satisfaction on Otto's face when she told him the visitors were from International Gallery, New York. Otto knew well their reputation.

Although more time to think about the situation and gather more news would have been her wish, she wanted to avoid any suspicion a prolonged delay in meeting them might cause. When she called back, she asked Elsa if Andre had called and when he was expected to be back.

Hannelore seemed mildly annoyed when Elsa told her there had been no calls from Andre since he left Sunday. That he had told Hannelore he was going to Mainz, without details, was not unusual. What was unusual was that he had made no contact with the gallery since leaving.

"Well, Fraulein Becker," Hannelore, of course, would never use an employee's first name, "when Andre does call, have him call me directly without delay. Now tell the visitors if they wish to meet me, then it must be at two p.m. tomorrow. I'll hold for their answer."

Elsa told Maria of the date and time, accepting the curt nod as approval, and told Hannelore they agreed. With that Hannelore hung up with no further words to be wasted exchanging pleasantries with Elsa, which, of course, she never did anyhow. Elsa didn't expect any.

As Elsa hung up, Maria rose and motioned to Greg, who was intently studying a large, beautiful porcelain figure of a unicorn and a young girl wearing a diaphanous robe stroking its mane. As Greg joined Maria, Maria thanked Elsa for her time and confirmed they would be back at the appointed time tomorrow.

Outside the gallery, Greg said, "Maria, why is it that every time I see a picture or anything involving a unicorn, there is always a young girl included?" Maria pointedly ignored the comment; unicorns and girls were not her concern, she said; what was her concern was the obvious delay given to them.

"Can't see us today! I'm sure Frau Hasenfeld is putting us off as they do when they hear 'insurance.'"

"Well," offered the more tolerant Greg, "It could well be it's all very legitimate. I don't think the receptionist was at all evasive. You know arriving unannounced without an appointment is simply a calculated risk that you'll get an immediate audience."

"Agreed," said Maria. "But it's worth the risk. There's always the chance that a surprise visit will catch them off guard. At least it lessens the time that an advance notice of our coming would give them to possibly alter or even hide information we need. It makes me all the more suspicious when we get the brush off."

"Maria, you always assume the worse. We have no evidence of any wrongdoing by this gallery; we are simply looking for information that may help us without themselves being suspected of wrongdoing."

"Greg," saying his name with some exasperation, "One of the chief attributes I believe necessary in this line of work is to always be suspicious and not distracted by a pretty receptionist, especially when it involves a

$560,000 fraud claim." Greg laughed. "Well, she is pretty! So since we have to wait until tomorrow, let's take a look at the city, okay?" he asked.

Maria didn't answer immediately; she still felt somewhat awkward in Greg's presence, although she had no reason to feel that way. He was and had been the perfect gentleman even after her promotion over him, but the offer of a walk seemed an invitation to a former closeness she wanted to avoid.

"Greg, I would rather go back to the hotel, update my notes to include this visit and what our line of attack should be; sure I'm suspicious. There's no doubt the painting in question came from this gallery. The best way to prove my suspicion wrong will be to prove to me they had no idea this was a copy"

"Okay, Maria, you're right. I guess I presume innocence until proven guilty while you order the gallows to be built in anticipation," Greg said with a laugh.

"Better to have it ready. I can always use it later if I don't need it this time," Maria countered.

Maria was not harsh or vindictive by nature, but experience had warned her that extending trust before proof was dangerous; it avoided the deep hurt that misplaced trust could cause.

"Well, I'm not ready to go back yet," Greg said. "I think I'll just walk around for a bit." Maria nodded, said she'd walk back to the hotel rather than take a cab since it wasn't that far.

Greg waived "so long" and turned to go down the Kurfurstendam lined with the bustling activity of a revitalized Germany. After a time, he located an inviting café and ordered a coffee and piece of cake served by an attractive waitress who spoke perfect English. Greg wondered if a German visitor stopping in New York would be served by a waitress speaking his native language.

Interesting, he thought, *how the twist and turns of my life have brought me to Berlin. Quite a far reach from my days at the seminary preparing to save the world. Well, saving artworks has its place in saving society, doesn't it? Or is it that the twist and turns that have led to Maria is what's really important?* He remembered well her concerns about her promotion and their friendship. Thoughts of Bobby and his devotion to Esther, whatever the costs to Bobby, continued to haunt him. Could he have the same devotion to Maria?

CHAPTER 11

YES, ANDRE THOUGHT IT WAS TIME TO RETURN TO reality, the quest need end. He had little hope that the Maestro would give in to Katya even if she followed his plea to try. However, even if there was little hope, he was going to wait another day.

He was pleased to hear Elsa's pleasant "hello," even at this late hour. Recognizing his voice at once, she quickly told him to call Hannelore immediately in the morning or even tonight.

"She's been quite cross that she could not reach you and told me to have you contact her at once when you called." Andre was mildly surprised. Admittedly, he had been gone a few more days than usual before contacting the gallery, but that should not have merited the urgency in Elsa's voice to call Hannelore "at once."

"Did she say what was so important?" he asked.

"No," replied Elsa, "but she has been quite on edge after she had a visit with two insurance people from New York. They met briefly in her office and, while I did not hear what they were saying, it was evident Hannelore was not comfortable with them. After they left she came to me and said there was to be another meeting, but she told me to schedule that only when you could be here. Then she went directly to Otto's studio."

"Well, I should be back the day after tomorrow, but I do not know for sure just when. I had better call Hannelore and find out what is the hurry. I'm just not sure when I'll be getting back for you to set a meeting time."

"Please let me know as soon as you can. It's nice to hear from you; you know you are very much missed when you aren't here." After a slight pause, she added, "By all of us, of course. Well, I'm glad you're okay. Goodbye."

Andre smiled to himself, he was aware that Elsa had some liking for him, as he did for her. They had dated on occasion, but it was more of just a friendly evening dinner or theater than any formal date. Andre and Elsa both knew that Hannelore wouldn't approve of any close relationship between them. She maintained that familiarity would lessen the necessary disciplinary control one should have over employees.

While Andre didn't share that concern, he avoided, whenever possible areas of controversy with Hannelore; it was just too unpleasant an atmosphere to work in when she was in high dungeon about something.

With some trepidation, Andre reached for the phone again, irritated with himself for his inability to overcome the feeling of a child facing a mother's reprimand. *Better to call her now and get it over with than wait till morning*, he reasoned.

Hannelore answered her phone and without so much as a "hello," demanded to know why he hadn't called earlier, and when exactly he would be back. Andre listened patiently trying to decide what he would use as an excuse.

He really didn't need any; he and Hannelore were equal partners insofar as his father and hers had specified their separate responsibilities and share of the profits. However, the actual stock had remained in his and his mother's name. Andre long ago recognized Hannelore's expertise in business and his complete reliance on her in such matters. That she was demanding his return was even more surprising because seldom was he ever involved with anything requiring a business decision.

"Andre, I must have you back here at once, please." The "please" caught him off guard. Usually, a direct demand from Hannelore contained no "please"; his curiosity was aroused but not enough to want to come back at once. He wanted to stall his return as long as possible while there was hope that Katya might contact him. Of course, he had no intention of telling Hannelore this because he would risk more of her ire if he didn't come up with a good reason not to come at once.

"Hannelore, I plan to leave Köln—"

"Köln?" interrupted Hannelore abruptly. "Köln? I thought you were in Mainz."

Andre thought quickly. "Yes, I was, but by happenstance I ran into the conductor of the orchestra we had just heard in Berlin. They were performing in Mainz. I told him that I had really been impressed by his Berlin performance. Since they were performing that night, he invited me to attend as his guest. I must say, Hannelore, I should have paid more attention to these concerts and developed the deeper appreciation you have always said was necessary." The pause from Hannelore was proof enough that Andre had fully perplexed her.

Finally, she said, "Andre, certainly this renewed interest in music is commendable. But if you're going to pursue this interest, then by all means wait until you have the opportunity to learn from someone eminently more qualified than a Polish conductor. Really, I can hardly see how this awakening could come from one visit to a foreign performance."

Andre couldn't help noticing Hannelore's practiced tone of disdain when she pronounced "foreign." He offered no comment.

Hannelore went on, "This is all very interesting, but what has it to do with you being in Köln and your not coming back immediately for a very important matter. I need your assistance to resolve what could be a troubling matter."

Andre was not comfortable with being in a situation that prevented him from being totally forthright. He was not by nature manipulative with people or with the truth, but to tell Hannelore the total truth would be, to say the least, most unpleasant. He didn't like his inability to assert himself against her. Since their youth he had always deferred to Hannelore's wishes; now he was resolved to wait at least one more day for a call from Katya.

"Hannelore, it is a bit complicated; after the Mainz performance, the director invited me to Köln where he was introducing a new arrangement of a Bach concerto. He thought it would prove most interesting for me to hear a first-time performance and experience the audience reaction."

"Andre, I am trying to understand what you are saying, but I find it hard to believe that this 'Polish' conductor would have such an influence that your love of music blossomed so quickly. Nevertheless, you can have other opportunities with much more qualified persons to further your musical interest, so please come at once so that this matter can be resolved."

There was no denying the edge in Hannelore's voice clearly implying that any reply other than his agreement to come at once would be unacceptable. Andre was determined to find a way around this impending disruption of his plan.

"Hannelore, can you at least give me some reason as to why this meeting is so important that I be there?"

"Andre," an exasperated Hannelore was losing patience, "this matter could affect the gallery negatively if not answered with dispatch. Your reputation will add much to offsetting any implication of impropriety on our part."

"Impropriety?" Andre asked sharply.

"Well," continued Hannelore, "anytime insurance people come questioning I am concerned. Although I am quite sure there is nothing we have done to merit suspicion, you never know how they will interpret things. So please come at once."

Andre, sensing she was about to hang up in the full belief he would be on his way, said, "Hannelore, wait a moment. I cannot come today, it will have to be the day after tomorrow. I promised Herr Mylovic to attend tomorrow's concert, at which time he will tell me whether or not he can accept my invitation to spend a few days in Berlin. As you can imagine, his schedule is very tight and..."

An audible gasp from Hannelore followed by, "What did you say?" interrupted him. She repeated again her question adding, "What was that about an invitation?"

"I said that I invited Herr Mylovic to spend a few days as my guest in Berlin. I thought it was a proper gesture to repay him for all the kindness he has shown me the past few days."

"Andre, I am at a loss to ever understand your lack of sensitivity in matters concerning what is and what is not acceptable in our cultural circle of friends. I have talked to you before about your, at times, almost deliberate attempts to embarrass people. My friends are important to our gallery; by criticizing, or worse, ridiculing their opinions and beliefs is not appreciated by them or me!"

Andre was well aware that this conversation was not going to result in a pacified Hannelore, but he had no choice. He was not going to risk, however remote, the chance Katya would have succeeded in convincing the Maestro to come to Berlin.

"Hannelore, I cannot imagine that even your close circle of friends, possessing this extremely strange attitude toward persons they do not even know, could be offended by the visit of this world-renowned composer and conductor."

Hannelore replied icily, "This is an affront to me and my friends' sensibility. The man is Polish; whatever his accomplishments, deserved or otherwise, cannot change that fact." Andre knew there was no value in furthering the conversation.

"Hannelore, the Maestro will give me his answer sometime tomorrow. If he accepts, I certainly cannot withdraw my invitation. In any event, I will leave after tomorrow's evening concert. Should he be able to come, I will be in Berlin to meet the train; if not, I'll tell Elsa to schedule the meeting you want. In any event, I can't be more specific at this time."

Andre could envision the tensed muscles of Hannelore's jaws and the thin line of her lips as she said there was no value in discussing matters any further. She made it clear that he had an obligation to return as soon as possible and that any adversity caused by his tardy return would be laid to his account. After telling him to call Elsa about his plans as soon as possible, she hung up without further comment.

As Andre laid his phone down, he felt a strange feeling of liberation. Should, by chance, his offer be accepted, his arrival in Berlin, not only with the Maestro but with Katya as well, would make for one interesting visit with Hannelore. He was determined, however, not to miss an opportunity to be with Katya for a few days. He must know more about this lovely creature who had so captivated him. Their brief encounter had only heightened this desire.

Hannelore hung up the phone in exasperation. The visit that afternoon with the two investigators had not gone well.

CHAPTER 12

ELSA ESCORTED GREG AND MARIA INTO THE CONFERENCE
room promptly at 2 p.m. and called Hannelore to announce their arrival.
Hannelore entered and motioned them to keep their seats. She wore a
tailored dark blue suit trimmed with white. Her hair was drawn back but
allowed an ample amount of blonde hair to rest on her shoulders. The
single diamond necklace and sapphire pendant with earrings to match
Greg estimated at a value that would pay the rent on his flat for several
years. He couldn't help a discrete glance at the exquisite legs Hannelore
crossed as she seated herself and presented her card.

Maria noted with some amusement the effect Hannelore was having
on Greg. She knew her somber two-piece gray suit contrasted sharply
with Hannelore's sartorial perfection. Maria answered quickly to Hannelore's abrupt question about the purpose of their visit. It was evident to
Maria that Hannelore wasn't interested in a prolonged conversation. She
handed Hannelore her and Greg's cards and without further introduction explained that her company carried the insurance for their client,
Art World.

A Renoir painting, sold by them as an original, was later proved to
be a copy. Hannelore showed no emotion, simply asked what that had to
do with Von Kunst Gallery. At this point, with a nod from Maria, Greg
entered the conversation.

He said he had contacted the proprietor of Art World, who professed
no knowledge of the transaction since he had taken over the gallery fairly
recently. He told Greg that the previous owner, Kurt Kohl, had decided

to sell out and go elsewhere. He had no further contact with him but confirmed Kurt Kohl's signature was the one on the receipt for the sale. At this comment, Hannelore didn't show the shock she felt, believing that her advice to Kurt to make himself scarce had been well taken. She asked again what this had to do with her gallery.

Fortunately, Greg said he had been able to locate Kurt, who affirmed he had sold the picture as an original, and that the picture had come from Von Kunst Gallery clearly marked as an original. Maria watched Hannelore's face for any show of emotion at this news. There was none. Hannelore was inwardly angered that Kurt had allowed himself to be discovered. She quickly replied with complete calm that she was not always current on matters concerning individual transactions with the various outlets that purchased from their gallery.

However, she was sure that if the painting in question was a copy and not an original, a switch must have been made by Art World.

Maria was convinced that Hannelore knew far more than she was admitting to but decided a direct challenge would not faze this woman. Maria simply said that the matter could be quickly cleared if she could have a copy of their invoice declaring the painting to be an original. If that were so, then their only recourse would be to pursue Kurt Kohl for fraud. Hannelore, still evidencing an outward calm, agreed that the insurer had every right to pursue Kurt for this falsification. However, she wanted her partner, Andre von Kunst, to be present when she showed them the invoice and to finalize the matter. He was now traveling and not expected back for a day or two, she would contact them as soon as he was back.

With that, Hannelore stood up signaling the meeting was over for her and extended an ice-cold hand in parting. How much the investigators now knew about her relationship with Art World or how much Kurt had revealed she didn't know. Why Kurt had done such an idiotic thing was beyond belief. He knew his success had been her making, so why would he have risked all of this? Her greatest fear was that a further probing would lead to questions as to how Von Kunst gallery came into possession of this original in the first place. This was one of the paintings that were to be sold only through the channel set up with Count von Linglesdorf to private U.S. purchasers.

CHAPTER 13

GREG AND MARIA WORKED WELL TOGETHER DESPITE her promotion over him. One morning Maria came over to Greg and showed him a claim that Brad had just laid on her desk.

"Hot Potato," she said seriously. "Sid told Brad to give it to me. Unfortunately, it's a claim from a gallery that Brad wrote the policy for. Greg, I'll really need your expert help."

Greg agreed readily, always pleased at the opportunity to be working with her.

Maria filled him in on the details of the case. A claim had been filed against one of Sid's insured, Art World, for fraud. A painting had been sold as an original for $560,000 to a purchaser who subsequently died. His estate claimed the painting was a copy, not an original as stated on the receipt. Maria gave Greg a copy of the receipt stating the painting was an original. Greg set out at once to visit Art World.

His reception by the gallery owner, who said his name was Georg, was cordial. After introducing himself, Greg produced the receipt and asked if he could see the file pertaining to the sale of the painting. Noting the date on the receipt, Georg explained the sale had been conducted before he had bought the gallery. The previous owner had taken all records. He verified that the signature on the receipt, Kurt Kohl, was the person from whom he had bought the gallery, but since then had no contact with him. Greg explained that without locating the original seller it would be impossible to determine the origin of the picture. Since it was the object of an insurance claim, any possible information would be greatly appreciated.

"Well, it does sound urgent," said the owner. "May I ask what the claim is about, was the painting stolen?"

Greg was hesitant; he didn't want to cut off the only lead he had, but didn't know how much of the details he should disclose. He decided that getting information about Kurt was the better risk and it would do little harm to tell the facts.

"It seems that the painting was sold as an original to the gentleman named on the receipt who, unfortunately, died shortly after the purchase. His estate is now in liquidation. Since the painting was an item of some value, the estate's executor requested an appraisal. My company was the insurer of this gallery at the time the picture was sold. Naturally, we're concerned that this new appraisal claims that the painting is a copy, not an original."

At the mention of the painting being a copy, Greg noticed the owner showed a renewed interest.

"A copy, you say?" the owner sounded surprised. "I would think that anyone purchasing a picture for that price would have made sure it was an original."

With that, Georg shrugged his shoulders and said, "Well, I really can't help you. I have no idea of the past history of the gallery. This Kurt offered it to me at a good price so I bought it. I don't see any need to inquire here about the claim. As far as I am concerned, I don't think there is any reason to involve this gallery with past events."

Greg decided there was nothing more to be gained from this interview and, thanking the owner, he left.

His priority was locating Kurt Kohl. Greg was only a few steps out the door when the owner quickly placed a long-distance call.

Greg thought there was the possibility Kurt was known by other storeowners in the area who could provide more information. He inquired at several but found little information useful. But there was always the possibility Kurt would have gone more into the Village to sell some pieces for cash. Dealers in the Village carried inventories more varied than his and catered more to the tourist trade that frequented the area. He decided to at least explore the possibility the next day.

The next morning Greg got up planning an early visit to Greenwich.

He enjoyed getting there early before the regular day began and watching the community become slowly aware another day had actually arrived.

Greg had a secret envy for this community where they lived their lives according to their own time schedules, which meant, in fact, no schedule; just follow the flow of events. If a late-night party meant sleeping in and ignoring the faded opening time on their shop door, so be it. If the customers were really interested, they'd be back. If not, they weren't interested anyhow.

As Greg enjoyed his coffee and munched a fresh bagel, the sun's early tentative rays crept through the alleys and tried vainly to penetrate the soot-covered windows of the not-to-be-wakened denizens in their lairs. Greg knew there would still be a wait before any of the shops opened. He enjoyed the quiet and his coffee.

His thoughts gravitated to Maria. She was always point north on his emotional compass whenever he tried to relax. Just how much of his nonchalance about her promotion was genuine? He thought about the enjoyable months she worked beside him before the promotion.

Hadn't he hoped that the promotion would keep her in the firm? As soon as other galleries heard she had taken a position with them, she was deluged with offers. She had confided in Greg that while she was flattered and, maybe, a little bit tempted to explore them, she wasn't in the habit of job-hopping. But it made him nervous; he didn't want her to leave, and it wasn't for the firm's sake. He wanted her near, but he soon learned the nearness he wanted came at a high price. Marie held to her determination to keep him at a distance.

His coffee and bagel were about finished, but it was still too early to expect much activity in the Village. The sun had done all it could in the alley and was advancing more into the main avenues. It warmed him and he decided to reorder another round of coffee and bagel.

He thought again of the circumstances that led him to this early morning watch. He continued thinking about Maria and tried to again analyze his reasons for staying with the firm after he had been passed over by her. Yet, in all truthfulness, it wasn't that she became his boss; he honestly believed she deserved the position. It was more the loss of her as a colleague, a peer, when they both could share ideas and thoughts on the same level. It was after her promotion that things changed.

The sun's rays now touched him; he was tempted to sit a while longer and just enjoy its warmth, perhaps another bagel and coffee refill were in order, but he resisted and reluctantly left his reverie of past events, motivated by the knowledge Maria would be awaiting his report.

She was all business now, not impolite, but certainly keeping her distance. After he told her of his visit to Art World and apparent lack of success there, she only nodded and agreed with his idea to explore this area. She made it clear that a positive report would be appreciated.

He paid the bill and ventured down the street. Some shops were just beginning to show signs that life was returning. He glanced at the various shop windows, noting which ones might be worth a visit. Just as he was about to cross the street, he caught a glimpse of a small picture propped up against the corner wall behind a window lettered *Bobby's Stuff*. He stepped over for a closer look.

His first impression was that it was a Pizzonie; however, if it were an original, he doubted it would be resting here among Bobby's Stuff. *Probably a copy*, he thought, *but a very good one*. Out of a curiosity to examine it, he decided he'd come back when 'Bobby' opened up; that is, if 'Bobby' was one of those who bothered to open at the time their weather-faded signs announced. Bobby's barely readable sign said 8:30 a.m.

There was still a half hour to go, so Greg decided he'd wander around for awhile and come back. He was just turning away when a young fellow approached the door and after a bit of fumbling for a key stuck in one or the other pocket of a well-worn pair of jeans put it in the lock.

"Bobby?" ventured Greg. The lad shook his head as he said, "I'm Jim. Bobby will be along later. I just open for him and do some straightening up before the day starts."

"Could I come in and take a look at the picture I see in the window?" Greg asked.

"Sure," Jim said, smiling. "Bobby will be along shortly, I'm sure," he said with enough uncertainty that Greg allowed 'shortly' to be more euphemism than fact. As they entered the store, Greg allowed the 'Stuff' 'lettered on the window was well represented on the cluttered counters inside. Greg went over and picked up the picture. To his surprise, a close examination convinced him it was an original. He was all the more interested after noting that penciled on the reverse side of the picture's lower corner was "Art World."

He turned to Jim. "Jim, do you know how much Bobby wants for this picture?"

"I can look it up," Jim said. "Bobby has a card file. Since I watch the store from time to time while he is out scouring flea markets or sidewalk throw-a-ways, he lets me make a sale for him. Are you a dealer? If so, you can get a twenty percent discount."

"Well, that's great," Greg responded, enjoying the young man's enthusiasm. "But do I qualify if I'm only an insurance rep?" Jim paused; he didn't want to kill a sale for Bobby and figured a "rep" would qualify.

"Sure," he said, "let me get the card." Greg was intrigued that the picture was truly an original and all the more surprised when Jim announced that the price on the card was $150.00 less, of course, the twenty percent.

Evidently, Greg thought, *Bobby isn't very well versed in the value of some of the "Stuff" he carries.* Greg nodded at the price quoted. He turned to the young man. "The price is okay, but I would like to know more about the painting before I decide," he said.

Jim looked doubtful. "I really don't know any details, and the card file simply states the price. Bobby might have other records; you'll need to ask him."

"Could we give him a call?" queried Greg.

"Bobby told me phone calls were simply an annoyance, and if people asked for him just to take their number and he'd call them," Jim said.

"Well, he might lose sales that way, wouldn't he?" asked Greg.

Jim laughed. "I don't think that bothers Bobby too much; he told me that if he had a loaf of bread, some cheese, and wine to cover the needs of a day, that was enough. Anything more was surplus."

Greg laughed in return. "Well, Jim, it seems Bobby has more interest in Omar Kyam's philosophy than art. Tell you what, I do want to know more about this picture. I'll buy it and then I'll come back later and talk to Bobby, okay?"

"Sure, Bobby will be glad to talk to you, and I'll tell him when he comes in. He should be here in around an hour and a half or so. Funny, I don't think I ever met this Omar guy in here." Jim was glad for the sale; Bobby always gave him a few bucks if he sold something. He wrapped the painting for Greg and gave him a receipt, thanking him.

"Well, thank you, Jim; be sure and tell Bobby I'll be back." Greg shook Jim's hand and left. It wasn't that long since his bagel and coffee, but another one wouldn't hurt to pass the time. Then he'd call Maria and update her about the picture.

While sipping his coffee and nibbling his bagel, he unwrapped the picture and turned it over. He noted that the back covering was quite new. This was not unusual for older paintings where the original covering, usually a light paper or cardboard, had become discolored or torn. It made a better impression for resale to at least have a new covering. No doubt Bobby had done that; however, Greg was still curious after noting the penciled "Art World." He wondered if the original backing was just covered over. He took out his penknife and carefully cut off the backing. The original was still there, and affixed to it was a printed label, "V K G," Berlin, in old German script. Greg was now all the more curious about this painting and its tie to Art World.

He decided putting off any call to Maria until he talked with Bobby. He sat for a while longer enjoying the sun then got up and started for 'Bobby's Stuff.'

Jim was still there, and as Greg entered, Jim called into the backroom, "Hey Bobby, the guy I told you about is here."

"Okay," echoed a reply, "be right there." Soon a tall, sandy-haired figure emerged slowly from the doorway evidencing no need to hurry. He paused to brush some of the evidence of cheese and bread from his shirt and then looked up at Greg, who couldn't help smiling at the removal of the crumbs.

"Hi," he said, extending his hand, "I'm Bobby. Jim tells me you bought the picture I had in the window and wanted some info about it."

"Yeah," Greg said extending his hand to meet the proffered one. "I know that artist. I was curious how you happened to get hold of it. Originals of his are hard to find."

Bobby looked surprised. "Original, you say?"

"Yep, no doubt about it. Didn't you know it was an original?" Greg said.

Bobby smiled. "Man, I haven't a clue about most of the stuff I have. If I can buy anything cheap enough that I guess a tourist will go a few bucks more, I'll buy it. The fellow who gave it to me said it was an original. Of course, I had no way of knowing if it was or not, so thought I'd give it a try and price it a bit higher."

"This artist is not well known," Greg said, "but he does have a serious following of collectors. His specialty, as seen in this scene, is rivers, and that's what attracted me to come in and see if it was an original, which I doubted."

"Then you must be an expert to know the difference," Bobby said, shaking his head.

"Well, I do work in the field of art," Greg replied, "so I should know something about paintings. In fact, that's why I came back. I'd like to know more about the picture and from whom you bought it if you don't mind."

Bobby laughed. "I got it for nothing from a guy who said it was an original and was worth more money. But he'd been drinking and I figured it was the drink talking and really didn't believe him. Anyhow, as we talked he started to tell me he was really bummed out about life. You know the kind of story a drunk tells to explain why he's into drink. Kind of an apology, I guess, for letting himself go like he had."

Greg nodded. "Yeah, it's sad when circumstances overcome a guy. But you say he gave you this picture for nothing?"

"Yep, he insisted. After I listened to his sad tale of love lost, he said that I had been such a good listener he wanted to give me something. I said that wasn't necessary, but he got up went out and came back with this picture. 'Here,' he said, 'take this. It's a nice piece and it's an original.'

"I told him no way. I said, 'Hey, you've had a few too many and I don't want to take advantage of you, I didn't mind listening so you keep it.' Well, he kinda got mad and said I had no right to take away his pleasure of doing something nice for someone. I wasn't about to argue with a guy who was becoming upset, especially when too many beers were involved. So I thanked him, took it, and after a few minutes he got up and left."

"You know, Bobby," Greg said, "I'd really like to know where this guy got the painting. Did he say anything about it, or why he even had it?"

Bobby paused. "To be honest, although I tried to pay attention to the guy, I confess my mind would wander as he talked, so I might have missed something. I really only remember he said something about being an art dealer and somehow lost his gallery because of his trouble with his girlfriend. I just don't remember the details, sorry."

"Hey, Bobby, nothing to be sorry about, but would you be willing to help me find this guy? Maybe someone at the bar remembers him or knows his name. Could you take me to the bar?"

Bobby looked surprised. "Say, you must really have an interest in this picture, mind if I ask why?"

Greg laughed. "I owe you that much for sure. The real reason I bought this picture was because of this. He turned the picture over and showed Bobby the penciled note "Art World."

"That's it, Art World!" exclaimed Bobby. "Now I remember he said that was the name of his gallery and for some reason I noted it on the back; guess it was so insignificant I just forgot about it until you showed it to me."

Greg then lifted the paper farther and showed Bobby the inside label. "VKG Berlin." Bobby had no idea what it meant.

Greg said, "I really need to find this fellow, Bobby, here's why." After Greg explained the reason to find Kurt was hopefully to learn if the picture under investigation, sold as an original, was known to be a copy, Bobby was intrigued.

"You know, Greg, that's fascinating. I've never been involved in an investigation of any kind, but determining who is ultimately responsible for a half-million dollar fraud, if that is what it is, sure puts a heavy responsibility on you, doesn't it?"

Greg nodded. "Yeah, but it's exciting. You meet some interesting people like yourself, and the unexpected surprise of finding things like this original Pizzonie in an unlikely place."

"Do you go to that bar regularly?" Greg asked.

"Yep, but I really don't drink much," Bobby said with a defensive half shrug of his shoulders. "It's more for the contact I make with other guys from the 'Village.' We usually meet Fridays and just jaw-bone, compare notes on what's hot or cold."

Greg asked, "Have you seen this guy there before?"

Bobby hesitated. "I think I have seen him there from time to time although until the night he gave me the pictures, I had never spoken to him."

"Okay, today is Friday, would you take me there tonight?" Greg asked. "I'd like to talk to the guy; perhaps I could get him to give more details about his reasons for leaving the gallery."

"Sure," Bobby said. "Come by around seven. It's not far from here so we can walk there."

"Sounds great," Greg said, shaking hands with Bobby. "I'll be there. Now I'll get back to the office and give my boss an update. She's pretty demanding that I show some progress on this case!"

Bobby raised a questioning eyebrow. "She, you say, you work for a woman? Isn't that rather difficult?"

Greg laughed. "Not really, you'd have to meet her to understand that working for someone smarter than you are, male or female, is what you have to accept in life. I respect her highly; I respect her competence in this field."

"Well, now," Bobby said, "that's refreshing. Sometime I'll have to tell you about a gal I met who was smarter than I was too."

"I'd like to hear about her, for sure. Well, so long, see you tomorrow," Greg said with a friendly wave as he left.

Maria was in her office and looked up as Greg tapped gently on the half-open door. "Well, I wondered when I'd hear from you," Maria said with just a touch of reproach. "I understand you didn't have much luck at Art World, you don't think the owner was very straightforward, do you?"

Greg shook his head. "No, I don't, but there was little I could do to find out more. Nevertheless, I have a good lead on finding Kurt."

Maria was pleased to hear of the lead through Bobby.

"Sid and Brad are quite upset over this claim." Maria paused. "Brad especially. It seems he wrote the policy when it was a small gallery. If Art World really deliberately sold a copy as an original, this would reflect badly on his underwriting judgment."

As Maria talked, Greg couldn't help seeing the notation on her desk calendar, "Dinner with Brad." *Hmm*, he thought to himself, *it seems her prohibition about co-workers of different sexes becoming too intimate in the workplace extends only to me.*

Maria caught his glance at her note and the slight tightening of his mouth. "A problem with that?" she asked.

"With what?" Greg feigned innocence.

"The note on my desk calendar you were reading. While it is lying in the open, it is still rather rude to read it," Maria said with some irritation.

Greg bristled at her tone. "Maria, I was not purposely scanning your calendar, but, yes, I couldn't help seeing your date with Brad. I admit it and, considering our talk about office relationships, it surprised me."

"It's not a date," Marie replied defensively. "Brad is really concerned over this case but doesn't want to discuss some ideas he has about how we should react if the claim proves true."

Greg decided it was better to drop the issue, sensing Maria's obvious irritation.

"Sorry, Maria, my fault. I truly didn't mean to pry. I guess there will always be that touch of jealousy in me. I'll admit that I can't always hide my disappointment at being shut out of your life." Although Greg's words touched her, there was no alternative to her decision to distance themselves. They had grown too close while working together; her promotion over him necessitated a break.

Maria said nothing and Greg turned to leave, telling her he'd get back right away on the results of his attempt to meet Kurt. Maria watched him go; she knew he was hurt, she knew, too, that her present relationship with him was not what she personally wanted; she also knew it was as much in his own interest as hers. He was a good investigator and whatever success came his way had to be on the merits of his work, not his relationship with her.

She also knew that Brad was not at all displeased with her keeping Greg at a distance. It gave him a few more opportunities to talk to her. The request for dinner, she rationalized, was legitimate considering the circumstances that Brad was her boss, not the other way around, and yes, Brad was pleasant to be with.

CHAPTER 14

BOBBY WAS READY WHEN GREG CAME. THE WALK TO
the bar was short as Bobby had said and was quite empty as they entered.
They took a table in a far corner of the bar and ordered a sandwich
each.

"Well, I hope Kurt's thirsty and comes in," Greg said.

"Yeh, me too," agreed Bobby. "Stories about lost loves are always
interesting!"

"That reminds me, Bobby," Greg said. "You made the comment about
a gal you knew who was smarter than you when I told you I worked for a
woman. Any 'lost love' involved, may I ask?"

Bobby shook his head. "Not really lost in the sense that there is a
deep regret, but I do feel her loss. After all, I was married to her; in fact,
I think I still am, as far as I know, that is."

Greg couldn't hide his curiosity, "Bobby, excuse me, but I would think
a person would know whether or not they were married."

Bobby smiled. "You're right, but I don't think either Esther or I have
ever done anything about a formal ending; it just didn't seem important,
I guess. You know, maybe we just feel that the spirit of our love is what's
important, not a physical proximity."

Greg smiled. "Now that's pretty profound, Bobby, care to expand on
that? I mean, after all, if I love someone, I sure would want to have her
with me."

Bobby nodded. "In most circumstances that would be true, but in others, like mine, it wasn't." Bobby paused, as if he wasn't sure he wanted to continue in this direction.

Greg sensed this and said, "Well, Bobby, I'm sure that is a very private part of your life; you needn't talk anymore about it, I respect that."

Bobby looked up. "It's not that I don't want to talk about it, it's just that it's hard to explain in terms someone like you could understand."

Greg looked surprised. "Someone like me? Why would you say that?"

Bobby smiled. "'Cause from what you said about wanting to have the person you love with you. How am I going to explain that presence is not the most important part of love and make it sound believable?"

Greg thought about Maria; he was admittedly fond of her, but did he love her? He knew beyond a shadow of a doubt he wanted to know her better; however, would that knowing lead to love? Was having to know a person completely that important? Wasn't there an innate instinct that signaled this is the one? How about the love-at-first-sight testimonies? People just trying to justify irrational acts, choices?

"Bobby," Greg leaned forward, "I'm intrigued. Try me, really. I need to hear your explanation, perhaps it will help me understand my own feelings about someone."

"Someone being your boss perhaps," ventured Bobby with a grin.

"Hey, don't jump to conclusions, Bobby," Greg countered. "Why would you say that."

"Because I think the first signs of love, like spring flowers, have to have a warming, and that warming is in the form of respect, and you have already said you respect your boss very highly, right?"

"Whoa, Bobby, you are going to fast for me. I'm no philosopher, and I'll soon be over my head in this discussion about signs and warnings and such. Can't you make this a little more concrete, give me some example I can relate to?"

Bobby looked at Greg for a moment. He had never told anyone the full story about Esther; it was very private, and, as he said, it would be hard to make it believable.

"Okay, Greg," Bobby finally said. "We haven't known each other very long, but your offer to return the painting because I didn't realize its value, yet you have every right to keep, indicates to me you are an all right guy, so let me tell you about Esther."

Bobby pushed his half-eaten sandwich aside and leaned forward on his elbows when his eye caught sight of Kurt entering.

"Whoops," Bobby half whispered, "don't look now, but Kurt just entered the bar."

Kurt was just adjusting himself on a barstool as he surveyed the room before ordering his drink. He saw the two in the corner and thought he recognized the one, but wasn't that sure. Taking his drink, he started toward Greg and Bobby.

"Heads up, Greg. We don't have to worry about meeting Kurt, he's coming this way," Bobby said quietly.

"Say, pardon me for the interruption," Kurt said lightheartedly to Bobby, "but I swear I've seen you before, haven't I?"

Bobby laughed. "You sure have, don't you remember the picture you gave me sometime ago?"

Kurt paused. "So that's where it went! You know, I was going through my inventory; I kept a few pictures for myself after I sold the gallery, and when I saw one was missing, I could not remember what I had done with it."

Bobby laughed. "No offense, but I can understand your not remembering right away, you had been in the suds. I was sitting alone when you came in, and you came over to me and asked if you could sit down. You did and we chatted for quite a while. You told me you had been an art dealer and something about losing the gallery because of, I think you said, girlfriend."

Kurt scratched his head. "This is bad, I must have really been out of it. I sure don't remember those details, but I thought I'd seen you before."

"Sit down." Bobby motioned to an empty chair. "Meet Greg, he's the lucky guy who bought the picture you so kindly gave me. He says it's an original Pizzonie"

Kurt laughed. "I gave it to you?"

"Yep," Bobby said. "After I listened to your sad tale about losing the gallery, you went out to your car and came back with the picture. You were insistent that I take it, and you said it was an original. At first I refused, but you started getting upset and since you had had a few too many, I really didn't want to agitate you. I said thanks and took it."

"Well, that ought to teach me a lesson not to mix booze with a sob story. So anyhow," Kurt looked at Greg, "you bought my Pizzonie. Hey, you don't have to tell me, of course, but I'm curious, can you tell me what you paid for it?"

Greg looked at Bobby, hesitant to say anything. Bobby said with a laugh, "Why not? Its all the more ridiculous that Kurt gives me an original, not knowing what he's doing, and I sell it for a hundred fifty dollars not knowing what I'm doing."

Kurt looked at Bobby in disbelief., "You gotta be kidding! Man, that picture was worth ten times that at least!"

"Yeah, now you tell me!" Bobby said with a wry smile. "But I'm no art expert, I deal in secondhand junk, and besides how would I know you weren't just talking through the froth of your beer? I got it for nothing, so a quick one fifty seemed like a good deal to me."

Kurt just shook his head. He looked at Greg. "Did you know it was an original?"

"Yeah." Greg nodded. "In fact, to be honest, that's why we're here. I asked Bobby how he got the picture and he told me the story. So I said I'd like to meet you. What really interested me was the notation Art World on the back. Bobby tells me your gallery's name was Art World. My company insured it. Unfortunately, we have a claim that a picture sold as an original was a copy. The new owner of Art World identified the signature on the receipt for the painting as yours."

Kurt nodded. "So here we go, I don't deny selling that picture but then, as now, I swear it was delivered to the gallery clearly marked as an original. In fact, I was so convinced that when I first heard that it was being claimed to be a copy, I was going to fight it and have another appraisal done. When I called my partner in Berlin about the claim, the reaction was violent.

"Instead of verifying the painting and supporting me, my partner told me she was exercising her right to buy me out and to do nothing more."

Greg asked Kurt, "Have you eaten?"

Kurt shook his head.

"Well then, food and drink on me. I'd appreciate hearing more about how the sale of the gallery came about and why your partner reacted the way she did."

Bobby motioned to the waitress. The three chatted pleasantly while Kurt ate his sandwich. When he had finished and the waitress had refreshed their drinks, Greg asked, "Seriously, Kurt, do you have any doubts that the picture was an original?"

"None, I could not believe the Berlin gallery would ever have made a mistake like that. I was convinced that the buyer's estate was making a claim that I could prove was false. That's why my partner's reaction so surprised me."

"So you had to sell without any further explanation?"

Kurt nodded. "None, she demanded that I clear out all documents and turn them over to her bank attorney as required in our agreement should a buyout occur. I did that and she then told me never to make contact with her or the gallery. I was stunned. I mean, we really seemed to have a good relationship that went beyond just business. I confess I thought she had real feelings for me."

Kurt sat silent for a moment. "You know, it was just an unfortunate turn of events that caught me by surprise. It happens when your head is turned by a pretty face and a fabulous figure."

"Yeh, that's what you started to tell me the night you gave me the picture," said Bobby. "I must admit sounds interesting."

"Hey, do you guys really want to hear my story? I mean, it's nice to sit here and talk, but it could be boring. After all, what's so new about boy meets girl, boy loves girl, and girl leaves boy?"

Greg said, "I'm sure Bobby and I both would like to hear more."

Bobby nodded affirmatively. "You know you're right, in principle; it's an old story but everyone has their own personal experience that gives it a uniqueness that is always interesting to hear. At least for me it is."

Greg nodded. "I agree with Bobby, why, when two people meet and there seems to be a solid relationship developing, suddenly or not so suddenly, it's over? The eternal question, why would what seemed so right in the beginning seem so wrong at the ending?"

Kurt looked up. "Well, it was an interesting ride, let me tell you. Here I had a small gallery, making a few bucks, and I read an ad wanting to find an U.S. partner for a European gallery. More on whim than real hope, I answered the ad.

"Next thing I get a phone call from Germany. It was a woman, Frau Hasenfeld, and she said she had received my reply and was planning to come to New York to meet with others who had replied. I offered to meet her at the airport and she seemed pleased, said that would be nice. Man, I have to say the woman coming toward me caused heart palpitations.

Well, to make the proverbially long story short, it was a whirlwind ride that I enjoyed but to no good end, believe me.

"In retrospect, I think I let myself give into the deadly sin of believing my ego. I convinced myself that she was really drawn to me as I was to her. There was never an indication that she had any other motive than to establish a partnership with someone she could trust.

"After it all ends, you sit alone and try and analyze what went wrong. What danger signs you ignored along the way, then before the beer washes over your ability to think clearly, you do see, much to your regret, what you should have seen."

"So," asked Greg, "what should you have seen?"

Kurt frowned. "I should have asked more questions, especially about her explanation that while most of the transactions between us would be direct; there was a so-called pre-existing arrangement with a private broker that she wanted to continue. It would involve certain works of art that would carry an additional code that would be handled by this agent.

"My responsibility was simply to clear these at Customs and then store them for pickup by this agent. She said our joint gallery would be paid a flat fee for this service. When the agent came to pick up the painting, he would sign a receipt, give me a sealed envelope, and I would deliver both to her agent bank. I wouldn't need to be involved any further in the transaction.

"Well, at the time I didn't really think too much more about it. After all, the agreement existed before our partnership; I didn't see why I should object. And as I said, it seemed reasonable. She did invest a goodly sum of money in the renovation and expansion of the gallery. So when she explained that the shares in the partnership would be apportioned according to each investment, that seemed in order. She also said that either one of us could buy the other out by purchasing the other's share.

"I didn't bother to read the small print in the final agreement that allowed the sale to be immediate, without recourse, upon payment of the original investment plus fifteen percent. I guess I was so taken in by her, her generosity in investing in the gallery, and the attention she paid me that I accepted what she proposed without question.

"Her visits to New York were the high points of my life. I gotta tell you, I was proud to be seen with her, and when she hosted a reception at the gallery, all the big names came. I enjoyed the spotlight to be sure. Of course, the time we spent together was like nothing else I could compare with. She made me feel like I was just one of the most fortunate finds in her life. I guess I really began to fall in love with her in spite of the one thing that really bothered me."

Greg jumped in at his slight pause, "Man, from what you have said so far, I can't imagine anything could have bothered you too much."

Kurt shook his head. "Well, one thing did. I was really surprised at her reaction toward my mention of anyone of my acquaintances who were Jewish or belonged to any ethnic group she didn't approve. I also learned early on during her first visit to avoid as well any reference to the war. Honest to God, I got the impression she felt Germany should have won!

"Anyhow, what caused her to force me out was that she claimed I had deliberately sold a copy of a painting as an original."

Greg asked, "Do you still believe it was an original?"

"Hey, why was I to doubt it wasn't? The invoice they sent clearly showed it to be an original…Well, whatever, I'm out and that's it. I haven't decided what to do next. I'm okay financially, but I don't doubt she could make my life miserable if I tried to do something here. I think I'll move up north, Maine perhaps, and open up a small gallery. I was still able to keep a starter inventory; you have one of those I kept, so I should do all right.

"You know, I still remember her voice as she ripped me apart. I thought it was a person I never knew. Perhaps that's it, I never knew her. Well, it's been great meeting you guys. I'm going to have to take care and watch my beers before I lose anymore inventory!" He laughed as he said it, thanking Greg for the sandwich.

As he got up to leave, he turned to Greg. "I don't know what else I can tell you, but I'll give you my card and I'll call if I remember anything more."

Greg nodded. "Thanks." Kurt shook hands and left.

"Frankly, I think he is telling the truth, has nothing to hide," said Greg. "But that's not the impression I get from the present owner of the gallery. So shall we go?"

As they left the bar and were walking back to Bobby's place, Greg said, "Thanks for your time in helping me find Kurt. I'd still like to hear your story about Esther sometime."

"Really?" asked Bobby, somewhat surprised that Greg had remembered. "It's still early. We're almost at my place, so why not come in and I'll make us some tea, or coffee if you like."

Greg said, "Tea will be fine," and followed Bobby into his shop.

The next morning Greg asked Brad and Maria for time to give them an update on his visit with Bobby and Kurt.

Brad said, "Well done, Greg, seems like the trail now leads to Berlin."

Sid's deep voice came from the doorway. "Just stuck my head inside to hear what was going on. Looks like you all have got this well in hand. When will you two be leaving for Berlin?" He nodded to Maria and Greg.

Maria spoke up quickly, "No need for two of us to go; since it's my case, I'm sure I can handle the details."

"Absolutely not going to let you go alone. I have no doubt you can handle the investigation better than any of us; you'll take Greg with you and that's final," said Sid emphatically, then added, "Besides, you'll need some one to carry your bags!" Sid laughed heartily. "Anyhow, just keep me posted. I don't like five hundred thousand dollar claims."

CHAPTER 15

ANDRE HAD RESIGNED HIMSELF TO THE FACT THERE was little chance the Maestro would give in to Maria's request to visit Berlin when the phone rang.

"Hello," he said eagerly. Too late to hang up, she had to decide quickly to cast doubts aside and accept the invitation or decline it. "Herr von Kunst?"

"Yes!"

Katya continued hesitatingly, "Am I disturbing you?"

"No, no, of course not. How nice to hear your voice, and dare I have hope of good news?"

Katya smiled at his eagerness but was still anxious about her own doubts. She decided not to discuss the matter over the phone. She admitted holding him in suspense gave her a certain pleasure and hearing his excited voice, her confidence rose.

"Herr von Kunst, the hotel café is still open. If it is not too late, could we meet there now?"

"I'll be there waiting for you," he answered instantly. "But please, do I come with hope or," he said with an unmistakable note of sadness, "do I come prepared for the worst?"

Katya couldn't resist the female urge to tease.

"Perhaps," she said, trying to hide the coyness in her voice, "what you consider as good could prove to be the worst. I'll meet you in about fifteen minutes in the café."

She hung up before the somewhat bewildered Andre could press the issue further. Her hand was still trembling as she laid the receiver down. She glanced at the picture of her parents, *Dear ones, you have taught me both faith and tolerance, I believe you would encourage me to do this.*

She sat down on her bed, head in hands, *Why*, she thought, *am I making this out to be such a momentous decision? It is simply an invitation to visit Berlin from a very likable young man. It will be made perfectly clear to him that there is no obligation to stay should circumstances arise that necessitates our departure if earlier than expected. There is really is no reason for this to weigh so heavily on either my or the Maestro's mind. Or is there some reservation on both our parts, if unspoken, that there might be more attraction than I now admit to?*

He was already seated at a corner table when she entered; there was no mistaking the look of pleasure on his face as he rose to greet her. He took her hand and gently helped her to her seat.

"Fraulein Preznoski, I keep hearing your words that the good may be the worst! How can that be? Worst could only mean that you cannot accept my invitation, a thought I can't really endure."

"Herr von Kunst, our meetings have been quite brief; we hardly know each other, and your invitation on such short acquaintance is most puzzling to the Maestro and to me. I dare say that whatever motivated you has no doubt been a strong curiosity, and what you are curious about I would like to know."

Andre smiled. "Before I try and explain what I am afraid is unexplainable, may I be so bold as to request that our past few meetings have been cordial enough to allow us to use our first names? The formality of the German language does not lend itself to an open conversation when discussing a matter of personal importance. Please understand that I am not presuming on a friendship with you that entitles me to this request, but I am so impressed by you that discussing my, as you put it, 'curiosity' makes the use of the formal language a barrier to expressing myself freely."

"Well, I must admit Herr von Kunst," Katya gave a warm smile, "while your family name is no doubt one you are proud of, 'Andre' does pass over the lips a bit more easily as I'm sure 'Katya' would than Fraulein Preznoski." They both laughed, sensing a new level of intimacy had been reached.

"Katya." Andre liked the sound of her name and the smile of approval on her face. "You ask me to explain what I have been trying to explain to myself. I can only confess to a fascination that came over me as I watched you on stage playing your violin. You played with such grace, the very movement of your arms, the gentle swaying of your body, the lightning fast strokes of the bow, a wisp of jet-black hair falling across an ivory cheek, all so captivating.

"How or why all of this swept over me bringing a desire to know you more I cannot explain, except it was undeniable. I only know that I had to meet you. Perhaps that would be sufficient to satisfy whatever curiosity I had. It was a strange feeling that I confess I had not experienced before, and I had not yet even met you.

"Now, after our brief meetings, I confess the desire has not lessened at all. To the contrary, it has increased and is the reason for my invitation to Berlin. I would hope that a few days of relaxation would permit me to know you better, and hopefully you would find me pleasurable to be with."

Katya tried not to stare at Andre. He spoke with such intensity that she was both embarrassed at his description of her yet deeply touched and flattered. She had to admit to her own desire to know him better. She needed to overcome the lingering doubts she had about going to Berlin. The Maestro's words still haunted her. She did not want to believe that people for no other reason than ancestry or nationality would be shown the disrespect, if not open hatred, that he said she could expect.

"Andre," she said his name with a slight hesitation, "I have a question that I must ask you."

"Katya, please feel free to ask whatever question comes to your mind."

She went on, "I told you before I was a Polish Jewess, didn't I?"

Andre nodded. "Yes, you did."

Katya watched him intently as she said, "Would you please tell me what your immediate reaction was to that?"

Andre responded quickly, "Katya, I clearly remember you telling me. I offered no response then because, were I to say it was of no concern, you would no doubt not believe me. I am not unaware of the attitude that prevails in some circles of German and other societies. I am sorry such an attitude prompted you to declare your status, so to speak. I was embarrassed for you, for your need to know if that revelation would affect the friendship I was offering you, am I right?"

Katya nodded. "Yes, you see, I have been warned over and over that people like me are not welcome. I could not wait until perhaps we became better friends and then disappoint you."

A look of sadness came across Andre's face. That this beautiful, talented creature had to live with what could only be called the guilt of her birth; guilt that would force her to make a declaration of her heritage before she could be assured of his acceptance.

She watched him closely. *Could that look of sadness be, as she feared, a genuine regret on his part of having to face, for him, this unpleasant reality?* She wasn't prepared for the sudden reach of his hand to cover hers. It was warm and firm. Though unexpected, this intimacy was not unwelcome; she made no effort to withdraw from his touch.

Katya spoke softly, "Andre, it is getting late and you have been patient, and I must say, very persistent, but in a flattering way, about our coming to Berlin."

She paused and Andre braced himself for the inevitable "I'm sorry but," then could hardly contain his pleasure when he heard, "We'll be glad to accept your invitation."

Katya almost laughed at the expression of equal surprise and joy that met on his face. She quickly followed with the proviso that the invitation had to be open-ended. There was no offense intended, but she had promised the Maestro they would be free to leave if at any time circumstances made this necessary.

Andre had little doubt that the Maestro had made sure this would be understood as a price for accepting. Andre resolved that whatever circumstances arose, it would have nothing to do with his or Hannelore's behavior. Katya was amused at how quickly Andre agreed to her provision.

"Andre," she slowly withdrew her hand from under his and smiled at his light resistance to her movement, "it is getting late; this has been a rather exciting day to say the least. The Maestro will be gathering us early tomorrow for rehearsal. I'll call you in the morning. Good night, Andre, and yes, I am looking forward to our visit." She rose with a warm smile and walked from the café as Andre watched admiringly. Andre returned to his room and sat for a while as he thought ahead about their coming visit. One thing was certain, he would make sure to plan some separate entertainment for the Maestro. He would leave the schedule open enough to assure he would have some time with Katya alone. He fell asleep smiling.

He woke early with the exhilarating thought of having Katya with him in Berlin. He knew she would be at rehearsal until later in the morning. Since she had said they usually departed around noon the day following a concert, he decided to go ahead and use the time to make reservations.

He called Elsa. Her cheerful "Hello, Von Kunst Gallery" was pleasant to hear.

"Elsa, hello to you," he answered, then quickly said, "I need a favor."

Elsa smiled at the word "favor." The difference was that Hannelore would call and say, "Fraulein Becker, call Herr such and such at once..." there was never a please or certainly never a favor. Hannelore's calls were commands from a superior to an inferior; if she didn't understand what made Hannelore so controlling, Elsa accepted Hannelore for what she was. The fact was she could overlook Hannelore because of Andre; Andre, the perfect gentleman, who asked favors that could easily have been given as orders.

"Of course," came Elsa's friendly answer. "What can I do for you?"

"First of all, please tell Hannelore that I plan to be back late tonight, and I would like her to have dinner with me and my guests at Jacques tomorrow evening. You can also arrange for that meeting she told me about for the next day preferably in the early afternoon."

"Did you say 'guests,' Andre?" Elsa couldn't hide the curiosity in her voice.

"Oh yes," Andre tried for nonchalance, "would you please make the dinner reservations for four. I am assuming Hannelore will agree to join us. Also, please call the Karpinski. I'd like to reserve two adjoining suites with a sitting room in between for five nights, starting tomorrow. Please ask them to include a nice flower arrangement with a basket of fruit, coffee, and a wine and cheese selection."

"Certainly," replied Elsa, biting her tongue against a curiosity-inspired question.

"I'll pass this information on to Hannelore at once, are there any other details I should tell her?" Elsa knew that Andre avoided talking directly to Hannelore whenever it appeared there would be some controversy. This avoided his having to answer a volley of follow-up questions from her on an issue he didn't wish to discuss over the phone, or, for that matter, to discuss at all.

"No, nothing more Elsa," Andre replied to her question, sensing the bitten tongue. "As said, I plan to be home late tonight and I'll meet my guests at the train station tomorrow afternoon." After Andre hung up, Elsa admitted to a strange feeling that Andre was not very forthcoming about his impending visit with his guests. The fact that he wanted her to pass on the information to Hannelore was not unusual, but there was definitely a different tone, perhaps almost one of hesitation that was not usually his way of talking with her.

CHAPTER 16

IT WAS EARLY, HANNELORE DID NOT LIKE ANY INTER-
ruptions before noon, and the Gallery was empty. Elsa went over to Otto's
studio and knocked gently.

"Come in," was softly spoken. Elsa entered and saw Otto hunched
over a small painting he was painstakingly repairing for a customer. He
didn't look up at once, no disrespect intended, but Elsa knew he was at
some critical point and needed to finish it. She liked Otto; she admired
his skill and care with which he approached his trade. The feeling was
reciprocated. Otto appreciated the way Elsa asked questions about what
he was doing and showed a true interest in his work.

He finally looked up and gave a rare smile. "So what brings me the
honor of your presence?" he asked. Elsa paused; she really didn't know
how to begin and wondered even if she should. After all, what was
between Hannelore and Andre was none of her business, but she had
often wanted to ask Otto. He had been with the gallery for years and
would know more about them than anyone else.

Otto sensed her hesitation and waited; he knew that something was
troubling her. She was not a complainer, but sometimes when Hannelore
had been especially contrary or even rude, she would come to Otto for
comfort and his reassurance. Otto knew that while it was difficult to
accept Hannelore's abruptness, she was that way with everyone and he
told Elsa not to take it personally.

"Elsa, is something wrong?"

"Otto, I had a call from Andre yesterday. He hadn't communicated with the gallery for several days, which was not like him. I told him Hannelore was very upset and wanted him to come back at once. She seemed very upset about two visitors she had a couple of days ago who had asked several questions about a work of art." At this, Otto, remembering Hannelore's asking him a few days ago if there were any new events in the art world, raised his brows questioningly.

"Do you know who they were?"

"I only spoke briefly with them. The women had a slight accent but spoke perfect German, the young man with her was evidently American. But what was strange," Elsa continued, "was after I told Hannelore the information that Andre had asked me to give her. I could tell she was upset that he was not coming at once. She mentioned that he was bringing a guest and I could tell she was not very pleased at that news. But then he called this morning and told me he would be back late tonight and would meet his two guests tomorrow afternoon. He also asked me to book two suites at the Karpinski."

"Two guests? Well, I wonder who they could be, did he say?" asked Otto.

"No, he didn't give me any more details except that he wanted me to make dinner reservations at Jacques and to ask Hannelore to join them. Otto, I can't remember a time when Andre would not have immediately responded to a request, or better said, a command from Hannelore. I could tell she was upset at his first call, and when I give her this latest news, well, I can really expect a very strong reaction especially when I tell her he is coming with 'guests' and the arrangements he wants."

Otto looked at Elsa for a moment before asking,

"Elsa, this is all very interesting, but I don't think you are visiting me to talk about telephone conversations. I know you too well, so what is on your mind?"

Elsa nodded. "Yes, you are right, Otto, but I really have no right to even be asking you about people and their personal lives."

Otto smiled. "I don't think you are asking about 'people'; I suspect you are thinking about two people who we both know very well, am I right?"

Elsa nodded again and said, "I hope you won't think less of me for asking you a question I have no right to ask. If you do not want to answer, I will just apologize for asking."

Otto waited a few moments, and then said, "Elsa, I have known you for many years, I have seen your loyalty to both Hannelore and Andre, and frankly there is no reason for you to apologize for any question you could ask me. I assure you I will answer, that is if I have an answer!" His reassurance was enough for Elsa.

"Otto, I just doesn't understand what causes Andre to be under such domination by Hannelore. It has always puzzled me, yet today, for the first time, I have heard Andre say and do something contrary to what Hannelore wished. Otto, why does Andre let Hannelore have such control over his life?"

After Otto finished talking, he looked at the silent Elsa, who had listened to all he said with little interruption. He had been as honest and open as he could be with many guarded remarks that he knew would only raise more questions in her mind. Elsa sensed that Otto was going only so far as he could, so she refrained from asking for answers she knew Otto would or could not give.

After a brief silence, Otto said, "So, Elsa, there isn't much more I can say, but for whatever reason, Andre and Hannelore are still as one; if indivisible, I can't say."

Elsa rose to go. "Otto, thank you for taking time to tell me this. I'll never turn down an invitation from Andre, but I'll not suffer from false allusions. Now I must call Hannelore and pass on Andre's message. No doubt I'll be grilled on details I can't provide, which will just infuriate her all the more; dare I confess I enjoy her irritation?"

Otto grinned. "I'm sure you do and with justification, but don't misunderstand what I have said about Hannelore. I believe you to be beyond anything Hannelore could aspire to be in beauty, brains, or personality. Perhaps in time Andre's eyes will be opened."

Elsa blushed. "Why how nice, Otto; with that complement I'll leave you to your work and go face the tigress," she said laughingly as she left.

Otto sat in silence. He remembered Elsa's comments about the two visitors who had come to the gallery. Apparently, their visit had concerned Hannelore. *Visitors, perhaps investigators?* he smiled to himself. *Well, dear Hannelore, you'll soon need more than your charm.*

Hannelore answered Elsa's ring with a sharp "Yes," since she knew it was only Elsa or Andre that had her private number. She wasted no time on pleasantries, as usual, but she was even brusquer when she was in pursuit of answers. Elsa passed on the information Andre had given her.

At the mention of the two hotel suites, Hannelore abruptly interrupted, "What do you mean 'two hotel suites'? Andre said he was coming, for reasons I cannot fathom, with this foreign person but never mentioned another as well. Did he explain?"

"No, but he did ask that I make dinner reservations at Jacques for tomorrow evening and to ask you to join them for dinner."

Elsa heard with delight Hannelore's sharp intake of breath; she knew Hannelore was at a loss of what to say, and Elsa wasn't about to offer any help. She waited a while and then with all innocence asked, "What shall I tell Herr von Kunst?" Hannelore was caught off guard. Inwardly, she raged, *How dare Andre put me in this position. After all, I made my displeasure clear about his bringing one guest, and now adding another is incomprehensible. Dinner? How could he!* She knew Elsa was waiting for an answer, and it infuriated her even more to know that her silence indicated to Elsa her indecision, not a characteristic she wanted displayed.

Well then, yes, she thought. *I'll come with Herr von Linglesdorf. As a member of the Kreis and well known as a music critic, it would be quite amusing to have him enter into a conversation with Andre's guests. Yes, it would be just revenge for Andre's unaccountable actions to have him hear how unlearned his guests really were about the world of music.*

"Fraulein Becker, tell Herr von Kunst that I will accept the dinner invitation, and please make sure that it is for five persons. Did he give a time?"

"Since Jacques is usually booked out in advance," Elsa quickly replied, "I was to ask him for a time between seven and eight. I'm to tell Herr von Kunst and, of course, you as soon as that is confirmed." Elsa neither questioned Hannelore's addition of a fifth person, nor who it would be; she knew better.

Hannelore said quickly, "Yes, do that, and call the two representatives who were here that a meeting with Herr von Kunst and myself can take place sometime the day after tomorrow. We'll confirm the exact time after I speak with Herr von Kunst. I understand he will be driving back this evening, is that correct?"

Elsa confirmed it was, and Hannelore hung up.

CHAPTER 17

AS MARIA AND GREG LEFT HANNELORE'S OFFICE AFTER
their two o'clock meeting, they decided to walk back to the hotel.

"Well," said Maria, "Nothing more we can do but wait until the other
partner gets back. At least the receptionist was cordial enough, but Frau
Hasenfeld is one cold fish."

"Yeah," Greg agreed, "but you have to admit, she sure is a looker!"

Maria sniffed. "That's why you males are not reliable investigators
whenever it involves dealing with a woman. You make it so obvious that
whenever a pair of shapely legs is crossed, your thought train derails. By
the time you get back on track, she has the advantage of the situation. She
can now direct the conversation in the direction entirely to her wish."

"Not true," protested Greg, "but there is nothing wrong in admiring
what's at hand to admire. After all, how many times have I told you how
beautiful you are and yet been able to keep my wits about me."

Maria felt the usual twinge of conscience whenever Greg reminded
her of his fondness for her; nevertheless, now, as always, he respected the
position she had taken with him after her promotion. He never pressed
the issue with her. Ignoring his compliments was her best defense; she
wanted to avoid any discussion of the matter that led to her disclosing
how much she missed the closeness they once had.

"Greg, as soon as we are back at the hotel, I'll wire Brad and give him
an update. Do you have anything I should include?"

"No, Maria. I think you have it well in hand. I'm just thinking how
silly it is for both of us to be here in Berlin, waiting with time on our

hands and not trying to enjoy what we can. After all, if I did as good a job as you say, then there should be some reward for it."

Maria tensed further at his words. She never doubted his promise to accept their situation without rancor, but never-the-less she was always on the defensive.

"Maria," Greg continued in a lighter tone, "let's not be so overly cautious. I think that in a situation such as this, we can lower some of the barriers that you have set up for my protection, as you say, and enjoy an evening dinner and a show."

Greg paused, then continued, "Can't we trust ourselves to share some time together. It is doubtful there are any watching eyes here in Berlin to tattle on us if we enjoy an evening meal and a show. Now really, Maria, there is no reason you couldn't loosen up a bit, unless of course, you don't want any contact with me unless it is business related."

Maria shook her head. "You know that isn't true, sometimes I just don't know what to do about us. I do miss the closeness we once had. Yet, if because we are here and allow ourselves the indulgence of a return to something like we had in our earlier relationship, if only for an evening, then how much harder is it going to be to return to the relationship I feel is necessary now?"

"Maria," Greg smiled, "I know you well enough to respect your will and determination to do what you believe to be right. I don't think a one-evening interlude will suffice to dissuade your resolve in this matter. Besides, I doubt I have any ability, nor would I try if I thought I did, to breach the emotional fortifications you have built. Let's put all of these thoughts aside and just simply enjoy an evening as two friends would, okay?"

"Greg," she said, "tell you what. I think it would be nice to do what you suggest. In fact, there is a movie I would like to see that I noted was playing in a small theatre here in Berlin. It will be in German, but I can give you a quick overview of the story. If you agree and won't be bored, okay?"

Greg was in no way going to dampen the moment with thoughts of sitting through a German movie he would not understand. Her agreement included a dinner, which was much more important to him. At least it would give him the chance to be with her in a more relaxed atmosphere.

"You're on!" he replied with an enthusiasm that brought a smile to her lips.

"Well, I'm glad that's settled," laughed Maria. "Now let's get back to the hotel and I'll wire Brad what's going on and you can choose a restaurant. A deal?"

Greg nodded and smiled his okay. After they parted in the lobby, Greg went directly to the concierge for restaurant recommendations. The concierge offered as first choice a restaurant not far from the hotel just off the Kurfurstendamm called Jacques.

Maria's call came shortly after he entered his room. The show she wanted to see, Gunter Grass' *Die Blech Trommel* had two showings, but the later one might really be too late for a dinner following. She wasn't so naïve as not to know what Greg would prefer. Perhaps inwardly she had to admit to the same preference.

When Greg called back, he said reservations were made. Maria felt a mixed feeling of guilt and pleasure. Yet, she had to admit, for reasons not clear to herself, attending the earlier show with dinner after would permit a more leisurely time with Greg.

Greg was pleased she offered no objections to his decision.

"Maria, what in the world is the picture about, I sure have no idea from the title?"

"Greg, give me some time to get dressed and then we can meet in the hotel café for a coffee. We do have some time before the show. That will give me the opportunity to explain the movie and avoid having to translate too much in the theater."

Greg agreed.

After a quick shower and a change of clothes, Greg went to the café and took a table where he could watch for Maria. He was thinking of what he wanted to say that would not violate his promises never to press her.

Yet, it was time to speak from his heart, time to explain his feelings while demanding no commitment from her. She needed to know that he had some personal decisions to make that did depend on her feelings about their relationship. He was not going to infer that this was an either/or about their friendship. Their friendship he never wanted to lose, but there was another level of involvement that had to be considered for his own piece of mind.

His thoughts came to an abrupt end as Maria approached the table. He caught his breath; this was not the investigator Maria, of the dark gray suits, white shirts, and pulled-back hair. The jade green sheath, while attempting to be modest, couldn't hide completely the undulating form that Greg found irritatingly seductive. Just how was he not supposed to notice what made the difference between simple friendship and something stronger when it involved persons of the opposite sex?

He couldn't help staring at the lovely creature who, smiling, seated herself before he could rise to assist her. Her auburn hair fell in soft waves to her shoulders, framing that always lovely face, now enhanced tastefully with a touch of color added to lips, eyes made even more luminous by the delicate shading of liner and shadow. She seldom wore makeup during working hours with the exception of light lip gloss. Actually, Greg had often noticed how little make-up her God-given complexion needed, and this evening she had never looked more inviting. This was the Maria of earlier days before the promotion imposed their more restricted association. He knew he must have been staring because Maria, slightly flushed, with the awareness of her apparent effect on Greg, said with an attempt at lightness, "Well, Greg, cat got your tongue?"

Greg said, "Well, I was waiting for someone else, evidently she isn't coming, but you are most welcome to stay. You will pardon, I hope, that the cat momentarily did have my tongue at the vision of such loveliness." Maria laughed and felt self-conscious. "Greg, I'm sorry. I guess I just got carried away a bit by the prospect of 'doing the town' as they say, something I haven't done in a long time. I didn't mean…well…I don't know what I meant…I mean, I didn't really…"

Greg held up his hand to stop her as he said, "Maria, please, for goodness' sakes you needn't explain. You are a beautiful woman going out for an evening properly dressed for the occasion. I'm just the most grateful guy who will enjoy the envious looks of those males who will have the good fortune to have seen true beauty."

"Oh, Greg, sometimes I do wish circumstances were otherwise, thank you for the compliment. Please let me tell you the story of the 'Tin Drum,' that's the English title of the movie. Remember, that's why we are sitting here, not to overwhelm me with kind remarks."

Maria hoped this conversation was not a prelude to the mood that would prevail at dinner afterwards. She thought, *I really didn't dress this way with the intention of impressing Greg or how he might react, did I?* "Well, Greg, to Gunter Grass," she said, raising her newly arrived cup of coffee.

As they left the theater, Greg confessed that the best part of the film was sharing popcorn with her. Maria laughed at his honesty.

"Yes, I know Gunter is a bit unusual, but I enjoy his unconventional way of making a political as well as a social statement. It forces you to pay attention. As I tried to explain in the café, the unwillingness of the boy to be born is symbolic of many who might wish, or have wished, that they were never born into a society they felt was unwelcoming. His drum became his defense; it drowned out the constant babble around him. He had no wish, was incapable in fact, of dialogue with an uncomprehending world."

"Maria, if that was a political statement. I'll need much more clarification regardless of what you told me prior to our going."

"Hmm," said Maria, "knowing you and flattering myself, I'd say you are just looking for another opportunity to wear down my resolve to keep our relationship friendly and mostly professional. I really don't think Gunter needs much more explanation, nice try."

"Touché," said Greg as he led her around the corner following the concierge's directions. "I allowed him to recommend a restaurant and this was his first choice." After a short walk, they came to a small, dimly lit sign that said simply *Jacques.*

Descending the short flight of stairs, they entered the softly lit, charming interior that had so impressed Katya. Maria felt the intimacy provided by the twelve booths placed in small alcoves. They afforded a view of the restaurants tasteful decor and the various paintings of French landscapes. *Not surprising considering the restaurant's name*, thought Maria.

"Greg," Maria marveled, "this is so beautiful, do thank the concierge."

"I'll thank him for sure if the cuisine matches the surroundings. I'll thank him doubly if the ambience and food are so pleasing that you'll forgive me for trying to soften a lovely lady's resolve to banish me from her presence."

Maria laughed. "Thanks for the warning. I'll be sure to eat heartily, my defenses will no doubt need fortification." Greg declared that he was sure that if what the concierge said were true, the excellent wines would make all fortifications vulnerable. Maria was enjoying the banter; it was refreshing.

"Oh dear," Maria feigned dismay, "I certainly will be on my guard, 'forewarned is forearmed,' isn't it?"

When Jacques came to lead them to their booth, they met Andre, Katya, and the Maestro, who were just leaving. Andre spoke to them in English while Maria answered his greeting in German. They both laughed.

Andre, ever ready to present Berlin's best face forward, continued in perfect English, "You have chosen one of Berlin's most excellent restaurants. You will enjoy your meal, I am sure."

"Why thank you," answered the lady in perfect German.

Andre laughed. "No offense, please, I just surmised you were American, and I like to practice my English whenever I can."

The lady smiled back. "Yes, we are American, but some of us, surprisingly, do speak other languages and I, too, like to practice them."

Greg smiled at Andre. "Unfortunately, I confess to being a one-language person, and I appreciate your English greeting. I was told that this is one of Berlin's best restaurants. How nice to have your confirmation."

"Do enjoy yourselves," Andre said as he took Katya's arm and, with the Maestro following, went to his car.

"What a charming fellow," Maria said to Jacques. "No offense, but the few Berliners I have met," thinking of Hannelore, "while not particulary unfriendly, certainly were not as outwardly friendly as that young man."

Jacques nodded. "Herr von Kunst is always the gentleman."

"Von Kunst, did you say?" said a startled Maria. "What a coincidence, my friend and I have a meeting with the owners of Kunst gallery tomorrow. Is he related?"

"Indeed he is, he and his mother own the gallery that has been in the family for generations. He has a business partner, Frau Hasenfeld, who is very active in the daily operation of the gallery."

He seated Maria and Greg with another gracious smile as he handed both the priced menu and the wine list to Greg, the non-priced one to Maria. He said he'd return shortly for their choices and his recommendations if they wished.

Maria laughed. "Well, since there is no price on my menu, I know who pays the bill, don't I?"

"Yeah," retorted Greg, "Sid!" They both laughed and Maria felt the mood lighten.

Jacques came for their order and they followed his recommendations.

The dinner was perfect, and they reminisced over past events in their lives that led them to join International Galleries and now here to Berlin.

Maria allowed, during a quiet interlude in their conversation, that her fortifications were harder to maintain than she thought.

Greg smiled. "I'll assume that you did and do enjoy my company at times. So, if you are truthful about enjoying the earlier times we had and the only reason we cannot have them again is due to our professional relationship, my solution is simple, let me explain."

Dinner ended and they thanked Jacque for the excellent meal and service. The night was warm and Greg suggested they walk back to the hotel instead of taking a taxi. Maria nodded in silent agreement. She was overcome by Greg's simple solution and tried valiantly as they walked to fight the tears that pressed for release.

They walked slowly, surrounded by the ghosts of a city once a cultural center that rivaled Paris. Now dismembered into three parts, one part cordoned off with a barrier stained with the blood of the unfortunate dying for the hope of freedom.

When they arrived at the hotel, they found a message that the meeting with Herr von Kunst would be tomorrow at two p.m. A car would be waiting for them at 1:40. They both gave a sigh of relief at the anticipation of a quick resolution of the insurance claim. Without a word being said, Maria and Greg's eyes met, reflecting thoughts beyond an insurance claim. The questions needing answers about their personal lives were far more important.

CHAPTER 18

AS USUAL, HANNELORE ENTERED OTTO'S STUDIO
with a brief knock that announced her presence but not for permission
to enter. The entire gallery was her domain, and therefore no permission
was needed for her gaining access to anyone. Otto had little regard for
Hannelore and never allowed her to intimidate him. She knew from past
experience that while Otto would do what she requested, it would be at
his own pace. He was presently hunched over a small Renoir cleaning
away paint a customer's young nephew had liberally applied.

Otto did not respond to her presence. It was a deliberate show of
his lack of respect for her. Hannelore knew his feelings but was aware of
his value to the gallery. It was not just for his artistic skills, but for other
reasons as well, that she restrained herself from forcing an issue about his
attitude. After a pause, she asked whether or not he had a moment for her.
Otto never paused or looked up from his work, only nodded. Hannelore
proceeded trying hard to keep the irritation she felt out of her voice.

"You remember a few days ago I asked you about any news in the art
world that would possibly affect the gallery or prompt the visit by the two
New York insurance persons?" Again only a nod. "Well, apparently while
there was nothing in the news that would give us cause for concern, my
meeting with them yesterday may prove otherwise."

Again a pause; she waited, her irritation rising at his insolent attitude
of non-response. The pause grew heavy; Otto kept on working inwardly
delighted at the discomfort he knew he was causing her.

Hannelore, now with a decided edge to her voice, said, "They're asking to look at documentation for a painting they said originated from this gallery and sold through our affiliate in New York. It appears that contrary to it being sold as an original, it has proved to be a copy. About a week ago I received a call from Georg about a visit from the male partner of the visitors who came here. He was inquiring about this painting. As you know, the question about its not being an original first came to light sometime ago when the executor of the estate came to Kurt with that information.

"A new appraisal had evidently proved the painting to be a copy. Instead of Kurt contacting us right away, he still insisted it was an original and wanted to challenge the finding. As soon as Kurt told me this, I was furious with him. Why would he try and sell a copy as an original? He knew that would be seen as fraud and would have disastrous consequences for us. He insisted the invoice from us stated it was an original and he had no reason to question it.

"Otto, since you are responsible for all transactions with New York, you must find that invoice that proves we correctly declared the painting to be an original. No doubt Kurt thought he could turn a quick personal profit in substituting a copy at the time of sale. In doing so, he has jeopardized our entire operation. I certainly could not trust him any further, and in accordance with our agreement, I exercised my right to buy him out.

"While Kurt never knew the details of our arrangements with the Kreis to use the gallery, he knows enough to arouse suspicion, and that we must avoid at all cost.

"Unfortunately, as I learned from my last meeting with the two investigators, they were able to find Kurt, and he admitted he received the painting from us, but claims the invoice declared it to be an original. The investigators said a review of our documentation should provide verification of my statement.

"Otto, I am sure we never would have sent a copy and declared it an original. Now I need you to check at once the shipping invoice. I will have to bring Andre into the matter. But in no way, Otto is there to be any indication to him of my major concern about unwanted investigations. We need to quickly resolve this issue. Tell only me what the invoice states and no one else, Andre included," she ended with emphasis.

Otto only nodded and continued his cleaning of the small painting. Hannelore, infuriated, fought the urge to sharply reprimand him for his lack of attention to what was a critical matter because she knew from experience that he had heard and she would get the information she wanted at his pleasure, not hers.

She left the studio making sure the closing door sent reverberations on impact. Otto laid aside his work and turned to look at the picture of Karl. Otto spoke out loud, as was his habit when addressing the picture, which he often did.

"So, old kommerad, it seems our young warrior maiden is upset. Investigators have come, good. Believe me, I have done what I have done over these past years for the good of Andre and your wife. If you would not have approved of the means, then forgive me, but I believe they justified the end. I have a foreboding that developing events will bring an outcome I have long feared. Faust, dear friend, could not have made a more disastrous pact with his devil than I have made with mine." Otto remembered clearly the conversation he overheard one late evening. A conversation replayed in his mind almost daily. It was between Hannelore's father and an SS officer, both assuming that the gallery was empty. The torment of bearing this knowledge alone, never able to share it, festered like a cancer, a hate for the Kreis that increased whenever he met any of them.

Otto gazed at the picture as he relived the horror of that night and its ongoing consequences.

"Dear Kommerad," he murmured, "I had no choice you must know that. How could you have forgiven me had I betrayed your family, who to this day do not know the truth of this illicit business we conduct? Although these vermin don't enjoy the victory they had been so sure of, their plans to convert the stolen goods to cash are proving successful. Yes, dear friend, with Hannelore's control over all the business affairs and my support, we are very successful."

Otto thought of all that had transpired since the Kreis had gone forward with their plans. He surmised that while Hannelore would not have countenanced the outright betrayal she would ultimately have to face, he knew she believed wholeheartedly in the cause of Aryan supremacy and what he and she were doing to support it.

It wasn't too long after the war ended and the economic situation had improved that Count von Linglesdorf had contacted Otto. He told Otto he must be prepared to fulfill his role as they entered the trade that had been carefully planned by them and Herr Hasenfeld. He reminded Otto of their meeting that evening several years ago when his future involvement with their program was laid out. Von Linglesdorf said with the clearest intent that any deviation on Otto's part or show of disloyalty would have the severest of consequences, consequences that would reach beyond Otto himself.

The Count said it was also time for Hannelore to become actively involved. Her business experience in controlling these transactions was needed. As planned with her father, her involvement would be kept secret from Andre. Andre would continue to concern himself with conducting the normal flow of sales and acquisitions. It was necessary to avoid any suspicion of the gallery's other venture that she and Otto would control. Von Linglesdorf wanted implementation of their plan to start as soon as possible.

CHAPTER 19

NOT LONG AFTER THIS CONVERSATION, HANNELORE
came to Otto's studio, demanding to know why it was taking him so long
to complete a repair for a customer of hers. Andre's customers always
received preferred attention from Otto; he enjoyed the complaints that
Hannelore had to deal with from her customers. Since he was the only
one in the city with the reputation of skills that customers were willing
to wait for, there was no loss of business, just irritation for Hannelore.
Otto decided now was the time to follow through on von Linglesdorf's
demand.

Otto ignored her inquiry about the work in question. Without turning around he told her to sit down, for he had something of great importance to tell her. Hannelore, taken aback by his tone, sat down almost
involuntarily.

Finally, he turned to Hannelore noting with some delight that she
was not happy with his initial abruptness in telling her to sit, like he
would a lap dog. Without a further word of greeting he said, "Fraulein
Hasenfeld, do you remember before your father's passing when he told
you I would have some information to share with you? It has to do with
a business arrangement he had made with a group of less than worthy
characters, himself included."

At this Hannelore started, "Herr Kranz, I highly resent this imperti-
nence. I am sure you are referring to the Kreis and to so include my father,
who did so much for you, is intolerable."

"I owe him nothing," retorted Otto. "Were it not for my skills and the need of my services in his nefarious scheme, he would have had me eliminated as swiftly as possible following Herr von Kunst's death. Be sure of that.

"What feelings of contempt I have for your associates needs no further discussion. The matter at hand is the conversation you and I had with your father before his death. It concerned matters I was to discuss with you at an appropriate time, do you remember?"

Hannelore thought for a moment and then nodded. "Yes, that there would be a time I was to be given some information by you and I was to carefully guard it. Why?"

"Your father and his cronies," Otto said with unmistakable disdain, "conspired during the war with members of the Ministry of Culture to funnel stolen works of art to this gallery."

Hannelore started, "Otto, how dare you infer my father or any of his friends conspired to receive stolen art. I'm sure that any such works brought here were properly and rightfully recovered from enemy nations. Besides, I know of no illegal art coming here, anyhow."

"No, you wouldn't, neither would Andre nor his mother. We, your father and I, since I had no choice, were careful that deliveries of these works were packaged in with legitimate deliveries to the gallery. Then late at night I would unpack them and put those marked for special handling in a secured place, the others placed as usual in the gallery or studio."

Hannelore sat quietly trying to understand what Otto was saying. She was resentful of his implications that her father and friends were involved in what she could not believe was wrongdoing. After all, anything that Germany had acquired during its defense against aggressive nations rightfully belonged to it. Her father had explained that any such acquisitions were rightful repayment for damages suffered by these enemy actions. Hannelore was angered by Otto's words but held her silence as Otto continued.

"Fraulein Hasenfeld, after I explain to you what your father and his cohorts conspired to do during the war, you will understand the entire success depends on your and my cooperation. You will no doubt gladly accept the additional burden this venture will place upon you. Your skill in business matters and my skill as a restorer and duplicator are necessary for the success of this business." Otto's skill was legendary, not just as a restorer, but from photographs of originals actually lost, he could recreate a copy with such accuracy that all but the most expert would judge it to be the original.

Hannelore was curious. "I am indeed honored that the plans my father made included me in this business you are about to reveal, yet I do not understand why you would be a part of it; you certainly have made clear your low regard for them. I am not unaware of your less than positive attitude toward me." He stared for a moment at this lovely woman whose outward beauty was matched by an equally ugly disposition.

Otto continued, "If present authorities discovered the plans your father and his fellow felons had made and carried out, you, I, and your friends, the Kreis, would be serving long prison terms; and this gallery would end abruptly." Hannelore was having difficulty comprehending Otto's comments.

"Prison? Why?" she asked, perplexed.

"Because, Fraulein Hasenfeld, as you were learning the business under your father's tutelage, every invoice for works arriving at or being shipped from the gallery carries your signature, now as then."

"Well, of course they do, and then I would forward the papers to you since it was your responsibility to take physical possession of arriving works and also to prepare for shipment those sold. It was and is all very routine. Whatever do you mean by threatening me with talk of prison?"

Otto was enjoying this conversation and the impact it was having on Hannelore. It was very evident that the papers crossing her desk she had signed without any questions about the originating source of these works. She had believed they were rightful property of the Reich sent to the gallery, her father explained, for safekeeping.

Her father told her that all invoices bearing the notation *sicherheit lager* were to be entered into a separate register and then forwarded to Otto. He said this was necessary because Karl and his family were not in sympathy with the cause of the Third Reich and wouldn't be pleased that they were performing this service.

She was not to mention this to Andre or anyone else. The seller's signed receipt, stating paid in full, accompanied all such designated invoices. It all seemed to be perfectly in order to her. She shared her father's disappointment with the Kunst family's attitude toward the government, especially Andre's, and dutifully never spoke of these transactions with anyone.

Otto continued, "Fraulein, I am telling you all of this because, as you remember, it was your father's wish I do this at a proper time. It appears your Kreis is now ready to exploit this ill-gotten treasure."

Hannelore frowned. "Why do you always speak so negatively, 'ill-gotten' and such? Whatever was done was proper and correct."

Otto continued, "Your late father conspired with your honorable Kreis to use their position in the Culture Ministry to divert works of art stolen from the homes of Berlin citizens and from homes in other occupied countries to this gallery.

"Entire museums and private collections in Belgium, the Netherlands, France, Poland, the Sudetenland, and Austria were transported in unmarked trucks to this gallery, usually at night. Your father, Hannelore, explained to Andre's father that these were works stored for clients of the gallery." He paused as Hannelore raised a protesting hand,

"Herr Kranz, you again keep referring to what was done by my father and friends as wrongful, even evil, yet the papers we processed had signed receipts of funds paid to the sellers. All was very correct. Since you were in charge of all those invoices I sent you, I never followed up. I never had a reason to determine the final disposition of those works. I assumed, since they were rightful property of the government, they were sent to us for temporary storage. I assumed they were to be distributed later to various museums and galleries after we won the war. That was your department; my duties only required entering invoices and separating them according to instructions.

"So why all this secrecy? Other works my father stored for clients were all accompanied with proper consignment documents. All that was done was legal." Otto didn't answer.

"As for those sent to you, that you claim were stolen, we had a perfect right to claim them as payment for the treasonable acts of their owners and the damage they inflicted on us. My father and his friends explained it very clearly how Germany had been betrayed after the First World War, had been exploited, had territories taken from her, was forced to make payments that caused us starvation and would make us a land of peasants. We had the right to try and reclaim these territories and to liberate large populations of people of German ancestry who wanted to be reunited with the Fatherland. They were oppressed and denied their rights by these foreign governments.

Otto looked at Hannelore with a sympathy she didn't deserve.

"Fraulein Hasenfeld, I remember you as a beautiful child, but with a mind so early poisoned, another evil deed for which I cannot forgive your father. But as you grew older, I had hoped you would see for yourself how blinded you had become to the facts. That kind of teaching you and others received poisoned many minds and, like poison, eventually killed. It led to the defeat and to the destruction of our beloved land.

"Whatever you and your friends think of the past as a time of lost glory, the reality is that the Third Reich was as evil a government as has ever existed on God's earth. They and those who have followed after who still hold to that heinous philosophy of Aryan Supremacy are nothing more, if not worse, than homicidal maniacs. If possible, I would expose them and their nefarious profiting; stealing and consigning to the ovens those from whom they stole."

Otto spoke with such vehemence that her own rage was overshadowed, but she recovered quickly.

Hannelore bristled at his words. "Otto, the Kreis are my friends and are still loyal to my father's memory. They, as my father did, hold fast to the belief in Germany's still to come rightful place among nations. Perhaps not through military might, but by electing the right members of parliament, they could affect an economic growth that would enable domination in world markets."

"Hannelore, I'm not going to argue with you. I have for good reason no choice but to reveal to you what has been carefully concealed. What I am about to show you, if it becomes known to the authorities, would be the abrupt end of the gallery. Not to mention long prison terms awaiting those involved, which includes your villainous Kreis members, you and I as well."

"Herr Kranz, you are not worthy to step foot in this gallery. I shall demand Andre to dismiss you at once."

Otto laughed heartily but cynically. "No, Fraulein, that you will not do. I would advise that before you approach Andre with such a demand, you wait until our coming meeting with your unholy group to discuss current plans, which, as I have said, involves you but not Andre.

"Fraulein Hasenfeld, my usefulness is one good reason why your accomplices are very unwilling to part with my services and why I advised you not to contemplate any action against me. You have, of course, seen these pictures upstairs on display but clearly marked as reproductions. Since a reproduction has little monetary value, they are still a good reflection of the original and can grace the walls of many a lovely home without apology. But as copies, they are not objects d'art and therefore are worth considerably less on the open market.

"Works of art like the originals we have are much sought after by private collectors who don't concern themselves with the source. The problem is that should some of these originals, thought long lost, suddenly appear on the market, there would be some embarrassing explanations demanded of the gallery. So they are going to be sold for considerable sums only to private collectors for the sake of their own egos and bragging rights to their closed circle of friends.

"The Kreis is now prepared to exploit this market, to move forward with plans made with your father to profit from their banditry. The war is over, many of our former enemies are more than willing to let bygones be bygones, especially when it serves their purpose. Many of them are now extremely interested to obtain for themselves supposedly lost works of art. As said, they have no concerns about the source of these works or the means to obtain them. Your father cleverly saw to it that you became the business manager of the gallery. Your position and the fortunate lack of interest in business matters by Andre has set the stage for the pursuit of a very profitable, if illegal, business."

Hannelore remained silent, her anger at Otto tempered by his words that the Kreis was about to venture into business and she was vital to its success. This pleased her; anything she could do to be of service to these loyal friends of her father, to further the goals they had planned, she would support wholeheartedly. Hannelore questioned how these special works were going to be transported without suspicion into other countries, especially the U.S.

"That, Fraulein Hasenfeld, is my value that the Kreis and you cannot afford to lose. It will be your and my responsibility to assure these originals will be delivered to future buyers without arousing that suspicion."

"How so?" queried Hannnelore.

"The details to establish an affiliate gallery in the U.S.," Otto said, "will be worked out between you and the 'Kreis.' Ostensibly, it will be a legitimate gallery and will conduct the normal business transactions of one. However, of far more importance to the Kreis will be the use of the gallery as a conduit for processing the transactions of these special works.

"My role is to assure the delivery of these works undetected. The usual methods of smuggling such works into the U.S. are clumsy. Sometimes they are tucked into suitcase linings or sandwiched between architectural blueprints or some such other devise long known to inspectors.

"What I have developed is a process known only to me. The secret formula rests in a safe deposit box. The bank has instructions to, upon news of my death or disappearance, turn the contents over to the authorities. The Kreis is well aware of this fact and my reasons for doing so.

"Now we are ready to accelerate the sale of these 'missing' works and, as I said, this is where you and I are to become more actively involved. We need to get a permanent gallery established in New York as soon as possible. Of course, from time to time we will sell some originals from our 'legitimate' consignment pool through normal channels—"

Hannelore interrupted, "Herr Kranz, really, I object to the tone you use in describing these plans; you just said 'legitimate' with the unmistakeable inference that it is not legitimate." Otto looked at Hannelore again with a mixture of sadness and dismay. None of what he had said or would say was going to change Hannelore's mind about the legality of what her father and her friends had planned. Her eagerness to enter into the execution of these plans was apparent.

Otto continued without acknowledging her objections, "Your father planned carefully with his collaborators not only to assure you of a secure financial future, but also to convert this purloined 'cache' into cash. This cash will in turn be funneled into the coffers of political organizations that are dedicated to promoting the election of candidates sympathetic to their idiotic plans.

"To further avoid suspicion, since the gallery enjoys such an excellent reputation, it is to be expected that some original works taken during the war would have been legitimately 'consigned' to the gallery for safekeeping. These are the works that will be sold with 'proper' documentation, which includes the proviso that if the consignee, or a designated agent, has not returned to claim the work within a specific time frame, the work becomes the property of the gallery."

"So there!" exclaimed Hannelore. "You just admitted these are properly documented and legitimate property of the gallery."

"I said," replied Otto carefully, "that it would be expected that 'some works' would have been legitimately consigned here. These are those works that your father convinced Andre's father that gallery clients had asked us to store for them."

"So why then," Hannelore demanded, "are you so insistent that these are not legitimately ours? There is nothing to hide."

"Nothing to hide? Interestingly enough, dear Fraulein, the paintings that we will offer publicly will have supporting documentation, documentation that is all forged."

Hannelore had heard enough. Evidently, Otto was just an embittered old man who refused to see the justification of Germany's right to these properties taken from those who could only be considered as enemies.

"Herr Kranz, you have done as my father requested, I believe it is now imperative that we both move forward with his and the Kreiss' wishes."

Otto agreed. "Your father was very clever in convincing Herr von Kunst that Andre's skills in developing the sale and acquisition of objects would free you to oversee the business aspects for which Andre had never shown much interest. This has worked out very well; your skill has been well demonstrated. Their plans for implementation remain their, my, and now your secret. Now come with me, I have something to show you.

CHAPTER 20

HERR VON LINGLESDORF USUALLY ASSUMED THE
role of spokesman for the 'Kreis.' He had been the most prominent
member of the Reich ministry with whom Heinz had developed the plan
to divert the stolen art to the gallery. When Otto called that he had
explained the plan to Hannelore, who was now eagerly ready to be a part
of its implementation, von Linglesdorf was pleased.

His meeting with Hannelore and Otto went smoothly. He had
always been Hannelore's confidant and mentor. His plan to set in motion
the sales of the stolen property, primarily to eager U.S. buyers, was exciting to Hannelore. Otto could only listen with disgust. Von Linglesdorf
outlined for Hannelore how the funds from these sales would provide
additional income for all of them personally. However, he reaffirmed that
a substantial amount would be used to support the election of political
candidates in sympathy with the designs of the Kreis.

Von Linglesdorf repeated again to Hannelore that the Kreis were
determined to establish a political base from which they could influence
programs that would further the desire to restore Germany to an economic power and achieve the goals that militarism had failed to do.

Hannelore's first responsibility was to establish a U.S. connection.
Her second, and just as important, was to coordinate with Otto the necessary documentation and accounting of these transactions. Andre was
never to know of this arrangement. His obvious dislike of the Kreis was
well known, as was his total lack of sympathy with any ideas of a German
rebirth on discredited philosophies of the past.

Herr von Linglesdorf also warned Hannelore that any suspicious actions of Herr Otto Kranz were to be reported to him at once. He was not to be trusted, yet, without explaining the details to Hannelore, he was quite sure Otto could be relied upon to carry out their directions if well supervised.

The gallery, with its impeccable reputation, would be a valuable asset in the success of their program. Hannelore's goal was to set up the procedure as soon as possible that would bring to fruition the plans her father and his good friends had made. Hannelore never doubted for a moment the legitimacy of the right to these works of art. It was their right to convert these treasures into cash to be used to establish a new and powerful Reich.

After Hannelore met with Otto and the 'Kreis,' she needed to find a gallery that would facilitate the illegal sale of "unclaimed" originals to the select customers provided by Herr von Linglesdorf. Of course, there would be sufficient legal sales of originals to give legitimacy to the U.S. affiliated gallery. Hannelore immediately prepared an advertisement for an U.S. partner.

CHAPTER 21

THE PLAN PROVED SUCCESSFUL. KURT KOHL, OWNER of a small gallery in New York, responded to her ad in *Art News*. Hannelore telephoned her interest in coming to New York to meet him.

Kurt was pleasantly surprised at the quick response from such a prestigious gallery and quickly agreed to the date Hannelore suggested.

Kurt met the arriving Hannelore with a large bouquet of flowers and impressed her with his welcoming charm. He hadn't been prepared for the striking figure who acknowledged with a bright smile the name on the card, Kurt, that he was holding as she came through Customs.

He escorted her to the Plaza Hotel, where he had already pre-registered her. His thoughtfulness impressed her. Since it was late afternoon, she accepted his offer that if she cared to have dinner later that evening, she would call, or if she would rather rest and meet him the next morning, that would be fine.

Hannelore did not feel exceptionally tired and after a short nap in the well-appointed room that Kurt had reserved for her; she decided to call him and accept the invitation for dinner. Kurt was pleased.

It was evident as dinner conversation progressed that Kurt was not interested in trying to impress Hannelore about his gallery. What was more evident to Hannelore was his open admiration of her. She enjoyed the difficulty he was having controlling his eyes. Her royal blue dress enhanced with a pearl necklace from which a sapphire pendant dropped perilously close to a delicate show of cleavage would challenge the most proper gentleman to maintain eye contact only.

112 | REGINALD KEITH

But Kurt remained the proper gentleman, and looking into sky blue eyes in an exquisite face graced by genuine blonde waves helped his control. His polite inquiries and offer to help her find a location or other alternative to his own continued to impress her.

Hannelore enjoyed the evening, and as Kurt returned her to the hotel, she expressed her thanks and eagerness to visit his gallery on the morrow. She said at his suggestion it would be fine to have a continental breakfast at eight a.m. at the hotel.

After Hannelore went to her room, she sat for a while considering how she would approach the subject of using the gallery as the conduit for the works of art that she and the Kreis wanted to deliver to special clients.

She decided that Kurt, apparently very interested in the partnership idea, might be a better choice even if his gallery was not exactly what she had envisioned as representative of Von Kunst Gallery. *Yet*, she thought, *it may be better to work with a more compliant partner like Kurt than a more inquisitive gallery.* She sensed it would not be too difficult to encourage Kurt to be as compliant as she wished.

Kurt admitted to himself as he re-entered the waiting taxi that he hoped Hannelore would find his gallery acceptable.

Breakfast was pleasant, and Kurt had to remark that never had he seen a woman look as good in the morning as she had the night before. Hannelore thanked him for the compliment, adding laughingly that it all came from a good night's sleep with a good conscience.

The gallery was more on the order of a second-hand outlet than an art gallery; the lettering over the door, *Kurt's Place*, did little to improve that image. Kurt sensed at once that he had really overstepped himself in even suggesting a partnership could exist between his and her galleries. He began to apologize as Hannelore walked through the clutter noting at once the amateurish works on consignment and yet occasionally seeing one that did show promise. The building itself was in need of a good upgrading and total makeover of the display area.

Hannelore reached into her large leather handbag and pulled out a note pad. She didn't talk, and Kurt sensed it wasn't the time for him to engage her in any conversation. She walked back outside and looked up and down the street and then studied the façade of Kurt's Place. Kurt watched her face for any sign of approval or disapproval as she kept jotting things into her note pad. Inwardly, Hannelore decided that Kurt and his gallery had more value than he might suspect.

Kurt said, "You mentioned at breakfast that you had other galleries you would like to visit. I would be glad to take you to them."

Hannelore said quickly, "If you really don't mind, I would like to visit one other gallery. It is the only one of the six, besides you, who answered my ad that I have an interest in seeing."

Arriving at the gallery, the receptionist looked surprised when Hannelore presented her card and asked for Mr. Raffide.

"Do you have an appointment?"

"No," replied Hannelore, "but I am sure Mr. Raffide will recognize the name, so would you please see if he is available."

The receptionist hung up her phone. "Mr. Raffide will be here momentarily, please have a seat."

Kurt nodded and said he'd simply browse around and not to hurry. He had the feeling he needn't be concerned about her hurrying on his behalf.

Mr. Raffide appeared with a smiling face and outstretched hand,. "Good Morning, Miss Hasenfeld. I am so pleased to meet you, but I confess, I didn't know you were coming today, please come to my office." Hannelore took the extended hand and followed him to the rear of the gallery.

After a relatively short time, Hannelore appeared quite suddenly, and with a nod to Kurt to follow, left the gallery. Outside the gallery, Kurt was tempted to ask some questions but again resisted the impulse. He hadn't been around Hannelore very long to learn there was an air about her that advised caution, better to let her have the lead. They walked about a block in silence when Hannelore said, "Kurt, I'd like to go back to my hotel, would you please hail a taxi for me? I'll call you later and perhaps we could have dinner. Meanwhile I do have some things I need to attend to, and you needn't come with me."

As New York luck wouldn't have it, a taxi was quickly hailed. As Hannelore entered, Kurt told the driver, "Plaza One," and quickly asked Hannelore if she was sure she didn't want him to at least escort her to the hotel.

"No need, I'll call you. Make dinner reservations somewhere for around seven." She motioned for him to close the door and left.

Kurt stood for a while trying to decide if he felt more like her valet than a possible partner. He laughed as he tried without much success to hail another taxi. "Guess even the cabs know its better not to upset her," he said to himself.

Hannelore looked at her watch. The bank in Berlin would be closed, but she knew Konrad would be accessible. She placed a long-distance call to his private number.

He answered promptly and, hearing Hannelore's voice, expressed his pleasure at her call. He was one of those who had Hannelore's confidence and was her personal contact in financial matters with the Kreis. He enjoyed the considerable funds that came to his bank through both the regular transactions of the Gallery as well as the separate transactions from the Kreis account. It was, of course, this latter account for which the Kreis paid him handsomely to personally ensure the account was kept coded and overseen by him only. He was also pleased at Hannelore's personal attention to him. His wife often complained, but Konrad explained that their evenings at the theater or dinner were a business necessity.

"Until two a.m.?" she once questioned.

Hannelore quickly explained she needed to have funds transferred to the bank's affiliate in New York.

"Done first thing tomorrow," Konrad replied. "Now do hurry back, I'd enjoy an evening dinner date soon as possible."

Hannelore laughed. "Well, of course, I'd enjoy that very much. Now thank you, I appreciate the good service."

With that, she hung up and went back to the notes she had taken at Kurt's gallery. A few hours later she called Kurt, who said he had made dinner reservations for seven as she requested. He would be by to pick her up at 6:30.

"Fine," she replied, "I'll be ready," and hung up. Kurt couldn't tell if she was inordinately abrupt or it was his growing sensitivity. Her take-charge attitude impressed and irritated him simultaneously.

He arrived at the hotel to find her waiting in the lobby dressed as before to his complete distraction. She had assumed early in life that her beauty was for a purpose, to be used as necessary to achieve desired goals, of course, with discretion. Tonight was a night for discretion; she didn't want to distract Kurt totally. That might be necessary later because the plan she had formulated would necessitate Kurt's acceptance, and she was prepared to use every advantage; his evident admiration would fit well with her plans.

Kurt had chosen a small restaurant that wasn't crowded and provided booths offering a good degree of privacy. Hannelore, after they were seated, took her notes out.

"Kurt," she began, "I want to thank you for your kindness in taking me to your gallery and the other. It was informative and now I want to get on with business and wrap up things so I can return to Berlin."

Kurt waited.

"You see, what I want above all else is a partner in whom I can place a great degree of trust. I cannot afford to enter a relationship that requires a lot of attention to details from a location so far away. From what I have seen so far, I really think I would be comfortable with you as that partner." Kurt was quite surprised.

"Hannelore, I am pleased that you would choose me, but I am also surprised because I know the other gallery is much more attractive than mine, I have to admit that."

Hannelore shook her head. "That gallery is of no interest to me; remember, I said trust is very important to me. You will discover these transactions can be complicated at times, and I must have full confidence in my partner.

"That would not be possible with the one we visited. I was under the impression Mr. Raffide was the sole owner; early in the conversation, however, Mr. Raffide said any meaningful discussions should include the other two owners, Mr. Greenberg and Mr. Grossmann. Well, as I said, hearing those names, the trust I need would be impossible."

Kurt was puzzled. "Do you know those gentlemen?" he asked curiously.

"No need to meet them." came the sharp reply. "Their names are all I need to hear."

"Oh, I see, you have heard something about them that doesn't please you?" Kurt was still perplexed. Hannelore looked exasperated.

"Kurt, their names, their names, don't you understand who they must be?" Kurt could do nothing but return a look of incomprehension that irritated Hannelore.

"Kurt, they must be Jewish." She said it with such a negative emphasis that Kurt half recoiled in his seat. He was at a lost for an answer. His business had involved many persons of different nationalities to which Kurt had attached no significance. He always accepted people on their own cognizance.

"Kurt," she continued, "evidently you belong to that great unenlightened group of people who, in ignorance, don't understand the danger such people as these are to society. In no way will I do business with them, and I would hold my partner to the same standard. Of course, that doesn't mean I would not sell to them as a customer, I just want to emphasize no business of a contractual nature is to be conducted with them."

Kurt tried to digest this surprising revelation that seemed to him to be so out of character for such a sophisticated woman. Kurt had no ready answer; he was not prepared to enter into a discussion with Hannelore about an issue he had given little, if any, thought.

He simply said, "Well, their loss, my gain, and thank you for having the trust in me. I will certainly do all that I can to prove it a well-placed trust."

"I am sure you will, Kurt," she said with a smile that drove all other thoughts from his mind except how pleasant it was going to be working so closely with such a lovely creature.

"Kurt," the warm smiled remained, "I want to be honest with you and mean no offense, but your gallery really needs a face lift and perhaps a better name if you are to represent our gallery in the U.S. I think the location is acceptable, and perhaps it will add a certain 'cache' if we emphasize its exclusivity.

"Kurt, I think the most important matter isn't the renovation, it's again what I first said, trust. My gallery has an excellent reputation, and we have many private clients who are U.S. citizens interested in buying very expensive and rare works of art. We also are very fortunate to have a restorer and reproducer of art who cannot be equaled anywhere. Many of his works are so skillfully done that it would take the most experienced art expert to be able to distinguish his copies from the originals. Now, of course, we never would allow a copy to be sold as an original, and we carefully make sure that copies are clearly identified as such.

"What I need for you to understand is that the originals we sell to the U.S. have to be handled with the most discretion. These customers want no publicity that would attract undue attention.

"However, these sales will be fewer in number than those that are copies. You will be notified of shipments coming to the gallery and the time of their arrival. You will need to be at Customs with the documents needed for clearance, which we will have sent you. The invoices with the prefix 'K' will be those special paintings to which I am referring.

"Those with the 'K' you are to store and not put on display. Our local representative will pick them up. This is an arrangement that has already been established and will remain outside of the normal activities of our mutual business. There will be no need to process such deliveries through the gallery other than for you to keep one copy of the invoice to be placed in a safety deposit box at the bank.

"Of course, there will be other originals sent for display and sale to the public who visit the gallery in the normal manner of trade. It certainly will enhance the gallery's reputation to be known as possessing these actual originals and drawings from some of the world's best-known artists. In this respect, perhaps a name like Art World might be appropriate, what do you think?"

Kurt was having a problem listening and comprehending at the pace Hannelore was talking. The soft blonde hair falling around her face and the gentle rise and fall of the pearl pendant didn't allow for much attention to her proposals.

"Well, yes," Kurt quickly tried, not quite successfully, to recover a measure of attention. Hannelore was pleased, no ice in the sky blue eyes she fastened on him.

"Hannelore," Kurt thought he had better be responding with more interest, "I think your plans are well thought out, and as far as the name goes, I like it. But I, too, must be honest with you when it comes to your mention of a face lifting. If you intend to have this gallery represent and display such works as you have mentioned that would attract the appropriate clientele, I'm afraid my finances might not be sufficient."

Hannelore had already surmised that would be the case and actually hoped for it.

"Kurt," she softly said, "of course it's understandable that not every business has capital for unexpected plans such as I propose. I wouldn't expect that and no need to be embarrassed by the need of funds to make the plans actual.

"I anticipated that my partner might need some funds to carry out the plans we made. Whatever funds are needed to make Art World a quality gallery will be available. Should additional funds be needed, you will only have to call me.

"Kurt," she looked at him intently, "the financial arrangements we make are secondary to the trust we must have between us. Do you have any questions so far?"

Kurt thought for a moment about the special handling of the "K" invoiced paintings but decided any questions about them might cause Hannelore to think he mistrusted her. He smiled. "I guess my only question is when do we start?"

"Tomorrow," Hannelore answered, pleasantly surprised at Kurt's unquestioning acceptance. "We'll meet at the bank, and I'll have the attorney there draw up all the documents we need. Kurt, I'm sure the attorney acting on my behalf will question the amount of money I will be investing and how the partnership shares will be divided.

"Personally, it doesn't make that much difference to me, but good business practice dictates that I, too, must answer to my partner in Berlin. Usually, the partner with the most investment would hold proportionately the greater number of shares. Do you agree?" Kurt knew without question that based on his financial position, Von Kunst Gallery would hold the controlling shares. He nodded his understanding.

Hannelore continued, "Of course, this will allow either partner to acquire the shares of the other based on the value of those shares at the time of purchase. My attorney can work out the details, but I wanted to ask you first if you would be in agreement with such an arrangement. I want you to be satisfied, Kurt; I want us to be trusting each other, more than just as business partners." The intensity of her gaze as she spoke decimated Kurt's ability to think rationally; he could only think of being more than just a business partner with this stunning woman.

After the meeting at the bank and all arrangements had been made and agreements signed, Hannelore told Kurt that all she needed was a floor plan of his gallery. Her architect would design the changes she had in mind. Since all business matters were now settled, she needed to return to Berlin but would return with the architect's proposals, and if Kurt agreed, they could proceed with the renovation. Kurt experienced a surge of anticipation at Hannelore's comment that when she came back, she would stay and help oversee the project.

Andre expressed a mild surprise at Hannelore's rush to get the plans ready for her return to New York.

"You're going back so soon? How long will you be gone?"

"Andre," came a quick reply, "this is really going to be very profitable for the gallery. I am excited to have the renovations done and be open to the public as soon as possible. It's a new adventure, you should be excited too."

"Well, you know me, Hannelore, I'm rather content visiting customers and acquiring new accounts here at home. Part of my surprise is that you never expressed much liking for Americans. Now you are willing to do business with them? While I have always trusted your judgment in business affairs, is this a costly venture for us, may I ask?"

Hannelore said with obvious pride, "Andre, it is one of the best arrangements possible. The money is coming from a private donor that our partner knows who has influence with the city officials. They are both interested in any project that enhances the property values in that area. Our expenses will be limited to my visits to the gallery on occasion. Even the plans I have made will be reimbursed by them."

Andre thought for a moment to ask about the private donor but decided Hannelore, in whom he had explicit trust, would have assured herself that all details were in order. He could only express his admiration for her ability to grow the gallery's business beyond the boundaries of Europe.

Later, at a meeting with the Kreis that Otto attended, Hannelore updated them with the details of her arrangement with Kurt to their delighted approval. When she explained how she had covered the financial arrangements with Andre, they were almost gleeful at her cunning. Otto's hatred for them all burned within him.

Kurt's obvious pleasure on her return with the plans was almost embarrassing to Hannelore as she entered Customs. She was sure bystanders were convinced Kurt was greeting his lover. She knew she would be able to use his admiration to good advantage.

The renovation went forward much more smoothly than Kurt imaged it would. When finished, a visitor had the impression when walking down the central aisle flanked by the graceful white columns in front of each blue-carpeted alcove that they were in the private gallery of some Italian duke.

Art World in bold gold script followed the curve of the arched window above the entrance. The announcement of the " invitation only" gala opening was a masterstroke of marketing by Hannelore. The invitation noted that several original works by Renaissance masters would be on display but not for sale. This was calculated not only to arouse the curiosity of the invited elite, but to place Art World as a gallery first, a business establishment second. Hannelore's strategy was to give an air of sophistication, of refinement, that Art World, while welcoming all, would be the choice of the most discerning clientele attracting many who would become "special" clients.

The opening event was, as the critics who were there testified, a smash. The collections on display were stunning, almost as stunning, they wrote, as the beautiful hostess and owner of Art World, one Hannelore Hasenfeld, partner in the prestigious Von Kunst Gallery, Berlin. The critics noted that several of the originals on display were works of art that had not been seen for decades and were presumed lost.

When questioned, the lovely Hannelore explained that their gallery enjoyed such a reputation that during the "late unpleasantness," families brought their treasures to the gallery for safekeeping. The gallery then purchased many of these works such as those on display from those families who decided to sell for financial reasons.

What was of added interest were the excellent reproductions of some of the originals that were placed next to them. The critics were hard-pressed to discern which was which, much to the hostess's delight.

She explained that the Von Kunst Gallery was fortunate in having in residence Europe's master restorer and copier. She noted that while originals were extremely expensive, it was her pleasure to be able to provide at a lesser price excellent reproductions to the public for their enjoyment. The critics concluded that the exquisite Art World gallery was a welcome presence and all the more pleasant to know that Hannelore Hasenfeld would be returning from time to time to personally welcome guests at future receptions.

Kurt was quite overwhelmed by the course of events and accepted his role as secondary to Hannelore. What was of far more importance to Kurt was the fact that she would be returning from time to time.

She was somewhat of an enigma. They spent most evenings together after a day overseeing the renovations. Dinner was a pleasant event, with much discussion over future plans. It wasn't long before Kurt tried to have an opportunity to be with her on a more intimate basis. He once suggested that after dinner, drinks could be had at his apartment. Hannelore countered with an offer for him to come to her hotel since it would be more convenient for her.

Those evenings, although not the reward of every dinner, were frequent enough to remain the focus of Kurt's attention, and anticipation of such times his most pleasurable thoughts. When it was time for her to leave New York, his regrets were soothed that last evening by her warm farewell and promise to come as often as she could because she enjoyed his company much more than just reviewing the gallery's progress.

The Kreis plan functioned smoothly. The majority of the "K" designated original works were sold to private American buyers attracted to the gallery. Von Linglesdorf's agent, installed as a salesperson by Hannelore, was responsible to inquire tactfully about a visitor's interest. If it developed that there was an interest in obtaining such works as the gallery could provide, he would advise the buyer of the difficulty in locating such works and, if found, of acquiring them. Transporting them to America would also be very problematic and costly.

If these potential buyers indicated they were willing to pay sufficiently to overcome such obstacles, the inquiries were then forwarded to the Kreis and Hannelore. Otto would confirm a requested work was available and a deal would be made. The work would be shipped at the agreed price through the channel established by Hannelore with the unsuspecting Kurt.

Hannelore was pleased that her ability to establish Art World as a conduit in fulfilling her father's plan was proving successful. Hannelore knew Andre must never be aware of what she was doing; he would have been shocked and totally opposed.

CHAPTER 22

ANDRE WASN'T SURE HOW LONG KATYA WOULD BE prepared to stay, but he wanted to be sure he had allowed ample time, notwithstanding her proviso that they be free to leave at will.

He thought the evening dinner would be an opportune time to introduce Katya and the Maestro to Hannelore. He calculated that a visit the next day to the gallery would impress the Maestro.

Katya called shortly before noon; rehearsal was over, and the Maestro had said they should be ready to leave around noon tomorrow.

Andre was pleased and asked, "If rehearsals are over, could we meet for lunch?" Katya had hoped that by mentioning rehearsals were over that a lunch invitation might be forthcoming. She hoped the hint was not too obvious. She was a bit chagrined to admit she wanted another opportunity to see him. Katya waited a moment before agreeing to lunch to avoid Andre thinking she was waiting for the invitation.

"That would be nice," she said, readily agreeing to meet in about an hour in the café across from the hotel where they had first met. She knew the Maestro would be taking a nap, but she wanted to avoid the possibility of his seeing her with Andre in the hotel. Andre was able to make train reservations and to arrange transportation to the train station with the hotel concierge before going to the café.

Katya was wearing a red pullover with black slacks. Her raven hair was pulled back, letting Andre have the benefit of seeing the full beauty of her face. She walked toward his table with a warm smile framing perfect rows of white. Andre caught himself staring. Katya pretended not to notice but was pleased. Andre rose and extended his hand as he helped her to a seat at the small table he had chosen in a corner of the café.

"Coffee and something to go with it?" he asked.

"Just coffee will be fine." She smiled winsomely. She watched him as he ordered two *kannchen kaffee*, treating the waitress with a kind respect. If there was one special quality about Andre that she had noticed from the beginning, it was his considerate manners for everyone he met. Even that first night in the hotel when the Maestro had been nothing less than rude, Andre had reacted with total respect and politeness. There had been nothing in their meetings so far that gave her any reason to believe that he wasn't honest, a good person, and a person to be trusted. If she had had earlier qualms about going with him to Berlin, they were gone now. Andre began excitedly to give her the details of his arrangements for their travel to Berlin.

"I have booked first class tickets on an InterCity express leaving Köln at one thirty-five p.m. arriving in Berlin at four p.m. The tickets for the train as well as transportation to the station will be available at the concierge. I plan to attend the concert tonight and then leave for Berlin."

"Drive to Berlin so late?" asked a surprised Katya.

Andre laughed. "Best time to drive; the autobahn isn't crowded and I can really enjoy some speed."

"Well, do be careful, it would be somewhat embarrassing to arrive in Berlin without our host to meet us."

"Indeed," replied Andre. "I'll be there to meet you and the Maestro and take you to the Hotel Karpinski, where I have reserved two adjoining suites. I have also presumed that after a rest, you and the Maestro would be so kind as to join my partner, Frau Hannelore Hasenfeld, and me for dinner at a restaurant that I assure you is Berlin's best."

Andre had to pause as the smile on Katya's face was fast turning to laughter as she held up her hand for him to stop.

"My goodness, Andre, we are not royalty! We very seldom, if ever, travel first class, suites are out of the question, and while we do enjoy a good meal, we are not accustomed to any special attention. You must understand that while I believe we are adequately compensated for our performances, the Maestro is very conscious of expenses, and all that you have outlined is going to certainly arouse his suspicion."

"Suspicion? Of what?" asked a puzzled Andre. A slight blush colored her cameo cheeks.

"Well, I think he will think you are doing all of this just to impress us and get him to start judging you in a better light."

"Really!" Andre countered with some force and, leaning forward again, took not one but both her hands in his before she could withdraw them, had she wanted to.

"Katya, I've said this before, I do not expect you to understand what I don't fully understand myself, but there is that quality about you that drives me to know you more. Every time we meet I am more convinced than ever of your uniqueness. Simply put, you have become very special to me. I just want to be in your presence as much as possible.

"If the Maestro is suspicious, he probably is right but for the wrong reason. I'm not trying to impress him or you by these arrangements. What I am doing is trying to show you how much I respect you both and want to make sure you are entertained in a manner you deserve.

"But above all, I admit that while I hope the Maestro derives some pleasure from all of this, I am not trying to buy his approval. That he must determine for himself. But yes, I am trying to make sure that you enjoy yourself as never before. If he has the suspicion that I want to spoil you, he is absolutely correct!" Andre finished emphatically.

"Well, I must say, Andre, you are indeed going well beyond what I think you need to do." Then, smiling coyly, Katya said, "But I think I'm going to like being spoiled a bit." They both laughed.

"Seriously, Katya, if there is any problem with these arrangements, they can be changed."

She shook her head. "No, really, it all sounds just fine, and I'll tell the Maestro. The leaving time fits our usual schedule, even if the final destination does not. Remember his condition that departure from Berlin is at his discretion, I must reaffirm that with him."

Andre smiled. "I remember that condition and fervently hope he will be as reluctant to leave as you will be when the time comes."

With that Katya rose to go. "Andre, you've been so kind, and I admit my pleasure at the prospect of spending some time in Berlin." After a slight pause, she added, "and with you, of course. Now I must get back to my room, rest a bit, and then meet with the Maestro to go over the evening performance. I'll need to bring him up to date on your extravagant arrangements that need give him no cause for suspicion." Andre watched admiringly as the lithe figure left the café.

Andre spent the remainder of the day in enjoying a stroll through the ancient city of Köln. He sat for a while on a bench overlooking Father Rhine. It reminded him of the day he had paused to take a walk up the path to the Frau Germania statue high on the river's bank, commemorating Germany's victory in the Franco/Prussian war of 1871. Since then there had been little cause to raise victory monuments.

The devastation of two world wars was spawned as Germany, claiming its right for *lebensraum*, invaded neighboring lands. No wonder there were constant fears that some day east and west would reunite and Germany would again embark on this quest for domination. He watched the flowing river; same river, new water. Finally, he got up and went back to the hotel to get ready for the evening concert.

He sat in his chair waiting with the same heightened anticipation for the concert to begin and the pleasure of watching her perform. The orchestra assembled, and he held his breath as Katya, in a black evening dress that followed the perfect contour of her form, strode purposefully to the podium. With the graceful nods of a first violinist, she directed the final tuning of their instruments.

What was it about this girl that so completely captured his attention? How many times had he asked himself this question with no reasonable answer to be found? As she took her place the Maestro ascended the podium and without a bow to the audience raised his baton and the concert commenced.

Andre's eyes were only for Katya and his envy of the violin held so closely between shoulder and cheek. Again, that enchanting profile, the alabaster whiteness of her skin accentuated by the blackness of her hair and dress. As she played, her sleeve fell back as if reluctantly giving her arm freedom to take command of the bow that danced with a vivacity that the eye could barely follow. The Maestro, long hair flying, body leaping, baton piercing the air, gave the impression of a man in pursuit on an unseen enemy, the Don Quixote of music came to Andre's mind.

The Maestro received the usual standing ovation with a slight bow. As he acknowledged the contribution of his orchestra, the applause rose to a crescendo when Katya stood at his beckoning. Her flawless rendition of the difficult solo in the third movement of Schostakovich's *Violin Concerto No. One* was still fresh in their minds. Her gracious bow with instrument in hand heightened the applause.

It was evident that the audience reciprocated the love the Maestro and his protégé had for their music. Andre had arranged for a bouquet of flowers to be delivered backstage with a note of congratulations and a reminder that all arrangements had been made as promised. He would meet them in Berlin tomorrow afternoon.

CHAPTER 23

HE ENTERED THE AUTOBAHN, TOP DOWN, PRESSED the accelerator to the floor, and began racing through the moon-silvered landscape. Andre arrived after midnight but wasn't extremely tired. The drive had been refreshing; the autobahn almost clear of major traffic permitted him to choose his speed and enjoy the warm wind whistling around the open cockpit.

He parked the car in the garage and stopped by Elsa's desk to leave a note telling her he'd call her in the morning.

With more pleasant thoughts about Katya, he fell asleep in his chair and woke only as the early sun's rays fell on his face. There was time enough to take a quick wake-up shower and shave before calling Elsa. She had already come in early in anticipation of his arrival, and Andre reached eagerly for the phone at the first ring.

Her voice was warm, her "Good morning, Andre. Welcome back" pleased him. Before he could offer a greeting in return, Elsa continued, "Shall I bring coffee?" She had made it a habit to offer a morning coffee. It gave her the opportunity to spend a few private minutes each day with Andre. He enjoyed starting the day with Elsa and her never-failing brightness and positive attitude.

They would enjoy the quiet time making small talk before Hannelore would join them. Elsa's presence always annoyed her. It was evident to her that Elsa's offer to bring coffee was only a ruse to see Andre. Perhaps, she once said, "Andre should discourage such intimacy with an employee."

Andre had laughed, said he had no intention to do that. He enjoyed the informal updates Elsa shared with him.

While Hannelore exerted much influence on Andre's life, she knew it was more a willingness on his side to let her do so, and she was aware that there was a certain point beyond which she ventured carefully when dealing with him. Her disapproval of Elsa's morning visits was mollified when Elsa cleverly included sufficient coffee for Hannelore and her favorite croissants.

This morning Andre was more interested in the reasons Hannelore wanted him back in Berlin than a routine update on gallery business, which Elsa quickly assured him was doing fine. Elsa couldn't add much to what she had already told Andre over the phone about the two visitors from New York. Evidently, their visit was the reason for Hannelore's request for him to return. She added that the news that he was bringing a visitor and later the news that it would be two annoyed Hannelore. Elsa tried to hide her own curiosity, but it was clear to Andre that she was as curious as Hannelore. He knew the unexplained addition of flowers and fruit for two separate suits didn't lessen this curiosity one wit.

"Andre, you really had us worried; it wasn't like you to not call for several days. Of course, that's your business, but you should at least let us know you are well," Elsa said with sincerity. Andre took her comment at face value and knew she was sincere in her concern. Looking at her across the small coffee table as they sipped their coffee in the moments of silence they reserved for private thoughts, he couldn't help comparing her with Katya and Hannelore.

Not that it was an attempt to compare them physically; the three were blessed with striking good looks. But Andre always tried to look into people, what made them distinct from others, what characteristics attracted him or repulsed him.

He made no effort to hide his dislike for the Kreis, yet he held Hannelore with all her misplaced affection for these men in high esteem. He excused her political blindness because of an overpowering father who filled her youthful mind with illusions of Teutonic, Aryan supremacy. Her father had fostered her relationship with the Kreis, who carried on the myths that so enraptured her.

When Andre was able to engage Hannelore in conversation on other topics or when they shared an evening together, she was a witty and charming companion. He was amazed at her business skills and total command of details. Her demeanor, however, toward others showed a hardness that was in stark contrast to both Elsa and Katya. They had inner warmth that was instantly transferred to others. They both were truly without guile.

Although he had known Katya for a very short time, he sensed a vulnerability that grew every time he met with her. It fostered in him a desire to protect, to shelter her from the hostile world she had been led to believe awaited her, especially here in Germany.

Elsa, ever at the ready to serve, had a genuine openness and was never one to force an issue or foster a confrontation. Her vivaciousness in relating events of the day was in clear contrast with the subdued Katya or the matter of fact mannerism of Hannelore.

Elsa possessed self-assurance without any of the self-importance that Hannelore too often portrayed. It gave Elsa the inner character not to let Hannelore's oftentimes overbearing manner affect her negatively. But there were times the temptation to strike back had to be held in check. The knowledge of Andre's and Otto's support helped her resolve to overlook any of Hannelore's less than friendly encounters; it was just Hannelore.

Elsa looked up at the clock and with perfect timing said, just as Hannelore entered the office, it was time to get down to the gallery. Hannelore nodded her acceptance of the departing Elsa's "Good morning" as she seated herself and poured a cup of coffee without a word to Andre. He was well aware that the coming conversation was not to be one of their friendliest.

"Well, how nice of you to return so promptly," she said with little concealed sarcasm. "Sometimes I wonder just how much interest you have in this gallery. I carry a great responsibility and very seldom do I call upon you for some assistance. Yet when I do, there should be a much quicker response to my request than you have shown on this occasion. It is quite inconceivable that your delay was due to an interlude with a Polish conductor of all things.

"I think my telephone conversation with you made it abundantly clear that your invitation to your guests was in poor taste. Perhaps you would be so kind as to offer a few words of explanation?"

Andre from long experience did not interrupt Hannelore's exasperated monologue, nor did he offer an immediate reply. What bothered him was Hannelore's extreme agitation. It was not like her; something was bothering her. It went beyond irritation at uninvited guests, his tardy return, or his comments about the Kreis. Those scoldings were always delivered with an air of self-righteousness, self-assurance. He detected now a slight note of panic, of fear even, and that disturbed him far more than just being scolded.

"Hannelore, I'm sorry for the delay in returning, but it's not unusual for insurance people to call on us, and you have handled such matters in the past without my help."

Hannelore hesitated; she didn't want to arouse any suspicion on Andre's part that this insurance inquiry was anything more than routine.

"Well, usually I don't need to bother you, but this inquiry is a first involving Art World, and I don't feel comfortable dealing with Americans. You seem to tolerate foreigners better than I, and I think you will be able to clear this matter without too much difficulty."

Andre's puzzled look reminded Hannelore that Andre probably didn't even remember the New York connection.

"Andre, don't you recall that we opened an affiliate in New York? I brought you the contract to sign, you must remember that." She wanted him to have a clear understanding that her concerns about the investigations were to avoid any question of the gallery's integrity. Andre, after a brief pause, allowed that he did remember the deal but had not really questioned it in any detail.

"You know, Hannelore, I don't remember the deal as much as I recall the many trips you took to New York. As usual, I suspect it has led to a very successful connection for the gallery, and I just accept that as further evidence of your expert management. I know I do take for granted how valuable you are and how much I leave to your capable hands while I enjoy the freedom it gives me. I apologize if my tardiness in getting back has caused you unneeded concern."

"Well, Andre, as you say, I did make several trips to New York, and some of them were lengthy and exhausting, but it was necessary to make sure the investment was profitable." Andre nodded his agreement.

Hannelore felt an inner satisfaction that Andre had then as now asked few questions about the New York gallery or Kurt. She wanted Andre to realize her concerns about the investigation were not misplaced. He needed to appreciate the importance of the New York gallery to the success of the firm but without its secret transactions with the Kreis. The plan had been running very smoothly until the two investigators arrived.

Hannelore was dismayed that, contrary to her explicit instructions for Kurt to make himself scarce, he had been located. Without Kurt, there would have been no connection to the Berlin gallery.

"Andre," Hannelore began in a less-confrontational tone, "you know we have a reputation that is highly respected, and we cannot allow ourselves to become the object of an investigation."

"Investigation?" Andre was puzzled. "Hannelore, we've had many inquires in the past about certain works of art, that's normal; you seem unusually upset by this visit." Hannelore's blue eyes were as cold as a winter sky and her voice as icy as the sea beneath.

"That idiot, Kurt, sold one of our paintings as an original, but it was a copy."

Andre started; it brought him to full attention, for this was no minor indiscretion.

"Why would he have done that?"

"Andre," she said, her face tense, "he claims that it was clearly marked as an original and he sold it for one. As you will learn from the two investigators, the purchaser of the painting died and his estate had it appraised and was told it was a copy. I had every confidence in Kurt, but he has proven to be incompetent. Of course, due to the seriousness of the matter, I dismissed him and purchased his remaining holdings in the gallery. I have since installed a new manager and expect we can put this matter to rest as quickly as possible." Andre was perplexed at Hannelore's recounting of these events.

"Hannelore, for a mistake, no matter if stupid or not, it seems you reacted quite severely. I thought the gallery in New York had been doing quite well; seems that one mistake, if unintentional, could have been met with a less severe reaction."

Hannelore looked at Andre trying to decide how much she dare tell him without arousing too much suspicion about Art World's involvement with the Kreis.

"Andre, as you know, we are very careful to make sure that the original works of art and the copies we sell are clearly marked respectively. This is the same procedure we follow on works shipped to New York. In this case, a copy, a very excellent one it seems, was sold, according to the investigators from New York, as an original.

"I told them this was impossible and that we could prove from our records that the invoice would clearly indicate we had declared it as an original and whatever substitution occurred would have been done in New York. They want to see that invoice. I instructed Otto to produce it and told the investigators that there would be no further discussion of the matter until you returned. I've scheduled that meeting for tomorrow afternoon, if you concur."

Andre nodded assent, then asked, "Have you seen the invoice?"

"No, when I asked Otto to verify the information, he said that he was sure it would have been correctly listed and he'd check his records. When he called me back, he said our invoice showed it was clearly listed as an original. After Otto said our invoice was correct, I felt it would be better to have you there when we meet with the investigators."

"Hannelore, I still don't understand the action you took with regard to your partner—"

Hannelore was quick to interrupt, "*Our* partner, Andre; after all, this involves you as much as it does me."

"Well then, wasn't it all the more important to have involved me before you took such action? It seems to me that it would have been a much simpler solution to acknowledge a mistake had been made and offer to repurchase the painting. If the estate wished to keep it, negotiate an acceptable price based on its value as a copy and refund the difference."

"You forget, Andre, that for some strange reason you made no contact with the gallery for the past week. I have had little chance to discuss the matter with you. In fact, you even refused to come when I did ask you."

Hannelore didn't like this criticism from Andre but knew it would be better not to press her defense; she needed his support.

"Well, Andre, perhaps you are right; however, I did feel it necessary to avoid any shadow of suspicion on our reputation. When I called Kurt in response to his call when the claim had first been presented to Art World, he maintained that the picture in question had been clearly marked as an original. He said he had sold it in accordance within the pricing guidelines that accompanied all pictures sent him.

"Kurt must have substituted a copy from his own inventory for the original for his own profit. Those copies always sell well. I am sure he had a supply of them in stock. So when I called Kurt back, I told him as much and such an inexcusable act would cause irreparable damage to our gallery.

"Naturally, I was looking to protect our interest. I told Kurt I was exercising our contractual agreement that either partner could buy the other out. I contacted our attorney in New York to execute the buyout and told Kurt to clear out all records and place them in a safe deposit box at the bank. I also told him that, in his best interest, he had better have no further contact with the gallery. Had he listened to me, none of this would be happening."

"Hannelore," Andre was visibly disturbed at this news, "I still do not understand why you took such drastic action without proof that Kurt did this deliberately. An honest error, a mix-up could have occurred in packaging if, as you say, copies were available. You have often said that the relationship with Art World was very profitable and you were very pleased with our partner. You certainly seemed to enjoy your visits to New York and promoting the gallery. The newspaper reports you showed me were very complimentary and that your receptions were very successful.

"Wouldn't this have been a good opportunity to enhance our reputation? An honest mistake immediately admitted to and settled? It would appear to me that your reaction to the matter will cause more questions as to why, if it were a mistake, you took such drastic action." Hannelore tried not to show her displeasure at Andre's continued questioning of her actions.

"Andre," Hannelore tried to keep her tone void of the irritation she felt, "I simply could not risk people prying into the gallery's internal affairs. We have been able to make some very profitable sales through the help of Count von Linglesdorf. He has contacts in the U.S. with important customers who do not wish to have their purchases made public." Hannelore sensed at once the mention of the Count was a mistake.

Andre, at the mention of the officious Count, was quick to ask, "What has he to do with our gallery, Hannelore? I was never aware that anyone from the Kreis had any connection with us. Did any of them have any connection with the gallery? You know how much I detest them, even if you call them friends. On this we can never agree, but out of deference to you I have tolerated them."

Hannelore knew she was entering dangerous waters. With a look of total innocence, she said, "No, only later when I talked about opening a New York gallery did the Count offer to help. He said he could supply names of customers who would be interested in buying some of our artworks, especially some originals. He explained, however, that these sales were to be very discrete and need not follow normal channels."

"Hannelore, the more I listen to you, the more concerned I am. What do you mean by not following 'normal channels'?"

"There's nothing to be alarmed about, Andre, it was simply a matter of not having to pay our partner a commission on art sales arranged by the Count and his connection in New York. The only thing Kurt had to do was clear the works at Customs and hold them for the Count's contact to pick up. We…they paid Kurt a small fee for handling the paperwork, and he was completely satisfied with the arrangement since it had been made long before our partnership. But in no way could I allow an investigation to involve these private transactions of the Count. After all, it was simply a courtesy I owed him, and it was very profitable for us. He was able to command an excellent price for these works and took only a small commission for himself. Andre, there is nothing more to say. If friends of mine and my father needed help, I gave it and gave it gladly."

Andre felt an uneasiness. "Hannelore, if the help you gave would in any way be detrimental to this gallery, I would be shocked and hurt."

Hannelore replied contritely, "Andre, please understand I only acted in the way I thought I should for the good of the gallery. I'll take your advice on how we should proceed to settle the matter. Believe me, everything is in order."

The conversation was only leading to more confusion in his mind, but the prospect of meeting Katya that afternoon began to crowd out his need to question Hannelore more. The deed was done and there was nothing more to do than meet with the investigators. Meanwhile, he wanted to make sure that he met Katya's train.

"Hannelore," Andre showed some impatience, "I just don't understand all of this and want to know more, but as you know, I have guests arriving this afternoon, and we have a dinner appointment with them for tonight. You will come, won't you?"

"Of course," she answered quickly, too quickly thought Andre, detecting a slight tone of annoyance. Andre decided he'd try to lighten the mood a bit before he left.

"You know, Hannelore," he said with a smile, "you really are a beautiful woman. No doubt your poor partner Kurt is more disappointed in not seeing you again than losing the gallery."

"Andre, please be serious," Hannelore replied, not without some pleasure at his words.

Andre laughed. "My compliment is sincere and offered to help you become a little less serious. While I also think the matter is serious, we can resolve it without too much trouble."

Hannelore was pleased at this. At times she wished she could have been able to include Andre in all the plans she and the Kreis had made. For the most part, she enjoyed a good relationship with Andre, although recognizing it was not possible to have the closeness a full understanding between them might have brought. Yes, they were intimate with each other, but only to a point.

"Andre," she spoke more softly, "I must tell you I am a bit disappointed about the arrangements you have made and that another guest, which I learned from Elsa, is coming. Who might the other one be?"

"Hannelore," Andre paused, "I really don't like to upset you when we get into areas in which we don't agree. You were certainly less than pleased when I told you on the telephone about my delay in coming and why. I just didn't want to upset you more until I could sit down with you and explain in person. Herr Karpinski's first violinist, his ward in her early years, always travels with him. She is a superb performer; you will enjoy her."

"Her?" Hannelore's eyebrows arched noticeably.

"Hannelore, after I made the invitation, he expressed to me the wish for her to come with him. There was no way for me to withdraw the invitation. Hannelore looked directly at Andre; she didn't want to spoil the more pleasant mood that had developed, but she sensed that Andre was being less than forthright with her.

"Andre, I don't want to make this an issue, but your whole story is your usual attempt to maneuver around situations you want to avoid. I hardly can accept that you just happened to neglect mentioning that your second guest, whom I remember from the performance last week, is a lovely young Polish girl. I do hope, Andre, that her coming was as unavoidable as you say."

"Oh yes, I should tell you that I have invited Count von Linglesdorf to accompany me to dinner with you and your guests. I told Elsa to include him. I would feel out of place without someone accompanying me. I really couldn't consider you my dinner partner, could I?" The import of what she said was not lost on Andre.

"You know," Hannelore continued, "the Count is very conversant about the music world and no doubt will be a welcome conversationalist at the table. I'm sure the exchange of ideas between him and your guests will be most interesting."

Andre hesitated; the invitation to the Count was not at all a pleasing bit of news. In fairness, he had not been open with Hannelore; this was no doubt her attempt to even up the scales when she knew he had two guests.

"Hannelore, that's fine with me. I'm pleased that you agreed to come to dinner as a favor to me, but I doubt the Count will find it a pleasurable occasion to be in the company of persons for whom he obviously has no regard. I know his and your attitude toward those who you think justify your prejudices."

Andre remembered the night of the concert when he had first heard Katya play and the negative comments Hannelore and her friends, especially the Count had made about the Polish orchestra. It was evident, they had said, that it failed to meet German standards, but that was to be expected.

"I would expect, Hannelore, that out of deference to me there will be nothing but a gracious acceptance of my guests."

"Why, Andre, I am surprised that you would think we would be impolite. You certainly cannot have an objection to hearing for yourself how deficient the cultures of other lands are in producing such artists as we have."

The mood was again becoming confrontational, as it always did when this subject came up. Andre was anxious to get past this unpleasant turn in the conversation, and yet his uneasiness with Hannelore's comments forced him to repeat his concern.

"Hannelore, the occasion of this dinner is to make my guest feel welcome, certainly not to engage in a conversation proving who is superior to whom."

Hannelore knew any further discussion was only going to antagonize Andre. She needed his support with the investigators and admitted to herself the invitation to the Count was done to do exactly what Andre feared, to embarrass the invaders.

"Andre, I'm sorry this invitation to the Count has irritated you. I'm sure that any unpleasantness can be avoided." There was a slight pause. Andre seemed relieved at her words and would have considered the issue settled; however, Hannelore was unable to resist laying all blame on Andre.

"You know, Andre, all of this could have been avoided had you not invited them in the first place, knowing our feelings for which you seem to have little regard."

Andre, who had just risen to go, believing he had a promise from Hannelore, straightened abruptly and stared at her. She would never change. He fought against saying the bitter words wanting to leave his lips. It was hopeless to believe there was any chance that Hannelore would ever free herself from the hatred and disdain for others that had been inculcated into her from childhood. Never would there be any chance of true compatibility with her. At times like these, he regretted those moments when their relationship went beyond their usual cordiality.

"Hannelore," he spoke softly, "I am sorry you believe my invitation was made with a disregard for your feelings. On the contrary, I made the invitation in the hope you would meet two people for whom my regard would give you some thought. If indeed I was willing to consider them as friends, would that not count for some consideration on your part to accept them as well, as people, regardless of their culture difference?"

Hannelore regretted her last words, not that she didn't feel he deserved them, but because it was evidently not serving her interest in gaining his favorable support.

Doubting her sincerity, but wanting to leave to meet Katya, he accepted with a sad smile Hannelore's attempt at an apology for her unnecessary comment.

"Well, I must be going, I was going to meet them with the company car and driver, but I think I'll drive my own car. You take the car and driver; it would be more convenient for you and the Count." He was sincere; she knew that whatever disagreements they had, Andre was never petty. Although at times she felt pangs of guilt over his gentlemanly attitude, her priorities allowed her to use what she believed to be a weakness in others.

As Andre left, Hannelore reached for the phone to call Otto. She wanted confirmation again that he had located the invoice they needed for the meeting tomorrow. His confirmation assured her that their invoice clearly stated it was sent as an original. Otto smiled as he hung up. He looked at the picture of him and Karl and nodded.

"Yes, Hannelore, I have what you need."

CHAPTER 24

THE INTERCITY EXPRESS PULLED INTO THE STATION on time. Andre hurried to the numbered car that held the seats he had reserved and waited at the steps. Andre could not conceal his delight as he gave his hand to a smiling Katya, whose firm, warm clasp thrilled him. The Maestro followed closely, showing little pleasure at this arrival in enemy territory. The look of delight on both Katya and Andre's faces did little to better his mood. After greeting Katya, Andre welcomed the Maestro, cordially extending a hand of welcome that was barely touched in response.

He led them to his BMW7000i, politely opening the rear door intended for the Maestro, who viewed the car as another display of undeserved opulence. Katya, with a demure smile at Andre, quickly slipped into the rear seat instead. Andre had no choice but to share the front seat with the Maestro, who immediately turned his face to gaze out at a city he had no desire to know. Katya was quick to speak and avoid what was apparently going to be a very silent ride.

"Herr von Kunst, we thank you for the excellent accommodations on the InterCity. The lounge cars were so comfortable."

Andre turned as he spoke to the Maestro, who was still looking out the window, giving no indication he heard what Katya had said.

"Sir, I do hope you, too, found the accommodations satisfactory."

Without turning, he replied not unpleasantly, "Herr von Kunst, indeed the travel was pleasurable. It simply amazes me how prosperous and efficient this land has become in such a short time, how fortunate." Andre had no ready response.

Katya said, "Yes, Maestro, it is good that we can travel in peace through countries once not open. I pray it will now always remain so."

Andre echoed her sentiment, "Yes, Fraulein Preznoski, may it be, so that we can enjoy the excellent talents found in other cultures like that which you, Herr Karpinski, and his orchestra have brought to us." The Maestro listened intently for some note of condescension in Andre's words that would enforce his suspicion of the young German's intentions, but heard none.

Andre accompanied then into the hotel reminiscent in style and ambience of the prestigious Hotel Adlon of better times past. The registration formalities went quickly due to Andre's prior arrangements.

Andre then asked that if the trip had not been too tiring, he would enjoy their company at dinner that evening with his partner and her guest.

Katya assured him the trip had been far from tiresome, but dared not go so far as accepting the invitation. The Maestro, knowing his lovely ward had slyly trapped him, nodded his assent.

Andre, inwardly pleased at Katya's obvious outmaneuvering of the Maestro, said, "I'm so pleased. Here is my card should you need anything. I'll be here at 7:30 this evening if that meets your approval."

The Maestro again only nodded, dismayed once more at Katya's obvious pleasure at the invitation he heard in her, "Oh thank you so much."

The bellman ushered them into the suite's sitting room, taking to heart Andre's words and grateful generosity to assure he granted their every wish. Katya drew a sharp breath at the suite's exquisite furnishings. On the rosewood table in the center was a large floral arrangement and bowl of fruit. These were flanked by a large platter of assorted cheeses and bread on the one side and a silver serving set of coffee and two bottles of champagne nested in ice were on the other.

While the orchestra had always had adequate accommodations, this was her first exposure to what could only be called extravagance. She turned to speak with the Maestro, who was having difficulty with the bellman who adamantly refused the Maestro's proffered gratuity.

"Vielen dank, aber alles shone bezalt ist," the bellman said, giving the Maestro a note from the management explaining that arrangements had already been made covering such details. The bellman asked if there was anything else he could do for them. The Maestro shook his head. As the bellman left, Katya exclaimed, "Maestro, have you ever seen a more beautiful room?"

The Maestro, still shaking his head, said, "That von Kunst, he leaves one with no pride. I am not a pauper, I do not need for him to pay even trivial amounts. Look at the extravagance of this hotel, these arrangements that I accept only for your sake, Katya. It is far more than we should expect from one who is almost a total stranger to us."

"Maestro, I don't deny he has a liking for me in a friendly way, and I confess to finding him pleasing to talk with. But is that so unusual for two persons to enjoy each other? If he has the means and is so inclined to show off his city and gallery, both of which he is so proud, should we not accept that graciously? Simply accept his generosity and be thankful?"

"Katya, I know you have been favorably impressed by this young man you have only known for a short time. I only ask that you do not let your emotions mislead you. Any further attachment to this man, as appealing as it may seem at the moment, can lead nowhere.

"They, he, are not our people; you will never be accepted. I cannot accept any situation without warning you that it could lead to your eventual sadness or disappointment. Katya, the very fact that Herr von Kunst can afford to be so charitable is proof enough for me that others have made it possible through their sacrifice."

Katya's face clouded, she fought again against his darkness.

"Maestro, you have no right to make such assumptions, you have no reason to imply such things. Or is there a reason I should know why you always react negatively to anything regarding Herr von Kunst?"

The Maestro held back the words he knew would crush her. Someday the truth will need be told, but it would serve no purpose now.

"Katya, I'm sorry, yes, let's enjoy what we may." *Perhaps*, he thought, *this visit will prove to her that whatever attraction she has for this man has been misplaced. Then this episode in her life will soon be a faded memory, the dark history of the von Kunst family's connection with hers, left mercifully for her sake untold.*

"Katya," he continued, "I did agree to come with you, and I will try to enjoy these surroundings with you for whatever time we are here. No doubt the coming evening will give us a good indication of how enjoyable that time will be. You know, dear Katya, your quick acceptance of the dinner invitation gave me no alternative but to agree. I am sure you did that deliberately. I believe I have seriously underestimated the wiles of a woman in ways that I will learn to regret."

Katya laughed and said she never knew she had "wiles," whatever that meant.

"Well, I think I'll take a little nap in my beautiful room," she said as she turned to go. She didn't want to hear anymore of the Maestro's doubts.

As she entered the bedroom and felt the lush carpet under her feet, she gave into the impulse to throw off her shoes and like a child jumped on the bed, whose softness could only have come from an eiderdown cover. She gave a sigh of pleasure.

Why oh why does the Maestro have to be so negative? she thought to herself. *Is there any real reason to doubt that Herr von Kunst is truly an honorable person who, to flatter myself, has found in me a person to admire and perhaps even more than that?* She felt a warm blush at her thoughts.

Why should he be held responsible for evils of the past? I find him extremely charming and, yes, I look forward to spending time with him for these few days. If we really find the time together to be pleasurable and enjoyable, then all the better. I personally enjoy that prospect and you, my dear Maestro, are just going to have to accept it. With such pleasant thoughts, she fell asleep on the soft covering without undressing.

The Maestro, turning to his own room, hesitated before taking a large apple from the bowl on the table. He grimaced at his silliness in regarding it as if it were forbidden fruit. Upon entering his room, he sat in one of the chairs by the window. He looked out on the Kurfurstendamn below, alive and bustling with activity as people let their affluence dictate their desires. Far down to the left he could see the ruined spire of the Kaiser Gedäctnis Kirche.

Yes, he thought bitterly, *do remember, as you so blithely walk by this ruin dedicated to the death of so many in a war you visited upon us. Now without so much as a passing thought you ignore what you should be remembering, your unpaid debt to the millions of lives sacrificed on your altar of Aryan Supremacy. Yes, remember well, because God or whoever there must be who renders judgment on evildoers will demand payment for these deeds. In what form, by what means, I do not know, but pay you shall.*

These thoughts flowed like a river through his mind from a never empty reservoir of bitterness. He, too, finally nodded off thinking of the unpleasant prospect of a dinner where his promise of civility to Herr von

Kunst for her sake would be taxed. Should her interest in the young German prove to be increasing to a point where it became necessary, for her sake, for him to reveal the connection of the von Kunst to her family, he vowed to do so.

CHAPTER 25

ANDRE RETURNED TO THE GALLERY AND STOPPED BY Elsa's desk to thank her again for arranging for his guests and confirmed the time for the evening dinner.

"I'm glad everything was as I ordered," Elsa smiled. "Jacques called to confirm that five guests would be coming, not four, and is there any special request other than your favorite table? I told him I'd call if there was any."

"Thank you, Elsa, for making all the arrangements. I am grateful."

"I really do hope it will be a pleasant evening for all," she said it so genuinely that Andre felt a good portion of guilt.

"I hope so too," he said, thinking with some trepidation about the Count and Hannelore. His concern was justified when he got to his apartment and Hannelore called.

"Andre, thank you for the car and driver. I hope you will understand if the Count and I do not stay the entire evening. I have much to do to prepare for our meeting with the insurance people tomorrow. Also, I am sure the Count will become quickly bored with the low level of discussion he must maintain in order not to overpower your guest."

Many times this tone, this arrogance, he dismissed as the usual Hannelore; this time he felt it was intended to remind him of her disdain for his guests. He was angered at her tone of condescension.

"Hannelore," he said, trying for self-control, "it could well be that the opposite will be true. I hope that the Count will not be too embarrassed to learn that there are those whose knowledge and expertise surpass his own."

Hannelore replied coolly, ignoring his comments, that they would meet him at the restaurant as agreed and hung up.

Andre's resentment subsided slowly as he replaced his phone. He resolved that should Hannelore and the Count be in any way less than courteous, he would be the one to excuse himself and his guest.

Katya awoke after a refreshing nap and started to consider what she would wear for the evening. For the rare occasion that called for a more formal appearance, she had two choices; a deep burgundy lace with short sleeves, a scooped neckline, and an empire waist. The other was a soft blue velvet that had a more open back, elbow length sleeves, a form-fitting waist that accented her slight but well-proportioned figure, demure but alluring. *Why not*, she thought, *after all, I am a woman*, and reached for the blue velvet.

The Maestro had no such problem; he wore a black suit without tails, the only variation from his conductor's suit. As Katya entered the suite from her bedroom, the Maestro, who had been waiting to escort her to the lobby was dismayed, his misgivings mounting at her appearance.

Never should I have brought her here, he thought regretfully. *She is beautiful, no denying that, yet so naïve.* He determined that whatever protestations Katya might have, their stay in Berlin would be as short as possible. There was little doubt by the look on her slightly flushed face above the stunning dress that words were unnecessary to express her anticipation of the evening to come. She noticed the Maestro's reaction and smiled, no doubt he was seeing a different Katya, and she was pleased.

"Maestro," she said gaily, "isn't this a pleasant interlude in our busy yet sequestered lives? I do hope for both our sakes you will take some pleasure from it."

The Maestro struggled to bring some semblance of a smile to his lips, the strain was noticeable. She viewed herself in the mirror once more before going down to the lobby. She wanted to make sure the carefully brushed raven waves that cascaded to her shoulder were all in place; yes, she wanted Andre to see her as more woman than musician.

She and the Maestro were early. They sat together on one of the lounge seats waiting for Andre. They didn't talk now, she thinking of the events that had brought her to this unexpected place. A few days ago this would never have been imagined. The Maestro prayed to whatever gods there were that he would be forgiven for placing her in such danger of misplacing her affection.

Andre was not expecting the vision of loveliness rising before him as he entered the hotel lobby. He could neither fail to see the friendly anticipation on her face, nor fail to see the consternation on the Maestro's. It flashed across Andre's mind that it must have been a woman like this that Lord Byron was remembering as he wrote, "She walks in beauty like the night of cloudless climes and starry skies."

Andre's words caught in his throat and sounded terribly constricted as he managed, "Good evening, Fraulein Preznoski, Herr Karpinski."

Katya was pleased at his evident surprise at her appearance and gave no indication that she noticed his strained greeting. The Maestro marked it well.

Jacques met them personally as they entered the restaurant.

"Herr von Kunst, how privileged to serve you and your guest. The table is reserved as you requested in the blue alcove, please follow me. You have arrived ahead of Frau Hasenfeld and Count von Linglesdorf. I'll bring them to you as soon as they arrive." Andre nodded his thanks as Jacques led them to their table.

The softly lit alcove enchanted Katya. The white linen table coverings glistened from candles placed in the center and from wall sconces. Their warm light was reflected back from the gleaming silver and china that graced the table. The intimacy was so pleasing that Katya was doubly disappointed that others would be joining them. The Maestro could not help but be pleased by the ambience of the restaurant and setting. *Perhaps*, he thought, *the dinner will be enjoyable after all.*

Hannelore looked in the mirror with satisfaction. She had chosen a black sheath, open wide to the shoulders and back with a white lace trim on the neckline that swooped as low as decency would allow. The full-length sheer sleeves ended with a touch of the same lace. The three strands of genuine pearls graced the fullness the neckline allowed. Their companions, a set of pendulum pearl earrings, almost touched the translucent skin of her shoulders. Her natural blonde hair was worn in an elegant French twist that allowed a full view of what the cut of the dress offered. The stiletto heels of her open-toed black pumps added an unneeded three inches to her already statuesque height.

Of course, she was aware of the effect she had on men, especially when she dressed this way, although she wasn't thinking of men tonight.

Her intuitive nature quickly surmised that Andre's interest was far more focused, for some inexplicable reason, on this Polish violinist. She doubted that it was the conductor who was Andre's reason for the invitation to Berlin. The lovely violinist was not just an unavoidable tag along. She almost felt a twinge of compassion for the poor Slavic girl and the conductor; both would undoubtedly feel so misplaced in her and the Count's presence.

Katya was enjoying their surroundings and sipping the delicious wine when Andre stood up. Jacques was leading a very elegant couple toward their table. The woman was a striking blonde exquisitely dressed with one hand on the arm of a silver-haired gentleman of aristocratic bearing. He was one of the most distinguished gentlemen Katya had ever seen. As they approached the table, Andre introduced them.

"Fraulein Katya Preznoski, Herr Karpinski, please meet my partner, Frau Hannelore Hasenfeld, and her friend, the Count von Linglesdorf."

Katya, not sure of the protocol, extended her hand to them both, but couldn't help a trembling that pleased Hannelore as she lightly touched it. Hannelore would later waste no time at the first opportunity to admonish Andre that his addressing Katya and the Maestro first had been inexcusable. She sensed it had been deliberate.

His partner! Katya felt an icy wind blow through her soul. She hardly acknowledged the Count as she touched the fingers of his outstretched and fully manicured hand. The Count, attempting perhaps to be congenial waved the Maestro, who was starting to rise, back to his seat, meaning it wasn't necessary for him to rise. The Maestro, viewing the wave as condescending, ignored the proffered hand and regained his seat. Katya, trying to hide any show of surprise beyond the betraying hand to Hannelore, was dismayed that the Maestro was so cavalierly treated by the Count.

It was not the ideal start for an evening of hoped for pleasantry. As they took their places, Andre knew, as he had anticipated, it would not be easy to introduce Katya and the Maestro here, but it was less risky than at the gallery. At least here there ought to be some degree of civility on the part of Hannelore and the Count.

His hope increased as the Count said, "Thank you, Herr von Kunst, for the invitation. It is not often I have the privilege of sharing a table with such notables as Herr Karpinski and the lovely Fraulein Preznoski." Katya smiled a thank you while the Maestro, with an ever so slight nod of acknowledgement, continued to study the menus Jacques had already conveniently laid on the table.

Hannelore tried not to make her continued study of Katya too obvious. Katya herself was having the same problem. Invariably, whenever their eyes met, they quickly avoided the contact as if it were simply unintended. Hannelore was clearly upset that this waif, this refugee, no matter how talented, could look so stunning. She doubted that contrary to Andre's explanation, she was simply here because the Maestro had insisted.

As for Katya, Hannelore presented a formidable image. Try as she could, Katya was having a problem fighting against a rising feeling of inferiority. Hannelore surpassed most descriptions of beauty. As Andre's business partner, she was no doubt extremely talented as well in areas far beyond Katya's comprehension. She began to have serious doubts about Andre's motive for this invitation. She remembered all the things he had said, his apparent sincere and openly confessed interest in knowing her better; now she could not help questioning what was the true relationship between him and this stunning woman. Was she his business partner only?

As Jacques left, the Count offered the observation to the Maestro that it must be indeed a rigorous life touring various countries. Alone the need for rehearsals and varying the program to provide a representative selection of requested pieces would be demanding. The Maestro nodded his appreciation of the Count's awareness of an orchestra's burdens. Perhaps the evening would have continued in this somewhat friendly vein had Hannelore not commented on what she noticed was a relatively small representation of German composers, Wagner totally absent.

The Maestro wasn't sure of her motive for the comment, but surprising himself he allowed it was a legitimate observation that deserved an answer that would not be confrontational.

"You observe correctly, Frau Hasenfelt. You see, I am aware of the great number of good orchestras you have in Germany that I am sure emphasize native composers in their programs. I have always tried to introduce as many compositions from other nationalities to provide a more eclectic program."

Andre had held his breath at Hannelore's observation about the lack of German composers and noticed as well Katya's tensing at the comment. Both were visibly relieved at the Maestro's answer. Katya felt it was a masterpiece of diplomacy considering what she surmised the Maestro could have said.

"Well," Andre spoke quickly, "while I am certainly limited in my knowledge of the world of music, I think there must exist in the world of both music and art, regardless of nationality, rooms for individuals representing many nationalities."

Hannelore, suspecting Andre was deliberately speaking out of deference to the Maestro at her expense, resented all the more his bringing such impudent persons to Berlin. She could not resist voicing her conviction that German composers were inherently more gifted than others

The Count surprisingly diffused what could have become an embarrassing topic. Affecting a conciliatory tone, he said, "Of course there will be differing opinions on this subject, and perhaps the best evaluation of the respective value of any work, be it music or art, is to be found in the public's response. Is a performance well intended? Is an artist's work in demand?"

Katya held her silence during these exchanges. She recognized both Hannelore's pointed attempt to coerce the Maestro into a debate and the Count's swift deflection of it.

Andre was pleasantly surprised at the Count's unexpected tolerant opinion on the matter, joining with Andre on allowing both positions to have merit. The crisis that Hannelore had hoped for now seemed past. Jacques soon returned with their selections excellently prepared and the remaining conversations continued on to matters of a more general and congenial nature.

After an excellent dessert of various cheeses, fruit, and wines, Andre declared that while the evening had been indeed pleasant, he was sure his guests needed to return to their hotel for rest after the day's travel.

With an exchange of pleasantries, the Count and Hannelore rose first and left to go to the waiting car. Hannelore was furious with both Andre and the Count.

"Why," she demanded angrily as they entered the car, "didn't you support me in what would have been an excellent opportunity to embarrass the two Poles? Hadn't I made it clear that accepting the invitation to the dinner was precisely to do that? And besides, I needed to show Andre how misplaced his evident attraction for this peasant violinist is."

The Count patted her hand comfortingly. "Dear Hannelore, you know how much my colleagues and I respect you and the contribution you have made to our mutual goals. The gallery under your guidance has provided excellent support, and you cannot let your zeal interfere with the greater need of maintaining the relationship we have with Andre. It is imperative that he continues to leave you to the business matters of the gallery. If his interest in the girl, who I must say is attractive enough, serves to further distract him from affairs of the gallery, so much the better. We cannot do anything that might cause him to have any less trust in you."

Hannelore sighed. "But she is just a peasant Pole who happens to play a tolerable violin. What possible interest could he have in her!"

"My dear Hannelore," the Count said, again patting her hand, "if I didn't know you better, I might think you were jealous! After all, Andre is a romantic at heart as you have often said, and evidently this young girl has touched it. So what chance has reason against such an emotion? Perhaps, Hannelore, that is your problem. No one has ever accused you of having a romantic heart. Therefore, it would be hard for you to understand the attraction that Andre might have for the girl. You would never allow such an interference in your life."

Hannelore thought a moment. "Count, is that a compliment?"

He laughed. "Depends, Hannelore, depends on whether you prefer rational ends to your actions or the consequences of irrational action when reason loses out to emotion."

Hannelore sniffed impatiently. "Of course the former."

Andre returned to his seat after his short farewell to the departing Hannelore and the Count. Although he had initiated the ending to the evening, it was not purely out of concern for his guest's need of rest. He wanted some private time with them without the others presence. Katya had not spoken much during the evening but had keenly watched the interplay between the others and above all watched Hannelore.

Katya spoke slowly, "Herr von Kuntz, your partner is extremely attractive, and I must admit I certainly feel a bit intimidated by her, but more importantly, I am sure she is somewhat annoyed at our being here."

Before Andre could think of an answer that would, however hopeless, defend Hannelore, the Maestro, shaking his head, spoke softly, "Katya, with all deference to our host, you think she is 'somewhat annoyed'? Dear Katya, that woman represents exactly what I have tried to explain to you will be the attitude of the majority of all the people we shall meet here. It goes beyond annoyed. It was a deliberate attempt to engage me in conversation with the intent to expose, so to say, my prejudices against German composers.

"Thankfully, our host and, for some reason, her companion diffused the issue, for which I am grateful. Needless to say, if provoked further, I would have had no reservation in expressing my heartfelt opinion not only about composers but people like her as well.

"Herr von Kuntz, I am sorry, but this evening has only confirmed my concerns that bringing Katya here was not in her best interest. I will not have her subjected to hurts she need not suffer. I hope you will understand, as we have already agreed, that we can depart as soon as we wished. I will make the arrangements to do that as soon as possible."

Katya turned abruptly to the Maestro and said with uncharacteristic force, "No, Maestro, I will not let one incident of perhaps unintended provocation dissuade us from enjoying a few days here. There is much yet to see and especially Herr von Kuntz's gallery. Besides, perhaps Fraulein Hassenfeld was not intending to provoke you as you assume."

The Maestro's look contained as much pity as surprise at Katya's quick comeback.

I must tell her the truth, whatever the reaction, he thought to himself. *She must be told the evil this family represents, not right here, but soon.*

Andre found his voice, thankful the Maestro had spoken before he himself made some inane defense of Hannelore's attitude, which he knew both had correctly judged despite Katya's kind attempt to moderate it.

Encouraged by Katya's remarks, Andre turned to the Maestro, "Yes, please, Herr Karpinski, please reconsider. I will not excuse my partner's ill-advised attempt, for whatever reason, to engage you in a conversation with unpleasant consequences. But if an explanation, not an excuse, will help, let me explain. She and her father have had a long association with the Gallery. While the world's condemnation of Germany's recent actions is justified, at times she feels prompted to offer some defense of uninvolved German composers against this bias. Tact is not one of her positive attributes, I admit. But I do again plead with you not to take this personally, her attitude is not to be taken as a measure of our hospitality."

The Maestro looked at Andre and admired, reluctantly, his valiant effort to defend his partner. He had no doubt that the defense was far more to dissuade him from leaving with Katya than a regard for his partner. The Maestro hesitated to make any further comment on leaving; he recognized full well that Katya would not readily accept a hasty departure after one unpleasant interlude. He knew she would accept his decision, would not make a public display of her disappointment, but he would risk a degree of alienation.

The classic horns of a dilemma, he thought, *whatever I do to intrude upon her evident attraction to this young Teutonic admirer will not be welcome.*

Finally he said, "Herr von Kuntz, I do not mean to be ungracious toward your generosity. Perhaps you and Katya are right, and we should not let this incident alone affect a personal decision whatever the motive. Let us take each day as it comes. If events place too heavy a strain on the situation, then I would expect you both to understand and accept any decision I would make as was agreed to prior to this visit."

Katya's sigh of relief did not pass unnoticed by the Maestro.

Andre was not unaware that the Maestro's antipathy toward him and all that was German would allow little tolerance for any similar occurrence as the one tonight.

The Maestro rose, "Herr von Kunst, it is late and I am weary. I do thank you for the evening's hospitality. We need to return to our hotel and the excellent accommodations you have provided. I recognize that both you and Katya, with your youthful energies, could carry through for several hours more."

As they all rose to leave, Jacques was leading a couple toward the booth next to theirs. *Americans,* Andre thought, *they have that casual air about them even as they walk.* Andre paused with a polite nod smiling appreciatively at the woman in her striking green sheath. He exchanged brief pleasantries with them, recommending Jacques highly.

Andre drove Katya and the Maestro back to their hotel. They were all rather silent, alone with private thoughts.

CHAPTER 26

AFTER LEAVING HIS GUESTS AT THE HOTEL, ANDRE
went back to the gallery to find Hannelore and the Count sitting in the
lounge sipping coffee. The Count greeted Andre cordially and thanked
him again for a delightful evening with his two guests. Hannelore was
quick to nod thanks and just as quick to offer an uncharacteristic apology
for what might have appeared to be a rude question to the Maestro.

"Well," answered Andre, not quite convinced of any sincerity in
her words, "You can make amends in person when they visit the gallery
tomorrow. I'm sure there will be time for that. I will ask Elsa to show
them through the gallery while we meet with the two from the insurance
company. The meeting should be short. As we agreed, if there was some
error by our partner in New York, we shall simply apologize and repurchase the painting. I'm confident that Otto's records will establish we had
correctly identified the work and our gallery's integrity."

The Count nodded; it irritated Andre that the Count was at all
involved in the matter. He knew Hannelore counseled with members of
the Kreis. At least if they gave good business advice, he should accept that
as a positive from her association with them. He had no reason to believe
that Hannelore would enter into any transaction that did not benefit the
gallery. He had to be careful not to let his personal antipathy toward the
Kreis interfere with the flow of business.

The Count motioned to Andre, who was intending to go to his apartment, to join them. Andre hesitated not only because he had no desire
to join them, but also he knew for the most part the feeling was mutual.

He knew he often annoyed the Count and the others whenever Hannelore included him with the group for an evening theatre attendance or dinner.

As Andre sat down, the Count shifted himself so that he could make better eye contact with Andre. He placed his hand on Andre's arm in a gesture of camaraderie. Andre resisted the impulse to withdraw.

"Andre, I have known you, your beloved late father, and your mother for years. You cannot doubt that my relationship and those of my comrades to your gallery and you has not been one of unquestioned loyalty. We all know how much you have contributed to its reputation and have established an admirable and profitable relationship with a very elite clientele.

"My friends and myself have confined ourselves to offering advice, although little is needed to be sure, to Hannelore on the necessity of maintaining close contacts with other benefactors and clients of the gallery. The others that we have influenced with are clients you would not have had access to in the normal course of business. No one can be all things to all people, perhaps a cliché, but nonetheless true.

"You see, your more progressive ideas, perhaps admirable in purpose, may be unrealistic or thought misguided by others. They may be offended by this open disregard of their sensibilities, such as entertaining persons with whom they would not associate. It could have a negative effect on our relationship with them. We need to ensure for the sake of the gallery that all of its clients feel welcome and avoid those situations that could distress any of them."

I believe you would agree with this would you not?

Andre nodded, but not because he agreed with the Count. His nod was affirming his own suspicion that it was another attempt to gain his understanding that these "others," like the Kreis, were dedicated in their desire to have Germany avenged. Andre was always amazed at their inability to believe in anything other than that Germany had been victimized and defeated by a jealous subculture of people who had betrayed the nation to its enemies.

"Herr von Linglesdorf," Andre avoided using the Count's first name although the Count had used his. "I certainly do not discriminate against our customers because of differing political views. However, if I am asked about a matter, I do respond honestly, as I must. But certainly, Herr von

Linglesdorf, should your friends be offended by me, I would advise you by all means to have them deal with Hannelore."

The Count was not prepared to drop the matter that easily. "Yes, Andre, all well and good, but there are other matters that can work against the goal of serving our clientele without offense."

Andre immediately asked, "Other matters?"

At this, Hannelore quickly interjected herself into the dialogue. She was unable to control herself any longer regardless of the Count's admonition not to irritate Andre unnecessarily. The Count was far more sensitive to the Kreis' need of the gallery than was Hannelore. The last thing the Count wanted was Andre becoming more inquisitive about the Kreis or their involvement with the gallery; before he could intervene, Hannelore took the lead in the conversation.

"Andre, I agree with what the Count is trying to politely say. He, as I, are disappointed with your relationship, I dare say friendship, with persons who are not welcome in our society. With all respect to your personal feelings, you must understand how your actions can be very detrimental to the gallery."

Andre seldom experienced real anger toward Hannelore and her friends except when their prejudices prompted them to utter disparaging remarks about others. He chose usually to ignore such comments and considered the source to be of no consequence; now he felt Hannelore had made a direct attack on him and the two guests he had invited.

His voice was hard. "Hannelore, are you and the Count insinuating that my two guests are to be considered among those you refer to as 'unwelcome' and are 'detrimental' to the gallery?"

The Count, aware this conversation was escalating toward a confrontation he wished to avoid, tried again to deflect its course.

"Andre, please," his fatherly tone angered Andre all the more, "you misunderstand us. We are not singling out your friends at all. As performers, they are accepted and that the theatre is full of admiring listeners is proof of that. Is that not evidence enough of our acceptance of them on those terms?"

Andre's anger continued to rise and it was heard in his voice, "Herr Count von Linglesdorf, do I understand you to say 'on those terms' means that as long as they are on stage and no physical contact is made with them, they are acceptable? But that extending a hand of welcome is not? Is their physical proximity likened to one having leprosy?"

The Count stiffened, his face flushed; now he, too, ignored his own warning not to irritate Andre. "Andre, you cannot be so ignorant as to believe that extending a hand of welcome to people who a short time ago contributed to and rejoiced in the destruction of your own nation is in any way acceptable behavior. Is that not the same as granting them absolution for their crimes against us?"

Andre looked at both the Count and Hannelore, his anger now mixed with dismay at what he was hearing. It was hopeless to think there was any chance of penetrating their impregnable wall of prejudice and in no way was he going to let them believe for an instant he sympathized with them.

"Count von Linglesdorf," Andre spoke slowly, "is it actually possible for you and your kind to be so blinded by the light of truth that you cannot see truth? How is it possible for you to regard as 'crimes' the actions of people defending their homelands from our aggression? Are you so ignorant of history, so obsessed with your twisted defense of Germany that facts are of no interest? How can the very lies that caused our destruction live on in your perverted minds?"

Hannelore was indignant; there was no mistaking her disgust with Andre as she said, "Andre, this is unpardonable of you, how dare you speak that way to the Count. How insulting to both of us!"

Andre knew it was time to end this conversation. Emotions had replaced reason. "Count von Linglesdorf, Hannelore, I cannot apologize for the truth you will not accept, but I apologize for allowing you to cause me to overcome my better judgment that should have kept me from this discussion. It serves no purpose other than to reinforce the wall already between us. I have a love for this gallery that exceeds any that either of you could have. That love will not be compromised by any attempt to bring me to condemn or disassociate myself from friends of my choosing, regardless of your misguided opinions.

"Now, please excuse me, Hannelore and I have an important meeting tomorrow. Apparently, there are implications regarding the integrity of this gallery, a gallery that you both profess to hold in the deepest regard. I certainly hope there is nothing revealed that would reflect unfavorably on it."

With that, Andre rose and left for his apartment.

Hannelore spoke first, "Gustave, we both should have followed your advice. It will not serve me well to have Andre so angry. I don't need him to be provoked enough to ask more questions than necessary about any connection you have with the gallery. As I understand from Otto, this was, unfortunately, one of the paintings destined for one of your customers.

"However, I am sure Otto will take care to produce the proper invoice that will avoid any connection with the Kreis. There is little doubt Andre would immediately stop any relationship that the gallery has with you regardless of how we would explain it.

"Thankfully, I know we can depend on Otto to continue to make sure all that we do remains hidden from Andre because he believes it to be for Andre and the gallery's ultimate good. However, his loyalty is directly tied to Andre; should Andre become too inquisitive, whatever he would ask of Otto he would get." The Count nodded and offered nothing more on that subject; it was better Hannelore never knew the truth of how Otto's allegiance was gained.

CHAPTER 27

AS ANDRE STARTED FOR HIS APARTMENT, HE NOTICED the light in Otto's workroom. He decided to ask Otto if there was anything yet to be cleared before tomorrow's meeting. Otto was seated at his workbench working on a small portrait with a noticeable tear in the middle. Andre always marveled at Otto's ability to mend and retouch with such skill that without a magnifying glass an expert would be hard put to find the repair.

Otto turned as Andre stepped into the room. "Hello, Andre." There was always warmth in Otto's voice even as there were shadows of sadness in his eyes whenever he spoke with Andre. Otto felt part traitor, part protector, and would have long since left the gallery had not doing so endangered both Andre and his mother.

Yet the hatred he had for all of the Kreis collectively or singularly did not transfer to Hannelore. Certainly, he disliked what she had become as a person. He had known her first as a beautiful, innocent, child, then watched her turn into a pawn in the hands of evildoers. This, done by her own father, who had so filled her mind with falsehoods that truth could find no place. Her circle of friends assured it never would. How gullible she was for all of her sophisticated demeanor. Otto could never fathom her total belief that the right of the victor to the spoils of war justified their traffic in stolen goods.

"I saw you with the Count and Hannelore in the lounge and hoped you might step in, but I know it's late."

"Never too late for a word with you." Andre smiled at the old man who had been a close companion of his father.

"I just wondered, Otto, if there was anything more I should be aware of for the meeting tomorrow. Hannelore told me that your invoice would clearly show that it was an original. She was very upset that the New York agent was going to fight this oversight, however it happened. Otto, do you have any idea how this mix-up occurred? I understand that all of our shipments go through you, don't they?" Otto nodded but gave no immediate reply.

Andre went on, "Well, there is the possibility that the appraiser for the estate in New York made a mistake. Maybe it really was an original and our agent was correct in challenging the finding. That's possible, isn't it? And I'm sure you would have known it to be correctly identified, right?" Otto again nodded but said nothing.

"Otto, we are ultimately responsible; the New York agent represented our gallery. I have no choice but to offer to buy back the painting, don't you agree?"

Otto nodded, finally speaking, "I know Hannelore is very upset, but I am human, Andre, mistakes can be made. There is a possibility that I made one, but I ask your trust to wait out tomorrow's meeting for me to explain what may have happened, but not now. I've been waiting to tell you many things for years, but please trust me, the time is not now."

"Otto," Andre spoke kindly, "your contribution and faithfulness to this gallery far exceeds whatever error you could possibility have made. Of course you have my trust, and that will be the last we speak of it this evening. Whenever you are ready to say more on the matter will be time enough for me."

Otto looked at the man he most loved in the word. All that he had done was to protect him and his mother and the action he had now taken was necessary; Andre needed to be told. Otto knew the order had been for the original, and he had deliberately substituted a copy. It was one of those paintings with the special code that marked it as one of the Kreis transactions.

He gambled that by declaring it to be an original, and that the New York agent, Kurt, would assume it was; then, if it were discovered to be a copy, it would cause an investigation. The investigation, Otto hoped, would lead to the discovery of the illegal trade of the Kreis without incriminating Andre. His own involvement and Hannelore's would be revealed, but this was a price that had to be paid. He had no other way of ending this trade; he could endure the deceit no longer.

As for the Kreis threats, he gambled his past loyalty would stand him in good stead. It would be hard for them to prove he had done this deliberately. He had a plausible excuse. The copy had erroneously been placed in the storage next to the original and in his haste he had taken it instead. After all, his copies were so excellent that even he could have overlooked that he had taken the wrong one for shipment. It would be hard for them to prove he had done this deliberately. But now there was the possibility that Andre would settle the matter before there was an in-depth investigation. Hannelore's reaction in firing Kurt might have aroused suspicions, but Andre's decision to allow it was an unintentional error and reimburse the estate would satisfy the insurance investigators.

Otto saw this turn of events with dismay. Andre, unknowingly, had thwarted Otto's plan to save him. He knew he still had to find a way to tell Andre all of this, the dealings the gallery had with the Count and the Kreis through his help and Hannelore's. He was growing old and dared not think of his passing and leaving Andre completely under the control of these criminals. A day of reckoning had to come.

He had no way of knowing how close that wished-for day was, how Andre's invitation to a young Polish violinist would lead to the fall of Von Kunst Gallery regardless of the substitution and settlement with the insurance company.

"Andre," Otto continued, "I can only repeat my apologies for a possible oversight that may have caused you this problem. As you know, Hannelore was very distressed over the matter; she certainly is not as forgiving as you are. Had you not agreed so readily to reach a solution that would satisfy the claimant, I'm sure there would have been a more intense investigation I would have welcomed."

"Well, Otto," Andre said, "I don't quite understand why you would welcome an investigation, I don't think the outcome would have been any different, we have nothing to hide, and I think the end result would have been the same. The gallery has to stand behind its agents even if the mistake is not ours directly. But as you said, anytime you wish to tell me more, I'll be ready to listen."

Otto nodded. "No doubt you are right, the end wouldn't have changed."

CHAPTER 28

ANDRE WOKE FROM A RESTLESS SLEEP EARLIER THAN usual. After he had showered and dressed, he went to the window overlooking the garden. He imagined he saw a young boy and girl, laughingly chasing each other around the fountain.

His reverie was broken by Elsa's familiar knock on the door. She hardly waited for his, "Good morning," to enter with the usual serving of coffee and croissants. She couldn't hide her pleasure at these morning opportunities to share light conversation with Andre before Hannelore joined them.

"Elsa," Andre greeted her warmly; he, too, enjoyed these morning chats. Elsa never failed to bring a cheerful smile and brightness into the room with her. "As you know, I have that meeting with Hannelore and the insurance investigators this afternoon. It shouldn't last long, but I will be bringing my guests to the gallery after I meet them for lunch. Would you be so kind and host them on a tour of the gallery until the meeting is over?"

"Why, of course," Elsa replied with more cheerfulness than she actually felt. She was not unaware that Andre's two guests included the attractive violinist. Of course, she told herself it was none of her business. She had no reason to question what Andre did with his private life.

She enjoyed immensely the evenings he invited her to join him. He was always attentive and complimentary, yet never gave an indication that he regarded her as other than a good friend. Her prior conversation with Otto had been sufficient to remove any hope of a deeper relation-ship; to deny the tinge of jealousy she felt was impossible.

As they finished their coffee, Hannelore entered from her side of the office. She reached for her own cup of coffee, ignoring Elsa's offer to pour, a signal that her presence was no longer necessary. Elsa quickly withdrew to the door, telling Andre that she would be ready to guide his guests on a tour of the gallery when they arrived.

"Tour the gallery?" A pair of ice blue eyes under arched eyebrows fixed on Andre. As she closed the door, Elsa couldn't avoid hearing Han-nelore's sharp question. It angered her how Hannelore spoke with Andre, and it angered her even more because she knew Andre would raise no objection.

"Yes, Hannelore," Andre replied with some exasperation, "I told you last night that I had invited my guests to the gallery and I expect them to receive a hospitable greeting." His tone was firm. Hannelore decided that the timing was inappropriate to discuss the matter further. She stood with coffee in hand and said she needed to return to her apartment but would like to discuss some matters with him shortly. He nodded and said, "I'll be here; just come in when you are ready."

Andre was irritated at the obvious dismissal of Elsa by Hannelore and even more by her sharp tone about the tour in front of Elsa. He often wondered why Elsa remained with the gallery considering her many tal-ents and Hannelore's visible coolness toward her.

His thoughts were interrupted by Hannelore's ring, "Are you ready to resume our conversation?"

"Yes," he answered.

When Hannelore came in, she said she was sorry if her reaction to his invitation to his guest was too abrupt. It was just that she was con-cerned for the gallery.

"Hannelore, I told you that I have invited the Maestro and Fraulein Preznoski to visit the gallery. I am sure, that contrary to your and the Count's concerns, there is no negative reaction to be expected, except for yourselves. I really don't want to discuss this any further, and I do expect you to extend a friendly greeting."

Andre resented these moments when he felt he had to defend him-self from Hannelore's evident displeasure; he couldn't help noticing that the trembling hand that held the cup betrayed her normal calm.

Hannelore quickly decided this was not the time to engage in any conversation that would further the discussion of the previous night. It was time to seek a truce with Andre and gain his support for the upcoming meeting. Composing herself, the eyebrows lowered and the ice melted. She refrained from any further comment about the upcoming visits by his guests; her focus was the coming meeting.

"Andre, I do apologize for the conduct of the Count and myself last evening, during the dinner and our conversation afterwards. Whatever our personal opinions are about certain events, we have no right to reproach you for yours. I believe we can continue our good relationship and just leave those topics alone. Naturally, I personally am concerned about an association with people that may bring reproach on the gallery; I must learn to defer to your decision on such matters and will say no more on this."

There were few times in their relationship when Hannelore showed this conciliatory attitude. He could never decide if it was genuine or simply a ruse to gain his favor. He wanted desperately to believe that there would be over time a softening in her attitude toward others and a breaking away from the Kreis influence.

I must always give her the benefit of the doubt, he thought to himself. *She really can't be held totally responsible for her misguided views. After all, what chance did she have to form her own opinions when her own father and his friends had so surrounded her with their warped outlook of the world.* Yet he knew he was making excuses for what he wanted to see rather than what he saw in Hannelore.

He smiled. "Thank you, Hannelore. I do believe your misgivings are unfounded, but I appreciate your concerns. The gallery has been the center of both our lives. I, as you, would never do anything to deliberately cause damage to its reputation. I guess I have a greater degree of confidence that the majority of people today are far less concerned with what you and the Count sees as cultural dangers. So we will agree to disagree on this matter and as you say, let's not discuss further what causes the rift between us. I really want to concentrate on matters on which we agree. I want more memories like those of times spent together enjoying the trips to visit other galleries or pleasant evenings without talk leading to dead-ends."

Hannelore couldn't help but be touched by Andre's words. Yes, there had been good times, but she knew in her heart that she had to do what was called for in fulfilling a higher purpose than her own desires.

"Yes, Andre, there are the good times we share, we need more of them. However, the meeting today is going to be very important, and I want to be sure that you understand that my actions, which you found too drastic, were truly to protect the gallery's reputation. I had no intention of bringing any suspicion of wrongdoing on our part."

Andre, while still troubled why she had acted so quickly in removing Kurt, answered with assurances that he knew her intentions to be well meaning.

"I don't think we have much of a problem, Hannelore. We have accepted the responsibility for correcting the matter. With our sterling reputation, we can prove to the investigators no fraud was intended, especially when we also offer to pay their expenses as well."

Hannelore was relieved. His solution, if accepted by the investigators, would surely stop any further investigation that she so feared. It was times like these that whatever remnant of conscience she had would stir guilt-bringing thoughts. She almost regretted the necessity of being involved with the Kreis in transactions that Andre knew nothing about. The separate books she kept showed a strong profit for the Kreis. These illegal transactions never crossed over into the legitimate business of the gallery.

Andre finished his cup and rose, saying, "Is there anything else you need from me, Hannelore? If not, I must be on my way to pick up my guest."

Hannelore showed no further displeasure at the prospect of the visit; she, too, finished her coffee and, with a smile as warm as was possible for her, shook her head.

"No, Andre, I believe you have found the best solution to the problem, for which I am grateful." She turned to go back to her side of the office. Andre watched the retreating graceful figure of a woman for whom he had such conflicting emotions. Then the image of Katya seemed to superimpose itself on Hannelore.

Andre blinked, got up, and hurried down to Otto's office for a last chat about the coming meeting.

Otto assured him he was prepared but did want some time with Andre as soon as possible after the meeting. They chatted for a while, and yet Andre could not mistake that look of sadness that crept again over Otto's face as they talked. Andre left Otto and then paused at Elsa's desk for a parting word.

"Elsa, I'm going to the hotel for lunch with my guests and will then bring them to the gallery. Thanks again for escorting them while I go to the meeting."

Elsa nodded and smiled but couldn't avoid the slight note of sarcasm slipping into her question, "Andre, I am so glad to be of service, but wouldn't it be nice if I could greet them by their full names. I don't think it proper to call her Fraulein First Violinist. I know they were in concert here, but I don't remember their names."

Andre started, "Elsa, I must have given you their names!" Elsa kept her innocent smile while enjoying Andre's evident embarrassment.

"Andre, in all the arrangements you have asked me to make there has never been a mention of proper names. I supposed you had some reason for that, but I think now it would be appropriate for me to know them." She laughed inwardly; Andre was in some ways so open that he gave away his thoughts without having to speak. She rested her lovely face on folded hands under her chin and waited expectantly for Andre to answer her.

His delay wasn't really that long, but he seemed a bit uncomfortable as he said, "The conductor is Herr Mylovic Karpinski, the violinist is Fraulein Katya Preznoski." Her name caused an uncontrolled flicker in Elsa's eyes. She remembered well the rave reviews about the orchestra and the precocious and beautiful first violinist.

Andre thought to himself as he left the gallery, *Is it possible I didn't want Elsa to know? Do I feel some guilt about this attraction for Katya because of Elsa?* He shook his head, *No place for such thoughts now.* He drove quickly to the hotel, giving his full attention to thoughts about the lovely girl he would find waiting there.

Katya's evident pleasure at seeing Andre coming across the lobby disturbed the Maestro no less than did Andre's own unabashed look of joy.

This has to end, thought the Maestro. *It has to.* Forcing a half smile at Andre's greeting, he followed as Andre took Katya's arm as if it was his given right and led them to the garden café for their lunch. Katya enjoyed the touch of his strong arm against her side.

CHAPTER 29

UPON ARRIVING AT THE GALLERY, ANDRE INTRODUCED them to Elsa, whose slim hopes that someday Andre might consider her as more than colleague and friend altogether faded when she looked at the young girl facing her. No one could convince her that Katya was here by accident, that she just happened to be in the tow of the conductor whom Andre had invited. She was here because Andre wanted her here.

I wonder, she mused to herself, *how all of this is being received by Hannelore. From the very first phone call from Andre about their coming and the reservations I made, I have the distinct impression that none of this is at all pleasing her. Well, if it's causing her some distress, that's some compensation for my own disappointment at what was no doubt just fantasy anyhow. Andre was and is beyond my reach.*

Elsa smiled brightly and was pleased at their obvious pleasure that she greeted them in Polish. Andre joined them with Elsa as they casually walked through the main floor of the blue-carpeted gallery.

Elsa sighed inwardly as she noted Katya's interest was much less focused on objects of art then on Andre. Neither could she neglect to notice how Andre treated Katya; there was a connection she could not fail to notice, nor could the Maestro. Elsa excused herself to hurry over to greet a couple who had just entered the gallery. To Andre's surprise, he recognized the couple as the two he had met last night at the restaurant.

As he approached, they both smiled and Maria, without introduction, said, "Hello, Herr von Kunst, how nice to see you again."

Andre, puzzled, looked at Elsa, who shook her head. "I didn't have a chance to tell them your name, and they said they already knew who you were."

Maria laughed. "After you left the restaurant, Greg and I asked the maitre'd who that charming gentleman was, and of course he told us your name. My partner," turning to Greg, who was discreetly admiring the lovely Elsa, "is Greg Sommers."

Andre smiled. "Well, I believe that takes care of all the formal introductions. I understand you have already met my partner, Frau Hasenfeld, so if Elsa will be so kind and call her and Herr Kranz, we'll go to my office."

"Thank you, Herr Von Kunst, for your time. Frau Hasenfeld was quite insistent that we wait for your return before we could discuss the matter fully," Maria said.

"I appreciate her wish to have me here," Andre said, "but very honestly I think that she includes me more for appearance's sake than need. She is really the business organizer and controls that side of the gallery's activities. We would be hard pressed to have a successful gallery without her expertise and, above all, her loyalty." You will soon meet Herr Kranz, who will be at the meeting. He is another valuable part of the gallery. He has been with us since I was a child. His reputation as a restorer and copier is unmatched anywhere. In fact, he is probably more critical to this meeting than any of us."

Andre was not unmindful that Katya and the Maestro were waiting to continue their tour. He said quickly, "We should proceed to my office and the others will join us there."

Maria and Greg stepped into the elevator, itself a work of art. The interior was richly paneled in fruitwood with a mirrored rear wall. This had been a later addition by Hannelore, who wanted to have a full view of herself before entering the gallery below. The floor was a mosaic of intricate wood pieces worn but polished. They were further impressed with the tasteful appointments of the reception area they entered from the elevator. They paused to look at the paintings on the wall, the lovely tapestried furniture, and the polished woodwork of the side tables.

Andre was pleased and proud at their voiced compliments as he led them into the conference room. Hannelore and Otto entered at the same time. After introducing Otto to Maria and Greg, Andre motioned them all to be seated. Hannelore nodded, and her smile of welcome was quite different than that experienced by Maria and Greg at their first meeting.

To Maria, it was quite apparent that Hannelore was in a much better frame of mind now. Otto was a different study. Not unfriendly by any means, but while he sat on the same side of the table as Hannelore, he was several chairs distanced from her and seemingly quite detached from the group in general.

More an observer, thought Maria, *than a participant*. Andre said Hannelore had given him all the details necessary. He was sure that the gallery's long-standing reputation as well as that of Herr Kranz would serve to assure them that however the mix-up had happened, it was not intentional. At this point Andre took from Otto copies of their house inventory and the shipping label and handed them over to Maria.

"As you can see, the inventory number that corresponds with the shipping label states clearly this was an original. However, Herr Kranz has explained to me that when he took the painting from storage, he unfortunately did not notice it was one of his expert copies that he placed in the packing case. In all his years this was the first time such a mistake has been made. I believe our records will confirm this has never happened before. You will agree that his copies are so excellent that he himself in the hurry to pack could have mistaken his own handiwork for the original. Perhaps our New York agent should have taken the pains to assure that it was an original, but, of course, having no reason to doubt the invoice, accordingly sold it for the price listed."

Hannelore tried to hide her shock at Otto's admission. Why had he not told her this before? Had she known this, all the things she had done to remove Kurt and buy back the gallery would have been unnecessary. From the look on Otto's face, it was apparent he had withheld this fact deliberately. Why would he do that? She intended to find out.

Maria looked at the documents and accepting what Andre had said, the possibility that a simple error occurred could well be true. However, there was no doubting the fact that the error, unintended or not, was going to cost her firm $560,000 dollars.

"Herr Kranz," Maria spoke kindly but directly to Otto, "evidently you have prepared many such shipments and invoices. No doubt from time to time errors do occur. May I ask when you first were aware you had made this mistake and what you did to correct it?"

Hannelore felt a chill. It was very clear this investigator was not going to accept Andre's explanation without some further clarification. The question implied that if Otto had made the mistake, wouldn't he have seen the error in time to advise Hannelore and she in turn could have told the New York gallery of the mistake?

Andre took no offense at the question; he admired Maria's thoroughness. Otto knew he had no alternative but to plead the forgiveness of an old man getting older. There was no way he could tell the truth about his deliberate attempt to expose Hannelore's and the Kreis illicit trade without endangering Andre and his mother.

Otto looked directly at Maria. "I was not aware I had shipped the copy until Frau Hasenfeld notified me that the New York gallery had a claim filed against it. I am very proud of the care I take in such matters. I could not believe I had made such a mistake until I went back to the storage room and confirmed the original was still there. Unfortunately, yet in some way to my credit, even our New York agent didn't discover that it was a copy. Had he, he would have notified us at once, avoiding all this unpleasantness. This whole affair is my fault. I take full responsibility for it."

Maria had little doubt he spoke the truth, but that there was a serious loss involved, the confession did little to resolve that matter.

She paused a moment, then asked again, very directly, "Herr Kranz, when you discovered your mistake, I assume you would have immediately told Frau Hasenfeld or Herr von Kunst. Wouldn't there have been plenty of time to have contacted the New York gallery and informed them of the error?"

She said this as she looked questioningly at both Hannelore and Andre. Indeed why hadn't they reacted promptly when told was clearly implied in her question.

At mention of her name, Hannelore sat upright and said sharply, "I assure you, Frau Skorkia, I received no information from Herr Kranz. Other than that earlier phone call advising me of the problem, I had no other information about the matter."

"Frau Skorkia, I did not tell anyone; others couldn't be blamed. I was so chagrined that I made such a mistake that I hadn't the courage to tell. I don't know what I was thinking, but, of course, when I heard of your arrival, I knew I must admit to the error. I am truly sorry, I indeed am responsible for all of this; I did not intend to defraud anyone."

"Herr Kranz." Maria studied the pained countenance of the old man. She was inclined to believe him. "I can only repeat that even if this was an honest mistake, my company is faced with a considerable loss."

Greg sat silently during the exchange with Otto. Something bothered him about the whole scenario. He knew Maria was trying to find an amiable solution to the problem without implying there was any impropriety on the part of the gallery. He acknowledged that Otto's story could be true, but his eyes were on Hannelore, but not just because of her looks. What he learned from his contacts in New York with the new owner of Art World and what Kurt said did not mesh with her claim of having no knowledge of the matter.

He thought more investigation of the involvement was going to be necessary before the matter could be settled.

As if he read Greg's mind, Andre spoke, "Frau Skorkia, Mr. Sommers, may I make a proposal that I think should be sufficient to settle this matter?" They both nodded; they liked Andre and had no reason to believe he acted in other than good faith.

Andre continued, "There is no doubt that the problem originated here. I have the utmost faith in my colleagues and believe no deceit was intended. However, we now know it was a copy and not the original it was purported to be. I would be glad to repurchase the painting from the estate for the full price paid or ship the original that we still have.

"In addition, since it has caused your firm some considerable expense, if you would prepare an expense report for those costs connected to your investigation, we would gladly pay that as well."

Maria and Greg looked at each other, but before they could respond, Hannelore, with a very distressed look, spoke, "Herr von Kunst, as your partner, I believe you have exceeded what would be expected of us."

Andre was taken aback at this. Why would Hannelore, after agreeing with him beforehand that this is what he would offer, now raise an objection, especially challenging him in front of the investigators? Otto was secretly pleased. Perhaps now with Hannelore's challenge the investigation that Otto had hoped for would result.

Andre sensed quickly that Hannelore's pride was in play here. She wanted justification for her abrupt handling of the matter with Kurt. It was apparent she wanted the majority of the blame to be placed on him, not the Von Kunst Gallery, for which she carried the most responsibility. She could not tolerate the impression that there was some fault to be found with her decisions. He knew that to be her nature; accept no blame for actions she took regardless of any negative consequences.

Maria spoke first, "Herr von Kunst, I think your offer to settle the

matter as you outlined seems very reasonable; however, I do need to discuss this with my partner and our home office as well. The sale of a copy
as an original is still a grievous oversight and that it was a pure error is
critical to an acceptable conclusion.

"My impression, from what I have heard and the reputation of your
gallery, leads me to accept the fact it was a human error without intent to
defraud. But, as I said, that is my own opinion; others will have to concur.
It appears that this may not be acceptable to your partner, and perhaps we
should excuse ourselves until we know your final decision."

Andre was reluctant to countermand Hannelore's position in front of
the visitors and accepted Maria's offer to excuse themselves.

"Frau Skorkia, I do appreciate your offer. I'm sure you both would
enjoy our lounge in the gallery. Frau Becker will be more than pleased to
provide you with coffee or anything else you might desire. I'll call her at
once to come and escort you down."

Greg thought the open opposition of Hannelore the perfect opportunity to make sure she hadn't the upper hand in the matter.

Greg spoke, "With all respect to you, Herr von Kunst, and you, Frau
Hasenfeld, while I am basically in agreement with my colleague's opinion, I am not entirely opposed to what Frau Hasenfeld has expressed as
a concern. Perhaps a further investigation is necessary. It might be best
to know in more detail how all of this came about, to determine just why
or how the proprietor, this Kurt, could have overlooked the fact the work
was a copy. I would think he would verify all works he sold regardless of
what the invoice said. Perhaps the outcome would be sufficient in arriving at a different settlement than what Herr von Kunst has so generously
proposed."

Greg was purposely baiting Hannelore, for whom he had a growing
dislike.

While he had no reason to disbelieve Otto's statement, he could not
shake the impression he was totally under the control of Frau Hasenfeld.
The conversations with Kurt kept haunting him, especially his references
to Hannelore and the evidently more than business relationship he had
with her. Her choice of him as a partner and the considerable sum of
money she had invested in his gallery didn't fit well with her protestations
of non-involvement.

With a gentle knock, Elsa entered the room with a very concerned
look on her face. With an apology, she asked if she might have a short

word with Herr von Kunst before escorting his guests to the lounge. Andre rose at once and excusing himself followed Elsa out of the room.

"Elsa, what's the matter?" Andre asked.

"Andre, something very strange happened, but I didn't know if I should have interrupted the meeting, but your call to come get the insurance couple gave me this chance. Your two guests left the gallery with the young girl very upset and in tears."

Andre was shocked. "Elsa, what happened, what did they say?"

"I really don't know. I had just stepped away for a minute to answer your call to come here. They were standing in the part of Otto's office where he repairs works. They were looking and admiring some paintings when I heard a gasp from the girl. I turned to look just in time to see she was pointing at one of the pictures. Then she turned to the gentleman with her and said something I couldn't hear. He immediately held her for a moment and then, taking her by the hand, started for the door. I asked what was wrong and could I be of help. He just shook his head and said, 'No, we must leave,' and they did."

Andre was perplexed. He had to know what the matter was, but he didn't want the present discussion with Maria and Greg to be disrupted at this critical point.

"Elsa, please take the two visitors down to the gallery, and then as soon as you can, please call the hotel and tell Herr Karpinski I will be in touch shortly. If at all possible, try and find out what has disturbed Fraulein Preznoski and assure them of my concern."

He re-entered the room with Elsa and with a very concerned look again apologized for the interruption.

After Elsa escorted Maria and Greg out, he turned to Hannelore. "Hannelore, why are you suggesting that we do exactly opposite to what we had agreed was an acceptable solution?"

Hannelore was defensive. "Andre, I just cannot tolerate taking the position we are solely to blame. We should make sure that our former partner who made the actual sale is held accountable, and if you insist that we pay what you have suggested, he pays a part. After all, while I did dismiss him abruptly, I negotiated a buyout that gave him a good sum of cash. Besides, your offer would indicate to my friends that we were guilty of incompetence and might damage their trust in us."

Andre was angered. "Hannelore, what your friends think of this gallery is inconsequential to me. They are not a part of it in any way, unless your close connection with them has allowed them to be. I have no inter-est whether they have trust in us or not, I certainly have no trust in them." Hannelore began to regret that her comments were leading in this direc-tion. Especially worrisome was Andre's alluding to her association with the Kreis possibly having a connection with the gallery.

Otto listened to all of this with a growing hope that Hannelore's willingness to carry the fight further would lead to the disclosures he wanted. He wondered if she was at all aware of this danger. Was she thinking that he was going to give her unlimited support?

Andre spoke, "Otto, I know you are sorry that the substitution has had ramifications beyond what any of us might have expected; do you think the New York agent should really have had the ability to know this was a copy, or was he simply too lazy or negligent to have taken a closer look? If the latter, then perhaps Hannelore is correct, and he should be brought into the investigation."

"Andre, I dislike any form of boasting, but as you know, my work is excellent. It would take a very expert eye to know this was a copy. Unless a person had a reason to doubt the authenticity, it would easily pass for an original. The only reason this error was discovered was that the purchaser's estate asked for an examination. I do not know this agent in New York, and certainly Fraulein Hasenfeld would not have formed a partnership with less than a very competent person. I believe he should have been able to see this was a copy. I think he carries some burden of guilt."

Hannelore was pleased at hearing this unexpected support from Otto. She had no idea of Otto's desire for an investigation.

"See, Andre, even Otto knows we should not be seen as having any serious fault; the majority of the blame lies with Kurt, and he should be pursued. I know you have no regard for my friends, but Herr Shoerstein is a very competent lawyer of my acquaintance through the Kreis. Would it not be advisable for me to ask him for an opinion as well? I'm sure if he is told the full facts, he could put your mind at ease about the justification of my opinion."

Andre was undecided about what to do. Perhaps Hannelore was right and he was too quick in making his offer without considering what responsibility Kurt should accept. There was the possibility that others outside of the Kreis might also think it was an admission of guilt. He was too preoccupied with worrying about Katya to give much further attention to the matter.

"Hannelore, ask your attorney his opinion today. I'm sure your closeness will ensure a quick and honest answer. However, it remains the gallery's responsibility to clear the matter. I'm inclined to follow my offer to them. Now I must find out why my two guests left the gallery so abruptly. I'll have to beg the two insurance people for a little more time and patience until we resolve the matter."

Andre went immediately to Maria and Greg. "I must apologize for this interruption. As you can understand, I do have a responsibility to hear my partner out, but I assure you that this gallery will stand good for whatever cost that we should bear. She is very defensive of the gallery, and I don't want to ride roughshod over her opinion.

"However, another situation has arisen of very personal importance to me; in fact, it is the main reason I'm asking for your indulgence. I need to clear the matter immediately. Would you agree to a postponement of our meeting until tomorrow? I'm sure it will then be possible to settle this without any further delay."

Maria sensed at once that Andre was very disturbed. She saw no reason not to agree with his request.

Maria turned to Greg. "I believe Herr von Kunst has been very gracious to us and we should respect his wish. It might, in the meantime, be in order to talk with our office and run these proposals by them. Do you agree?" Greg nodded; in fact, he was sure the delay would give him time to again review his notes on Kurt in the event more ammunition could be found to counter Frau Hasenfeld's assertions of innocence.

Andre insisted on calling for the gallery's car and escorted them to the door with more apologies. Maria assured him this was not necessary, but he insisted the car and driver would be at their disposal.

After saying goodbye to the Americans, Andre went immediately to Elsa. "You said they were looking at a picture in Otto's studio when you went to answer my call, do you know which one it was?"

"I wasn't that far away and turned as I heard her gasp. She was pointing at the large painting half facing this way, so I could see clearly which one it was. Here, I'll show you."

They walked over to the painting. Andre noted it was a reproduction; several of these had been done by Otto, and they sold well. It was a lovely landscape, peaceful and well suited to evoke a sense of tranquility in the beholder. Certainly not a scene to cause a reaction such as Elsa had described.

"Elsa, have you called the hotel?"

"No, Andre, I didn't think they would have had time to get back when you asked me. I'll call now."

"Thank you, but I'll call. I'm sure they are back by now. Meanwhile, please ask Otto to come here."

CHAPTER 30

THE MAESTRO ANSWERED RATHER GRUFFLY WHEN Andre announced himself. Before Andre could speak, the Maestro said that he and Katya would be leaving on the next train for Warsaw and no further services or contact from him was needed or welcomed. With that, he hung up.

Otto came into the studio as Andre replaced the receiver in bewilderment. "Otto, please come here and look at this picture." He explained what had happened with his guests. "Do you know why this particular picture would cause such a reaction?" Otto shook his head as much surprised as Andre.

"No, it is simply one of several I have made, and it's on display for the interest of anyone who might wish to purchase. In fact, we have sold several. The original has long since been lost as far as I know. I made the copies from a picture of the original in an old catalogue."

This was his stock answer to questions about his ability to make copies of paintings long since considered lost. Otto hated this deceit; he knew exactly where the original painting was that had been in this frame originally. He had no alternative but to lie for Andre's sake; why this copy caused such a reaction by the young lady, he had no answer.

"Andre, I have no idea to why this copy would have disturbed her so much."

"Well, I'll call Hannelore to come, though I doubt she will know anymore than the rest of us.

Hannelore had gone to her apartment after the meeting had closed

175

without a clear-cut settlement. The only reservation she had was what information Kurt would have supplied the investigators about her arrangement with Kurt involving those paintings destined for Kreis customers.

While Kurt never questioned her about the details, assuming it was, as Hannelore told him, an arrangement that preceded their partnership, he could, no doubt, have told the investigators enough to arouse their curiosity. She began to have some reservations, nevertheless; she was convinced she had done well in challenging Andre's proposal, Kurt not withstanding. Her thoughts were interrupted by Andre's call to please come down.

She crossed the gallery floor quickly to where Elsa, Otto, and Andre were standing.

"Whatever is the matter? What are you all standing around and staring at?" she asked in her usual annoyed tone whenever she was interrupted.

Andre quickly told her of Katya's reaction to the picture causing her and the Maestro's hasty exit from the gallery.

"Hannelore," Andre indicated the picture, "do you see anything in this painting that would have caused such a reaction?"

Hannelore glanced quickly at the colored landscape; obviously there was nothing there to be considered offensive. "You are dealing with a very emotionally disturbed woman," she said. "No doubt the picture brought back a memory of some unpleasant event that took place in a flowered field. You know how people in some of these more peasant societies have little regard for a woman's worth. I'm sure one of her countrymen took his pleasure with her as is common with them regardless of the inappropriateness of time or place."

With that, the matter was settled as far as Hannelore was concerned.

"But what were they doing in Otto's studio? It seems strange to me that they were allowed to just roam around the gallery. After all, this very show of instability could have resulted in her attacking the picture itself if it was so disturbing."

"Hannelore, they were here as my guests. Frau Becker was at my request showing them through the gallery; had they just wished to roam that would certainly have been acceptable. However, Otto's expert work, of which we are very proud, was certainly a part of the gallery they would have been entitled to see. If, indeed, the picture brought back such a memory as you suggest, I think a feeling of compassion, not derision would have been the proper response. Your unfeeling and total disdain for many people, Hannelore, never fails to amaze and disappoint me. Thank you for coming, now I must go and try to contact them."

Hannelore felt Andre's anger. That his response was a reproach did not elicit from her the need for an apology. One doesn't apologize for telling things as they are. Besides, the two persons in question were not worthy of any further conversation. Without further comment, Hannelore turned and left for her office. A quick glance at Otto as she left signaled she wished to talk to him. Andre thanked the others for their help.

Andre went back to his office concerned about his next step. He could not bear the thought that Katya would be leaving without his seeing her again. He began to think again of Hannelore's comments, her attitude toward others, especially if they belonged to nationalities she felt were inferior to her own. What about his own attitude? Yes, he had from time to time quarreled with her over this issue, but had he really been adamant enough in opposing her and the Kreis philosophy? Was it possible his attitude was too passive, even tolerant? He needed to speak with Hannelore. He called her office phone and asked if she had time to speak with him.

"Why, of course, Andre," she answered pleasantly, the earlier conversation in Otto's office completely forgotten.

Andre came in and took a seat across from where Hannelore was seated with a cup of coffee in her hand.

"Would you like a cup, Andre? I have it freshly brewed."

"No, thank you, Hannelore, I just wanted to have a few words with you about my guests. Hannelore, I just cannot understand this attitude, what exactly are the reasons for this dislike?" Hannelore sat back and slowly shook her head.

"Andre, the problem with you is your inability to think beyond the personal level. You seem so overly concerned with how the individual or, in this case, two individuals, are affected, that you cannot see the greater dangers which they represent. It's not a matter of disliking them, personally, whether we like them or not is secondary to the issue.

"The two alone are of no real threat, but the cultures they represent, if allowed to become dominant, can be. Therefore, no acceptance of persons from those cultures based on personal concerns or emotions can be allowed to cloud the issue. We have no choice but to make sure their ideologies are challenged on every occasion. Their very presence in our country could be construed by others that we accept them and would welcome them into our society. We have, as a nation, suffered in the past by showing a tolerance that should not have been allowed if we were to preserve our way of life, our superior culture."

Andre broke in, "Superior culture, Hannelore? In what way superior? Certainly I'm just as proud as you of the contributions people of our culture have made to the civilized world and so have others from their cultures, but to say we are superior? Was the recent performance of my guest's orchestra deficient in any way because they were Polish?"

Hannelore sighed. "Andre, really this discussion leads nowhere. You want a specific reason for my dislike for them. I can only repeat what I have already said; it is not personal, and that should answer your question. I might add, Andre, that this fact is what surprises me most about your attraction, evident to all, to the young violinist. She may be physically attractive to you, but a closer association will prove to you that she lacks those qualities of special worth."

Andre got up shaking his head sadly. He looked at the beautiful lady sitting on her couch, coffee in her hand, smiling sweetly at him. What more could he say? A further defense of Katya would be met with the same arguments.

"Hannelore, I must go. You are right, not in your beliefs about cultural superiority, which can only lead to the same disasters that it has before, but in our personal relations. How sad, you are such a beautiful and talented woman. As a business partner, I could do no better, but as a soul partner there is a great dry desert too great for our hearts to cross."

Hannelore laughed. "Oh, Andre, you sound so melodramatic, 'a great dry desert' indeed. Even if that's true, most deserts do have oasis for those willing to travel it. I believe we have been at those oases, haven't we? I suspect that from time to time despite your present mood, you will remember those moments that prove your 'great dry desert' is crossable.

"I'm willing to be patient, the oases are quite lovely, worth waiting for." His eyes met hers almost reluctantly as he had to admit to the truth of what she said.

"I have to go Hannelore, we need to speak again about the matter with the insurance people. Make sure you have your friend's opinion ready for us to discuss."

With that, he left. As he returned to his apartment, his thoughts were again on her comments about superior cultures. *How could reasonable and supposedly highly intelligent people become so twisted in their thinking? What rational could support such prejudices?*

He sat down in a chair overlooking the private garden behind the gallery. The fountain was still showering the playful nymphs frolicking at its base. He could still see the young girl with the golden curls sitting on the fountain's edge telling the young boy beside her of Germany's glorious past.

The ringing phone interrupted his reverie.

"Andre, I have Fraulein Preznoski on the phone wishing to speak with you."

CHAPTER 31

AFTER LEAVING THE GALLERY, THE MAESTRO AND Katya returned to the hotel without any exchange of words. The Maestro was perplexed; he had been standing next to her as they viewed the picture that evidently was the cause of her reaction. He saw nothing that was unusual; her abrupt plea to leave gave him no time to ask what was wrong. What had he missed? Frau Becker had been most friendly and, begrudgingly, he found the young von Kunst a pleasing host. Evidently, the ghost he had expected to encounter had not failed to appear, at least to Katya.

After a while, he knocked gently on her door and entered with her soft, "Come in." She was seated looking at the picture of her parents; tears stained her pale cheeks.

"Katya, I don't want to pressure you with questions; if you care to share with me what it was that upset you, I am prepared to listen.

"Maestro," she said softly, "you were so often in our home that you probably remember the picture that hung in our foyer?"

The Maestro nodded, "Yes, I remember every room very well. I was familiar with all the works your father had gathered. He had a valuable collection, and the one you refer to was one of my favorites. However, it was not the one we saw in the gallery, although similar in some ways.

"Katya, you were very young when we left. I think those similarities in the picture may have led you to believe it was the same one. After all, many years have passed, and your mistaking it is understandable. You need not to apologize for your reaction. It just re-enforces my reservations about coming here. To have incidents like this upset you, accidental or not, is justification to leave now and avoid future unpleasant moments."

Katya shook her head. "It wasn't the picture, Maestro. It was the frame."

"The frame?" he asked, perplexed. He had to admit that while he could recall the picture, the frame he could not. Since the frame was very incidental compared to the painting, why would Katya remember it so vividly?

"Katya," the Maestro spoke tenderly, "whatever has caused you this sorrow I need to know. It is important that you tell me exactly why this particular frame upset you. I have for years wanted to tell you the reason why I not only harbor a hatred for the criminals who destroyed so much of Europe, but especially the family of the young man for whom you evidently have a liking. Perhaps if you tell me what you saw, it will be what I need to know before I say anything more about the reasons for my hatred."

Katya, drying her eyes, said, "Maestro, no matter what I tell you, I do not want it to be evidence to support your hatred. Perhaps if I tell you, it will help you understand that your hatred serves no purpose if it seeks to destroy. Please, come sit by me and I will tell you what I saw, and why I have proof that frame was once in my home."

After she finished, the Maestro sat in silence, gently holding her hand. "Katya, I cannot answer for my hatred at this moment, but I believe that now after what you have told me, I have positive proof of what I saw with my own eyes years ago. Now it is time to tell you about it. Then we can discuss the justice or as you say, the injustice of my anger. Whatever, I doubt very much that you will wish to continue any association with Herr von Kunst after I finish my story.

"Do you remember the night the SS Officers came to your home?" Katya nodded; she had been only twelve, and since they spoke only German, she had had to ask the Maestro what they were saying. She remembered the sadness on his face as well as on the face of her parents.

"Yes, I remember you telling me that the German Command needed their home for headquarters and that my parents would have to move to a smaller home. You said they were told to immediately prepare an inventory of all their private possessions. These would be transferred to a safe storage facility until the time when their home would no longer be needed and they would be returned. You told me not to worry since my father, a prominent doctor, was held in such high esteem that he was being afforded this exceptional courtesy."

The Maestro looked into her tear-filled eyes and said slowly, "Katya, it was all a lie. Your parents weren't being relocated to a new home, nor was the inventory list to provide for a safe storage for their later return, which was never to be."

The Maestro paused as Katya turned her pale face from looking at her parents' picture, her eyes now filled with a questioning.

He sighed as he continued, "Katya, that very night after the SS left, your father told me to make arrangements to take you to England. He gave me the name of Lord Richfield and a copy of the letter he had sent to this English friend. Your father wanted me to know the details of the arrangements he had made. Above all, Katya, was his love for you and his concern that you would be protected."

The Maestro struggled with his own emotions as he began again to recount the past. "The next morning I telephoned Lord Richfield and gave him a brief recounting of the events of the past night and your father's request that we come immediately. He responded that in prior correspondence, your father expressed the fear that such a move was going to be necessary. Lord Richfield said we, of course, would be welcome and to bring your father and mother as well. When I returned to tell your parents, your father said they would only endanger you if they tried to leave with us.

"The Gestapo had already been there and, following instructions from the SS, informed your parents they were to be sent to a processing center and to prepare for immediate departure. It was evident that due to your father's prominence they wanted this to appear to be a very civil process, no sudden disappearance in the middle of the night. Your father still did not want to believe what he had already heard about the sudden relocating of Jews and others thought to be a danger to the occupiers. However, he was fearful this move was not going to lead to any good end."

Katya was still; she held the Maestro's hand tightly as if it was a living connection back to that heart-wrenching night when she said a sobbing goodbye to her parents. They had assured her this was just a temporary but necessary precaution due to the political unrest in their country.

"*Whatever happens, Katya,*" her father had said as he held her close, "*remember, that people are basically good. There may be times that through fear or ignorance they do things that later may be judged evil, but circumstances blind them to that realization. We must always have sympathy for their blindness, and with that understanding we avoid becoming blind ourselves. Katya, always keep your heart open. Do not judge the actions of people blinded by ignorance, what else could we expect? Without the light of truth shining in their lives, they will stumble in the darkness of that ignorance. Of course, in their stumbling they will cause hurt to others, but remember, forgiveness will ease the pain of that hurt.*"

Young as she was, Katya never forgot those parting words. They were a summation of many prior talks she had had with her parents. Her entire upbringing had been in an atmosphere of trust and understanding. The Maestro waited as he sensed Katya was deep in thought; when she looked up, he continued.

"Katya, as I was leaving your father for the last time, I heard voices in German coming from the library where many of your priceless paintings were hung. I looked in; they didn't see me. As I watched, two of them were taking down paintings from the wall. Another was standing by large packing crates with a list in his hand, evidently a copy of the list your father had prepared. As they removed a painting, he instructed them to write the number he read from the list on the back of the painting. Then he said to place the painting in the crate marked Von Kunst Gallery, Berlin."

Katya gave a start and turned even paler. "What are you saying, Maestro? You mean the paintings taken from our home were sent here to Berlin?"

"Katya, there was no mistaking that these paintings were being sent to this very same gallery; the crates were clearly labeled."

Katya was stunned; Andre's gallery had stolen her father's paintings! A sickness filled her; how could she deny the truth of what the Maestro said? It was proof that the frame she saw was not in this gallery by accident, but by intent. Tears again welled up in her eyes as she struggled to control the surge of resentment and betrayal rising in her heart. The Maestro, reading the distress in her eyes, decided he must continue.

"Katya, you might as well know it all." He tried to control his own rising anger as he relived the past tragedy now tearing at the soul of this young, innocent victim, deprived of a life with loving parents. "While in England with you, I made contact with some of my non-Jewish friends to find out if there was some way I could get your parents out of Poland. At a great risk to themselves, they were able to locate your parents. They had been taken to a concentration center in Auswitz. We soon learned that this was not a place of safety as the SS had implied, but a place of extermination." The Maestro buried his face in his hands; he could not bear the look of horror on Katya's face.

Finally, Katya, with a choking voice, said, "Maestro, for all these years you have known this, yet not told me. Why?"

The Maestro lifted a face now wet with his own tears. "Katya, what good would it have done then to tell a twelve-year-old girl the truth? For your own happiness I let the terrible ending of your parents' lives be unknown to you."

Katya said, "Why now?"

"Because, Katya," the Maestro's voice shook with emotion, "I could not bear any longer the possibility of you having an even greater attraction than you now have for this member of a family that were accomplices in the murder of your parents. It would have been a betrayal of the trust your parents gave me in caring for you. You had to know this.

"We should leave as soon as possible. There is not much that we can legally do; I have no written proof and only my word of what I saw. Even your identification of the frame will prove nothing; you also have no proof that it was the one from your home, especially since it contains another picture."

The phone rang, the Maestro answered, and from the chill in his voice Katya knew who it was. She heard the Maestro's brief and curt declaration that they were leaving and no further contact with the caller was wished.

As he hung up, Katya raised her face wet again from freshly shed tears. "No Maestro, we are not leaving without my talking to Andre. Of course I am crushed, but I cannot simply run away without hearing from him what part he played in this. He was very young; I will not condemn him without knowing how he was involved. If he was involved, then I must forgive him. All that I have seen and heard from him is contrary to what you would have me think of him. To say he is guilty because he was born into a family involved in such a terrible crime is unfair. The Maestro stared, uncomprehending this obstinacy to accept the truth.

"Katya, this is no time to speak of forgiveness, never can I forgive this family."

Katya continued before the Maestro could say more, "Maestro, that is the very reason I must see and talk to him. If indeed he was aware of this crime, although young, but aware, then I must accept that with deepest disappointment. However, I will still forgive him because unless I do, I will harbor this hurt until it turns into the hatred you have. That would dishonor my father; he taught me that while hating the effects of evil , I must help people avoid following evil desires. To do that here is no alternative but always to love and forgive, in so doing we save our own soul from being damned by that same evil."

The Maestro shook his head. He had often had similar conversations with her father sitting in his library before a warming fire as they debated the affairs of a changing world. He could almost hear her father's voice as Katya spoke. How well indeed had his friend instilled his philosophy into his young and loving daughter. There was no doubt he would have to allow Katya her demand; however, he could not resist a final attempt to dissuade her from this decision.

"Katya, with all love to your father and to you, is it not possible for you to see that premeditated evil acts, done with the full knowledge of the devastation the acts will cause, whether to a person or to a nation, forfeit any claim to forgiveness? Katya, evil does not deserve pardon, only damnation."

Katya shook her head vehemently. "No, Maestro, unless forgiven, the hatred will kill the one who cannot forgive. I love you, and I must in all love tell you I fear that you, too, will allow your hatred to someday kill you."

The Maestro knew the battle was lost. He took no offense at her words, he knew of her love for him. He only feared the day when she would have to realize that all the good her father had seen in an evil world was not sufficient to overcome it.

The Maestro gave a sigh of resignation. "Well then, Katya, I must call Herr von Kunst and much to my regret take back my words about us leaving."

"No," answered Katya quickly, "I shall call him myself. I do not want to discuss what has happened over a telephone, only in person. I believe he will be honest. Perhaps even offer that excuse you so quickly push aside. 'Sorry, I didn't realize, didn't know, and so forth.' Of course, any admission on his part of having been either a willing or unwilling participant will not alter in anyway my offer of forgiveness.

"But, I am human, I will not deny the sadness I will feel if it proves true he was involved, and that sadness will remain forever. Certainly, out of my love for my parents and in honor of their memory, there will be an emotional gulf I could never cross. But sadness is not hatred."

The Maestro's heart was itself saddened. As much as he had wanted to discourage her attraction for the young German, he had hoped it could be accomplished without the hurt of this revelation.

"Katya," he rose to go to his room, "you must do what your heart tells you. I have said all that I can. I love you; you know that. Whatever comes of this, I am willing to accept for your sake."

Katya smiled. "I need to thank you, Maestro, those words from your heart gives me great courage. How I have cherished your love and care through these years. You will never know the depth of my gratitude. Now I must face the first real testing of all that my father has taught me. The past that you have revealed to me was necessary, regardless of my current feelings toward Herr von Kunst. Now to see if I can offer true forgiveness, if indeed I look into the face of a man who possibly was aware of this evil and accepted his family's role in the murder of my parents."

The Maestro stood. "Katya, I know you must do what you feel is right. I have said all that I can about this tragedy. I will go now and rest a bit. I know you need some time to think." He bent low and placed a soft kiss on her brow and left her alone with her thoughts.

Katya was emotionally drained. It was evident that her feeling for Andre, despite their short acquaintance, had developed into a much stronger attraction than she had been willing to admit. She struggled with how to approach him. He had been young, just a teenager. How much of the family's business would he have been involved in?

She admitted that her social life had been almost totally under the Maestro's control. Her career, her love of music was the focus of her life. There was little time to devote to making contact with others outside her world of music. Yet she knew that whatever decisions he made were for her good. She never felt imprisoned, it was jut the way it was. Until now she had been very content with her life, her music. She looked at the phone, in a few moments she would be speaking to him; her heart began to beat rapidly.

A desperate hope was undeniably rising that in some way this most polite and attentive young man could put her fears to rest about his guilt, a guilt the Maestro avowed he could not avoid. The question was what then? What if indeed she was convinced he had no part, no knowledge of the crimes of his family? Would that be all that she needed to know? She was sure she had met a true gentleman who had, out of his generous nature and appreciation of her talents, provided this interlude as thanks. Perhaps to her own embarrassment she was assuming far too much about his feelings for her. Was she perhaps overlooking the fact that all that he was doing was just a show of kindness and nothing deeper? She reached for the phone. *I will not accuse, I will only ask for a moment of time to be with him. I must look into his face as we talk.*

Andre's eager "hello" was answered with an unmistakable quavering in her voice. His immediate concern was her greeting, "Herr Von Kunst," not Andre.

"I know we left your gallery very abruptly and what the Maestro told you about our leaving." She added quickly, "However, I'd like to talk to you directly about the reason for my departure, but I don't want to discuss it over the phone." She said it all so hurriedly, almost in one breath, that he could only listen until she finished.

"Katya," he ignored her formal greeting, "of course I want to talk to you. I am terribly sorry that something, a painting I believe, so upset you. I could hardly endure the thought that you would be leaving without my seeing you again. Please, when can I see you?"

He sensed the emotion in her voice as she spoke, "I want to see you as soon as possible. If the Maestro and I could come to the gallery yet today, I would appreciate that." Without hesitation, Andre insisted he would be there to take them to the gallery as soon as they were ready.

"No," Katya replied firmly but not rudely. "We do not wish to impose on your hospitality, you have done enough. We shall come by taxi within the hour if that is acceptable."

Andre was perplexed; Katya's voice, while not unkind, was decidedly distant, formal. She refused his second offer of transportation, only asking again if her suggestion to be there within the hour was acceptable. Andre agreed and decided it would be unwise to press the matter.

"Katya, I do not know what has happened to cause you this distress; whatever it was, I must know if there is anything I can do to help you. As you wish, I will wait here for you to come as soon as you can."

"Thank you," her voice still trembled. "It is important for me to see you. I do not want to say what I must or ask what I must over the phone."

After she hung up, Andre sat down again by the window. The fountain continued to shower the playful nymphs, but the girl with the golden curls and the young boy were no longer there, they had left long ago.

CHAPTER 32

IT HAD BEEN ONLY A FEW DAYS SINCE THE NIGHT OF the concert when the dark haired violinist had first entranced him. The events afterwards had shown promise of at least a growing friendship; how could it all end so abruptly in front of a painting in his gallery? What could she tell him that would justify such an abrupt wish to leave? Had Katya not intervened, the Maestro prevailed, they would have left without another word.

He sat a few minutes longer again trying to assess his own feelings. Just how much attraction did he feel for this girl? Was it simple infatuation, now satisfied by meeting her and finding her a pleasant person and no more? Would it suffice, having satisfied his curiosity and enjoying the pleasure of her company for a few days, to say a pleasant goodbye and wish her well? Was that it? Had he no wish to prolong the friendship beyond making sure that whatever had offended her a sincere apology was given?

Yet he knew his feeling was deeper than that, but what of her feelings for him? He believed she liked him, but to what degree? To what good end could their mutual attraction lead, given there was a good end? She was a talented musician with a bright future. There were many more concerts to perform across the world. He was a partner in an enterprise that depended much on his close-knit relationship with its customers. Would a relationship endure extended separations, extensive travel?

Had his behavior in following her across half of Germany truly been the irrational impulse he often confessed it was but powerless to have resisted? *It's a little late, Andre,* he said to himself, *to start thinking of consequences now. You pursued her, persistently, even much against the will of her guardian. It was your insistence that brought her to Berlin. Now she is coming to talk about an event that caused her grief, evidently caused by you or your family. Whatever, it has to be serious.*

He went down to the lobby and walked over to Elsa's desk. She was busily recording the events of the day in her journal. She looked up as he approached her desk. She knew the phone conversation had not been long, and she knew it had been Katya sounding quite sad. She said nothing, noting the look of concern on Andre's face.

"Elsa, I am expecting my guests to be coming soon. Please call me as soon as they arrive. She said she wanted to explain why she had left the gallery but not over the telephone. I am really perplexed about what she saw in that picture. I'm going over to Otto's studio again. Perhaps he has more thoughts on the matter." He found Otto, as usual, working on a reproduction.

"Otto," Andre hoped he was not disturbing him; a quick negative assured him he was not. "Fraulein Presnoski and Herr Karpinski are coming back to the gallery. She wishes to explain in person what caused her abrupt departure. Perhaps, if she wants, it would be good to have you here since it obviously has to do with the painting."

"Of course," Otto said quickly, and then added, "Perhaps it would be wise to ask Hannelore as well." Otto knew all of this revolved around the picture, he didn't know what could have caused the lady's reaction, but he felt uneasy. If there were questions to be answered, better to have Hannelore present.

Otto had gone over in his mind several times what could have been the cause. The picture was a common copy, nothing that should arouse suspicion. All the pictures hidden away had arrived years ago from the homes and museums that the Reich had systematically looted. The recent decision to start selling these to private customers, primarily in the U.S., had been carefully planned using Kurt as an unsuspecting accomplice. The Kreis was sure there would be no claimants for works taken from private homes. That problem was solved at the time of acquisition as the true owners boarded trains destined for the "Final Solution."

From the start, Otto had been the one to accept and inspect every shipment that arrived. He would carefully enter in his log each painting and its origin by name and address of the previous owner, private or museum. As for the frames that accompanied them, they were of little value in themselves. These were removed and stored separately. However, Otto found them very useful as decorative frames for reproductions such as the one now on display in his studio. Due to the commonality of many of these frames made from plaster molds, their identification with any particular work of art was doubtful. Otto felt secure in using them for display purposes.

The idea of having Hannelore present didn't appeal to Andre. He didn't relish the idea of her repeating in front of Katya her unwarranted comment that Katya's reaction was due to an unpleasant experience with a countryman in a flowered field.

"I don't know, Otto, if having Hannelore here will help matters. I'd rather wait to hear what Katya has to say." Otto nodded.

Elsa came quickly. "Your guests are arriving."

Andre murmured, "Thanks," and hurried to meet them. His face fell at the look of heavy sadness on Katya's drawn face and the open hostility on the Maestro's.

"Fraulein…" he started to say but stopped as Katya held up her hand.

"Herr von Kunst, what I have to say must be said quickly and in private. I beg you not to interrupt, it is going to be difficult enough to say what I must."

Andre nodded. "Please, let us go upstairs to my apartment," he said, motioning toward the elevator. They followed, and no one spoke as they stood in silence. Andre quickly stepped from the lift and crossed the foyer to open his apartment door. Katya noted the name "Hasenfeld" on the door opposite Andre's.

The thought of intimacy came and went quickly; it was of no consequence. Andre indicated a sofa for them to be seated and chose a chair across from them. Andre sensed Katya was waiting to speak and did not preempt her with the question weighing so heavily on him. Katya, fighting for composure, yet with glistening eyes started.

"Herr von Kunst, I have always looked for the best in people wherever I have been. My trusted companion, Herr Karpinski, is much wiser than I in the affairs of the world. He has always warned me that this tendency on my part to always trust and look for the good in people was destined to result in some disappointing experiences. He said that, unfortunately, I would learn sooner or later that people are not always what they appear to be. He warned that my belief in the innate goodness of people would prove to be misplaced." She paused to wipe the moistness under her eyes.

The Maestro sat silently, laying one hand consolingly on her knee. Andre stared at her and the Maestro with a genuine look of incomprehension, myriad questions crying for answers. He knew these comments were directed at him, but why?

Katya swallowed hard, the moisture in her eyes now welling above dark lashes; tears threatening, ready to fall on yet paler cheeks. She reached into her purse for a tissue, and Andre waited as she delicately stemmed the pending flow.

With a deep sigh, she continued, "Herr von Kunst, (Andre wanted so desperately for her to say "Andre"), I have had to admit more reluctantly than I care to that the Maestro has been justified in foretelling that I would suffer for my trust. I just never knew how much the hurt could be. I confess without embarrassment that I have enjoyed knowing you. Never before have I met someone who has fulfilled my expectations of genuine, human kindness, a person to whom I could offer my highest respect, besides the Maestro. Yet even for him have I sorrowed over his unwillingness to accept the possibility of human goodness being more prevalent than he believed.

"You became my proof, Herr von Kunst, that this goodness was possible, even in one the Maestro would find as the most unlikely." She paused again to fight the tears. Andre's confusion was now total. This confession of her fondness, her admiration, for him was a welcome surprise. Evidently, this admiration had ended.

"Herr von Kunst, I lost my parents very soon after your country invaded mine. The bitterness she fought so hard against, was, if unwillingly, forcing itself to the fore with her telling. My parents, knowing the danger facing them, had Herr Karpinski take me to England. I was never told the truth about my parents until today, after the visit to your gallery. Herr Karpinski told me that they had been murdered because they were considered to be worthless beings, not fit to live in the new world being born. They had committed no crimes, were guilty of no treason, but they were Jewish, they were cultural contaminants, there was no room for them or their kind."

Andre sat in total dismay; he tried to find adequate words of sympathy, yet was at a lost how this admitted tragedy affected him personally.

After the war ended, he had listened without much interest to the disclaimers of the people surrounding Hannelore and, by association, himself. The events revealed after the war as atrocities of the Reich were "gross exaggerations," they said.

What was beyond belief was the denial of Hannelore and her friends and their distorted justifications. They still held to their prejudices toward others of different cultures; what could he say now to Katya? Was it of any consolation that he, too, lost a parent? Would this be sufficient to have a shared sorrow? He knew there were to be no answers possible until what she saw in the picture that ripped open the wounds of the past was revealed.

"Herr von Kunst, while the horror of what happened to my parents, their untimely deaths, is hard to accept, what is to me the added horror is that your family contributed to their deaths."

Andre stared, stunned. He shook his head as the constriction in his chest took away speech. She looked directly into his eyes for the sign of guilt that would be there. His mouth opened, no words came. Katya, wondered, *Was this evidence of innocence? Or a mask for discovered guilt?*

The Maestro spoke, "Herr von Kunst, from the very first time that I met you in Mainz, the mention of your name brought back distressing memories and rekindled my hatred for your family that has never left my heart. Until today, I had no proof of what I saw with my own eyes one day long ago of your family's guilt in her parents,' my beloved friends, deaths. But this morning I have proof of their complicity. It is to be found on that easel standing now in your studio."

Andre could not believe this. His family? Murderers? How? His voice was a rasp, "Katya, Herr Karpinski, this I cannot accept. With all my heart I must refuse such an accusation against my parents. Yes, they were, I am, German, and with all the shame that we must accept for atrocities committed by criminal elements, we are not all criminals. Above all, I must swear to you that this cannot be true. You must explain to me exactly what you have seen that gives you the evidence of this crime."

The Maestro spoke again, "Herr von Kunst, until this morning I have tried to shield Katya from the truth about her parents' death. It was obvious to me that she was becoming attracted to you, and I wanted to avoid exactly what has now come to pass, the crushing truth of her parents' deaths and how misplaced was her affection for one such as you. You talk of proof? I was there in her parents' home and watched as the

Germans packed her father's priceless works of art into cartons clearly marked 'Von Kunst Gallery, Berlin.' But what proof could I offer and to whom could I go with this knowledge? My account without a witness would lead nowhere. I knew that. But today we have proof, a positive identification."

Andre was slowly trying to recover some composure. "Herr Karpinski, Katya, I do not doubt what Herr Karpinski said he saw. I see no reason why he would unjustly speak against us. However, that this picture is proof that works taken from Katya's home were sent here and my family was the recipient cannot be verified by this painting in question. This painting is only a copy, one of many of a very pleasant landscape of no special meaning. Far less value, I am sure, than those owned by Katya's family. I do not deny what you saw, but you must admit the conclusion you have drawn may be in error.

"During those terrible days, it may well have been that paintings of value were removed from danger and shipped to a safe place. It could well have been that, without any consent from my family, our gallery was temporarily used for storage by the government."

Katya listened intently. If what he said was true, why then did this frame remain here, but without the picture? Would it not have been passed on as he suggested? Although she would have liked to allow the possibility of what Andre said, her doubt had to remain. What the Maestro said next echoed her doubts.

The Maestro was undeterred. "Herr von Kunst, if what you suppose were true, would you then explain why evidence of what I saw, these objects, taken at that time would still be retained by your family? If all of these works were just awaiting transfer to a place other than here, why would this one have remained?"

Andre rose. "Katya, Herr Karpinski, please, let us go down to that picture. I need to know how this copy justifies your accusation."

He called Elsa, "Please, Elsa, call Hannelore and Otto to come with you to Otto's studio. My guest and I will be coming at once."

As they rose to go, Andre reached for Katya's hand; she didn't withdraw it.

"Katya, I can understand your suffering from what you have heard. Whatever transpired back then was unacceptable, but I know beyond any doubt that my parents were not involved, nor was I. But I must know the truth, that I am determined to do."

When they arrived downstairs, Elsa, Hannelore, and Otto were all standing by the painting. Hannelore's expression was clearly one of exasperation. Whatever Andre's reason for trying to calm this emotionally unbalanced girl and her unpleasant companion, it had nothing to do with her; she resented the intrusion.

Otto was again studying the picture with an uneasy feeling about the situation, a premonition of danger.

Elsa saw the look of distress on Andre's face as he held the hand of the lovely girl beside him. *No doubt he has a strong attraction for her*, she thought with a twinge of jealousy.

The Maestro said nothing; he waited for the feeble excuses that would follow what Katya would reveal. There was an awkward silence as they waited for this pale girl to explain the mystery of the painting. Without a word, she finally stepped forward and reverently with trembling hand touched the upper right corner of the frame. She kept it there as uncontrolled tears again swept down a sorrowful face.

Andre spoke first, "Katya, what is it, what does this mean, please!" Katya stepped back and still could not speak. The Maestro watched the extremely puzzled faces turning from the frame to Katya, to the Maestro, and to each other.

The Maestro's words came colder than a winter wind. "Herr von Kunst," the Maestro was fully prepared to enjoy the destruction of this young von Kunst in front of Katya, "would you be so kind as to count the grapes in the cluster that Fraulein Preznoski has just touched."

The Maestro's tone allowed nothing more than for Andre to step closer. "There are three," he said obediently.

The Maestro pointed to the opposite corner of the frame. "Please count the grapes in that cluster."

Andre said softly, "Five."

"You will note the remaining corners also have five grapes, only this has three," the Maestro emphasized.

At this point, Hannelore could no longer contain her anger. "Herr Karpinski, we are busy people, I have no idea how some missing grapes has anything to do with this gallery or the emotional reaction of your companion. The frame has evidently been slightly damaged, so slight that it was obviously overlooked. However, we often purchase entire collections at auctions or estate sales. Some of the pictures are worthy of resale, others are of no particular value, but the frames can be used, as this one, to frame better pictures or copies of works for resale. I am sure that is the case here. Whatever the cause of your young friend's strange reaction to this particular frame and its connection to her family, perhaps she would be so kind and explain so that we can end this matter now."

The Maestro turned to Katya. "Dear girl, I know the sorrow you must feel standing here and touching a frame that once graced the hall-way in your parents' home in Poland. It would be time to tell how you know this to be the one."

Otto froze. *Impossible*, he thought, glancing at Hannelore, who showed a face of almost contempt for the drama before her.

"Indeed, Fraulein Presnoski," the disdain in Hannelore's voice angered Andre, but he refrained from interrupting. "Do tell us how you can be so sure this is the one. Perhaps the similarity of this one to the one you remember from so long ago has confused you, understandably, of course."

Katya cast a defiant look at this unfeeling woman with her conde-scending tone. Hannnelore's manner so angered Katya that she found the courage to overcome any intimidation she felt. She wiped the last tear from her eye, glanced at Andre, and pointed to the corner of the frame with the missing grapes and began to speak in a steady, composed voice.

"One day, as a young girl, playing in my father's house, I climbed up onto a small table above which this frame hung holding another picture than this. I wanted to touch the grapes, they seemed so real to me. As I reached out and touched them, the table tilted and I fell, grasping the grapes that came off in my hand. My father came running hearing me fall. I was crying, not because I was hurt, but fearing punishment for breaking off the grapes. But my father, as usual, never meted out punishment for things unintended, if unwise. He picked me up, made sure I wasn't hurt, and told me to stop crying over a couple of unimportant grapes. Besides, he said he didn't think anyone would notice anyhow. Then he said that I must have really wanted those grapes for a little girl to take such a risk. I remember laughing and saying that I really thought they must be real and just wanted to touch them.

"My father said it really wouldn't be easy to put them back on, but perhaps he'd have someone try. So I gave them to him." She paused just long enough for Hannelore, with a slight but audible sniff of impatience, to interrupt.

"A touching story, of course. Since this happened long ago, it is reasonable for you to mistake it for the one you remember. Naturally, that memory could upset you, and I think your explanation why it did will be sufficient to excuse your unusual behavior. Now, I think its time we should all be back to the business of the day, thank you."

Katya looked straight at Hannelore, speaking with a firmness that caught all of their attention, "Frau Hasenfeld, this is the frame, and from what the Maestro has told me, it is the one taken from my home and brought here."

Otto, still apprehensive since hearing of Katya's first reaction to the painting, was now doubly sure that her accusation was accurate. He didn't remember this frame exactly, but he knew he recorded every picture and frame delivered to the gallery by description. If he went to his file, he would probably be able to verify her claim. He needn't have worried; what followed next made his research unnecessary.

Hannelore bristled at the nerve of this unwanted person daring to so openly challenge her. She spoke sharply, "Fraulein, excuse me, I have forgotten your name, but that doesn't matter, what matters is this unsupported accusation that we are in possession of a frame you think is the one taken from your home. I do not wish to be unkind, but unfortunately we have had from time to time people who have claimed ownership of works contained in our gallery. Their faulty memory, like yours, led them mistakenly to think the object to be the one lost. Of course, we were able to assure them they were not the works they thought them to be and like you they had no proof."

Katya's eyes lit with passion as she replied in a voice reflecting it, "My name is Katya Preznoski, a name I am proud of, it is a Polish name of long standing and this is the frame taken from the home of Doctor Professor Preznoski, my father."

Katya continued, "A few days later my father came to me with this necklace." She paused and reached for the necklace around her neck. She lifted it from her blouse, exposing a pendant with two golden grapes. She removed the grapes from the chain and went to the frame and held them to the exact place where they had once been. They fit perfectly and matched the others, although they were now gold, not the original light green of those remaining.

Katya resumed talking, "My father said that since I loved them so much to risk my life for them, he wanted me to have them forever as a remembrance of his love for me."

She stepped back from the frame. Otto, never one to underestimate Hannelore and her dedication to her cause, was not surprised at Hannelore's cavalier reaction to this inconvertible truth.

"Fraulein Presnoski, indeed this could well be the frame you remember. Quite a coincidence to be sure. But as I said, we purchase complete inventories and document piece by piece each objects, frames included, and an individual value is assigned to them. Herr Kranz keeps this information, and we will be glad to show you where this frame came from.

"Who was responsible for its removal from your father's home and what route it traveled before we acquired it will probably never be known. Those were troubled times. If indeed Herr Karpinski's recollection is correct, there may have been some justification for the action taken against your parents that neither you, at your young age, nor Herr Karpinski could have been aware of. You must accept that possibility; after all, your people were enemies of our nation, and treasonable acts deserved whatever punishment necessary to stop them."

Katya stared in disbelief. This woman was actually justifying the actions against her family, their death, inferring that it was a probable result of their treason. She struggled against a feeling arising in her heart that she had never felt before. Was this indeed the first awakening of the hatred the Maestro had assured her would come and what her father had told her never to allow?

Andre was completely at a loss as to how to respond, but he was incensed at Hannelore's unfeeling words to Katya. Objectively, Hannelore's explanation was plausible, but her manner of speaking absolutely inexcusable at a time like this.

Andre spoke firmly, "Fraulein Preznoski, I have no reason to doubt you or what Herr Karpinski has told you and I had no knowledge that this frame or any other object of that period came to this gallery for transfer. This is all new to me, but I intend to know more.

"Fraulein Preznoski, Katya, it is getting late and you have suffered much this day. From what has been said, much more needs to be done to determine exactly how we came by this frame. Herr Kranz, as he has already explained, will have a record of the transaction that brought us this frame. I must apologize for the words that should not have been spoken at such a time as this. I ask only that you allow me to have you returned to your hotel while Herr Kranz retrieves the documents we need. I need to know more myself, as to what transpired back then."

Although the Maestro protested they did not need the ride, in deference to Katya he accepted. He was somewhat taken aback at Andre's reaction and pledge to investigate further. He expected a far more vehement defense, somewhat more in line with his partner for whom the Maestro had no regard.

As they rode back to the hotel, Katya's emotions fought against the evidence of the frame and her heart's wish that all that Andre said about having no knowledge of the frame or how they obtained it was true. The attitude of his partner, her insinuation that whatever happened to her parents was evidently their own fault, burned in her heart. How could this woman be so cruel? Yet, she had to admit that the circumstances Hannelore described as to how the gallery obtained the frame could be true. But then how to reconcile this possibility with what the Maestro had seen that night in her home? She had to believe that Andre's promise to investigate further was proof of his innocence.

"Maestro," she turned to him imploringly, "we must give Herr Von Kunst the opportunity to study this matter, to offer proof that his gallery, his family, are innocent of any intended crime. Certainly, is it not possible that during those times that the gallery was simply a holding depot for such works as you saw and beyond the control of his family?"

The Maestro felt the urgency in her voice for the conformation he could not give.

"Katya, you heard at our dinner the opinion these people have for us, the disdain, the disregard. It was evident again today in the remarks of Frau Hasenfeld. She has no wish to see any further investigation into the matter. As far as she is concerned, it wouldn't matter if the family had been deliberately involved, it would be in her mind justified. However, to please you, I am willing to wait for whatever Herr von Kunst has to say, but I offer you little hope it will resolve anything."

The Maestro had a heavy heart. It was clear to him that Katya wanted to believe in the young German's innocence. Katya knew he had no witness, so she might believe he could have been mistaken as to the gallery's involvement if the invoices asked for proved the frame came from another source.

"Katya," he continued, "I do not even know what Herr von Kunst means by investigating further. He certainly has no interest in finding my claim true. Why should he bring reproach on his family and, of course, alienate you even more? You must not allow his professed innocence to influence you against me. I know what I saw and heard." Katya turned a pained but kind face to the Maestro as she reached for his hand.

"Dear Maestro, I never for a moment have doubted you, I believe you and what you saw. I only question that perhaps there is the possibility that what Frau Hasenfeld says is true. If so, it could explain how the frame came here from another source. I know you are anxious for me. I can understand your desire that I not be hurt, that my liking for Herr von Kunst will be the cause of that hurt. You are determined that I learn how evil this nation is and the von Kunst family in particular. Yes, the comments of that woman hurt, I could feel an emotion rising in me that I have never experienced before, and I feared it to be the beginning of the hate you so often express to me.

"Dear Maestro, whatever the outcome of this matter, even to the possible guilt of Herr von Kunst, I will not hate. I will forgive one and all, including his partner and her unfeeling remarks. I will make sure that only sorrow and disappointment remain of my now lost hope. Yes, I admit that I was sure I had found someone with whom I would have enjoyed being near and knowing more."

The Maestro shook his head; the more she spoke of the German, he knew there was more left unspoken.

CHAPTER 33

AFTER KATYA AND THE MAESTRO LEFT, ANDRE CALLED
Hannelore and Otto to meet him in the conference room. He arrived
before they did, deeply disturbed by what he had heard from the Maestro
and Katya's positive recognition of the frame. Without a doubt, it was
among those works the Maestro saw being removed from her home. The
question was, for him, whether or not it was specifically destined for his
gallery, or as Hannelore asserted, it was obtained from another source,
original source unknown. That question he had to have answered. There
was the possibility of Hannelore's explanation being correct, but somehow he could not accept that without the proof that he hoped Otto could
provide from his excellent detailed records.

His major concern now was having as much evidence as possible to
remove Katya's doubts. The Maestro's suspicions would remain regardless,
but Katya was his true concern. As these thoughts were going through
his mind, Hannelore entered the shared office space before Otto arrived.
She had met with Otto immediately after Katya left, ignoring Andre's
request to come at once.

"Otto," she had asked demandingly, "I certainly cannot recall every
item from memory that you seem to be able to do, but we need evidence
that we acquired this frame in the manner that I explained to Andre and
these two intruders of his."

Otto, before Andre's call, had quickly read the number on the back
of the frame and checked his registry. *Nummer* 667, *Renoir Bild Rauman*
668, *Beide Aus Poland Haus Nummer* 1266, *Linden Strasse, Preznoski.*

"Frau Hasenfeld, there is no question that the frame came directly here as the music director claims. We have the original painting stored." Otto waited.

Hannelore, with a face clouding with disgust, spat words of anger, "Herr Kranz, am I to believe that in all stupidity you allowed one of the articles that were delivered to us under the arrangements my father had made with the Kreis to be openly on display? You knew that these works were all to be kept secret and sold only under the strictest care. You knew that, did you not?"

Otto nodded, answering slowly, "Frau Hasenfeld, there is nothing more to say. I have often used frames from this collection for display purposes. Since the style is very common, I saw no risk in using them without their original painting. We never shipped originals with their frames because of the bulk and manner of packaging. You are aware that when these special paintings are shipped, they are disguised, as you know, as copies. We include them with shipments of copies to avoid undue attention. It has worked well. The frames have remained here. It seemed to be a waste not to use frames as I did this one. The chances of a discovery like this were never expected. You must admit it was hardly possible to think two missing grapes would have linked the gallery to your business in stolen art."

Hannelore could not contain her fury. "Otto, you idiot, by what right did you decide that you could use these frames, property of the Kreis, at your discretion? Again I resent your continual reference to these works as stolen. Now, you have no choice but to prepare an invoice showing this frame as among a group of works bought either from an estate sale or other common source or auction. Since it is a common frame, this should present no difficulty to you. Now prepare such an invoice at once, so that we can remove any possibility that this unbelievable stupidity of yours could lead to a discovery of our activities. These works are rightfully ours, regardless of how you and others of our socialistic government might regard them."

Otto felt the fury of her words, but they didn't have the effect she might have assumed. Otto made up his mind, now was the time. He nodded what Hannelore accepted as his agreement to do as he was told.

"Now," she said, still in an angry voice, "we must answer Andre's call, and I suspect he will be asking for evidence that does not exist. I'll go first and tell him that you are still researching your files. After a few minutes, you come in and say you need more time but you're sure you can find the needed invoice that will prove the gallery's innocence." She turned without a further word and went to meet Andre.

She was aware he would start questioning her about the comments she had made that he would consider uncalled for, as well as questions about the frame. Hannelore showed no sign of discomfort or worry, and before Andre could speak, she took the offensive.

"Andre, this has really gone too far; you almost gave the impression that you doubted my assertion that the frame came to us under normal circumstances. Then you added to this impression by telling these two foreigners that you wished to investigate the matter. Investigate, indeed, whatever do you mean! This just adds to the impression there might be something to hide. I know you probably thought I was being discourteous with my remarks to that emotionally distraught girl, but she needed to face reality. I am simply tired of these people and their constant whining about events they brought upon themselves."

She finished and sat down across form him. "Dear Andre," she spoke softly, reaching for his hand, "I am truly sorry that you are so upset by these events. Perhaps all the more so because these people to whom you have so kindly offered your hospitality and friendship are not cultured enough to appreciate it. You are being used, Andre, and I resent them for this as well."

Andre looked at her intensely; he knew her, and yet he did not. In a few short sentences, she had gone from justifying her unjustifiable behavior, chastising him for his attitude, castigating his friends and now, as his friend, proffering her sympathy for their ill treatment of him. Rather than spending time trying to understand her real motives, he was determined to satisfy in his own mind that whatever the Maestro had seen and now apparently confirmed by Katya was no more than one of those unfortunate tragedies of war. He intended to know that the circumstances that had deposited that frame in his gallery did not involve anyone with knowledge of its source.

Andre withdrew his hand from under hers, not quickly, but with a sigh of resignation as if there was going to be no satisfactory resolution for anyone. A light knock on the door announced Otto's arrival.

"Otto," Andre asked quickly, "have you had time to locate the invoice for the frame?" Otto shook his head. "Herr von Kunst," never in Hannelore's presence did he call him Andre, although Andre had asked him to, "I'm sure I have the record, but I assume it is no recent purchase so it will take a little time to trace it back. If it was a bulk purchase, I'll need to find it on what usually is a fairly long list of items."

Andre nodded his understanding. "Well then, please do so as quickly as possible, I am afraid without proof, Fraulein Preznoski will remain convinced my family was well aware of the source of this frame as her companion has avowed."

Hannelore arose to go, touching Andre lightly on his shoulder. "Andre, I'm sure our records will prove we had nothing to do with the matter. I would hope that once that has been established, your two guests will offer apologies for the unnecessary turmoil they have caused and remove themselves from our lives permanently!"

Otto's detest for Hannelore was now so complete that he cared not for his own safety, but was determined to bring her and the Kreis down without jeopardy to Andre and his mother. He never doubted for a moment that the Kreis would not allow anything to stand in the way of achieving their goals of a resurrected Germany. The profits from their trade in stolen works were needed for this end. Anything he did to cause the end to this business was to imperil his own and other lives as well. Would it, on second thought, be better to produce the lie she wanted? The second thought was only for a moment; he knew what he must do.

Otto stood. "I must get started, but it shouldn't take long."

He quickly departed, but Hannelore caught a glimpse of a face that disquieted her…was Otto smiling? As she started for the door, she turned again to offer an apology to Andre for this trivia that had so disturbed him.

Andre started, "Trivia? Hannelore, how can you be so callused? Even if our gallery is proved innocent, can you so easily dismiss from your mind the loss of her home, her parents, and the added insult of what Herr Karpinski saw, a household stripped of its private possessions, as mere trivia?"

Hannelore, with a tone of resignation, spoke sadly, "Andre, we have discussed many times and just as many times been unable to reconcile our feelings about past events; however, this inability has never been so strong that we could not set the differences aside for the most part and continue in an amiable manner until now. I believe I have shown a willingness, most of the time, to not let these differences interfere with a closeness we both enjoyed." The last was said with an unmistakable sadness.

"It is very apparent, Andre, that this young girl has had a very strong influence on you. I confess to be somewhat of hurt over this."

Andre felt a tinge of remorse. The beautiful woman before him, as desirable as she could be at times, was more remote from him now as never before. Her recent attitude toward Katya was inexcusable. He couldn't easily forgive this behavior toward Katya, whom he had come to not only admire but perhaps had allowed an even deeper affection to develop that he was unprepared to admit.

Katya evidenced a spiritual quality beyond her physical beauty, a quality that was never a part of Hannelore. Andre was now, more than ever, aware that this failing in Hannelore was of more importance to him than her intelligence and physical beauty. He knew this lack on her part, so much in contrast to that same spiritual abundance found in Katya, confirmed his conviction that a stronger relationship with Hannelore was never going to be possible. He knew that he could not embrace temporal qualities without the eternal ones.

"Hannelore," he began haltingly, "we have, as you say, for the most part been able to conduct ourselves and the business quite successfully in spite of these differences. Until now I have been able to regard those differences as inconsequential, if annoying, but tolerable as long as they were just expressions of misguided thinking."

"Until now?" broke in Hannelore.

"Yes, Hannelore, I have deliberately overlooked, or worse, ignored what I should have protested against more emphatically. It was the evidence of a deep seated and indefensible placing of human lives in categories. How twisted to determine these categories based on their value according to standards established by minds infected by a pernicious racial bias."

Hannelore stared at Andre as she said, "What a horrible thing to say, to imply that my friends and I have 'infected minds.' You dare call us mentally warped?" Andre knew there was no retracting his words; he had to speak his heart.

"I suppose that does explain it all, Hannelore, you have summed it up quite well."

Hannelore fought for composure; she rose again from the seat she had retaken after Otto left.

"Andre, I am going to my apartment. I am truly sorry that we have come to this point in our relationship. It seems irreconcilable. Life isn't always kind, but we mustn't let personal feelings interfere with facing certain realities when justice demands it. Andre, the rightness of my cause, at the cost of your friendship, compels me to follow my convictions." Hannelore turned and left. His phone rang; it was Otto.

"Andre, I must see you, but later tonight after Hannelore has retired."

Andre sensed the urgency in his voice. "Of course Otto, have you found what we need in your records?"

"Yes, Andre, yes I have, but I need to see you alone." Andre wanted to ask more, but Otto quickly said, "Please don't ask me for anything more until I see you. Call me when you are sure we won't be interrupted." Andre agreed and laid the receiver down as questions crowded into his mind.

After Hannelore left, Otto went straight to his studio and applied light pressure to a wall panel that slid to the right, revealing a narrow passage into a small room. Here he had stored all the transactions that had to do with the Kreis from the beginning. The invoices that Hannelore had without questioning passed on to him according to her father's instructions contained the damning information of their illegal trade. Otto quickly pulled the folder under slot number 667/668 and returned to his desk. As he had many times before, he looked at the picture of Karl and himself in their WWI uniforms.

"Yes, kommerad, the time has come, there is no other way to stop these years of betrayal. I cannot deliberately continue this deception by lying to Andre. I am not forging a document that will only allow Hannelore and her nefarious friends to continue their treasonable trade." He bowed his head; he knew that Andre must believe him and act quickly before the Kreis could act.

Andre called the hotel, the Maestro answered coolly. "Herr Karpinski," Andre said, "I just want you to know that I will have the answer you need to your questions by tomorrow morning. I would like to bring that information to you in person. You must understand my personal sorrow at the events that have caused Fraulein Presnoski such pain. I do not doubt that you observed an unfortunate and tragic event at her former home and my colleague, Herr Kranz, has told me he has the records we need and will be bringing them to me later this evening. I want to share these with you and Fraulein Preznoski in person. Will you tell me what would be a convenient time for you?"

The Maestro paused; he wanted to say that whatever documents Herr von Kunst provided would undoubtedly exonerate his family, and the Maestro would have no way to prove their validity. However, he had no choice for Katya's sake other than to say that Andre should call around nine in the morning. He wanted to be sure Katya's sleep was not disturbed. He wanted to be sure she had as much rest as she needed; he then hung up.

Katya was just about to retire but overheard the Maestro's conversation.

"Maestro, did Andre say what he was going to call us about tomorrow?"

"Katya, evidently he has found whatever documentation he needed to prove to us the innocence of his family. You must realize, Katya, that whatever he produces, we can never verify. I'll admit we probably have no choice but to let him present what he has. My deeply felt advice is that we leave this place regardless of evidence that could easily have been contrived. Katya, you have heard and seen enough to know that I am right, regardless of your personal wish to have it be otherwise."

Katya nodded; he was right. She felt in her heart that Andre was the kind soul she found him to be, but the circumstances surrounding all that had happened, regardless of what could or could not be proven, she would never feel at home here, for there were too many Hannelores. She would try and place in her memory the best of what had happened. Those moments of closeness she had felt when she was with Andre were genuine. The guilt, or lack of it, made no difference to her regarding his family, she knew he was innocent. Yes, better to leave now before any more hurt occurred.

CHAPTER 34

IT WAS LATE WHEN OTTO, RESPONDING TO ANDRE'S
request, entered with a light knock. He declined the seat Andre offered.
"Andre, before I tell you what I must, please come with me, I have something to show you." He turned to go and Andre had little choice but to
follow.

They descended to the gallery floor and then into Otto's studio.
Without a word, Otto went over to a mural on the far wall of the studio
and reached up to touch a door of a small chapel. He then turned and
started for the door but paused to pick up the picture of him and Andre's
father.

He looked at it and speaking softly, as if no one else were around,
said, " Dear kommerad, what I am about to do should have been done
so long ago, but I saw no way without endangering those you and I have
loved. Please forgive me if I failed to do earlier what you would have
wished."

Setting the picture down, he continued out of the studio, beckoning
Andre to follow. They went down the narrow corridor leading to the side
door exit and when Otto stopped, Andre waited expectantly for Otto
to open the door. Instead, Otto turned to the opposite wall and reached
up to turn the overhead light fixture to the right. Andre watched fascinated as a panel in the wall slid open, revealing a descending staircase.
Otto motioned for Andre to follow. At the bottom of the stairway Otto
opened a door into a rather small room with nothing much in it. Andre
looked questioningly at Otto but said nothing.

Otto spoke, "Do you remember, Andre, after the war, the Allies sent inspectors to this and other galleries looking for stolen art?" Andre nodded vaguely remembering the visits, but as a young teenager he didn't pay much attention to them, he was just glad the war was over.

"In order to allay any suspicion that we had anything to hide, I showed the inspectors the passageway to this room explaining that we used it to store works of art for safekeeping. This show of honesty and our open records seemed to satisfy them and they searched no further. If they had, this gallery would have suffered a very different fate."

Otto, reaching almost to the ceiling, pressed an invisible switch. The entire wall pivoted open. Andre gazed in bewildered amazement as a soft light bathed row after row of shrouded objects rising like tombstones before him.

"Otto, what is the meaning of this, I never knew such a room existed. What are these covered objects?"

Otto didn't answer but stepped into the room and approached the nearest object, gently lifting its cover. Andre stared, and his trained eye immediately recognized a famous work long since considered lost or destroyed during the war. He was stunned. With a sinking heart, he knew what he was seeing was evidence of terrible crimes, and his family was guilty of them. The Maestro was right.

"Otto, before you try and explain to me, an explanation I expect to be the truth and of little comfort to me, tell me, does Hannelore know of this?"

The downcast look of sorrow that had not left his face since he had entered Andre's apartment was answer enough as he nodded yes.

"Otto," said Andre slowly, shaking his head in disbelief, "I need to know what all this means. Evidently, you and Hannelore have been willing accomplices in this, as well as my family and hers. And what about the comment you made about a danger to 'loved ones'?" Otto could not speak as he saw the look of betrayal come to Andre's face.

Andre spoke softly, "Otto, whatever the truth, I must hear it. Why have you and Hannelore kept this from me all these years? I suspect it is because you both know I would never have allowed this. Perhaps Hannelore has in her twisted mind a rationale that justifies these treasures being here. I have heard her comments about such objects belonging to her country by right of conquest, but you, Otto, but from you I would never expect such behavior, an acceptance of such crimes."

Andre stared again at the shrouded rows and the horror they represented. Otto, do we still have the original picture that was in the frame Katya saw?"

Otto whispered, "Yes." Then, gaining some courage, he continued, "Andre, the story I have to tell has been withheld from you because of my fear of the consequences that would follow and not an ungrounded fear. Hannelore herself does not know the real reason for my being an accomplice to this evil trade."

Otto paused. Andre sensed there was much more to hear. Before Otto could continue, Andre said, "Otto, come, we must go to my apartment and decide what is to be done, and I want a complete explanation. You have some very important things to tell me before the sun rises on a very different day in my life."

After they entered Andre's apartment, he offered Otto a brandy, gratefully accepted. Sipping it slowly, he looked at the log fire, saying nothing at first. Andre studied the old man bent with age, holding his glass between two veined hands that were instruments of a dying art. Hands that had contributed in no small way to the success of the gallery's legitimate business as well as the reprehensible trade of the Kreis. He had known Otto from his earliest childhood, had listened with fascination the story of how his father had rescued Otto from certain death in that early war. Now to learn that Otto had entered into this nefarious trade that his father would never have condoned? Could there be a valid reason for his betrayal?

He waited patiently for Otto to speak; he knew the old man was deep in thought. Andre himself was struggling to comprehend how Hannelore could have been so influenced by her father and his friends that she could have betrayed him so completely. The gallery would be ruined when the truth of these transactions was revealed, as they had to be. *Hannelore, Hannelore, how could you!* Andre sat back in his chair and joined in watching the dancing flames. Finally, Otto raised his head and extended his glass for Andre to replenish.

"Andre, what I need to tell you will hopefully bring some clarity to my behavior and remove any doubt about my loyalty to you and your mother."

"Otto, I am ready to listen."

Otto began, "Hannelore thinks it is a threat the Kreis made against my life that has kept me loyal to them. Andre, that threat was of no consequence."

Andre was puzzled. "What then, Otto, could have induced you to cooperate in a trade you knew to be illegal?"

"Andre, what is important right now is for you to make sure the authorities move quickly to apprehend these criminals based upon what you have seen and my testimony. There are literally millions of dollars in illegally taken artwork stored here. Unfortunately, many have already been sold to private collectors, primarily in the U.S., through the agent that Hannelore set up in New York for that purpose. The money raised is for use in supporting the election of representatives to the government that are sympathetic with their goals. The Kreis and Hannelore envisioned a new Germany, perhaps not militarily superior, but so strong politically and economically that their lost military objectives would be achieved by other means."

Andre could hardly believe what Otto was saying about Hannelore being actively involved. Regardless of her political and racist opinions that she never was shy in sharing, it was inconceivable that she was an active participant in this trade. Inconceivable that she would use the gallery as a conduit to achieve ill-conceived goals. And what of his own family's involvement? They must have known.

"Otto, what about the reason you were a part of this?" Otto stared into the fire again.

"Andre, let me tell you how it all began. Many years ago, while Germany was invading these neighboring countries and rounding up the so-called undesirables in our own country, Hannelore's father devised a plan to acquire the works of art that were taken from the homes of these unfortunate people, from museums and from any source. He conspired with his cronies in the government, primarily those you now know as the Kreis, to set up a procedure to route all these confiscated works to this gallery."

Andre broke in, "Otto, how could my father have condoned this? It is against all that I remember of his attitude toward what was happening in Germany. He was even opposed to my joining the *Jugend Korps*."

"Andre," Otto labored to talk, "there is a terrible truth to be told; first, let me go back to the beginning regarding your father. Hannelore's father, Heinz, was able to convince your father by showing him forged documents that many of these works were being stored at the request of residents for safekeeping or had been sold outright to the gallery.

"Your father accepted this for a while but after trying personally to contact some of these customers to thank them for their trust and business, he could not locate them. When he inquired as to their whereabouts, neighbors gave vague or conflicting answers out of fear of any involvement of course. When he told Heinz of his concerns, Heinz said that these people had simply moved away because of the political unrest, and that was the reason the pictures were given for safekeeping. Heinz was clever enough, but your father continued to voice concerns about his inability to find any of these customers.

"Then, when Heinz came to him with plans to expand storage space, the space you have just seen, your father said it was inconceivable that so many works would be coming to the gallery for the reasons Heinz gave. Heinz told him that the government was going to use the gallery for storage of paintings taken from conquered lands, your father protested that he would never allow his gallery to be used for such a purpose."

Here Otto paused and looked at Andre. The anguish shown on his face instantly reminded Andre of that moment long ago when the news of his father's death reached them. Although the officer who brought the news came with a personal letter of commendation from the *Fuhrer*, Otto had left the room with much that same expression as now. Andre had never forgotten it. He had always wondered but never asked.

With a great effort to control himself, Otto began, "Andre, what I am telling you will require immediate involvement of the police. They must act at once to apprehend all who are involved, Andre, that includes Hannelore and, of course, me. There is yet more to tell."

Andre was trying desperately to comprehend what Otto was saying, and what more could there possibly be to tell?

"Otto, this is beyond what I could ever have imagined, the thought of my father being involved with anything as reprehensible as this is unthinkable."

Otto's voice became almost inaudible, "Andre, your father was killed because Heinz knew he was a danger to their plans."

Andre drew back. "Otto, what are you saying, what did my father's partner have to do with his death? My father died in battle, didn't he?" Otto's look of sadness pierced Andre's heart. Did this mean that Hannelore, his partner for all these years, had been an accomplice to his father's death as well?

He had to ask, "Otto, does Hannelore know of her father's involvement in my father's death? And if he died in battle, how could Heinz have been responsible? Otto, this is all too hard to understand, to even believe, although I have to believe you, but Hannelore?"

Otto quickly replied, "No, Andre, while Hannelore unfortunately came under the spell of her father's teachings and those of his cronies after his death, they were careful not to reveal to her his part in your father's death. Rightly so, they were afraid that Hannelore as much out of her love for you, yes, Andre, in some strange way she does love you, it was their fear that even she would not accept that her father could have done such an evil thing. There was the possibility that she would turn on them, accusing them of lying about her father and refusing to cooperate further.

"Hannelore is an idealist, she doesn't realize the deadly consequences of blind idealism. I loved Hannelore as a child, but as she grew older, I could not understand how this beautiful, intelligent creature evolved into such a rabid devotee of a lost cause. How could she accept the justification that what the Kreis was doing was righteous, just recompense for crimes against Germany? She embraced totally the concept that others were inferior to the 'super race.' Aryan superiority needed to be preserved, lesser races legitimately excluded, or worse, exterminated. As I watched this transition in her, I came to dislike her intensely and even more because of her betrayal of your trust.

"Now, to answer your question as to how Heinz could have been directly responsible, it involves my reason for being a part of this evil." Again Otto paused, the memories too painful. How would Andre react to the betrayal he was about to reveal? Finally, he drew a deep breath and continued, "I was working late one night in my studio, in the back room where I worked on smaller objects, and was not readily visible to anyone who didn't know I was there. I finished what I was doing, turned out the work light, and rose to go. Just as I stood, I heard voices coming from Heinz's office. I didn't know he was even here late as it was, so I was curious. I approached his half-open door and when I saw the uniform of a Gestapo officer standing with his back to me, I stopped and listened to them talking. Heinz was very agitated. What I heard so startled me that I stepped back and knocked over a small display stand. The noise brought Heinz and the officer out of the office.

"Heinz was furious and could tell from the look on my face that I had heard him tell the officer to arrange for your father's induction into the army. Heinz had early on through his connections received military exemptions for himself and your father. Now that he was sure your father was going to investigate further the source of artworks being deposited at the gallery, Heinz had to avoid this at all cost.

"Heinz then told the officer that Karl had to be eliminated, yet in a way to avoid any suspicion of foul play. Karl was too popular to risk scandal. He had a plan."

Otto could not stop the tears. Andre waited, too stunned to talk. Gaining composure, Otto struggled to continue as the weight of suppressed memories burdened his speech.

"Heinz then told the officer that even though your father had an exemption from service, the need was now to remove him. 'Naturally,' said Heinz, 'the good citizen that he is, he will comply with a request from the army to join again, due to special needs. Unfortunately after a short time he will give his life for his country, a fallen hero for the Fatherland. I am sure that can be arranged very conveniently, right?' Obergruppenfuher Kleinschmidt had replied quickly, 'Of course.'"

Andre stared at the old man. "But, Otto, why didn't you say something, you could have prevented my father's death!"

Otto looked up, shaking, a tear-stained face spoke brokenly, "Andre, you do not understand how evil they were. Naturally, I could not believe what I heard. I told Heinz that his betrayal of a friend could not be allowed, and I would tell Karl at once.

"Heinz laughed at me, then said, 'I would advise you, Herr Kranz, to be careful.'

We went into the office, and Herr Hasenfeld called Herr von Linglesdorf on the phone. Heinz told him what had happened and asked his advice on what to do with me. Evidently, von Linglesdorf dissuaded Herr Hasenfeld from taking any harmful action against me; he had a better plan.

"Herr Hasenfeld hung up smiling at me. 'Herr Kranz, Herr von Linglesdorf has wisely reminded me that you are too valuable an asset to dispose of as I would have. He has a better suggestion, we need to assure that we obtain your services for the future.'

"I told Herr Hasenfeld that his betrayal of Herr von Kunst was so evil that I would prefer death rather than to serve him. At this he laughed and said he believed me, but they did need my talent. Then Heinz spoke so softly that I had to strain to hear him and the soft tone carried a deadly earnestness that gave little doubt as to his intent to make sure I was listening.

'Herr Kranz, Herr von Kunst has unfortunately demonstrated once too often his traitorous tendencies toward the Third Reich. I have no ill will toward him, but my loyalty must first be to my country regardless of any other consideration. Should my wife behave in this same way, I would not hesitate to do with her what must be done with Herr von Kunst.

"'As you know, this gallery has been designated as the depository for the works of art that have been rightfully confiscated from families or galleries that have come under the control of our country. However, this is a highly confidential undertaking that requires absolute secrecy. Those who know of this undertaking are certain members of the Ministry of Culture; it is not for public knowledge.

"'We are planning to establish a channel of distribution that, after the war, will be used to sell these 'lost' works to private investors. They will be willing to pay considerable sums for them.

"'Herr Kranz, your skills of restoration and copying ability will be needed in cataloging, evaluation, and preserving these works of art. Your service, when the time comes, will also be needed in disposing of these works in a manner that arouses no suspicion as to how they were acquired.'"

Otto continued, "Andre, I stared in disbelief, and I told them, 'Never, never will I betray Herr von Kunst or work for you in any capacity. He has only shown me kindness. To be a part of this conspiracy is unthinkable.'

"Herr Hasenfeld then said in a voice that fully conveyed his conviction, 'You do not understand who the betrayer was, the seriousness of the matter, and how necessary to use whatever means at hand to accomplish our goals. It will only take a word from me, and not only will Karl be eliminated, but his wife, his son, and you will be accused and convicted of treason. The consequences will be fast and effective. I suggest you rethink your threat. Otherwise, we could arrest both Andre and his mother as accomplices in Herr von Kunst's betrayal. You do know the penalty for treason, don't you?'

"He looked directly at me and then at SS Kleinschmidt, who smiled at my look of open revulsion. I remember well the chill that wrapped itself around me like a shroud as I realized the full impact of Herr Hasenfield's threats."

"Heinz continued. ' Now, we are going to need your good services and expertise to continue our business. However we will not hesitate to find a replacement for you if we have to, and rest assured any attempt on your part to expose us will result in the unfortunate circumstances for Andre and his mother I have referred to. Is that understood?'

With that Heinz told me to go about my business and not to forget his warning. SS Kleinschmidt added his assurance that whatever Herr Hasenfeld had promised, it would be followed explicitly."

Andre looked again at the old man. What a horrible dilemma for him. Permit the sacrifice of his closest friend in exchange for saving the lives of his wife and son. Yet, in reality, they would not have permitted his father to live regardless.

"Otto," the old man raised his head as Andre spoke, "why now, what has happened to make you change your mind and accordingly, if what you fear is true, my mother and I as well as you are in danger, are we not?"

"Yes, we are, but I finally came to the decision that I could initiate an investigation without implicating any of us. It would result in the apprehension of these criminals before they could act. That's why I deliberately substituted a copy for the original picture. It has caused the investigation I had hoped for. It would be hard for the Kreis to risk retaliation based on what could conceivably be an honest mistake. I hoped they would decide I was not intending to betray them, the risk of acting against you too great.

"However, that you were so willing to indemnify the loss defeated my whole purpose. It now appeared there would be no further investigation. In fact, had it not been for the Polish girl, Katya, identifying the frame, which led to Hannelore's demand that I create a false invoice, the crisis would have passed. Actually, Andre, I could produce that invoice; the matter would then be settled and the gallery saved."

Andre shook his head. "Otto, this has to end, regardless of the consequences. I am responsible for never having had the interest in being more involved in the business side of the gallery. Hannelore was so efficient, there was no need, but that is no excuse. And now you tell me that Hannelore has actually asked you to prepare a false invoice to prove our innocence?"

Otto nodded. "Andre, that was impossible for me to do. Admittedly, I kept the knowledge of your father's death from you for the reasons I have said; however, to directly deceive you, as Hannelore wanted, was impossible for me. This command of hers to prepare a false receipt proving the frame came to us by a legitimate purchase convinced me I had to act regardless of the risk.

"Andre, all that I have told you must be brought to the attention of the police at once. You are a good friend of Herr Dietz, the chief inspector; we must be before him the first thing tomorrow, before I have to answer to Hannelore. I doubt she will accept excuses for any further delay in having that invoice. Will it be possible to see him at once?"

Andre was trying to assemble his thoughts, trying to organize them into a rational pattern of action. His first concern was for Katya; there was no avoiding the truth that his gallery, if not himself, was guilty of acquiring stolen works of art. The realization that many of these works came from homes whose owners were doomed to pay with their lives, like Katya's parents, crushed Andre's conscience.

"Otto, there is no doubt that going to the authorities will put this gallery out of business. I have no choice but to either accept that fact or conspire with Hannelore and allow you to present a false invoice. I don't doubt that the invoice will be accepted as being authentic. Together with the reputation of the gallery, it will add much credibility to Hannelore's assumptions that the gallery came into possession of the frame by legitimate means. The Maestro may have his suspicions, but he has no proof to back his claims. I am sure that he will not give up trying to influence Katya against me, a pressure she does not deserve. Of course, admitting to this crime will make any further pressure from the Maestro unnecessary. There really isn't a choice is there, Otto?"

The old man seemed to have aged even more as he told his sad story and now listened with a heavy heart to Andre. He had no doubt what Andre would do, but he resolved to make sure that the blame would fall on he and Hannelore and not Andre.

Otto shook his head; he knew there was no other choice.

"Otto, you said the original painting is still in our possession." Otto nodded. "I want you to take the frame, put the original painting back in it, and wrap it carefully. Please do that as soon as we get back from our visit to Herr Dietz. While it is too late tonight to contact him, I am sure he will make time for us as soon as I call him tomorrow."

"Andre," Otto smiled sadly, "do you really think I'll be coming back to the gallery with you? After what we have to say, it is possible neither of us will be back."

Andre shook his head. "I know Hans well. My word will be sufficient to assure him of our cooperation in helping him round up the perpetrators. It will just be you and I who go to Hans. Hannelore must not know of this visit, I cannot trust her, how sad to have to say that, how sad. Well, Otto, there is nothing more we can do tonight. Let's get some rest if that's possible."

Otto looked at the young man he loved so much; perhaps he should have kept the secret, it would have been so easy to have done so; a simple forged document and all would have gone on as before. Yet there was no turning back, this had to end.

"Andre," Otto said as he rose to go, "you cannot blame yourself. The sacrifice of your father and my testimony will surely stand well for you. Hannelore, the Kreis, and, of course, myself are the guilty ones. I can assure you that will be the revealed truth. I don't expect to sleep much. I'm going to pack the picture now and put it in a safe place in my studio. Please call me as soon as you know when we can go to Herr Dietz."

"Really, Otto, how could they think that they actually could find support in this day and age for such bizarre goals? No one in present-day Germany would embrace again the philosophy that almost destroyed us forever as a nation. We have learned a hard lesson, Otto. We are proud to have overcome those past sins and become a symbol of democracy."

"Andre," Otto shook his head, "I do not believe for a moment that the numbers who would embrace this idiocy are large, but remember, Andre, what unbelievable power the Third Reich secured for itself without ever having the majority of the people behind them. Even the election of that maniac was achieved with barely much above thirty percent of the vote. People can convince themselves of anything that will feed their bellies or further their advancement if at the cost of others.

"Sorry, Andre, this holds true today and, believe me, not just in Germany alone. There are those who will sacrifice every vestige of a morality if they are offered a means of attaining selfish desires, or promises of food if they are hungry, a roof if they are wet."

Andre's face mirrored the anguish of his soul. "Otto, how was it possible for all of this to go unnoticed by me? I failed to realize that their impassioned hatred for others, their disdain for all people that they believed to be their inferiors was not just idle talk."

"You must realize, Andre, that it was planned from the start that you would not be involved in the business of the gallery, so how could you know?" In the silence that followed, a question that could not be answered, Otto reached a reassuring hand to rest on Andre's shoulder.

Finally, Andre said, "Otto, tomorrow will be a day never to be forgotten. I doubt either of us will sleep well tonight, but we must rest. As soon as we are finished with Herr Dietz, I must reach Katya and the Maestro as well as the two investigators from New York. It is clear that the gallery is guilty; they need to know that. My offer to purchase back that one painting will pale in the light of the liability I face regarding all the other illegal transactions. The authorities will need help from your records, Otto, to locate the persons who purchased these works of art."

Otto nodded. "I'll do all that I can, Andre, but the actual transactions that were carried out in the U.S. were kept there, no doubt in a secret lock box. My records will reflect the source of our entire inventory and exactly which ones were shipped to New York while Hannelore handled all the financial transactions through her bank connections. The New York investigators will have to pursue that through authorities there.

"Well, as you said, Andre, tomorrow will be a day not to be forgotten. I'll leave you now to attend to the painting you want wrapped." As he rose to go, his lined and aged face showed both the strain of events, but also a look of long-awaited peace.

After Otto left, Andre went to the office he shared with Hannelore. He turned on the light and walked over to stand in front of the full-sized portrait of a beautiful, young, uniformed Aryan girl smiling in jubilation as she saw a future filled with promise.

Tomorrow he would ask his friend, Hans Dietz, head of Berlin's criminal investigation department, for an immediate audience. He would bring all the names of the Kreis members. Otto's warning was clear; any of the plotters would be capable of carrying out their threats against Otto, himself, or his mother if they thought it would prevent the discovery of their business.

"Hannelore, how could this be?" he asked the smiling girl out loud. Yet thinking back on the many discussions, disagreements, and comments from the Kreis, he knew 'how this could be.' He sat down in the chair that had been his father's. From sheer emotional exhaustion, he sank into a restless slumber filled with a montage of strange images. One of them was of marching men under flying banners with the French tri-color but with a black swastika in the center; the leader was a half-bare young girl with blonde hair, wearing the brown Maidenkorp uniform.

The telephone's ring broke his uneasy slumber. Elsa's warm voice asked, "Kaffee, Andre?" Her cheerful voice jolted him into awareness that for everyone but he and Otto, it was the start of a normal day. His first impulse was to say, "No, thank you." He hadn't even had time for his wakeup shower and felt a bit groggy from his troubled sleep; however, the pleasing moments spent with her each morning over coffee always gave his day a better start. Elsa always came with a winning smile, never out of sorts, and her distinct air of serenity seemed to declare her prepared-ness to accept whatever life would bring. He told Elsa coffee would be appreciated.

He felt that today he needed her presence as much as ever before. Hannelore had said upon leaving last night that if Andre didn't mind, she would probably not join him for their usual early morning briefing. Perhaps later in the morning would be acceptable. As far as Hannelore was concerned, Otto's producing the forged receipt would put the matter to rest. Andre now thought, *Yes, Hannelore, later in the morning will be just fine, by then I will have had time to visit with Hans.* Elsa arrived with the coffee; she couldn't help but notice that Andre had evidently just awak-ened from sleeping in his chair.

"Andre, did you sleep all night there? My goodness, that can't have been very comfortable! You must still be tired. I know it was a very tax-ing day for you and I truly am sorry for your young friend's discomfort. Indeed it would be painful to have such sorrow-filled memories brought back so unexpectedly, I feel sorry for her, I do."

Andre could only nod. He knew there would be a different a reac-tion from Elsa compared to Hannelore, who no doubt actually enjoyed Katya's grief and felt it well deserved. Andre motioned Elsa to take her usual seat.

Elsa was curious as she sat down and poured his cup of coffee. This was not the usual Andre with the bright morning greeting she loved to hear. She looked at him closely; there was no escaping the new lines that had seemingly formed overnight under tired eyes. She did not often see the stubble of beard. She felt a tinge of fear that something was seriously troubling Andre. She refrained from asking questions; better to let him speak when he was ready.

Andre watched as she poured the rich coffee into the china cup and extended it with her delicate hand, touching his briefly. Her smile was bright; she didn't want her consternation to be obvious. Andre appreciated her show of warmth and after a few sips from his cup spoke, "Elsa, don't be in a hurry to rush downstairs. Hannelore won't be coming in until later this morning." Elsa was delighted; any extra time with Andre she accepted gratefully. He watched as the image of the dark haired Polish violinist seemed to appear beside her. Elsa saw his gaze was directed at first to the empty couch beside her and then toward the portrait of the beautiful blonde hanging on the opposite wall. She was apprehensive; she knew that something serious was troubling him as he again fell into silence.

Hannelore, Elsa, Katya; of the three he knew Hannelore the longest, understood her the least. Elsa he had known for several years, always impressed by her steady presence. Andre always marveled at her graceful manner in greeting people and her ability to quickly put them at ease. He reflected on the many pleasant evenings spent with her at the theater or dinner. He knew she enjoyed being with him; yet neither had shown an interest in deepening this mutual affection any further. *Was this by a silent, mutual consent?* each asked themselves privately, afraid of the answer.

Katya, known for only a short time, yet he had to admit his fascination with her had increased, not diminished, with each occasion they met. He wanted to know more of her, to understand her more, her wishes, and her desires; in light of what he had learned from Otto, that prospect was fading fast.

Elsa watched and knew his gaze was fixed on Hannelore's picture. How could she deny the feeling of jealousy, no matter how unjust? Andre had never given her reason to believe he considered her as more than a good friend. She recalled the conversation she had had with Otto and her admission to him of her attraction for Andre. She remembered also that Otto could give her no real reason to believe that Andre reciprocated in any way other than as a good friend.

She had realistically given up any hope that he would feel any differently; the young girl in the portrait was too formidable an opponent, or perhaps it was now the intriguing violinist. Although Andre's acquaintance with the dark-haired beauty from Poland had been for only a short time, he was impressed enough to have invited her to Berlin. *Perhaps,* thought Elsa, *Hannelore is not as invincible as I had assumed.*

Suddenly turning to Elsa, Andre realized with some guilt that she must have noticed his fixed gaze at the portrait.

"Elsa, forgive me, I guess recent events have been a bit distracting."

Elsa ventured a soft, "I know," and said no more.

Andre was silent for a few more minutes, silently sipping his coffee that Elsa replenished without a word. She sensed again he was troubled but refrained from any questioning.

He looked at her and, more as a statement than a question, said, "Elsa, you have been with the gallery ever since you graduated from the university, haven't you? I am so pleased that you have stayed these years, you have added much to our success. I do hope you have been happy here."

His tone disquieted her; the "have been" seemed to indicate a possible ending, no encouraging "and you always will be" followed. What was the reason for his present mood? It was so unlike him.

"Andre," she spoke with lightness in her voice. She hoped it would help relieve the increasing concerns she was feeling. "Ever since that first day I came for the interview and was so surprised that you actually hired me before I could leave gave me a confidence I have never lost. You have been a source of inspiration to me, and my commitment has been to never let you down. I couldn't imagine a position that could have given me more joy than I have experienced working here. You have been so kind and generous."

Andre couldn't help but notice the omission of Hannelore's name in her kind remarks although she would have no reason to include her; Hannelore had never been overly friendly to Elsa from the start. They sat a while longer drinking their coffee and enjoying the small pastries Elsa had always included, avoiding the danish that was Hannelore's favorite. If Hannelore appreciated the coffee and special attention, she never said so.

Andre remained silent as a river of memories carried him back looking for tell-tale signs that would have alerted him to Hannelore's perfidy. Perhaps the most telling one that should have sparked a greater interest was the founding of the New York gallery and her frequent and sometimes extended visits there. She never offered to discuss the matter other than to show Andre at each month's end the sizeable contribution made by the New York gallery to the total profitability of the Berlin gallery. For Andre, that only confirmed his trust in Hannelore's business expertise.

Elsa finally asked softly, "Andre, I don't mean to pry, but you do seem to be troubled about something. May I be of help?"

Andre smiled. "Elsa, you are too perceptive. I didn't know my concern was so obvious." He looked directly at her; she was aware of an unusual tension in his voice. "I cannot say too much more right now, but before the day is out there will no doubt be some disturbing events. I want you to know none of this concerns you directly, but it will have profound effects on the gallery."

Andre's gaze intensified as he asked, "Elsa, have you ever been aware of any transaction that caused you to question it or arouse your curiosity? For example, does the inventory list show the source of the item, where it was purchased, from whom?"

Elsa shook her head. "No, Andre, the list I get is simply an inventory by item, no details. Your questions bother me. I suspect that something is wrong, isn't there?"

"Yes, Elsa, but I cannot tell you more. Believe me, it is not because I don't trust you, but I must see this through without involving others who have no part."

Elsa asked nothing further, she only wished she could provide him some comfort. The silence returned; Elsa felt a sadness descending over her. She couldn't help but notice his repeated glances at the picture on the opposite wall. Each time there would be a different mood reflected on his face. One of worry on a furrowed brow then softened to sadness, or a pained concern on tightened lips, then a return to Elsa with apologies.

"Elsa, I am sorry, I'm not the best breakfast partner this morning, am I?" Elsa smiled with certain sadness in her eyes. "Andre, I know you are concerned and have a heaviness of heart that I only wish I could lift for you. Be assured, whatever the problem I will do all that I can to help, you know that, don't you?"

Andre was touched by her genuine tenderness; he nodded, and then glancing at the clock said with a sigh, "Elsa, I wish we had more time to talk, but I must make an early appointment. If the investigators from New York call, please assure them I will be getting back to them sometime today."

"Of course, Andre, is there anything else I can do?"

Andre shook his head. She rose to leave, reluctant that this time together had not been the usual one of pleasant sharing. She paused at the door with the coffee tray in hand; she spoke with shyness, "Andre, whatever the problem, please know that your words of appreciation, your trust have always meant so much to me. You will never understand how I have cherished the memories of those times you have honored me with an invitation to dinner, the theatre, a concert, or shown other acts of kindness. Truly, the anticipation of knowing you would be here has made my coming to work a joy, thank you." Before Andre could offer a response, she left.

Andre was startled; Elsa had never spoken so openly about her feelings. It touched him. Yes, he had enjoyed the times spent with Elsa. Yes, he knew that she no doubt had a certain fondness for him as he did for her. But he never spent much time thinking deeply about their relationship; certainly not to the extent that Elsa's words would indicate she did.

Meeting Katya, however, was a different experience. It was more of an invasion, an attack on his emotions, unexpected and all the more disturbing for that reason.

His relationship with Hannelore had been from early youth, with Elsa for several years. He was comfortable for the most part with his relationship with them both, but nothing comparable to the feelings Katya had aroused. But why? Why this constant state of deeply questioning his motivation to know her. It was an obsession. His attraction to this lovely creature could not be denied, she had touched him deeply. She had stirred emotions never before experienced. Now he was faced with an undeniable reality. He would have to reveal to her an awful truth, possibly ending any chance of knowing her enough to find the answer he sought.

His mind was jumbled, he could think no further about relationships. What was about to happen would probably make all his personal wishes irrelevant.

He finally reached for the phone and was quickly passed through to his friend, Hans Dietz. Andre's request to see him as soon as possible was granted. Hans knew Andre and his parents very well and knew the matter must be serious for Andre to make such an urgent request for an immediate meeting.

Andre called Otto, "Bring all the documentation you can, Otto. Hans will need sufficient evidence to permit the police to act quickly. I am not going to involve Hannelore at the moment. We need to know what Hans advises based on what we have to show him."

CHAPTER 35

ANDRE AND OTTO WERE QUICKLY USHERED INTO HANS' private office. Hans extended a large hand in warm greeting to Andre and did the same when Andre introduced Otto. He didn't know Otto personally but said he knew of him from his reputation as one of the best restorers of art. Otto acknowledged his kind words with a slight nod and grasped the extended hand firmly.

"Well then, Andre, what is this urgent matter? It has been sometime since we sat together and solved the problems of the world; I suspect your visit means we have another."

Hans was quite elderly, a large man with a youthful demeanor that belied the bristle-brush gray hair above a ruddy complexion. He should have retired a few years ago but had been asked to stay longer due to his years of experience as chief investigator for the City of Berlin. He had been close to Andre's father and was taken by surprise when he heard of his sudden induction into the army. He had called at once to Andre's home only to hear that Karl had already left. He was extremely saddened to hear of Karl's death soon after; his own life took a sudden turn when the Gestapo arrested him for his membership in the Socialist Democratic Party.

"Hans, I'm going to ask Herr Kranz, Otto, to tell you what he told me last night. I believe it better to have this information come from one directly involved in what will prove to be evidence of a continuing sickness in our land. The scandal, Hans, that will result from what you are about to hear will no doubt involve me and be the certain end to Von

Kunst Gallery. My ignorance of these activities that, as owner of the gallery, I should have known about is of little comfort or excuse." Hans raised his eyebrows questioningly as he looked at Andre's earnest yet downcast face.

He turned to Otto, "Well then, my friend, please proceed."

Otto carefully traced the development of the trade in stolen art from the moment he became involved. Hans listened intently as Otto described the evening he uncovered the plot and the threat against Andre and his mother that forced him to cooperate.

At the mention of the Kreis, Otto handed Hans a list of its members. Hans stiffened but said nothing as he read the name of Count von Linglesdorf. As Otto talked, he would from time to time place other documents before Hans and pause as Hans would quickly look at them, jotting down notes for further discussion, then nodding to Otto to proceed.

Otto's recounting lasted for more than an hour as the pile of documentation on Han's desk kept apace with the discourse.

With a final sigh of audible relief as if his imprisoned soul was set free, Otto placed the last document he had on the desk and fell silent. Hans sat back in his chair with one hand holding the list naming the Kreis members.

Hans finally sat upright and looked at Andre. "Dear friend, you are right, this is very serious and must be brought before the magistrate at once in order to arrest these named conspirators. I have some knowledge of these persons from past activities, however, nothing that could be substantiated until now. You realize that although these reprobates have said what might be considered as derogatory statements against the government, those opinions alone would not be sufficient grounds for action, but the evidence supplied by these documents will be. The physical presence of the artworks on your premises will shut any door of escape for them.

"Andre, you and Otto must understand that you cannot avoid being included in those against whom the State will move. I completely understand and believe you, Andre, when you say you were unaware. That may have some bearing on how you will be judged and Otto's testimony will be in your favor. You and your mother are the owners of Von Kunst Gallery; perhaps the court will accept to a point that you didn't know of these activities. I'm afraid the fact remains, you should have.

"Now, Herr Kranz, I personally have no reason to doubt your involvement was involuntary and done to protect Andre and his mother. Very admirable, but unless the threat against Andre and his mother can be substantiated, it will be of little value in your defense. Otherwise, it will be difficult to hope for any degree of relief from a charge against you of being in full compliance with the other perpetrators. Sadly, both of your admissions places me in the uncomfortable position of placing you under arrest immediately." Andre nodded his understanding, Otto as well.

Hans went on, "However, if we want to shoot the bigger bears, we should try and save the cubs. I'll call the magistrate at once, notwithstanding the yet unproved threats against you and your mother, Andre, the matter will require immediate action against all of those involved to avoid their possible flight."

With that said, Hans reached for the phone connecting him directly to the magistrate. A quick, "Good morning," from Hans was followed without pause with a curt request to see the magistrate, followed immediately by, "Thank you." This terse conversation was clearly a sign of a close relationship that didn't need unnecessary pleasantries to accomplish immediate concerns.

Hans rose and, motioning Andre and Otto to follow, went to an adjoining door, knocking lightly as he opened it. The magistrate rose, a thin man with snow-white hair above a matching short-trimmed mustache. Clear blue eyes peered through Prinz-Nez glasses resting on a very thin nose. Narrow lips were tightly closed; without words he motioned them to be seated in front of his desk, void of any surface article save a picture of a young German officer with an array of medals and ribbons adorning his uniform.

The magistrate nodded to Hans. Hans proceeded to quickly recount Otto's testimony and handed the documentation over. The magistrate, after a quick review with an experienced eye, asked in a deliberate, low voice, "Herr Dietz, you are convinced this to be a true and accurate recounting of current criminal activities?" The magistrate said it more as a statement than a question.

Hans said, "Yes."

"Are you requesting permission to immediately arrest the following persons for complicity in these crimes?"

"Yes."

As the magistrate read the names, Andre felt an inner pain as the name Hannelore Hasenfeld was read into the arrest order. It affected him even more deeply than hearing his own. Hannelore arrested? A criminal? He could hardly imagine her horror, her rage of indignation that he would have betrayed her and her righteous cause. Andre was surprised at the speed of all that was happening. After reading the names, which the magistrate in freehand wrote down, he attached them to a printed form extracted from a desk drawer. After signing it, he handed it to Hans.

With hardly a glance at Andre and Otto, he asked Hans, "Will that be all?"

Hans requested that since Andre and Otto were two material witnesses, he be allowed to retain them under his cognizance to help in the investigation. The magistrate nodded his approval. Hans rose to go, motioning to Andre and Otto to come as well.

When they re-entered his office, Andre asked, "Hans, how can the magistrate act so quickly without a complete investigation before action is taken?"

Hans laid a hand on Andre's shoulder. "You know, Andre, there are many of us who have an unshakeable trust in each other to do what is right. We, who have lived under a regime that forbade any deviation from 'orders' under penalty of death, have vowed to never again follow an order that violated our sense of justice, even if that would mean imprisonment or death on our part. Believe me, there are more Germans than you can imagine who would now follow this philosophy than to ever again allow such a criminal element to rule our land."

"Hans," Andre asked, "does this mean that Hannelore must be imprisoned?" Hans nodded. Andre was silent; the thought of Hannelore being taken away even with the evidence against her justifying it pained him.

"Hans," Andre asked imploringly, "I know she is guilty, but instead of having her arrested at the gallery, may I bring her to your office myself? Just as the magistrate has permitted you to keep us under your cognizance, may I ask you to extend to me that same trust for Hannelore?"

"Andre, you realize that should Hannelore understand what you have done, from what Otto has said, she would not hesitate to warn the others. Do you want to take that risk?"

Andre paused, for all her misconceptions and this current revelation of her involvement in the Kreis activities, he could not bring himself to see her summarily arrested and imprisoned.

"Hans, I will take that responsibility. Otto has confirmed that she had no knowledge of the threats against my mother and I. After all, it is one thing to be involved in what she has been taught was a just cause, but she would be horrified that a premeditated murder by her father was a justifiable means to further that end. My father was always kind to Hannelore as a child; that her father would have done this, I believe this truth will crush her."

"Very well, Andre, but I will expect you to be prepared to escort her to my office when necessary. Meanwhile, I'm going to initiate proceedings against the Kreis members at once."

Hans watched as Andre and Otto left. *Well now*, he said to himself as a grim smile stretched itself under a brush mustache, *Herr von Lingles-dorf, it's been a long time, but that old saying is again to be proved. "The wheels of the gods grind slow, but exceedingly fine." Yes indeed and I shall watch with the utmost pleasure as you and your ilk are placed under those wheels.*

The Kreis had been extremely careful as the war ended to make sure any records of their dealings with upper members of the Culture Ministry were "lost."

Hans, however, had gained personal knowledge of the involvement of some of the Kreis members in the illicit traffic of stolen or confiscated goods. His information came from a cousin, Erik, a clerk in the department of Culture, where Count von Linglesdorf and most of the Kreis worked. Erik had come across documents directing certain shipments not to be recorded in the general directory but to be referred to Herr von Linglesdorf for further disposition.

When Erik told Hans what he had discovered, Hans asked him to get copies of these documents as soon as possible. Erik was never heard from again. Hans dared not make any inquires until the war's end. When he did inquire, Herr von Linglesdorf who had been "De-Nazified" for lack of evidence, said the records showed nothing other than a notation that Erik Proust's failure to report to work was due to his death during an air raid that previous night. Hans was convinced that the Count had had a hand in Erik's disappearance.

Hans vowed that he would keep a close watch on this group for any future evidence he could use against them. Now he had it.

Andre and Otto drove back to the gallery in silence. Both were aware of the serious consequences that their actions would have on their own lives as well as others and the gallery itself.

Andre entered his office from the garage. There was a message from

Elsa waiting for him. Maria Skorkia, the New York investigator, and Herr Karpinski had both called requesting he call them.

He called Maria first; he explained that unexpected events had arisen and would she please be patient for a few more hours. Maria hesitated, but since he had been so cooperative, she agreed. Before she hung up, she said that her New York office was agreeable to a settlement along the lines he had proposed.

With great anxiety he next called the Maestro, whose impatience was evident.

"Herr von Kunst, why the delay in giving us the promised evidence of the gallery's innocence? After all, Herr von Kunst," his voice barely concealing his sarcasm, "it should not be difficult for you to *find* what you need. Actually, I have no expectations of any other proof other than that which would establish your innocence. I know what I saw, but I am well aware that I have nothing more than an empty frame to base my claim on. It is also evident to me that Fraulein Presnoski will be more than willing to accept anything that could be used as evidence of your innocence, regardless of the past activities of your family. So please, let us have our meeting so that we can make our preparations to leave and put this unpleasant interlude behind us. Fraulein Presnoski has suffered enough pain that this visit has caused her."

Andre knew that all that was about to happen would prove the Maestro right. He also knew that whatever possibility there had been to develop any closer relationship with Katya was lost.

"Herr Karpinski," Andre's voice was so subdued that the Maestro strained to hear him, "I certainly understand your concerns. However, there has been a series of developments that have precluded my resolving this issue as quickly as I had hoped. May I only say that what you will soon learn will erase any doubts you my have about my integrity, or lack of, to resolve this issue. I assure you I want the truth as much as you do. I will be back to you before the day is out. Would you please grant me that time?"

The Maestro was somewhat taken aback at this somber reply. He sensed a deep concern in Andre's voice that convinced him to agree.

"I have no desire to prolong our needed discussion, Herr von Kunst, but in deference to your reasons, we can wait a few more hours. Please call as soon as you can. I doubt there is anything more that we wish to do in your city, so we should be here at the hotel."

Andre hung up. The thought of having to face the Maestro and, above all, Katya with the awful truth was weighing heavily on his heart. He sat back and swiftly traced the torrent of events that had swept him into this maelstrom of deceit and betrayal. In a few short days, his pursuit of an unexplainable desire to follow this enigmatic, captivating beauty was ending with the collapse of his beloved gallery. The betrayal by his lifelong partner, Hannelore, was beyond comprehension.

The phone's ring demanded attention. It was Hans.

"Andre, as promised, we don't waste time, we have taken all those named into custody. We do have one major problem; I doubt we will be able to hold them too long without substantiating their involvement in the death threats. Otherwise, they will have to be released pending trial.

"Art theft is, of course, serious, and when the physical evidence that Otto says is on your premises is verified, I'm sure long prison terms will be the result. But if the threats they made against you and your mother and Otto are true, there is a danger they might through other channels succeed in carrying them out. I'll put nothing past them. I have reason to believe that from my prior knowledge of them, especially von Lingles-dorf. I'll explain later. I think it necessary that you bring Hannelore in as soon as possible."

Well, Andre thought as he hung up, *the beginning of the end is at hand. Its time to confront Hannelore with the news of the exposure of her and the Kreis involvement in the traffic of stolen art.*

He had barely thought the words when the door from Hannelore's side of the office virtually flew open. Hannelore's face was ashen; she rushed over to Andre's desk. She stood there, gathering her breath, one hand to her throat, breast heaving, eyes aflame. Finally, she gasped out, "Andre, it's impossible! I've just had a call from Count von Linglesdorf's wife. The police came and took him away! I called Frau Bruckner, she said her husband had also been arrested and she had heard from the other wives that their husbands were also taken. Evidently, all my friends have been arrested! What can this mean?"

Her agitation was heightened at Andre's lack of any response.

"Andre, I know you have little regard for my friends, but you must help me find out what is going on. I'll call our attorney as soon as you can determine what the charges are. I'm sure he can help them; that is the least we can do!"

Andre looked sadly at this distraught yet beautiful woman, always in control, now shaking before him.

"Have you no idea, Hannelore, why they would all be taken into custody so suddenly?"

Hannelore, still standing, suddenly seated herself, or better said, half collapsed into the chair by his desk.

"Of course not!" she responded, and Andre could see her indignation rising. "There are always those who have had nothing more on their minds than to discredit my friends. It is because of their open criticism of a socialist government. A government that does not support the need to see Germany regain its rightful position in the world needs to be replaced. My...our insistence that Germany has been unfairly penalized has antagonized those who keep groveling before world opinion.

"I suppose these persecutors have drummed up some bogus charge just to harass them, nothing substantive to be sure. Now please call one of your friends and find out what is going on!" Andre looked at his partner with a sadness that unnerved her; he made no move toward the telephone.

"Andre, why aren't you calling?" A note of panic, suspicion, was in her voice. Harshly, accusingly, she asked, "What do you know about this, why aren't you trying to help me?" Her anger was fueled by fear, as Andre remained silent. With rising anger she demanded, "Andre, why are you so silent? You do know why this is happening, I demand you tell me!"

"I will, Hannelore, I will."

The sadness on his face was now in his voice. Hannelore, her anger spent, now stricken by fear fell back in her chair.

Andre spoke slowly, his words seeming to weigh heavily in the air between them. "Hannelore, you know that Fraulein Presnoski recognized the frame in Otto's studio as coming from her home and presented proof that would verify that."

Hannelore suddenly sat upright and indignantly said, "Andre, you cannot mean that on this simple girl's statement, proven or not, was grounds for my friends' arrests? This is unbelievable. How did the police get involved before we had the chance to present our proof of innocence?"

Andre's voice was so low and choked with emotion that Hannelore had to strain to hear him. "Hannelore, I have worked with you, known you since we were children together. I have placed full confidence and trust in you and your management skills. I'm saddened that you have not returned that trust to me."

Hannelore sat upright. "What ever do you mean, Andre? I have conducted the business of the gallery with excellent results, have I not?"

Andre nodded. "Yes, Hannelore, as far as the business that we do as a legitimate gallery, you have. But there's business you and the Kreis have conducted that can only be regarded as a deliberate misuse of my trust. What you and your 'friends' have done is a perverse use of trust. You trusted me to live the good life, leave the affairs of the gallery in your so very capable hands, so capable that until the matter of the frame, things would never have changed.

"It's my fault as owner of the gallery to have never questioned activities that, had I not had this unfailing trust in you, prudence would have required of me. I never questioned your opening of the New York gallery, believing it to have been a good, legitimate business decision. I admit that I, at times, wondered about the trips you took or the length of time you spent there; I trusted you and felt that any questioning would offend you, so I just let it go. I believed that whatever you did was for our good. Of course, I have from the very beginning never understood your association with the friends you have in the Kreis and that this affiliation was a danger to the gallery never crossed my mind. It should have; now that they have been arrested the truth will out.

"They're not just a group of harmless malcontents. They have a lingering hatred of those who, in their minds, were and are responsible for Germany's loss of the war. They are a group of diabolical plotters who will let nothing, individuals included, stand in their way of achieving the nefarious goal of a resurrected Germany. A Germany again established on long-discredited principles. They have no desire to have our nation respected for its repudiation of past atrocities, its determination to be an example of democracy in practice. Oh no, they want a return to the practice of extreme racism, of discredited Aryan supremacy. But they are clever, they know militarily it would not be possible, but politically, with the right people in government, the same goals could be achieved. I should have taken much more seriously their comments about the need for Germany to return to its former glory, as they remembered it. I considered such ideas as idle talk, the sour grapes eaten by men emotionally starved.

"Hannelore, I had no idea that these men influenced you and that you would have willingly and knowingly become an active participant in their plans. I had no idea that they had found a way through you and the gallery to financially support those who could help them gain their destructive political goals. My sadness knows no bounds."

Hannelore was stunned. *How much did Andre really know and from what source?* With Hannelore, going on the offense was her immediate response whenever she felt an accusation or blame was coming her way.

"Andre," she sat very straight, then leaning forward she spoke forcefully, "yes, they have been able to use funds that I have willingly given from my rightful share of the gallery's profits. Have I not the right to use what is legitimately mine as I wish? You have no right to criticize me or my friends for our beliefs. We have the right to use every means available to convince others of the rightness of our cause. In a way I detect a suspicion that you believe I have used proceeds from the gallery to help my friends. That is absolutely not true, but what I have done with my own money is my business, and I resent your intrusion into my personal affairs.

"It appears to me that my friends have been arrested for their opinions, how strange to be arrested for the very principles the democracy protects. Are you afraid that the reasons we offer for the need of a change will eventually be embraced by more and more people until that change is effected?"

Hannelore sat back in her chair convinced that she had effectively rebutted whatever suspicions Andre had of any illegal activities her or the Kreis had with the gallery.

Andre marveled at how adept Hannelore was in deflecting his remarks. He could, in other days, have probably been persuaded by her had he not stood in that subterranean chamber and listened to Otto's account. He thought to himself, *I wonder, Hannelore, if your defense of using any means will include accepting your father's role in the murder of my father.*

Andre spoke softly; Hannelore still heard the sorrow in his voice, saw the sadness in the eyes focused on hers. "Yes, Hannelore, you are right, as obnoxious as I hold the prejudices you and your friends have toward people not of our culture, this attitude is not punishable by law. However, by the same measure, I have every right to speak out against these attitudes.

"But it is intolerable for me to be actively involved in furthering these odious beliefs. All the more important is that while your friends cannot be arrested for breaking moral, ethical laws, they can be arrested for breaking civil laws to attain their immoral ends."

"Andre, I have no idea what you are talking about. Are you implying that because I use my money I earned from the gallery and spend it on causes you don't approve of, you are morally involved? If this is your thinking, then it follows you would be justified in dismissing me, right?"

"No, Hannelore, I wouldn't be justified on those grounds, but I would be if your association with the gallery involved in any way the breaking of civil laws." He looked directly at her as he spoke. She showed nothing of the sudden realization that he might be aware of more than he was admitting to know. But how could he know of the gallery's function as a conduit for the sale of the purloined artworks? He had no knowledge of these; they were not a part of the gallery's legitimate inventory.

She was absolutely convinced she had taken every precaution to avoid his ever knowing of the connection. Even the mistake Otto had so stupidly made was in no way connected with the frame. Otto's invoice would prove it legitimately belonged to the gallery. Besides, all parties involved seemed ready to accept the explanation that a simple mistake had been made and to accept Andre's offer of a complete reimbursement.

That would have settled the matter had it not been for that neurotic Pole and her damnable frame. That, too, would soon be resolved when Otto presented his proof of the gallery's innocent purchase. Hannelore's impatience was growing.

"Andre, you are really annoying me with all this morality jargon. I came here to ask you to help me find out why my friends have been arrested. Evidently, you know far more than you have admitted, but instead of helping, you just lecture me on moral laws and such. You and I have argued constantly about the views of my friends being unacceptable to you. To continue that discussion now solves nothing."

Andre nodded and drew a deep breath. "Hannelore, you are right, and neither you nor the Kreis will ever comprehend that a moral law is higher than a civil one. The arrests of your friends are solely based on their and your breaking civil laws. I contend, Hannelore, that you all broke the civil laws because you disregarded the moral ones. Had you followed a moral course, considered what is inherently right for a society, not the disregard for its rights as evidenced by you and your friends, the tragedy we face would not have occurred."

Hannelore looked sharply at Andre. "Andre, you seem to be including me in all of this as if I were guilty as well. Now you continue to belabor the point about moral transgressions causing a so called 'tragedy.'"

"It is a tragedy for the innocent who must suffer the consequences of those who break the law. Yet it is a triumph for justice when the moral law receives satisfaction through a judgment against the breaking of the civil law. In other words, Hannelore, you may think you are escaping the consequences of breaking a moral law. This disregard will be your and the Kreis undoing. You believe your ends justify your acting above all laws, moral or civil; be aware that when exposed and convicted of breaking civil laws, moral laws win as well."

Hannelore shook her head in exasperation. "Andre, you really are annoying me with all this philosophizing about moral and civil laws. I certainly hope you understand what you are saying because I do not. I simply came to ask your help for my friends who are in trouble, but instead I am subjected to your openly hostile attitude toward them and me as well. You talk of crimes committed, yet none are named."

"No, Hannelore." Andre returned Hannelore's hostile gaze with one of compassion. "It is not my duty to name the crime; that is the duty of the magistrate, who has issued the orders for the arrest of your friends and you as well."

Hannelore could not have reacted more violently than if Andre had physically struck her. She stiffened, face chalk white. With her whole body trembling, she managed in an uncomprehending voice to ask, "Andre, you cannot mean what you have said, 'my arrest'? Impossible! Have you allowed enemies of my friends and me to persuade you to believe lies against us. Is that possible?"

"No, Hannelore, it is not possible. I would never allow unsubstantiated accusations to influence me against your friends and above all you. The accusation comes not from others, but from your betrayal of my trust. Hannelore, I cannot imagine a sadder day in my life than today, I am at a loss to find words that could express my sorrow, believe me."

Hannelore struggled with the realization that Andre was in earnest about her arrest and her betrayal. She rose, still struggling to gain her composure, but gathering strength from the rising anger and indignation she felt toward Andre.

"Andre, this is unbelievable of you to speak of betrayal. What betrayal could be greater than your betrayal of me? You're taking the word of some inconsequential girl of questionable emotional stability who has captured your affection for reasons I cannot comprehend over my word."

"Hannelore, I do not deny that my friend's recognition of the frame as the one coming from her house has led to this crisis." It hurts me deeply to believe that you think I would react this way on the basis of her reaction and the Maestro's accusations without more proof. And why would I not believe you when you said that Otto could produce evidence that the gallery came by the frame through a very normal and innocent purchase, not by theft?

"No, Hannelore, you are wrong to think so. The arrests are the direct results of illegal, proven actions by you and the Kreis. I am not going to say more here. What more there is to be said will be said before Hans Dietz in his office. In order to save you embarrassment, he has permitted me to bring you to his office as well as myself, because, you see, I am also under arrest."

Hannelore paused; still standing by Andre's desk, she leaned forward placing both hands flat on the desktop so that she was directly in front of his face.

"Andre, I have no idea of what you are talking about. All this about arrests and crimes you say are coming from the incident with the frame. Otto will be producing the proof that the gallery had no way of knowing the origin of that frame. If you think that there is a case to be built on supposition rather than fact, I am surprised.

"Now listen to me, I will not take this humiliation lightly, nor will my friends. Be assured that after this matter is cleared, I will bring charges against you for initiating a false arrest. I will do all I can to take control of this gallery." She pushed back with eyes of ice still fixed on Andre. She waited for a reaction from Andre, especially about her threat to take the gallery; Andre knew there was not going to be evidence of her innocence coming from Otto. To the contrary, the evidence was going to result in imprisonment and dissolution of the gallery. The sadness in his eyes and smile disturbed her.

"Hannelore, we must go now, Hans is waiting for my call that we are coming. As I said, he has been kind enough to allow us to come on our own without an escort."

Hannelore sniffed her disdain. "My, how kind! Without an escort, as if I needed an escort! I look forward to this appearance; you might warn your friend that those responsible for this outrage will be called into account! How ridiculous you are going to feel, Andre, you and your unfortunate friends. I'm sure they will be glad to exit the city as soon as possible. Hopefully, they leave with some remorse for the trouble they have visited on you, their gracious host. Now, if you will excuse me, I'll be a few minutes getting ready. Would it not be in order to have Otto come with the proof of our innocence? I am sure your Herr Dietz would appreciate that; it might save him the embarrassment of pursuing a non-existent crime."

Hannelore's confidence that nothing would come of all this except her exoneration and that of the Kreis was firm, she was back in control.

"Andre, please have the car ready in front of the gallery. I'll call Otto and have him bring the documentary proof that will absolve us of any wrongdoing." With that, she left, striding purposely to the door leading to her apartment and was gone.

She immediately called Otto. "Herr Kranz, you certainly have the needed invoice by now, do you not?" she asked curtly without any pleasantry.

"Of course," he replied in kind.

"Then come at once and accompany Andre and I on an important visit." They both hung up with equal smiles of victory on their faces.

Andre sat for a moment; the die was cast, no turning back. He reached for the phone. "Otto, Hans called, he has all the Kreis members in custody and Hannelore knows this but not the reason. Hans knows we are coming. "

"Yes, I know," Otto replied. "Hannelore just called me, she was very agitated and wanted to make sure I had the 'proof.' She has no idea of what is coming, does she, Andre?"

"No, Otto, she is confident that what you are bringing will 'turn the tables' on me."

"Andre, this is the end for us, isn't it? I don't know whether or not I have done right." Andre heard the dejection in his friend's voice.

"Otto, there can be no question of right, it is justice long overdue, and we both know and accept that whatever the cost to us, it is a choice made that had no acceptable alternative. Now we must leave."

He knew that Hannelore believed she had the upper hand. *She has no idea what lies behind all of this,* he thought to himself. Otto's disclosure of their trade and the eventual revelation that his compliance with the Kreis was due to the threat against Andre and his mother would be a shock to her, and the knowledge that her father was instrumental in the death of his father would be devastating.

She would never believe that, regardless of what Otto said. Even Hans confirmed that Otto's word alone about her father's role in Karl's death and his threat against Andre and his mother, without proof, would be hard to verify. Otto had no further proof to justify his claim of coercion to join with the Kreis. The case would be prosecuted alone on the illicit trade in stolen art and the gallery's responsibility in allowing this, with or without Andre's personal knowledge; knowledge he should have had.

Elsa watched as Hannelore and Andre left the elevator and crossed the lobby toward the waiting car. Hannelore was dressed in a dark suit, her blonde hair pulled straight back in a tight bun. A firm set to her jaw accompanied her purposeful stride. *A modern Brunhilde*, thought Elsa, *going on the attack, she lacks only sword and helmet.*

Andre came over to her desk. "Elsa, should there be any calls for Hannelore or myself, just take the message and we will get back to them shortly." As he was talking, Otto came from his office carrying a rather large briefcase and went to the car. Elsa looked at Andre's drawn face before her. She felt a heavy sadness as she remembered his words that this could prove to be a day not soon forgotten.

"Is there anything I can do for you, Andre?" The concern in her voice touched him.

"No. Elsa, not now anyhow, but it is a comfort to have your support. I appreciate that so much." He gave her a smile of appreciation as he turned to go to the car.

Andre got into the driver's seat with Hannelore sitting silently beside him, her thoughts on her coming vindication. Otto, sitting in the back seat, held the briefcase that contained evidence to the contrary closely to his chest.

Hannelore thought about Andre and what he could actually know about the events leading up to this meeting. They had had their moments together, political differences not withstanding, in all a good relationship. She could find no other reason for this situation other than it was a result of allegations brought by the Polish intruders that would soon be proved groundless. It was always the same; these culturally deprived people would take any opportunity to bring shame on Germany.

It was the continuing conspiracy of persons like these to keep Germany emasculated. It justified all means necessary to stop them. How could Andre be so blind? How sad the war had ended as it had. But at least many of their enemies had met a just fate for their actions, but all too many had survived.

Filled with confidence, she entered Hans Dietz's office with Andre and Otto. Hannelore was prepared to launch a frontal attack as the best defense. She didn't wait for Hans to speak first. She knew him from prior meetings at social events and his reputation from comments the Kreis had made about him. They hated him and his obsessive pursuit of them after the war. They never forgot his relentless efforts to find evidence of their complicity in crimes of the Reich. His attempts to portray them as criminals using every tactic available led to nothing of substance. When the investigating tribunal had finally released them all, they openly gloated over his failure. But Hans was never convinced of their innocence and continually monitored their every move.

"Herr Dietz, I demand an immediate explanation of this totally unacceptable and illegal action you have taken. I cannot imagine that you would accept unfounded accusations against Andre, my friends, and myself. It is unfathomable, especially when made by a couple of itinerant troubadours. It is shocking and humiliating to find oneself arrested and friends actually incarcerated based on such spurious claims." She stopped and with hands on hips and waited for an answer.

He had known her as a young girl and had watched with dismay as she associated herself with the group of racists he so hated. He was saddened when she began to echo their warped philosophy. He never fully comprehended Andre's defense that she had been unduly misguided and influenced by her father's early teachings.

Hans feigned surprise. "Fraulein Hasenfeld, I am sorry, but what do you mean by accusations made by 'itinerant troubadours.' I have no knowledge of such accusations by them against any of you." He paused, enjoying Hannelore's apparent loss of words.

"Herr Dietz, you are toying with me and I do not like it. What other reason would there be for you to have taken this action? Right in my own gallery these intruders openly accused me of being involved in taking works of art from this pathetic little violinist's home. Who else could be behind this? And they didn't even have the courtesy to wait for us to produce proof that we were not involved, proof that Otto has brought with him."

Hans shrugged his shoulders. "Well, Hannelore, what you say is interesting, but as I said, I have done nothing based on any accusations from the persons you allude to. The reason for this preliminary meeting is to simply record that you all have been made aware of charges pending against you concerning illegal transactions in stolen art. I have the authority to immediately arrest you on the evidence we have; however, due to my highest respect for Andre, I am going to release you both under my cognizance.

"Andre, as owner of the gallery, please come with me. I need to have you sign that you have been made aware of these pending charges. Please excuse us, Frau Hasenfeld and Herr Kranz, we won't be long."

As they entered the conference room, Hans turned to Andre. "Evidently, you haven't revealed much to Hannelore, have you? I can understand that, probably a very wise decision to wait until we can talk about how we should proceed. From what Otto has given me, you know she is also facing criminal charges with very unpleasant consequences.

"Andre, I want to make sure that those I have presently under confinement stay that way. I'll have to prove that the charges are serious enough to avoid their being released pending trial. I have had too many unpleasant experiences in the past. Persons I was instrumental in tracking down have been released on their own cognizance, never to be heard from again. I am sure even at this late date, there are still those safe havens available to them. However, I believe that when the evidence located in your gallery is revealed and Otto's testimony is heard, these perpetrators' imprisonment for a long time is assured. Assured, that is, if they are here to stand trial. I must have grounds to prevent their release pending trial.

"Now, what I would like to see happen, and I think you would too, is for Hannelore to turn states evidence, as I am sure Otto will as well, and both testify against the Kreis. This will help to prove your innocence as an active participant in this crime and will help obtain a lesser charge against Hannelore and Otto.

"What I need is evidence of crimes they committed that are more serious than art theft. I need evidence to support Otto's claim about the threat to you and your mother's lives and Karl's death. Evidence supporting his claims would assure an even longer prison term for the majority of these vermin and permit me to continue to hold them until trial."

Hans paused, "The problem, of course, is that Otto says Hannelore did not know of the plot against your father and was not aware of threats made against you. So there is no hope of confirmation of his claims to be had from her. Otto's testimony alone will not be sufficient, but I have a plan. I know this slime, I know that they were directly involved in many of the Nazi's atrocities. Yet they live and thrive among us enjoying the freedom they denied others.

"Andre, they are cowards, I have seen them turn on one another in a feeding frenzy if it meant saving their own hide at the expense of another. I am willing to let one of the lesser involved off with a lighter charge if he will testify to the veracity of Otto's statement. The major focus for me is von Linglesdorf. I want the highest possible sentence leveled against him." Andre sensed the intense hatred in Hans's usual dispassionate voice.

Andre listened but with heavy resignation said, "Hans, I really doubt you can get any of them to give away any of the others. They are so bound together with their perverted ideology that I'm sure they will unite on this."

Hans nodded. "I understand, Andre, but believe me, they have no honor. They're willing to betray their country, and they will betray one another. As for Hannelore, can you assure me that she will be available to us if I release her to your custody? I am going to be open to some criticism by allowing you three to be free at this time, but I have faith in you, Andre, not to betray this trust."

Andre nodded his thanks. "You can be assured of that, Hans."

Andre welcomed any chance to help Hannelore, despite her recent threats against him. He knew he had wounded her, her reaction understandable. He had no reason to hold her responsible for her father's role in his father's death.

Hans was concerned. "Andre, I know you wish to protect Hannelore as much as possible. I confess I find that hard to fathom in the face of the evidence before me. But if you wish to save her, then you must gain her cooperation and willingness to testify against the Kreis."

Andre remained silent; he could not deny his wish to protect Hannelore. To convince her to testify as Hans suggested he doubted was possible. If in the past she had always refused his request to break away from them, he was sure her intense loyalty would prevent her doing so now.

Hans spoke again, "Andre, you are sure that she has no knowledge of the events leading to your father's death?" Andre nodded.

"What was her relationship with him?"

Andre thought back. "My father showed her every kindness he could. Often, Hannelore herself would tell me how much she liked my father, even if she couldn't understand why he never acted pleased with her family's political beliefs."

"Andre, tell me, are you so sure that Hannelore won't remain loyal to her friends even if she was told of her father's role in your father's death? Hannelore seems driven to see Germany restored politically to power. Those past atrocities involved persons far removed from her. I don't think she and her kind internalize these victims personally. She has no connection with them, they don't even exist to her, why would it be different with your father?"

Andre nodded. "Hans, I understand your point, but there is in Hannelore, strange as it may seem, evidence of a line she will not cross if it affects her personally. The possibility that her own father would perpetrate such an act against a person they both knew, who had been kind to them all, would be incomprehensible. It would be an admission that her father was other than the hero she held him up to be. This wound would be so severe that defending those who did such a deed would not be tolerable, even if it included her father.

"That her father would do this to her, she would consider as a betrayal of her love. I say this because of what Otto has said. He is sure that the reason that the Kreis has never dared intimate that they had anything to do with Karl's death is that she would turn on them as liars and break off her support.

"No, I believe this is her vulnerability, the revelation that must come could win her to our cause. What she hears today will be devastating enough. I don't want to bring up her father's role in my father's death until after she hears what Otto says."

"Andre," Hans said earnestly, "I suggest you take this opportunity to have her make a clear confession and cooperate in every way she can."

As they re-entered the office, Hans looked at Hannelore, who was visibly out of patience and irritated at her exclusion from their private conversation.

"Frau Hasenfeld, I suspect the proof you are alluding to that would prove you and others innocent of any wrongful activities is in that briefcase Herr Kranz is holding. Have you read it?"

Hannelore shook her head. "No need to. I know what he has, so do you," she replied, implying that Hans was lying about having no knowledge of the accusations made by the Polish troublemakers. He was just toying with her; it infuriated her all the more.

Hans went on, "Perhaps, then, before we discuss this any further, I need to ask Herr Kranz to give me the documents he has that have a bearing on these charges. Would you agree?"

"Certainly," Hannelore replied with full confidence. What Otto would present would vindicate them all and force Hans to admit he had acted impulsively to harass her and her friends.

Hans said, "Thank you." Looking again at Otto, he asked, "Herr Kranz, please give me what you have."

With a nod from Hans, Otto slowly opened his briefcase and extracted several folders that he laid on the desk in front of him.

Hannelore was perplexed, she thought, *A simple invoice reflecting the fact that the gallery had purchased the frame legally was all that was needed. What had these folders to do with this matter? What is Otto doing? He doesn't need anything more than the simple invoice I told him to prepare.*

Hans looked at Otto. "I think it would be wise at this time, Herr Kranz, that you give us a summary of what these folders contain."

Otto nodded and took another folder from his case. As he began to read from a carefully prepared history, starting with his employment by Andre's father, Hannelore impatiently interrupted him.

"Herr Kranz, we are not interested in a recital of your association with the gallery. Please just produce the evidence pertinent to disproving the false claims against us."

Hans quickly held up his hand. "Frau Hasenfeld, this is my hearing, I'll decide what we will or won't hear." Turning to Otto, he said, "Please continue, Herr Kranz."

Otto continued to read, the mention of her father's name jolted her composure as Otto recounted the association her father had formed with the Kreis. He explained how Herr Hasenfeld and the Kreis members conspired to have the gallery designated as the depository of art treasures being taken from conquered lands.

Hannelore stood up and protested vehemently. "This is absolutely not true. Why, Otto, would you be making such a ridiculous statement? You know as well as I that people fearing the consequences of war brought objects of art to us for safekeeping. If, from time to time, we were asked by the government to store works taken as rightly due us as recompense for attacks by enemy countries, this was entirely justifiable. Your statements would imply my father and his friends were conspiring to do something criminal. I demand your apology and retraction of such remarks. Besides, there is nothing to substantiate your claims. This is deplorable behavior on your part."

Hannelore remained standing, waiting for Otto's apology. Hans once again held up his hand to indicate he wished no further comments from either Hannelore or Otto.

"Frau Hasenfeld, this is not a formal hearing. I will entertain a request to speak from anyone, but at my pleasure. You are not to so rudely interrupt, is that clear? Now please be seated as Herr Kranz proceeds."

Hannelore seated herself but not without a withering look at Otto. Otto ignored her and looked again at the papers in his hand. He proceeded to read in detail how the Kreis and Hannelore's father set up the receipt and storage of the works of art being transferred to Germany. He explained that the objects taken from Berlin families with affidavits supposedly consigning them to the gallery for safekeeping were falsified.

Hannelore was again on her feet at this point, but before she could utter a word, Hans said, "Frau Hasenfeld, if you insist on interrupting, I will immediately have you removed from this hearing, formally charged, and locked up with your colleagues." Hannelore, trembling with anger, gave a baleful look at Otto as she retook her seat.

Hans continued, "What you are hearing, Frau Hasenfeld, is not the worse, I would advise you to stay seated because if there is any humanity in you, the pain of what you are about to hear should be unbearable." He nodded to Otto to proceed. In a voice now choked with emotion, Otto began to read again.

"Herr von Kunst began to have concerns about the families depositing their possessions in such numbers that he decided to call on them personally. He wanted to determine what the cause was for their concern and to thank them as well for the trust in him. I was present the day he came into the gallery quite upset. He told Herr Hasenfeld that he couldn't locate any of the families who had left these treasures. Apparently, they had simply packed up one night and left without a forwarding address or explanation. Herr von Kunst said it was evident that neighbors were deliberately evasive about giving him any information.

"Herr Hasenfeld explained to Herr von Kunst that when people came to consign their works, it was because they felt uncomfortable with the political situation and were joining relatives in other countries. He showed Herr von Kunst some of the affidavits to substantiate this. Herr von Kunst remained skeptical and told him that he intended to investigate further. He told Herr Hasenfeld that if some of the rumors he heard had any truth, he questioned how voluntary these consignments had been. He said that he would never countenance the gallery becoming a tool of the Reich. If there were any political connections between the consignment of these works and pressure on these families by the government, the gallery would have no part of it.

"The folders I have put on your desk will prove conclusively that Herr von Kunst's fears were justified. Herr Hasenfeld and his select friends were part of a conspiracy to funnel stolen works through the gallery.

"Frau Hasenfeld was well aware of these transactions, kept all the records, and I controlled the storage, inventory, and shipping. I was well aware of the illegality of this trade. I can swear that neither Andre nor his mother had any knowledge of this business."

Here, Otto paused. "Herr Dietz, included in one of the folders I have given you is my personal account of a crime that far exceeds the illicit trade I have described."

Otto turned and sat down. Hannelore stiffened. She had fought desperately against the urge to stand and challenge Otto outright about his yet to be proven allegations. She looked instead at Andre questioningly and asked very softly, "Andre, what is happening, why is Otto doing this? What other serious crime is he referring to? You must believe me, Andre, what Otto is talking about needs to be explained to you. I just never wanted to bother you with unnecessary details about a business that can be totally justified."

Andre met her gaze directly. There was sadness in his eyes, a sadness that told her there was nothing she was going to say that would convince him of her ability to justify what she had done.

"Hannelore, I will let Otto explain all of this and more when we are back at the gallery. The conspiracy he is about to reveal, the evil deed your friends were capable of doing, had you known, I believe you would have ended any relationship with them."

"Herr Dietz," Hannelore spoke sharply as she rose, "it is incomprehensible that you have taken the action you have against prominent people, including Andre and myself, and without verifiable cause. I promise you there will be consequences. I have heard enough of the story Herr Kranz, for some reason, has fabricated against us. Especially against Herr von Kunst, who has provided him a good living, far beyond what his talents alone would merit. I wish to go now unless, of course, you wish to imprison another innocent person," she added sarcastically.

Hans looked at the beautiful woman before him. *Too bad*, he thought to himself, *she really doesn't comprehend what she is going to be faced with when all of this comes to light. No doubt from her reaction to Otto's comments, she probably really believes that what she and her cronies have been doing is justifiable. Just goes to show that intelligence is no barrier to forming prejudices that fit one's goals. Whether morally sound or not plays no role.*

Hans spoke quickly, "Frau Hasenfeld, believe me, on the evidence I have, immediately imprisoning you would not be judged as having wronged an innocent person. However, out of deference to Herr von Kunst, you are all free to go under his and my cognizance. Just be aware that serious charges are pending against you. It is upon your honor to commit yourself to being available when the time comes, and it will come shortly. Yes, you may all go after you sign acknowledgement of the charges pending."

After she signed, with an imperious sniff of disdain, Hannelore went to the door, and without waiting for Andre to open it, exited the office.

In the car, Hannelore turned to Andre, "I am naturally very upset by all of this and your own involvement. Evidently, you have been influenced by Otto's story. Yet you have taken no time to talk to me before all of these accusations were made. And now there is the inference that you have something else to tell me that exceeds the lies that already have been told. Now just what is that?"

Andre shook his head. "Not here, Hannelore, wait until we are back at my apartment, then Otto will explain better than I could. And please remember, Hans has been very gracious in granting us our freedom, your cooperation is going to be very critical in determining how much freedom we will eventually have, if any!"

"This is all so ridiculous," Hannelore almost snorted her anger. "All because of the ridiculous charges brought against us by this frivolous girl. Certainly by now, Andre, you must have regrets for bringing these persons to Berlin."

"No, Hannelore, no regrets. And despite your insistence on believing they are the ones who have brought charges, they are not. However, if their presence and recognition of the frame has been the cause of revealing the dark side of Von Kunst Gallery, whatever the consequences to us all, in the name of justice it is well done."

Hannelore's impatience was obvious. "How can you be so blind? To me, using as a financial source material rightfully obtained during the course of a war justifies the idiom 'to the victor belong the spoils.'"

Andre didn't respond at once; it was evident that who was the victor was not clear to her, perhaps never would be. He knew from many past conversations that no rebuttal from him would cause Hannelore to concede this point.

Finally, he spoke as they neared the gallery, "Hannelore, you speak of evil. You are going to learn at a heavy price what is truly evil."

Hannelore was taken aback at Andre's aggressive tone; she was not used to being spoken to in that manner.

Sensing his mood, she simply nodded. As they entered the gallery, Elsa stopped him at her desk. She couldn't fail to notice the continued absence of Andre's usual gay greeting or the current stony look of what might be called defiance on Hannelore's taut face.

Looking at Andre, Elsa said, "Maria called. She didn't seem to be upset, but she wanted you to please call as soon as possible. However, the Polish conductor also called, and he seemed very upset that you could not be reached. Is there anything I should tell them should they call again, or do you have a message I could call and give them?"

Andre thought for a moment, *Is it better to face Hannelore with Otto's confession before or after meeting with the investigators?* It was clear to Andre that Hannelore thought all that she and the Kreis had done was entirely proper action to take in their fight for justice. Better to face her with the truth now and gain her cooperation that Hans had said would be important for them all.

He gave Elsa a wistful smile. "Elsa, please call the Americans back with my apologies and tell them I will call later with a more definite time when I could meet with them. Tell them I am sorry for being indefinite right now, but they will understand when I do meet them. Then please call Herr Karpinski and ask if I could see him and Fraulein Preznoski around three this afternoon at their hotel."

Elsa said, "Of course, I'll make the calls now."

"Elsa," Andre added, "please hold all calls to Hannelore, Otto, or myself. I want no distractions, please."

Elsa nodded.

CHAPTER 36

AS THEY ENTERED HIS APARTMENT, ANDRE MOTIONED to Hannelore to take the chair separated from the settee by the small mahogany serving table. He didn't speak immediately but walked, as he often did, to the window facing the rear courtyard where the circular fountain still played.

He remembered again those early years and the hours spent there with her. The bench under the arbor, now empty and moss covered had been their special place to talk. Hannelore liked to bring up the topic of boys and girls. Especially after the vacation in Spain, she'd embarrass him with remembrances of their time on the beach. *But Andre*, she would taunt, *your must admit it was fun, wasn't it?*

Now in the silence of the room Andre could not help but ask himself again, *Why, as we have grown to adulthood, did the passing years have to so change our relationship that the closeness we had once is lost?* He turned and looked at Hannelore, who had been watching him at the window.

She spoke as he faced her, almost reading his mind, "Yes, Andre, we had many good times together in that courtyard. It was our private world, wasn't it? I remember you saying once that the happiest days of your life were those spent there with me. I think you were only ten or eleven when you said that you would marry me when you got older. Of course, as you grew older, you forgot all about that, didn't you?"

Andre smiled. "No, Hannelore, I never forgot, not then, not now. Marriage to you would have been any boy's dream. But you know as well as I do that any such commitment requires a deep common bond, far beyond the physical. As we both grew older, it became very apparent that our ability to reconcile our ever more diverging views about life was becoming more remote. We have discussed this before and both know the impediment this issue has been for us to ever marry. We never could have had the closeness that a marriage would need. In fact, Hannelore, you are already married, married to your cause and the despicable group from whom you could never divorce yourself."

Hannelore studied him for a few moments. "How sad, Andre, that you could never see the righteousness of my beliefs. But it would have been no problem for me to set that part of our lives aside and enjoy all the other pleasures we know would be there for us. Andre, do you remember the English teacher we had?"

Andre nodded. "I remember."

Hannelore spoke softly, "Can you remember the poem she had us memorize?"

"*Maud Muller*," he answered, amazed as always at her sudden mood change. The question was, did she do this for effect, or was it genuine? He should know by now but didn't.

"Do you remember the closing verse?" she asked quietly. "I'll say it for you, 'For of all sad words of tongue or pen, the saddest are these; what might have been.'" They looked at one another in silence.

Elsa's light knock announced the arrival of coffee. As she entered the apartment, she was not unaware of the very subdued mood. Neither one spoke to her. Hesitantly, she asked if there was anything else needed. Andre seemed to return from a far distant reverie to answer.

"Yes, Elsa, please tell Otto to come. And thanks so much for the coffee." As Elsa left, Andre sat down and poured Hannelore's coffee, taking none for himself at the moment. He forced himself away from the intimate mood and looked at Hannelore, now expectantly awaiting the promised explanation Andre had said would be given when they were back at the gallery.

"Hannelore, Otto will be here shortly." Andre paused, he didn't quite know how best to prepare Hannelore for what was to come. "I assume you are waiting for him to produce the document that will prove our innocence?"

"Of course, Andre, and then we can bring a quick end to this outrage and talk of arrest. I still cannot understand how Herr Dietz would jeopardize his position by arresting prominent people on such a flimsy accusation. Otto's proof will quickly put an end to all of this."

Andre watched her as she spoke with such certainty and confidence that Otto would be bringing what she had demanded of him. How else would she expect Otto to respond to her demand other than to produce the falsified receipt? Otto may not have liked his association with her and the Kreis, but Andre knew Hannelore believed Otto would follow orders, as a subordinate should. That was his duty, and he was paid well to do it.

"Hannelore," Andre faced her directly, "you told me last evening Otto would find the document proving the frame had been purchased in the normal course of doing business and that we had no knowledge of its prior history, is that right?" Hannelore nodded.

"But you still haven't received that proof. Is there the possibility that it is lost or misfiled? After all, Otto is human, this could have happened; if so, what then? We'd have no proof?"

Hannelore was irritated; the whole affair was becoming absurd. She literally snapped at Andre, "Andre, it will be found. Otto remembers seeing the invoice, but he doesn't remember the exact time period. It takes a little time to research the back records, be assured he will find it."

Andre kept his eyes fixed on her. "Yes, Hannelore, I suppose it would take a little more time, especially when he has to be careful how he prepares it so there is no doubt of its authenticity."

Hannelore froze with her cup halfway to her lips; she slowly lowered it back to the table without drinking. She thought quickly that Andre was trying to unnerve her, trying to make sure that whatever Otto showed up with, Andre would have reason to doubt it. He could then continue his misguided attempt to support the claims of this Polish tramp, regardless of the consequences to the gallery.

She felt her threat to wrest control of the gallery from him even more justified now. With a firm voice and eyes again the color of winter blue ice, she said, "Andre, how I pity you. It is so sad to see how you have let your emotions mislead you. Your recent attitude, your actions, all so void of reason, it saddens me to think where this will lead you, all of us." To Andre, the icy eyes belied any pretense of sadness. Hannelore continued, "What you are accusing Otto of doing is remarkable considering how much you supposedly trust him."

"It has nothing to do with my trust in Otto, Hannelore. But from what I have already heard, I confess your secretive dealings with the Kreis, an activity you have so carefully kept from me, would seriously challenge my trust in you. There may be good reason that Otto could be prevailed upon to prepare a document to cover for one that never existed, not to deceive, but to protect me."

"Protect you? From what?" Hannelore registered genuine surprise. "Are you afraid, Andre, that your pride will be wounded when you have to face the facts that what your young friend accused us of has no basis?"

"Hannelore," the sadness was now back in his voice, "did it ever occur to you that there is a line of deceit that some will not cross whatever the cost? Did it not occur to you that what you ordered Otto to do was for him the line he could not cross?"

Hannelore's eyes narrowed. "What are you talking about, Andre, what order?" I simply asked Otto to find the receipt for the frame proving it was obtained in the ordinary course of business. Why do you say I ordered him to prepare one? Whatever do you mean about a 'line of deceit'? I certainly wish Otto would hurry. You are talking nonsense, Andre, you will see."

Andre shook his head. "No, Hannelore, it is you who must finally see. In spite of your blindness caused by years of association with the Kreis, the protection I refer to goes unfortunately much deeper than even you would suspect. It will be better to wait until Otto comes before we discuss this any further. Otto is not coming with deceit; he is coming with the truth, a bitter truth."

Hannelore looked sharply at Andre, "You speak of truth? The truth is that what Otto has portrayed to you and before Herr Dietz as criminal activity will be proven to be the exact opposite. You have yet to give me a chance to explain. Why I never tried earlier to tell you what I was doing was because of your very often outspoken resentment of our wish for a new Germany.

"Why, Andre, why wouldn't you also wish to have a strong Germany? A nation freed from the influence of those who wish to keep us in bondage? Don't you see, Andre, it was our right to use every means possible to further the cause of returning Germany to its rightful place among nations. It takes money to do this. What better source of funds than to use profits from the forfeited objects our enemies lost due to their attacks on us. We had a right to these works of art as recompense for the suffering they inflicted on us."

Andre looked at Hannelore and shook his head. "Hannelore, what you say changes nothing for me. Now as then, I cannot understand how so intelligent, so gifted a person as you could succumb to such a twisted philosophy proven in time to self-destruct and its believers as well.

"What is about to be revealed concerning your dealings will find no sympathy in our courts. In fact, Hannelore, the more you and your colleagues expound this philosophy, the more assured we are of receiving an increased severity in our sentencing. Our only hope is to cooperate fully with the prosecution of all those involved in this crime, including you, Otto, and myself."

Hannelore bristled with indignation. "Never," she shot back, "never will I confess to a crime I didn't commit. My father's memory dare not be besmirched by a twisted repentance for a crime not committed."

"Perhaps," Andre kept his voice low, "you will see things differently after you hear what Otto has to say when he comes. Hannelore, do murder and betrayal qualify as crimes in your definition?"

"Andre," Hannelore was indignant, "how silly, of course murder is a crime, but killing is not necessarily murder if done in self defense to protect yourself or your country, you know that. Betrayal can be worse than killing, just as those who have betrayed our country are to be considered criminals of the worst kind and deserve the highest punishment."

"I suspect, Hannelore," Andre smiled sadly, "that the greatest difference between us is exactly the issue of who betrayed whom. I offer you the incontrovertible truth that those who espoused, and still do, the sick philosophy that led us into a war of murderous aggression, the price for which we will pay forever, are the real betrayers. Fortunately, many, but not all, have received the 'highest punishment' you so rightly said they deserve."

Hannelore turned her head away from him, her anger rising at his unjust implications. Andre said nothing more and walked to the window overlooking the rain-drenched courtyard, the moss-covered, empty bench, the fountain playing with the rain. Silence again descended until Otto's gentle knock. Otto entered quietly and at Andre's beckoning sat down beside Andre facing a now very hostile Hannelore.

"Well, Otto, you have much explaining to do," she snapped, "but first give Andre the receipt you have found so we can settle that matter at once."

Andre spoke quickly, "Hannelore, before we look at any documents, you need to listen to what Otto has to say. I want you to listen closely. Otto will be talking about those matters of trust, betrayal, and, yes, even murder...such things as you and I were just discussing. Perhaps you will see things a bit differently regarding loyalty when he is finished. Otto's loyalty to me and my mother has caused him no little pain of conscience as he served your unholy group in order to save our lives."

Hannelore stared at Andre in disbelief, "Your lives?"

"Yes, Hannelore, our lives. And what is worse, he had to commit crimes because of this loyalty, and will these crimes, because they were committed out of loyalty, save Otto from punishment? I rather doubt it. Yet I would hope his motivation will grant him some reprieve. But, Hannelore, the worst is yet to come. The crimes committed by the Kreis and, sad to say, your own father, went beyond the trade in stolen treasure. It has much to do with the means they were ready to take to protect their crimes. Before we talk any further, I want you to listen to what Otto has to say."

Otto reached into the small folder in his hand and lifted out several sheets of handwritten notes. Otto began slowly to read his recounting of the events that he had already told Andre.

Hannelore was expecting to hear profuse apologies from Otto about it taking time to find the needed invoice and her attention sharpened as Otto began recounting an occurrence in the gallery that she had never heard before. Gestapo? Her father? What was this tale of conspiracy between her father, the Kreis, and the Gestapo? At the point Otto was saying that her father ordered the Gestapo to make sure Herr von Kunst, now a traitor, was to be inducted into the army and killed, Hannelore shouted out in horror.

"Otto, you liar, what are you saying? Why are you doing this! This is nothing but lies to save your own skin! Andre, you can't possibly believe this."

Otto stopped; he turned to Andre and Hannelore. "You both were there the night the Gestapo came, and we never saw Herr von Kunst alive again." Otto struggled with sad memories now crowding in as he recounted his sad story to Hannelore. He looked at her as she stared at him in shocked disbelief. Andre sat with bowed head on hands.

Otto composed himself and continued, "Shortly after the death of your father, Count von Linglesdorf paid me a personal visit. He reaffirmed the need for me to remain loyal if I had any concerns for the well-being of Andre and his mother. It was evident the war was coming to a close. He assured me that he and his colleagues would survive to carry on the plans they had made regarding the treasures they had stored at the gallery. I had no reason to doubt their threats, so I complied with their wishes.

"But as the years went by, I knew I had to do something that would expose them. I deliberately substituted a copy for the original painting that was on the declaration of the one we shipped to New York. I was in the hope it would be discovered to be a copy and initiate an investigation. It did, and I thought it would be considered an innocent enough mistake. I would say, when questioned, that in my haste I had inadvertently placed the copy in the packing crate.

"We all know how good my copies are, so even I, in haste, could make that mistake. I calculated that the Kreis, Hannelore, would take some immediate action that might arouse suspicion.

"I was right. You, Hannelore, quickly shifted the blame to the New York office. It was naturally still in your and the Kreis's best interest to keep your activities free of suspicion. You could have said that it was an innocent oversight on my part compounded by a wrong assumption by the New York agent. Of course, you didn't, you pressured Herr Kohl to sell and disappear, exactly what I had hoped for. Your actions now aroused the suspicions of the insurer whose investigators recently came here. I was encouraged when you told me of their visit.

"My hope died when Andre stepped in. His offer to acknowledge the error and to recompense the purchasers' estate and all costs of the investigation would end the matter and my plan was foiled. There it probably would have ended had it not been for the visit of the young violinist, Andre's guest, who recognized the frame as coming from her home.

"I knew how we came by it, so did you, Frau Hasenfeld. You knew we had to prove the purchase of the frame was a legitimate one, and so you demanded that I prepare a receipt to substantiate that claim. I knew I could not, whatever the consequences I had to stop. There is no document to prove our innocence, Frau Hasenfeld. That frame held the picture that came from Fraulein Preznoski's home, and that picture is in our storage chamber. What Herr Mylovic saw is what happened happened not only to the Presnoski's but many others."

Otto looked directly at Hannelore, who was trying to comprehend the incomprehensible. Her mind raced, *Why is Otto deliberately destroying the gallery itself a betrayal of the Kreis's trust in him? That they had forced him to cooperate with threats against Andre and his mother was another fabrication. Can Otto be believed? Of course not! That my father disagreed with Andre's father was well known, but to plan his murder? Never! This meeting Otto described had never happened! Were my father alive, he would deny the whole as a fabrication by Otto to absolve himself.*

But, Hannelore now thought, *betrayal is what traitors do. My father called Andre's father a traitor? A man who had taken my father in as a trusted partner, a man who had never shown me anything but kindness, a traitor? Yes, he may have disagreed with my father on the politics of the time; even though Andre and I disagree about the Kreis and its philosophy, we remain close to one another in other ways .I can never imagine doing physical harm to Andre. Yes, I might have to take legal action to save the gallery and its purpose, but in the end it will save Andre too. What Otto is accusing my father of doing is unbelievable. Otto is lying.*

Otto waited for a moment watching the struggle now mirrored on Hannelore's face, then he continued, "That's when I went to Andre and told him the whole story. He knew the danger we would all face if the Kreis had any time to carry through their threats. He called Herr Dietz at the magistrate's office, there, Frau Hasenfeld, as you know, I presented the proof I had. What you didn't know was that one of the folders I gave Herr Hans contained what I have just told you. Andre had already told Herr Dietz over the phone about our activities, the circumstances leading to his father's, death and the threats against him and his mother. That was enough for Herr Dietz to immediately arrest and hold the Kreis members before they could take any action.

"Frau Hasenfeld," Otto's voice was subdued, "to your credit, neither I nor any member of the 'Kreis ' dared to tell you of the role your father played in Herr von Kunst's death. We all knew how you worshiped your father. The Kreis feared you would react negatively and accuse them of lying about your father and possibly end cooperation with them. Had I told you, you certainly would not have believed me then, as you don't now. To you he was an honorable man and all that he did was for the good of his country; betrayal of a friend was out of the question. As misguided as you are about politics, no one believed you would support or condone what the Kreis and your father did."

Hannelore was ashen faced; she made no attempt to stand. She looked at Andre, then back again at Otto in complete disbelief. *How can they*, she thought, *devise such a cruel lie against my father? To what purpose? An attempt by Otto to build an excuse for his claim that he was forced to participate?* Hannelore's expression remained frozen in disbelief. She fought for composure.

Finally, Otto spoke again, "Fraulein Hasenfeld, you know of the storage facility beneath the gallery. When that is revealed to the authorities, there will be no question of our guilt. The physical evidence will be sufficient, as will my documentation and testimony. What I haven't told you is the reason I did not stop this business long ago. It was the threat against the lives of Andre and his mother."

Hannelore finally spoke in a strained voice, "What you are saying, Otto, accusing the Kreis and my father of this reprehensible crime, is totally without proof. It is clear to me that all you are saying is simply self-serving. It's an obvious attempt to distance yourself from an activity that rewarded you very handsomely. Now that there is an attempt to find this to be a crime, which it is not, you are becoming cowardly."

Otto shook his head. "No, Hannelore, I speak only the truth, sad as it may be for you to hear it."

Andre spoke up, "Whether or not there is proof at this time, Hannelore, in time proof will come. I personally have no reason to disbelieve Otto."

No one spoke. A heavy silence, Hannelore's face still chalk white, lips a thin line across a pale mask, eyes unblinking. Otto looked questioningly at Andre, who, face in hands, watched Hannelore. The wall clock never sounded so loud, each tick seeming to punctuate each unspoken thought. An eternity of emotions passed in the heavy silence suddenly split like a gunshot with the ringing of the phone.

Elsa was apologetic but reminded Andre he had said to call if she felt it to be urgent. She said that the Americans had called earlier but not to disturb him if he was busy, but they needed to get back to New York soon. However, the Maestro had just called to say they were leaving for Warsaw that evening. He was convinced that Andre had no further interest in them and there was nothing more to be said. Elsa felt Andre should know of this at once. Andre thanked Elsa and hung up. He looked directly at Hannelore, who appeared almost paralyzed.

"Hannelore, we must quickly come to an agreement. Otto and I are going to support the prosecution against the Kreis. You have already heard Otto's recounting of what you and the Kreis have conspired to do, and he has sufficient damning evidence. As for proof of the plot against Andre's father or threats against him and his mother, that can wait for another time if necessary.

"What is important for you to understand is your involvement in selling stolen art will result in a harsh penalty unless you cooperate. It's your only hope of some mercy being extended to you. I have promised Hans to call him back with your decision. Should you decide not to cooperate, then you must return to the magistrate's office and face a formal arrest and confinement until trial. If you will cooperate, then you can remain free with Otto and me until then. I doubt that the court will accept your reasons for what you have done as being valid or serve as any kind of justification. All of us, Hannelore, cannot escape the evidence resting row upon row in our subterranean gallery of shame."

Hannelore looked at Andre; she was still chalk white, her lips now slightly parted, her eyes less hardened, now a look of bewilderment more than belligerence, more questioning than demanding.

"Andre, how can this be true about my father?" As she asked imploringly, the remembrance of the many times her father had told her of Herr von Kunst's disloyalty gnawed at her conscience. Her gaze faltered, a slight mist formed in the corner of each eye, she shook her head slowly looking down at the floor, thinking, *Was her father capable of such a betrayal of his partner? Of death threats? Her friends of so many years, the Kreis, partners in such a horror?* She wished she could convince herself that Otto was lying; in all the years she had known him, there was never an instance of any characteristic other than complete integrity. In fact, she had to admit that his willingness to cooperate with the Kreis, for whom his dislike was always apparent, had disturbed her.

On one such occasion after he made a derogatory comment, she asked him directly why he did stay. His answer was simply, "It's not for you to know," and refused to comment further.

But now she knew, and that knowledge lent veracity to all that Otto said. As for her friends, they had known this. They had used her by building on the confidence her father had instilled in her the righteousness of their cause. All the while they were accomplices to the murder of Andre's father and holding Otto hostage with threats against Andre. She remembered bitterly how often she and Andre had argued about her association with the Kreis and his rejection of all they espoused in the name of German superiority. How sad that the closeness she had always wanted with Andre had been thwarted by these differences. Now that wished for closeness with him was all the more impossible.

Regardless of her fondness for her father, had he ever intimated that he was capable of doing to Andre's father what Otto claimed, she would have rebelled. Yet she had accepted what she had been told were necessary measures against Germany's enemies. She thought about all the reasons she had been told that justified these actions. She had accepted at face value that the danger to Germany by people of so-called sub- cultures justified any means to stop them.

Now she faced the reality that this philosophy could include the capacity of her own father and friends to betray one of their own countrymen, Andre's beloved father. He who had never shown her anything but kindness. She knew she never would have allowed herself to be so deceived had she known all of this. The pain of realizing how she had been used was too deep to dwell on. The thought of the public humiliation, of being arrested, incarcerated, was too much to bear.

Knowing what she did, what she faced, fact and feelings had to be brushed aside; she must fight back. After all, it was still not proven what Otto claimed. Even if he told the truth, what proof did he have of the alleged plots? As for Andre's belief, she would gain no credibility before the court if she tried to justify her involvement, then perhaps he was right. She would follow his advice even if inwardly she didn't agree. After all, people did make honest mistakes. Her confidence began a slow return as she looked up again at Andre.

"Andre, perhaps what we did will be viewed negatively by people who don't understand what we were trying to do for the good of Germany. However, I find it distasteful to speak against my friends. Of course, if there were proof of what Otto has claimed, I would think much differently, but Andre, he naturally would want to save himself if he could. I think he is lying."

Otto said nothing. Andre paused before saying anything. He knew Hannelore well and her ability to rationalize a justification for anything she did. Her long silence, he knew, had allowed her the time she needed to work through all the information Otto had given. Even if there was the possibility that Otto was right, he knew she would seize on the fact that he had no proof. Her answer confirmed this.

"Well, Hannelore, we need a decision from you."

"If you are sure, Andre, that if I follow your advice and simply explain what I did, express sorrow if it was misguided, I might be treated more sympathetically?"

"Yes, Hannelore, Hans himself recommended this approach. However, you cannot expect total exoneration, but he feels sure a lighter sentence will be the result. As for your colleagues, he offers no such hope. His line of defense will be that you were an impressionable youth negatively influenced by your father. After his death, these older men who had been his friends continued to influence you. They all, your father included, shared responsibility for what they led you to believe."

CHAPTER 37

ANDRE HAD CALLED THE MAESTRO BEFORE LEAVING to meet Maria and Greg. The Maestro was not inclined to accept Andre's request to come back to the gallery.

"It would serve no purpose," he said harshly. "I am sure you have carefully prepared whatever would be necessary to convince us of your innocence."

Katya knew at once with whom the Maestro was talking, and surmised that the Maestro was refusing a request from Andre, probably to meet again. There was a pause in the conversation. Katya looked inquiringly at the Maestro.

"Just a moment," he said to Andre. "Katya," looking at her questioningly, "Herr von Kunst wants us to come to the gallery. He has something he needs to show us, a phone conversation will not suffice." Katya hesitated. She was still reliving the memories of her home and her loving parents that the frame had brought back so forcibly.

To actually touch an object that had been in her home was an experience she could not describe. Yet, she still could not bring herself to accept that Andre or his family were the criminals the Maestro portrayed them to be. There must be another explanation. She desperately hoped Andre would have an explanation that would prove he and his family had come by the frame innocently.

"Maestro," she implored, "we do owe him this last chance, please accept." The Maestro nodded his head resignedly.

"Herr von Kunst, out of deference to Fraulein Presnoski, we accept."

After the Maestro replaced the phone with a none-to-steady hand, Katya said, "I do hope that what Herr von Kunst has to share will clear him and his family of any wrongdoing."

The Maestro spoke with unusual sharpness, "Katya, I saw what I saw, I heard what I heard. Why do you let your misguided optimism continue to doubt me?" Katya felt the sting of the rebuke. It was true; she did hope that even if the Maestro was right about the gallery receiving her family's art, it still did not prove Andre himself guilty. She could only apologize to the Maestro for his taking her optimism as a challenge.

A short while later, the front desk called to say the car from Von Kunst Gallery had arrived. Katya's evident pleasure at the prospect of seeing this young German barbarian again did nothing to improve the Maestro's displeasure at having to return to the gallery. He was tired, he wanted to return to Warsaw, and he really had no interest in hearing again protestations of innocents backed up by documentation he could never verify. He had no witnesses, no proof.

Andre had asked Elsa to call him as soon as they came and to have Otto and Hannelore meet them all in Otto's studio, Elsa included. She knew the reason for the visit from what Andre had told her the evening before in his apartment. She had listened to his explanation of what Hannelore and the Kreis had been doing with shocked disbelief. He told her that she would be called upon to testify about her duties and knowledge of the gallery's business, as would all employees.

She told Andre that his guests were here and then called Otto and Hannelore to come to Otto's studio. She asked the Maestro and Katya to come with her. As they seated themselves on one of the viewing couches, Elsa studied Katya with a touch of envy.

There is good reason for Andre's attraction to this girl. It goes beyond her hard-to-deny beauty and innocence. How ironical; she is, without doubt, the cause of all the unpleasantness that was soon to befall all of us, yet through no fault of her own. If only she hadn't seen that frame…

Elsa's thoughts were interrupted by the arrival of Andre followed closely by Otto and Hannelore. Hannelore, more subdued than normal, stiffened notably at the sight of the Maestro and Katya. She could not totally conceal her anger at the two whom she held responsible for the coming collapse of her tidy world. She was also perplexed at why Andre had called them together. She took a seat to the far side of Katya, yet where she could watch her without being obvious. Otto placed himself along side Elsa. Andre walked over to a shrouded canvas on an easel facing them. He spoke directly to the Maestro and Katya, "I know your visit to Berlin has not been what either of us had envisioned. There is no way I can describe my disappointment and sorrow for the sadness it has caused, especially to you, Fraulein Presnoski. I share with you the sorrow you must feel at the loss of your parents, a loss caused by the evil acts of evil men. For I, too, lost a loving father through a deed all the more evil because of deceit and betrayal of a friendship. I would probably have never known this and the subsequent crimes committed by this gallery had you not seen the frame that came from your home."

At this, the Maestro suddenly came to attention. He had come prepared to hear explanations and see evidence of innocence concerning the gallery's acquisition of the frame. Without proof, he expected his claim that the von Kunst family was involved in the theft of Katya's parents' works of art would be denied. Now he heard Andre say without qualification that there were "crimes committed by this gallery" and "the frame that came from your home."

Andre paused; he moved closer to the covered canvas and looked directly at Katya as he spoke, "Fraulein Presnoski, you have suffered much in the past few days. I wish to cause you no more sadness, but I must bring all that has been said against you and the Maestro concerning the matter of the frame and my family's involvement to an end."

With that, Andre lifted the canvas from the picture. Katya gasped so loudly that she startled them all. She covered her mouth as she stared not only at the frame, but also at the picture it held, as it had so long ago in the hall of her parent's home.

The Maestro was the first to speak, "Herr von Kunst, am I to assume that you are admitting that not only this frame but the original picture as well came directly from Fraulein Presnoski's home to this gallery, as I have claimed?"

"Yes," Andre said.

Hannelore stirred uneasily as she watched the young woman who could not take her gaze from the picture in front of her. The Maestro had no immediate comeback. He was taken off guard by Andre's simple, "Yes," without any further defense. Finally, Katya shifted her gaze to Andre. Their eyes met. Andre had no ready answer for her questioning eyes, and she felt compassion for the sorrow she saw in his.

Otto finally spoke up. "Herr Karpinski, you and Fraulein Presnoski must understand that Herr von Kunst had no knowledge of the involvement of the gallery in this business. It is the result of a conspiracy formulated during the war by Herr Karl von Kunst's partner, Heinz Hasenfeld, together with a group of prominent businessmen. Herr Hasenfeld, of course, is now dead, but those who were also involved and participated in the theft not only of this picture but also of many others are now imprisoned awaiting prosecution. I have already given verbal and written testimony to this fact.

"Evidence of this horrid business is presently resting at this gallery. I was involved from the beginning; why I was an unwilling accomplice will come out in the coming trial and need not be explained here. What is important for you to know is that the von Kunst family from the beginning had no knowledge of these activities.

"Furthermore, I could have produced proof of the gallery's innocence that you would have found difficult to disprove without evidence to the contrary on your part. You must understand that Herr von Kunst, of his own free will, decided to expose this illicit trade, knowing it would bring an end to his gallery. He himself will have to stand trial as owner and partner of the gallery regardless of his own innocence. I intend to make sure that he is cleared of any involvement. Frau Hasenfeld is committed to do the same."

At the mention of her name, Hannelore started; she realized that Otto had just publicly implicated her. The Maestro and Katya both turned to look at her.

Hannelore protested at once, "You must understand that what Herr Kranz has just said is his version of what will undoubtedly be revealed to be a justifiable result of what happens in the confusion of war. Of course, I am aware that what happened to Fraulein Presnoski's family is unfortunate. These are consequences that result from regrettable acts by governments such as those who chose to attack Germany. These aggressive actions may or may not have been the personal choice of each citizen."

The Maestro spoke measured and slowly, "Fraulein Hasenfeld, am I to understand that in your view, what your country did to others, both in your own country and in those it occupied by aggression, was justified? Leaving generalities alone, let's be specific, do you believe that Fraulein Presnoski's parents were deserving of death and the confiscation of their property? Was it because they not only lived in a country you claim to have been an aggressor, but more importantly because they belonged to a group of people your government classified as sub-human and therefore justifiably exterminated?"

"Herr Karpinski, we did what we had to do for our own protection."

Herr Karpinski shook his head in disbelief as he turned to Katya, "Dearest, have you need of any further proof of what I have told you about this land, these people? Evidently, there is nothing more that needs to be said, I hope justice will prevail."

"Herr Karpinski," Andre spoke quietly, "there is indeed much more to be said. Fraulein Presnoski has been wronged; property stolen needs to be returned. I would suspect that this work alone is not the only one that was taken from her home and delivered here. Herr Kranz was responsible for recording each and every work delivered to this gallery and its source. I had him research his records for any other works of hers that we may have.

"I suggest you delay your departure a few days so that we can ascertain what property belongs to Fraulein Preznoski, or in the event it has been sold, to work out a compensation."

To Katya, Otto's declaration that neither Andre nor his family had played a part in the tragedy that befell her family was a confirmation of her inner belief of his goodness. Elsa, realizing all the more what Andre was doing and how devastating it would be for him personally, fought against the tears forming in her eyes. He had been so wonderful to work for, ever the gentleman and a joy to be with, now all to be destroyed through no fault of his own. She looked at him and at Katya. What really existed between them?

The Maestro was perplexed. Evidently, this Herr Kranz had a conscience that compelled him to finally decide to put an end to this criminal activity. Apparently, his participation had been forced, by what means it would be interesting to know. As for Hannelore, there was no mistaking that this woman had no conscience. She would gladly see any and all destroyed who didn't believe in the philosophy espoused by her and her kind. Sadly, it appeared there were many who would yet agree with her. As for Andre, the Maestro was deeply stirred by the fact that the young German could have easily covered for these crimes. Yet he did not. It took character to do what justice demanded when faced with such dire personal consequences. Otto broke the silence when he turned to Katya and said, "Fraulein Preznoski, Herr von Kunst has alluded to the fact that there may be other works of art that belong to you; this can be determined quickly." With that, Otto tilted the painting forward and retrieved a small card and handed it to Katya. He asked her to read out loud the number on the back. She read slowly "Six–six–seven, six–six–eight, Preznoski, Section 1 A."

"Thank you," Otto said as he lifted a rather large register lying on a desk next to the easel. He quickly turned the pages and then stopped. He looked at Katya, and read, "Number Six Hundred Sixty-Seven, Renoir Pastoral Scene, with frame Number Six Hundred Sixty-Eight, Delivered Seventeenth July, 1941. One of fifteen from Warsaw, Poland, Residence of Professor Presnoski, 1226 Linden Strasse. Owner and wife deported, one child, location unknown. Prepared document certifying owner had sold collection."

With that, Otto handed a document to Katya. She was hardly able to read it through tears forming as she heard the name of her parents and the address of her former home. The document declared that Professor Presnoski had sold his private collection containing the following works to Von Kunst Gallery, Berlin, for 120,000 Reich Marks. A list of the paintings followed. Herr Preznoski's signature was at the bottom, witnessed by Count Dieter von Linglesdorf, procurator for Von Kunst Gallery, Berlin.

Katya looked at Otto in disbelief. "My parents sold you their collection?" She looked at the Maestro. "Maestro, then what you saw was the gallery rightfully taking possession of what my parents had sold them." The Maestro shook his head. "You see, Katya, how easy it would be for them to claim it was a legitimate sale; who could prove otherwise? Except I know the truth, your parents would never have sold their collection under circumstances that wouldn't have provided for you. The document is patently false."

Andre broke in, "Yes, Katya, sadly it is all false. Every work of art that came to the gallery through members of the Kreis was channeled to Hannelore and Otto. My father became suspicious of this and it cost him his life." At this, both Katya and the Maestro looked questioningly at Andre. Andre held up his hand, "The details of my father's death will come later.

"The business of the gallery was organized so that I was given responsibility for building sales and cultivating a relationship with our clientele. Hannelore took over all the business affairs, and frankly I was pleased to have it that way. Of course, this permitted her and her friends to use the gallery as a conduit for their trade without involving me. This illegal trade would not have come to light had you, Katya, not recognized the frame. When Otto came to me with the truth after refusing to falsify a receipt proving we acquired the frame legally, I could do nothing other than report these activities to the authorities."

Katya was perplexed, turning to the Maestro, "You said yourself, Maestro, it would have been hard, if not impossible to disprove their claim that they had no involvement had they produced that false receipt. Is it then not true that what is happening here is proof of what I have always believed? That you cannot judge every individual to be evil just because they are of the same nationality or culture as those who do evil things? It seems to me that Herr von Kunst has proven without any doubt that goodness exists where you might not expect it, and perhaps to a greater degree than you would have thought possible."

The Maestro offered no immediate response; what could he say that would convince Katya that her obvious attraction for the German clouded her vision?

Andre looked at the Maestro, whose impassive face assured him that he had gained little credence with him.

Turning to Otto, Andre asked, "Otto, your record states that a total of fifteen works were taken from the Preznoski residence, correct?" Otto nodded. "Wouldn't you also have a record of those sold and those still in our possession?" Again a nod.

Andre looked again at Katya. "Fraulein Preznoski, if it wouldn't distress you too much, would you like to view any of the other works that belong to you that we may have." Katya thought a moment; at first she wondered how much more she could endure, the closeness of her family already so real as she gazed at the picture. Then again, Andre already said they were her property; perhaps just seeing them would strengthen her bond to the past.

Otto had turned to the ledger when he heard Andre's offer. "Herr von Kunst, there are still seven in our private gallery."

Katya spoke, "Herr von Kunst, yes, I would like to see those that you have."

"Well then, you shall, will you all please follow me."

Without a word, Otto touched the church door in the mural.

Andre led the way down the corridor with the Maestro and Katya following. Elsa walked with Katya, apologizing for not having had the time to know her better. She expressed her sympathy for what had happened to her family.

"I do understand what it is like, Fraulein Preznoski. I, too, lost mine in a moment's time. War is so monstrous!"

The Maestro overheard Elsa; he turned and said with unmistakable bitterness, "Too bad, Fraulein, that your people have never learned that lesson, not even today."

Katya looked sharply at the Maestro, but he turned away before she could speak. Instead she looked at Elsa with a voiced apology for the Maestro's rudeness. Elsa liked Katya. She felt that she would like her even more given the chance, even admitting that there was a tinge of envy for the attraction Andre evidently had for her. But how deep this attraction was, and if equally shared between them, Elsa could only wonder. She only knew that she herself gladly accepted whatever affection Andre shared with her.

As they walked down the corridor, Katya asked, "Fraulein Becker, just where are we going?"

Elsa shook her head. "I really don't know exactly, I only learned after your first visit that the gallery was involved with stolen art. Actually, how it was done and where the art was kept I did not know and don't even now; I expect that is where we are going."

Katya said, "If Herr von Kunst had used a false document to prove their innocence, no one would have challenged him and none of this would be happening. Instead, as I understand it, he will lose the gallery and face imprisonment. Herr von Kunst must be very unusual; perhaps that is why I surprised myself when I accepted his invitation to come to Berlin. I confess I wanted to know more about him."

"Yes," Elsa said, "I can understand that, I believe Andre is exceptional and has been a wonderful person to work for. I admire him greatly." Katya sensed her words carried more feeling than perhaps Elsa was aware of herself.

They had arrived at the sealed entrance to the lower gallery. Otto pressed the appropriate brick and the door opened. Everyone was silent as Otto switched on the subdued lighting. The Maestro, Katya, and Elsa looked in awe at what appeared to be rows of graying tombstones. Andre stepped over to Katya and took her hand.

"Fraulein Presnoski, please be careful, the light is dim, but I want you to come with me. Herr Kranz has the ledger with him that gives us the exact location of every work that our records show as coming from your home."

Otto had paused by a shrouded canvass near the end of the first row. He beckoned to Katya to come. Andre, still holding her hand, led her forward, the others followed closely. Without further comment, Otto lifted the cover. Although she had prepared herself, Katya still could not control the shock of seeing another of her parents' pictures, this old Dutch masterpiece.

The Maestro's anger burned inside. To think that here before him and Katya were his beloved friends' possessions, torn away by these barbarians. He directed his angry stare at Hannelore, who stood a few paces away from the group. What little emotion she showed was one of defiance. To her it was a total desecration to allow these two from a country that shared the responsibility for the evils that befell her land to now try and claim possession of what was no longer theirs.

Andre sensed the tension and wanted to spare Katya from the unpleasantness that he was sure was coming. He spoke quickly, authoritatively, "There is nothing to be gained by any further comments from any of us at this time. I wish that Fraulein Preznoski be left to her own thoughts and memories in silence. If she should wish, Otto will lead her to view the other works; they are all grouped together here."

Katya looked through streaming tears thankfully at Andre, then motioned to the Maestro to come and stand by her. Andre stepped back a respectful distance and indicated to Hannelore to do the same. Katya nodded to Otto, and with the Maestro at her side, followed him as he reverently lifted each cover for as long as Katya wished to view it. Occasionally, she would reach forward and gently caress one, remembering fondly in which room it had hung, and the activities that had taken place there. Others seemed to cause a deepening pensiveness, as if some particular memory was bound to it. The subterranean room became a cell of lonely remembrances, captured and imprisoned as the owners themselves had been.

Finally, Katya smiled at Otto. She had noted with thanks how tenderly he had showed her each painting and it was evident he suffered with her. In a way guiltless, he still shared the guilt of being a part of this travesty against the young girl. She turned and led the Maestro back to where Andre and Hannelore were standing. She avoided Hannelore as she spoke to Andre, "Herr von Kunst, this has been a difficult journey for me. I thank you for your courage in bringing this dark business to the light of truth. How unfortunate for us both to have had such sadness touch our lives. Yet we accept what we must and cannot change, but providence has brought me here. I am able to understand even more what my parents taught me about forgiveness. It is all the more precious to forgive an evil deed when one could justifiably withhold such forgiveness."

She looked at Hannelore, who remained impassioned. Katya smiled. "I am sorry for you, Fraulein Hasenfeld, you have had to walk a path that can bring you no joy and only sorrow to those that may have crossed it, I being one of them, and I would forgive you for it, should you ask." Hannelore offered no response.

Andre was moved to tears; as for the Maestro, there was only more bewilderment at his young ward's capacity for compassion. He felt none!

"Katya," Andre said softly, "you need not rush away should you wish to stay longer."

Katya shook her head. "No, I am ready to go. In a way, I have been home again, thank you."

They started toward the exit as the Maestro, seething inside at what he had seen, dropped back alongside Andre. He grasped his arm and turned him back to face the shrouded rows.

"Herr von Kunst," his voice trembled with rage, "do you have any understanding of the devastation, the horror, the shattered lives, the suffering of the many like Fraulein Preznoski, who were deprived of home and family to live as orphans? Are they not here represented by grave cloths covering the evidences of their buried lives? How can you find any justification for the lives that were sacrificed on your bloody altar of racial supremacy?"

Andre could not have felt physical lashes more intently. He, too, felt anger that such evil could have befallen his nation. But at the same time, he believed that the soul of his people was not forever lost. There was redemption to be gained by people doing what he was doing when the truth was revealed. Katya's spirit was proof of the forgiveness at hand if repentance was genuine, restitution made, and future actions proved a horrid lesson had been learned.

Andre met the Maestro's gaze. "I offer no justification, Herr Karpinski, but what must be learned is that the evil that occurred was deeply rooted in hatred toward others. Perhaps we must be on guard that a hatred, which allows no mercy, no forgiveness, will only lead to dire consequences for those who so hate. In the end, they may suffer even more than those to whom their hatred was and is directed." The Maestro found no reply; he turned to join with Katya, who had gone ahead.

When they had regained the studio, Andre spoke to the Maestro and Katya, "I believe that in your own interest you should remain for just a few more days as my guests. It would help to have you formalize your claim and to have an evaluation placed on the works already sold and the ones we still have. A court-appointed expert, I am sure, will handle such details.

"The Maestro was not all pleased at the prospect of remaining any longer in the hated city. However, he was hesitant to leave without the details concerning Katya's rights being determined. He looked at a very pale and drawn young lady, to him still a child, all the more so due to her ever-present readiness to forgive what need not be forgiven.

"Katya, this has been exhausting for you; for me it goes beyond that. I would just as soon leave this city as we planned as soon as possible. But, with respect to what lies here that belongs to you, I'm inclined to stay and make sure there are no mistakes in obtaining all there is that is yours."

Katya had no reservations that Andre would not take care in assuring all her property would be secured for her. She knew the real reason she readily agreed to stay was that there would be an opportunity to talk to Andre alone. The Maestro's agreement provided a welcome opportunity to do this without admitting to the Maestro her own desire. Andre, hearing the Maestro express a wish to return to their hotel, said the car would be at their pleasure not only now but for any occasion during their prolonged stay.

Katya thanked him again for their generous accommodations. Only Katya, who gave him a warning look, heard the Maestro's muttered comment, "The least he could do."

After they entered the car, Katya reminded the Maestro that it was evident, as she had surmised from the start, that Andre and his family were not involved. His willingness to expose it all was proof enough for her. The Maestro shrugged his shoulders.

"Katya, we may never know why he has done this; deep in my heart I have a suspicion that, unbelievably, he has done this for a personal reason."

"Oh, and what might that be? I would like to know your thoughts."

The Maestro shook his head in the manner she knew nothing would prevail against it. They fell silent. After a while, the Maestro said suddenly, "Katya, what will you do in the future?"

Katya, surprised, said, "What a curious question. I would hope I am professional enough to hold my position with the orchestra, are you contemplating letting me go because I am friendly with the enemy?" A light sarcasm accompanied her question.

"No," the Maestro was very serious, "I am just fearful of losing you. Now that you will be so independently wealthy, you may not wish to play anymore."

Katya stared. "Wealthy?" she had never thought for a moment what the recovery of this property would mean materially. Her immediate thoughts remained on meeting Andre alone. The Maestro said he was still very doubtful about Andre's true motive in exposing an activity that certainly spelled ruin for himself and his gallery.

After Katya and the Maestro left, Andre reminded Hannelore and Otto that they needed to make sure their statements that Hans had requested were ready for him in the morning. He suggested that they come to his apartment later that evening to finalize the matter. They both nodded and left.

Andre turned to Elsa, "I know you have questions beyond what I have already told you, but I think you need to understand why I have done what I did. I am no hero, Elsa, I was almost tempted to ask no questions and let the matter pass even with Otto's confession. Now, you must be hungry, what say we call Jacques and see if he has a booth for us, would you agree to that?"

CHAPTER 38

OTTO WAS FIRST INTO THE APARTMENT. ANDRE GLANCED through the statement; he knew Otto would be factual. Otto said he included the matter of his father and the threats against he and his mother. He knew he had no corroboration but felt it should be made a part of the record.

At this, Elsa looked up sharply. "What threats, Otto?"

Andre held up his hand. "Elsa, after you have witnessed Otto's signature, we can talk."

Nothing more said, Otto signed his statement and left. Andre handed it to Elsa to sign, saying she was welcome to read it. Andre called Hannelore's apartment that he was waiting. She said she'd be there momentarily.

"Elsa," Andre said, "I'll want to read Hannelore's statement very carefully before you sign. You can then read it as well. I think that both of these statements will tell you the full story better than I could. After you have signed them, it would be prudent to make a copy of theirs and mine as well. If you wish, you may read them later since it is getting late."

"Andre, you can't be serious," Elsa replied quickly. "Do you think I could possibly sleep before I know all that has transpired, especially what concerns you?"

Hannelore entered without knocking, as usual, and glanced disapprovingly at Elsa's presence. Involving an employee in such a private matter was totally inappropriate.

Andre took the offered papers from Hannelore, saying, "Hannelore,

I'd like to read this now before you sign and leave in case there is something we should discuss."

Hannelore snapped back, "Andre you told me to write an account of what I know; that I have done, there is nothing to discuss. What I have written I have written."

"Hannelore," Andre sighed, "I wish only to help you. I know the people who will be reading this and will be sitting in judgment. I want to be sure that it will be received as positively as possible. I cannot condone what you did, but nevertheless, I don't want you to suffer unduly. As wrong as you were, I cannot believe you acted out of anything other than the misguided belief you were furthering a good cause. It is so sad that you could not see how wrong it all was."

"It wasn't wrong, Andre," Hannelore's tone was defiant. "Now I am tired and want to sleep." With that she laid the statement on the table between them, signed it, and without another word and another disapproving look at Elsa, left the apartment.

As Andre sat back to read her account, Elsa began to read Otto's. There was a deep silence accented by the resonate ticking of the great clock that soon began to accompany the soft sobs coming from Elsa. Andre looked over at Elsa, whose cheeks were awash in a profusion of tears. She lifted her head and in a voice almost inaudible said, "Andre, how could it be possible for Hannelore's father to do what he did? It's a betrayal of the worst kind! His own partner! Poor Otto, you have often told me how much he loved your father. How awful that he had to live with those he hated the most to protect his friend's son and wife. Did Hannelore know of this?"

"No," Andre was emphatic, "for all the wrong she did, for all the twisted logic she used to justify herself, when the truth of her father's betrayal was revealed, she firmly believed it all to be a lie. She thought Otto told the story only to justify why he continued to work with them. And besides, he has no proof. Without that proof it becomes only hearsay, and the courts won't consider it as support for Otto's claim."

Elsa laid Otto's statement down. Her look of compassion touched Andre as she said, "Andre, is there anything I can do? I am so shocked at what happened to your father. Perhaps it's true that Hannelore didn't know what her father did; she certainly held to the same principles he did. To me that makes her just as guilty. I am sorry, but I feel only disdain for her and her feeble attempts at justification. You are so kind, Andre;

even now you try to protect her as much as you can. She doesn't deserve it. I'm sorry if I am speaking out of place, but I feel so angry that all of this is happening to you and yet you have no fault in it."

"No fault, Elsa?" Andre said. "I wish I could convince myself of that, but I cannot excuse myself that easily. The fact remains, I could have paid closer attention, could have asked more questions, but I was enjoying life too much. If I did have doubts, I'm sure I was quick enough to set them aside as inconsequential. Elsa, thank you again for your support. It really is late, we both need sleep."

Elsa nodded, then hesitantly looking away from him, said, "I guess since I've gone this far presuming on our friendship, I'll dare go a bit further, but please stop me and don't answer if my next question probes too far."

Andre reached out and gently lifted her head. "Elsa, look at me, please, there is no need for you to apologize for any question you may have, believe me."

Elsa found comfort in his words and the kindness she saw on his face. "Things are developing so rapidly that I may not have the chance to ask you what I have no right to ask, but it is important to me to know more. You have said yourself that if Otto had produced the false evidence that Hannelore had demanded, that would have been enough to prove the gallery innocent. The Polish conductor himself admitted that he would have had no way to disprove the evidence."

Elsa again lowered her gaze, and Andre again had to raise a now tear-stained face.

He saw the slight flush rising to her cheeks. "Elsa, please, what is it that you wish to ask me."

She again took courage from his kind voice. "Andre, I have not had too many occasions to speak with Katya, but on those occasions I did have, I found her to be a fine person. She is very beautiful and talented and, of course, very upset at what she has learned here about her family and the gallery's involvement. It has distressed you as well. Andre, what I want to ask is this, all that you are doing that will result in the loss of the gallery and perhaps prison for yourself, has it been for her sake?" She watched his face as a slow smile crossed his lips,

"A good question, Elsa, one that many others would like to have asked, I'm sure. Your honest question deserves as honest an answer. I agree with you that Katya is a fine person. I'll admit that I wanted to know her better and that was the reason I invited her to Berlin. Unfortunately, events have prevented much opportunity to develop any closer relationship; whether or not that would have happened, we'll never know. But what is important to know is that by whatever means the revelation of what Hannelore was doing had come to me, I would have done what I did. I had no choice out of honor for my family and for those families that suffered, now memorialized by the paintings we have seen."

Elsa had no doubt about the honesty of his answer. She also had no doubt about his attraction for Katya. She had to admit as she looked at him that it didn't sadden her that he had had little opportunity to know Katya better.

"Andre, again I apologize for asking so much. You have been so kind to me and have answered so honestly. Yes, it is late; we must get some sleep. I'll use the guest room."

Elsa rose to go. Looking at Andre, she couldn't resist reaching over and kissing his cheek.

"That's for good luck tomorrow." She smiled. "You know that whatever comes I'll be there to help in any way I can. I thank you again for your honesty tonight.

"Yes, I'll admit, without your asking, that I have always been jealous of your relationship with Hannelore. I have never fully understood how she seems to control your life even to the point of her plans always taking precedent over ones you may have made with me. I confess I was hurt at times, but I never said so, it wasn't my place. I guess this evening I feel bold enough to tell you this.

"Whenever you had made plans with me to go to the theatre, or have dinner, then only to call me and say you were sorry but you had to change plans because of her, I was so disappointed. I always acted like it really didn't matter, but it did."

Andre nodded. "Yes, Elsa, but you never gave me the impression that you cared one way or the other. I confess that I just took you for granted; not in a careless way, but simply to avoid a conflict of interest. I knew if I told her I had made other plans how ungracious her attitude would be and you would always graciously accept a change, so I chose to give in to her. I am sorry for being so insensitive."

Elsa smiled. "No apology needed, I know from much experience that Hannelore would never have countenanced your turning down a request from her because you had made plans with an employee, especially me. I am telling you this not because I expected it to be different, I just want you to know that I was disappointed at missing an opportunity to be with you. You are a very special person, Andre. I suppose that's why I am being so open with you this evening. I want you to know that, and yes, you might as well know that I am also jealous of Katya. So there, now you know that I am not as nice as you thought I was."

Andre couldn't help smiling. Elsa's tone was so lacking of any meanness that her words might have conveyed, and he knew she meant him well. There was no reproach, just acceptance of reality. She smiled once more as she left his apartment through the door that led to the general office and guestroom.

As she left, the great clock sounded a single deep tone. *One hour past witching time*, he thought to himself. He was tired to be sure, but more mentally than physically. He thought about Elsa's comment about being jealous of Hannelore, but more so about Katya. With Hannelore it had more to do with her apparent possession of his time, but he sensed a much different reason concerning Katya. That touched him. He had been honest with his answer. He was not doing what would lead to the demise of the gallery because of Katya; she was simply the cause of his having to face justice.

As for his attraction to her, he had admitted that as well. Elsa's admission of some jealousy on her part toward Katya, without malice, was intriguing. Did she really have feelings that went beyond the simple friendship they professed to have for each other? He knew there were times when it must have, both sides, but they seemed to have sidestepped that issue; tonight was the closest they had come to facing it. He could think no more; he was tired. When he awoke the next morning, he was still in his chair.

CHAPTER 39

IT WAS EARLY MORNING WHEN ANDRE, HANNELORE, and Otto entered Hans's office. He greeted them and indicated a seat for each. He had prepared coffee, refused by Hannelore, but accepted gladly by Otto and Andre. There was silence as Hans read the preliminary statements before him. They weren't lengthy, and he was satisfied that the contents were sufficient in detail to prepare a more formal deposition.

"Fine," Hans said, looking up, "this is what I need." Directing his gaze at Hannelore, he said, "Fraulein Hasenfeld, in reading your statement, I get the distinct impression that you wish to defend an unlawful act with an ideological justification. I can understand your reason, but unfortunately, the trial will not be about ideologies. The facts are clear; you will be accused of dealing in stolen art with sufficient evidence to assure you a long incarceration. I might advise you to put yourself at the mercy of the court by an admission of guilt with a very contrite demeanor."

"Yes," Hannelore spoke harshly, "I know you would want me to do that rather than your having to face reality. There are still enemies of our country who would do everything possible to keep us from our rightful place among nations. We have a duty to stop them. There is no better justification for what you say is a crime than to use proceeds derived from property taken from our enemies while at war, to strengthen our nation, and prevent this aggression from ever happening again."

Hans shook his head. "I have, at Andre's request, gone a bit further in advising you what might be your better course of action. I have been involved in many cases like these; I know how the judges will react to your testimony. I'm sorry I cannot dissuade you."

Hannelore glanced at Andre. "Yes, I don't doubt that Andre has interceded for me with you. My only regret is that I could not convince him of our cause, because then he would have been a true partner and would have joined with us. But because I could not convince him, I could not tell him."

"Fraulein Hasenfeld, despite your ideological differences with Andre," Hans said, "I would appreciate that what you have just said be a part of your public testimony when the time comes. While I have assurance that the crime for which you and your colleagues are under indictment for will be easily proven, there is another more serious matter. It is Otto's accusation that the Kreis and your father planned the murder of Andre's father. And it was Herr von Linglesdorf himself who made the threat against Andre and his mother.

"These accusations seemed to be unproven. Proof of them being true would lend much credence to Otto's reason for participating in this illegal activity."

Hannelore sat upright at what she knew in her mind was a blatant lie. "Just what do you mean, Herr Dietz, by 'seemed'?" Hannelore said demandingly.

"Of course they are unproven because they are simply lies. Herr Kranz has invented the story to help himself. We all know that."

Hans looked directly at Hannelore as he spoke, "It may be that this is a very sad day for you, Frau Hasenfeld, for I did say 'seemed'; might I be more direct, now we know."

Hannelore stared. Even Otto and Andre looked inquiringly at Hans with surprise. Hans continued, "I know these characters well, especially Herr von Lingelsdorf, for whom I have never given up the hope of bringing to justice. He possesses a true criminal mind, he has no morals or compunction to avoid doing anything that would advance his goals regardless of the severity of the means, including murder. Yes, Frau Hasenfeld, your friend the Count and your father conspired to have Andre's father killed as assuredly as if they had fired the fatal shots themselves."

At this, a scream from an ashen-faced Hannelore pierced the relative calm of the proceedings. "You lie, you are all liars, what you say is impossible, my father would never have done what you say, nor would as fine a man as Herr von Linglesdorf. You'll do everything possible to support your already weak case against us." As she spoke, the flush of anger replaced the whiteness in her face.

Hans looked at her calmly as he said, "Fraulein Hasenfeld, as much as I believe you betrayed Andre's trust in doing what you did, I believe you have been betrayed even more by those who used you in carrying out their evil plans."

"You do know Herr von Brubach and Herr von Bruckner very well, don't you? They are close associates of Herr von Linglesdorf in the so-called Kreis, aren't they?" Hannelore nodded but said nothing, the hatred in her eyes said enough.

"It is interesting to me," Hans continued, "how quickly loyalty among persons of the Kreis's ilk evaporates when it means their skin as opposed to their co-conspirators.

"While I dislike giving one criminal an advantage over another, justice permits this if a greater justice can be achieved. In this case, the offer of a lesser punishment for the two I have just mentioned, if they would cooperate with me, was effective. It was apparent they were aware of the circumstances leading to the death of Andre's father, but were not participants.

"They learned of the details later from Herr von Lingelsdorf himself. He bragged to both Bruckner and Brubach how proud he was to have orchestrated Herr von Kunst's death and gaining Otto's loyalty by threatening the lives of Andre and his mother.

"Both of these men have given me sworn statements to this effect. We were fortunate enough, because of their statements, to locate the Gestapo officer Herr Kleinschmidt, who was in Herr Hasenfeld's office the night to which Otto refers. While elderly, he is in good health, and faced with complicity in this plot, he is willing to testify for the prosecution.

"Fraulein Hasenfeld, if your father were alive, he would be standing alongside Herr von Lingelsdorf, accused of murder, of murdering his own partner, and that is the sorry truth."

There wasn't a sound in the room. Andre buried his head in his hands; Otto seemed to look beyond the room to an unseen place, Hannelore, immobile except for her rapidly heaving chest, fastened her eyes on white-knuckled hands clasped tightly in front of her. Hans offered no more words. There was a certain degree of sympathy for this beautiful but misguided woman before him. He thought the punishment brought by his news was greater than any the court would possibly give.

Finally, Andre raised his head and looked over at Hannelore. He got up and went over to her, sat down beside her, and softly said, "Hannelore, this is a sad time for both of us. The past has overtaken us and our future together is possibly coming to an end. Exactly what will be the final outcome will, of course, depend on the court.

"What is important for you to know is that I hold no malice toward you. What your father and the others did only confirms to me how intelligent people, people like yourself, can be so persuaded by others to accept false teachings.

"Hannelore, now is the time for you to reject the past, and plan for a new beginning. We are both young enough that when all of this is past and we have paid our debt, there can be a future."

For the first time in his life, Andre saw true tears forming in the corners of Hannelore's eyes. She unfolded her clenched hands and to his profound astonishment, turned, put her arms around him, and wept bitterly on his shoulder. There was no other sound except those anguished sobs. They all waited until Hannelore raised a tear-stained face to Andre, seemingly oblivious to the others.

"Andre," the sobs now subsiding to a level that allowed her to talk, "what can I say? I grieve for what was done to your father; he was always so kind to me. What I am hearing is almost beyond my comprehension. Yet, I did believe what my father and then his friends told me about the need to defend Germany, it seemed so justifiable. I know how many times you tried to persuade me otherwise, but I thought you were the one who didn't understand, wouldn't understand. It all sounded so reasonable, Andre, the need to keep our culture pure and untainted by inferior ones.

"But if that ideal could only be served by deeds so evil that the killing of your innocent father was justifiable, then no, Andre, they were wrong, and so stand I, just as condemned. Please forgive me. I cannot face this shame to know I have lived in the company of men so evil and not recognized it is a burden I cannot endure." She sighed and fell silent.

Finally, Hans said, "It is a sad day, Andre, when such truths cause such grief. There is not much more to be done here today. I have the statements and will prevail upon the magistrate to bring this to a hearing as soon as possible. Unfortunately, no matter how quickly we resolve the issue, the international press, and some of our own, will use this crime to prove that the criminal heart still beats in Germany.

"You are all free to go under the same provisions as before. Please be ready to present yourselves to the court when called."

While they were driving back to the gallery, Hannelore faced Andre.

"Andre, your kindness is harder to bear than if you would show some hatred toward me. You have that right."

"No, Hannelore, there is no hatred for you, but for the evil ideas that invade and poison minds that lead to situations like this, those ideas, those I hate. I hate the loss of a closer friendship with you because of the ideological chasm that we could not bridge. We have lost a future that could have been rewarding. The present brings destruction of a gallery that was the pride of my family for several generations. Yes, I hate those promises of false glory that are damned from the start when they can only be nourished by innocent blood."

Hannelore nodded. "Yes, I know, but I know too late."

As they entered the gallery, Elsa glanced up from her desk and quickly sensed there were no words needed from her. Otto left for his studio.

Andre and Hannelore took the elevator and as they exited in their common foyer, Hannelore took Andre's hand. "Andre, I ask once more for your pardon, may I hear it?" Andre was touched by this genuinely contrite plea. "Hannelore, you need never ask that question again. I forgive you for everything with all my heart. Now, please, get some rest."

Hannelore's tears flowed as she pressed his hand and went to her apartment. Andre entered his still feeling the pressure of her hand and the image of her tear-stained face.

His thoughts about he and Hannelore were interrupted by Elsa's call that Fraulein Preznoski was on the phone for him.

"Herr von Kunst," her voice was barely audible, "is there any possibility I could see you alone?" she asked hesitatingly, unsure herself why she was asking.

"Of course," was his immediate reply; his joy was so unmistakable that her reservations vanished.

"Katya, please, and did we not agree it was to be 'Andre' and 'Katya'?"

"Oh yes, you are right, Andre, I like that."

"Good, so do I. Regardless of this present situation, I do not want us to distance ourselves. That would only add to this tragedy. Now then, when and where would you like to meet?"

"I would rather it be someplace new. You know, I haven't really seen much of your city, do you remember you told me that there is a lovely park here?"

"Of course," Andre replied at once. "The Grünwald, it is beautiful."

Andre felt an excitement at the prospect of seeing her again that lightened his mood considerably for the first time in days.

He added quickly, as if he wanted to give her no time to reconsider, "I could call for you whenever you are ready"

Katya had to suppress a laugh at his evident excitement, which pleased her. She hadn't actually thought he would be so quick to set a time, but it was opportune.

"Actually, this afternoon would be fine. The Maestro has gone to visit some smaller museums and indicated he needed to be alone. I'll just leave him a note." It wasn't accidental that Katya made the call to Andre in the Maestro's absence.

Andre agreed to give her a half hour or so after she declared she needed it in spite of his intention to be there within minutes. She quickly studied her small collection of clothes, none really appropriate for park visiting, other than the one she wore the day she met him in the café in Köln. It was the only one that seemed appropriate, and there was a pleasant memory associated with it.

She quickly penned a note to the Maestro and on second thought decided to omit any mention of Andre. She simply said she, too, wanted to see some of the city and was taking a walk, probably one of some duration, so not to worry.

Andre came down from his apartment shortly after Katya's call and went to Elsa's desk. "I know Hannelore has gone to her apartment and, if possible, don't put any calls through to her unless you think they are really important. The magistrate made it very clear to her that he had proof of her father's complicity in the death of my father. She has taken that news very hard. For all her faults, I believe she would never have agreed with the Kreis or her father's actions against my father. Yet, she never would have believed Otto's account without the proof she learned today. It was a terrible truth for her.

"Otto is in his studio, should you need him. You can always rely on Otto for help."

"I gather you won't be here?" Elsa posed the question as innocently as possible. She wanted to avoid giving the impression she knew Katya's phone call had any connection to Andre's obvious plan to leave the gallery. Andre smiled, Elsa knew her innocence failed.

"Elsa, I am going to met Katya. She called and requested that we meet, and I want to do that. I've admitted to you that I wanted to know her better, but there has been no time. I cannot let her leave the city under these circumstances without my being sure that she has no malice toward me. I couldn't endure that, although in some ways I would deserve it."

Elsa tried to suppress the unavoidable urge to jealousy. She had no claims on Andre, he had been honest, but all the same, she did have her own feelings for Andre. She couldn't deny that the thought of him going to Katya was not pleasant.

She forced a smile. "Of course, Andre, you should. She has suffered a lot, and I would not want her to think any less of you because of this. I mean that. I do, I really do."

Andre paused and took her hand. "Elsa, please remember what I have told you. You mean a lot to me, and I know you understand why I need to see her."

Andre turned and went to the garage for the car. He didn't see Elsa's hand move quickly to her eyes.

Andre recognized Katya's outfit as soon as she entered the lobby. She smiled when he said it was a good omen because the last time he saw her wearing it was on a very pleasant occasion. Except for a few pleasantries, they drove to the Grunwald in relative silence. As they entered the park, it was obvious to Andre that Katya was struggling to begin a conversation.

"Katya, I am sure this has been a sorrowful journey for you. The memories of a life secure and comfortable suddenly disrupted by black-booted hellions entering your home. In the matter of a few days, you had to leave for a foreign country, never to see your parents again. Then, years later a citizen of the country that has caused all this evil and grief pursues you from city to city. After his persistence wears you down, you accept the invitation to be his guest. This all the more surprising since this young nuisance is a member of the family whose name has been a festering sore in your guardian's soul.

"Now the truth is revealed and all that the Maestro saw has been verified. But, Katya, now you know the full story. You must believe that my family and I have been victims, not participants."

"Andre, you must understand I want to believe that, or I would not have called and asked to see you. I know we had planned to have some time together to know each other better; events have intervened, haven't they?"

Andre nodded; without speaking, he took her hand and led her to a bench overlooking the water. Katya sat back, closed her eyes, and bowed her head. Neither spoke.

Katya thought, *How, what am I going to say to him? It never should have happened, this coming to Berlin. Better never to have seen the frame and let the past be buried. What benefit was this resurrection of treasonous thievery?*

It would not restore her parents or her home. Old wounds torn open seldom heal without a deepening scar. She didn't resist as Andre again took the hand he had let go as he seated her.

Andre spoke slowly, "I have a reason to tell you how I, too, have been betrayed, but not in order to become your equal in suffering. I can never equal that. What I need to tell you is that which I hope will convince you of my personal innocence."

After Andre had finished recounting everything that had happened and been exposed since her coming, Katya's tears flowed between the locked fingers covering her eyes. Her black as midnight hair fell across the porcelain cheeks now also wet. She sobbed softly, then lifted her head, turning to Andre.

"Oh Andre, why, why, is there such evil to be found in the human heart. I do suffer for you, how horrible to lose your father at the hand of his own partner. How tragic that your partner became so convinced of the justice of their cause that she, too, betrayed you. And now you will lose it all because I saw a missing grape! How ironic!"

Andre was still holding her hand as he said, "Ironic? Perhaps not, perhaps it's justice finally using the very person who had been so wronged to right the crime." He looked down at the delicate hand he was holding and remembered how the tapered fingers held the bow that flew across the strings.

Her fame was still ascending, even greater recognition lay before her, by what right had he to interpose himself in her life, especially now? He looked at the tear-stained face that could not be more beautiful. He had seen in the short time he had been with her an inner beauty that surpassed the physical beauty that still overwhelmed him. She had showed no malice, voiced no reproach.

"Katya," Andre's voice carried the burden of his question, "it matters not whether I personally or my countrymen collectively have caused these injustices to you and others, we are all guilty. But, Katya, when you offered forgiveness to Hannelore, did that include all of us, those who should have known but did nothing? Can we share in your forgiveness?"

Katya slowly shook her head. "Andre, I have no right to forgive beyond that which has been done to me. I cannot forgive on behalf of others the injustices done to them. Yes, I can, I do forgive you completely because you ask me to. I believe the goodness in your heart would never have allowed you to become a part of these crimes. But as for the others you speak of, they must in turn ask for that forgiveness themselves just as you have done when face to face with the victims they meet."

Andre nodded. "Yes, they must, you are right." Andre fell silent and thought how the time he had hoped to spend with her was so different from what he had anticipated when he had invited her.

Katya sensed in his silence the same regrets she had. She turned her head to look out at the placid waters reflecting a golden path to the lowering sun.

"Andre, see the golden path?" He followed the pointing finger and nodded. "Isn't it beautiful?" Katya sighed. "Yet it cannot be walked upon, can it?"

"No, Katya, it cannot," Andre said softly. "But doesn't it hold out the promise that there are other paths just as beautiful that can be?"

"I don't know, Andre, I don't know." They watched without speaking as the gold turned a deeper orange and a slight breeze began to break the smoothness of the path just as events were now breaking their life's paths. The same breeze brought a slight chill that prompted Andre to place his arm across her shoulders. He felt her nestle unresistingly to his side.

Finally, Katya broke the spell, but she didn't move away,

"Andre, you would have liked my father. He, too, would have looked for other paths to follow if the one at hand was unreachable. He certainly would not have turned back if the goal he wanted lay ahead. Maybe it's the philosopher in you that reminds me of him."

"Me, a philosopher?" Andre laughed. "I think not, dear girl; you place me too highly. I just try and see the world as honestly as I can. I will not give up the hope of a world that will follow a moral code that respects the right of every individual to live without fear that others will take what they have."

Now Katya laughed in turn. "Why, indeed, you are a philosopher! Andre, you know I am Jewish. I was taught, as they say, at my father's knee. He used to read to me from the Torah. One passage I remember clearly because my father said if the world followed it, then we would have the world you just described. Haven't you ever heard of the Ten Commandments?"

Andre thought for a moment. "Katya, I'm afraid that like many others, we've read or heard, of course, but we didn't listen very well."

"It's never too late, you know. It is because of my father's constant reminder that hate consumes the one who hates more than the one who is hated that I can forgive when asked. That doesn't mean, however, that I will hate if forgiveness isn't asked. I will always be ready to forgive, but how can you forgive if you are not asked? I will not hate. I am so sorry for the Maestro; he is a very unhappy man. In his mind he is justified in railing at past injustices and he can do nothing about the past; his hatred will deny him any peace."

She remained close to Andre; as she looked up at his face, was she expecting the oh-so-gentle kiss he gave her? She lowered her head without saying anything and pressed her fingers to his lips to stop the first words of a coming apology.

The sun's golden path, now completely broken up by the breeze-driven ripples, was dimming. Andre felt a slight shiver pass through Katya's still close body. He knew regretfully they needed to go. Katya looked up again, a warm smile on her face.

"Andre, this has been so nice, but I must return to the hotel. I am sure he is back by now and even though I left him a note, he will worry."

Andre nodded. "The Maestro really watches over you, doesn't he?"

Katya laughed. "Yes, he does. Sometimes I wish he didn't watch so closely, but I understand his caring. I love him for all the care he has given me. I owe him much."

Andre hesitated, then said, "Katya, you have your own life to live. I understand how much he must mean to you, but you must feel free to make choices that will bring you happiness as well."

"Andre, happiness can not be bought through selfishness without regard for the needs and feelings of others. How could I put my happiness first if it were to cause the Maestro pain? After all he has done, his teaching me my music, his constant care, his need for me as an important part of his orchestra? I don't mean to say I am irreplaceable, not at all, but he has come to rely on me and my duties as his first violinist."

Andre attempted to keep his voice lighter than his hopes, "Katya, I appreciate you all the more for your caring attitude, but then I must ask, is there room in your life for me?" Katya didn't answer; she still held his hand tightly as she rose to go. They walked silently back to the car.

Finally, Katya, sitting next to him as he drove, said, "Andre, there is no question of there being room for you, how could there not be? You already have a place in my life that will never be lost, memories of a time, although short, that are and ever will be as precious as any I could have. I have seen in you all that a girl could appreciate. Yes, there is room always and just as we saw that golden path on the lake, it was beautiful, but we couldn't walk on it. As you said, there must be other paths that can be followed; we just haven't found them yet. For now we must follow the paths we have, mine leads to Warsaw and a coming tour to America."

They arrived at the hotel and Andre escorted her inside. The Maestro, from a chair where he had been reading the daily paper, saw them enter. He had not intentionally been waiting for Katya; she often took long walks. He had come down for the paper and decided to sit awhile in the lobby to read and, as was his want, to observe people. Andre and Katya entered the lobby. There was little doubt they were enjoying each other's company. He watched as Katya gently led Andre out of the main flow of traffic to a slight alcove by one of the columns. They seemed to be engaged in serious conversation, so he resisted the urge to interrupt them immediately by contriving a need to see her at once.

He watched the German now holding both Katya's hands as he talked looking earnestly at her upturned face. He begrudged the gnawing awareness that, except for Andre's haughty female partner and the odious count she brought to dinner, everyone else had admittedly been like the young von Kunst. They showed nothing but politeness and deference to them both. He had to admit attendance at his concert had been excellent and so were the reviews; however, he couldn't let these thoughts interfere with the need to find nourishment for his hatred of these perpetrators of past crimes, regardless. The greatest enigma was Herr von Kunz's willingness to expose the illegal traffic in artworks conducted by his own partner. His own career and that of his gallery were destined for ruin, and he could have covered it up!

More despair than anger filled him as he watched their lips meet in a close embrace. He waited until Katya had entered the elevator before he went himself to go up to their rooms. She was standing in the central room looking out the window and turned as he came in.

"Well, Maestro," she said smilingly, "did you enjoy your tour of the museums?"

"Interesting it was, Katya."

Katya frowned. "Dear Maestro, You seek only the proof of your conviction that all here is, if not evil, then at the least not worthy of your presence. Are you then not just as prejudiced as you accuse them of being?"

"Katya," the Maestro walked over and put his hand on her shoulder to turn her so that he could face her directly, "I was sitting in the lobby reading when you and Herr von Kunst came in. I could not but help to see your parting. I assume then that you have found some goodness in this land? If so, may I ask what this means for me?"

"What it means for you?" Katya showed genuine surprise. "Whatever do you mean? I have no idea what it means for you other than the vindication of what you saw in my parents' home so long ago. Your festering wound, I hope, will now begin to heal, and the restoration of what belongs to me deserves my deepest thanks to you. For it is because of you, against your own wishes, that allowed me the privilege of coming to Berlin. That you accepted the invitation from a person for whom you had good reason to dislike, let alone trust, and you did it for me; do you think I take that lightly? I do not!

"But I do know that a person like Herr von Kunst, Andre, does exist. He is a person of genuine character, capable of extending a friendship and respect of the truest nature, demanding nothing more than a belief in his honesty and integrity. Certainly, Andre has exhibited all of those qualities, especially when you consider what he now faces because of his honesty."

The Maestro looked at her intensely. "Katya, you have no doubt from what you have said and naturally from what I saw, formed a strong attraction for this young man. I know you too well not to realize this. I have in the past admittedly introduced you to what I considered to be fine young men and never have I seen or heard you extol their virtues as you have for this young man. I think it is very natural for me to ask what it means for me."

Katya smiled. "I think I have said all I can say. I owe you the thanks for the opportunity to meet a person who has confirmed my faith that there exists one in whom my trust and affection would be well placed; perhaps that is all that was necessary, to know he exists.

"Now, what it means for you is that you have a first violinist who loves you very much and is looking forward to some days of rest in Warsaw and an exciting concert tour in America." She reached up and kissed him tenderly on the cheek just ahead of the betraying tear.

As Andre left the hotel, the tender kiss and warm embrace were much with him. He sat in the car for a few minutes, as if driving away would close a chapter in his life that would never be reopened. Yet certainly Katya had not closed the door on a future meeting. She had to be pragmatic; she explained that the next few months would make contact difficult. But she promised to write and update him on the tour and tell him the itinerary, including when they would return to Poland. Of course, she would welcome his visit at that time.

"That," Andre had said with a wry smile, "would depend on whether or not I'm going to be free to travel, the court will decide that!" He knew himself that asking anything more of Katya was unreasonable. There was so much of the unknown that lay ahead. With a parting glance at the door of the hotel where they had entered together and he had left alone, he started the car.

As he entered the gallery, Elsa told him that Hannelore had not come down from her room, and Otto was still in his studio. Andre knew why her matter-of-fact report on everyone's whereabouts was delivered without the usual lightness in her voice.

"Elsa," she heard the slight tone of pleading as he said her name.

She said quickly, "Andre, please, you do not need to tell me of the afternoon. After all, you were honest enough to tell me more than I deserved to know before you went to her. It is your private life; I am not so close that I am owed explanations.

"Elsa," Andre repeated her name now with some exasperation, "not so close? After the recent conversations we have had, I daresay we are both very much close to one another. No, you haven't asked for a report, and I do not consider it a report when I share thoughts and feelings with a friend as close as you are to me. In fact, I need to talk, but we won't right now.

"But there will be time enough. Katya and the Maestro will be leaving tomorrow, and I have no idea when we will, if ever, meet again. So much of the unknown lies ahead for all of us that planning for the future has to wait for current affairs to be settled." He smiled and was pleased at the understanding one she gave in return.

Otto was intently bent over a restoration of an old Roselli. He glanced up as Andre entered but turned quickly back to the object at hand. Andre waited as a steady hand added an ever so delicate touch of shadow to a wall. When Otto withdrew the brush, Andre said, "Nice touch, meister," looking over Otto's shoulder as he spoke. He was always amazed at the man's skill. Andre often imagined that Otto in an earlier time would have himself been one of the masters instead of a restorer of their works.

Otto turned to face him. "Andre, please sit down. I cannot imagine that I have done what I did, except that I could not bear to continue to work in association with the Kreis. I was truly fearful that some day inadvertently something would happen to force them to carry out their threats against you.

"They were heartless in their action against your father. It was proof enough for me. Anything that might have caused them to fear discovery of their trade would be sufficient for them to devise a way to eliminate us all.

"They were clever enough to have convinced Hannelore of the righteousness of their cause. While she may not ever have condoned a direct attack on us, accidents do happen. She would have, in a twisted way, been sorry for us but considered it a work of fate.

"It's true, Andre," Otto shook his head sadly, "I saw that so clearly when she asked me to falsify a proof of purchase for that frame. I just couldn't continue with this deceit. Now the gallery, you, face ruin, an undeserved fate. As for Hannelore and I, we are guilty. I should have found a way much earlier to have stopped all of this. Well, so much for what I should have done, now it is done and events are moving forward.

"While you were out, Elsa passed a call through to me from Herr Dietz. He said a hearing has been set for two days from now. They are anxious to clear this matter quickly. They have a plan for restitution in place and want to be ahead of any negative press reports. I took it upon myself to call Hannelore and advised her of the date. She didn't say much, actually thanked me for the call, and hung up."

Andre rose to go. "Yes, Otto, events are moving rather quickly, and frankly, I am glad. We need to get the matter settled so we can learn our own fate. I'll talk to Hannelore again; I really want her to be careful of her attitude before the magistrate. I still care that she receives as light a sentence as possible."

Otto shook his head. "Andre, you always amaze me how you continually find reasons to excuse her. I wonder if she ever appreciates the loyalty you have extended her. I believe she has always taken you too much for granted, but that's your business, not mine."

"Otto," Andre laughed, "I don't know myself why I allow her so much control, and it just hasn't mattered to me. I suspect I wasn't aware of the impression those early years together made on me. She was always so sure of what she said that I deferred to her. After all, I was the younger one. I looked up to her and felt honored that she paid so much attention to me. So what more can I say? Justified or not, I do care much for her and that I'll not try to deny or defend."

Otto smiled, if sadly. "No, you won't, and I wouldn't expect you to anyhow."

With a wave Andre left Otto and went back to Elsa. "Were there any other messages, Elsa? Otto told me of Han's call and he, in turn, passed it on to Hannelore. Is she still in?"

"As far as I know, Andre, unless she left by the back entrance, which I doubt. Shall I call her?"

Andre shook his head. Elsa continued, "The lady from New York called and said she'd call later, or you could call when you got back. I told her I had no idea when you would be back, but I'd forward the message." She couldn't resist the emphasis on "I had no idea," which Andre chose to let pass.

"Thank you, Elsa. I'll call them; I need to see Hannelore and discuss the hearing coming up shortly. That was the reason for Han's call."

He went to the elevator and, exiting in the common foyer, went and knocked gently on her door. With no response, he tapped more loudly, the force of his knock made the unlocked door swing inward. The sound of Wagner's opera *Tristan and Isolde* no doubt muffled the sound of his knock. Not wanting to alarm her he called out, "Hannelore, it's Andre, your door was open. You must not have heard my knock. May I come in?"

He waited, then assuming the music still overcame his voice, and he ventured more into the sitting room where the music was playing. Hannelore was sitting with her profile toward him but was apparently engrossed in the music she loved so much. He was about to turn and leave without disturbing her when she lifted the slim hand resting on the side table. It beckoned him to come closer. Isolde was just beginning to sing the "Liebestode" as Andre came to her.

With alarm he saw the empty glass and the small, empty vial resting next to it. Hannelore turned a pale face with eyes half-closed above the deepening blue under them.

"Andre," her voice a whisper, "on the table is a letter for you. I did not expect you back before I left." Andre took her hand and pulled her toward him.

"Hannelore, for God's sake, what have you done? I must call a doctor at once!" He tried to go, but the weak hand gained a sudden strength and held him tightly.

"No, Andre, I must go. I cannot stay and face the shame I have brought upon us all. I am not as heroic as Isolde, but I, too, have nothing more to live for. Perhaps if I had realized long ago the error of my life and listened to you, it could have been different.

"Andre, what could have been between us is now lost forever; others have now entered your life; perhaps you will find in one of them that which I failed to give, I envy them. Whoever wins your heart will have won none better. Sadly, it will not be Hannelore. Andre, I could not face a future with such a burden of guilt. Your forgiveness was all I needed to be at peace, please hold me."

As he lifted her toward him, she put out her arms and clasped them gently around his neck. With a sigh, her last soft breath kissed his cheek, her arms slipped away, and he knew she was gone. Andre wept. Isolde's song ended.

CHAPTER 40

THE LAST OF THE CARTONS CONTAINING HANNELORE'S
property were being packed and labeled for storage. His own possessions
and furniture with the exception of the desk where he was sitting had
already been transferred to the studio and quarters he would now be sharing with Otto. His thoughts drifted back over the events of the past few
days.

The trial had been delayed two days due to Hannelore's death. The
funeral had been private, attended only by Andre, Elsa, and Otto. They
listened somberly as Andre's friend, Pastor Ulrich, read a short passage
from the book Hannelore never read. The pastor, Andre, and Otto then
lifted the bier and guided it into an empty vault in the von Kunst family
crypt. Andre had insisted on it, despite his mother's initial hesitation.

Andre and Otto's sentencing had been light, no imprisonment due
to their cooperation and the information provided in Hannelore's last
written testimony.

Herr Bruckner and Herr Brubach's damning evidence against their
cohorts in the Kreis confirming their conspiracy against Andre's father
and he and his mother won them a light five-year sentence. As for von
Linglesdorf and the others directly involved in the death of Karl von
Kunst, the judges did not allow sentencing for the crimes of art theft and
conspiracy to murder to run concurrently. This assured that the total time
to be served would in all probability exceed their life expectancies based
on their current ages. Hans was pleased that his long quest for justice had
ended well.

The court had appointed a committee to locate all legitimate heirs.

The U.S. authorities armed with this information from a willing Kurt recovered the records of the illegitimate sales and instituted proceedings against the American buyers.

The court had no recourse but to revoke Von Kunst Gallery's license.

Andre was relieved when the elderly Schmidt brothers, who had been contemporaries of his father and owned a much smaller gallery, stepped forward and purchased the Von Kunst Gallery. They planned to move into it from their smaller location, bringing their name with it. Von Kunst Gallery was now history.

The Schmidts had always admired Andre's father. Since they had concentrated more on local contemporary works, they had not been a major competitor. They had graciously extended an offer to Andre, Otto, and Elsa to continue working at the gallery. They appreciated the value of Andre's talent and client base, Elsa's expertise, and Otto's skills.

Andre left the desk where he had been sitting and walked for one last look out the window to the gardened courtyard below; did he hear the laughter of bygone times? He turned and looked at the now empty wall where the full-length portrait of the smiling young invincible maiden had hung. He could still see her and all the now lost promise held in her glowing smile. He closed the door behind him, glanced at the nameplate *Hasenfeld* on the entrance to Hannelore's apartment, entered the elevator glancing one last time at the entry foyer, as the door closed on a past and happy life.

He approached Elsa's desk and with feigned formality asked, "Fraulein Becker, would you care to join me for dinner?"

"How very kind of you, Herr von Kunst," Elsa replied with affected surprise. "However, I must review my appointments; if free, I shall be glad to join you."

"Dear lady," said Andre, "there should be no need to review your appointments. If you have recorded them correctly, there are no other times available for anyone else but me!"

"Well, now I must indeed be more careful, you are right," Elsa said with a bright smile. Reaching for her coat and taking his outstretched arm, they started for the door.

Otto, sitting at his easel, turned to watch them leave. As he turned back to finish the shadow on the wall of the restoration before him, he paused to look at the picture of his old kommerad and give a quick salute.